Trusting Desire

Gilded Passions Book One

By Alice Langdon

Jenn —
Always follow your heart! You Rock!
Love,
Alice Langdon

All rights reserved. No part of this publication may be reproduced, distributed, or transmitted in any form or by any means, including photocopying, recording, or other electronic or mechanical methods, without the prior written permission of the publisher, except in the case of brief quotations embodied in critical reviews and certain other noncommercial uses permitted by copyright law.

This book is a work of fiction. The characters, dialogue, places and incidents are of the author's imagination and are not to be construed as real in any way. Any resemblance to actual events or persons, living or dead, is entirely coincidental.

DISCAIMER: This book includes adult situations, violence and sensitive issues that some people might find disturbing. Please read at your own discretion.

    Trusting Desire
    Copyright © Alice Langdon
    ISBN: 978-0-9909678-0-4
    Cover art by Michael Canales
    http://mjcimageworks.com/283159/other-work

    Cameo Books
    Printed in the United States of America

DEDICATION

To "boy" from "giw."

And to my parents, for their unwavering support.

Chapter One

Colorado: 1880

The rough gravel tore into Gabriel's palms as he crashed to the ground.

"That's the last time you destroy my property, you son of a bitch!" the brothel owner shouted, storming out the doors and pushing past the two burly men who'd thrown Gabriel out. "If I ever catch you in my establishment again, you're finished!"

Gabriel flipped on his back and squinted past clouded vision. Jesus, how the hell did he get here? One minute he'd been sitting at the poker table with a good hand, and the next . . .

Damn, he'd done it again.

"It never would've . . . happened," Gabriel slurred, sprawled on the ground, "If your four-flushing customers hadn't accused me of cheating. I'm a skilled player, dammit. I won that game fair and square."

The heavy amount of alcohol coursing through his veins did little to mask the throbbing pain.

An obnoxious chuckle buzzed from the brothel owner's crooked nose, and he rocked back on his heels. "Skill? A steaming pile of horse shit's got more skill than you."

Gabriel propped himself up, wiped the blood from his bottom lip and glared at the stone-faced brutes standing behind the bastard. "Do you always have your customers fight your battles for you?"

"Don't test me, deadbeat."

"Or what?"

The brothel owner yanked open his coat and pulled out a pistol. He aimed at Gabriel's chest. "Or I shut that trap of yours forever and make it look like an accident. No one cares about you, you filth. It would be so easy. Now git!"

Gabriel scowled and spat blood from his bruised mouth. In a last effort to annoy the man, he took his time getting up before stumbling away. But it wasn't easy, and every muscle hurt, right down to the bone. It was a miracle he hadn't broken anything.

The walk through town had never seemed so difficult, and his wobbly legs felt heavy as stone. The day grew hotter by the second. The sun hadn't finished climbing, so it couldn't be past noon. He pulled out his cracked pocket watch and squinted, attempting to make out the blurred numbers.

Eleven o'clock. Once again, he'd managed to get drunk and in some kind of trouble before noon. If only he could live through a day sober enough to leave this godforsaken town, to head for the place he'd spent his best childhood years. But these days, he couldn't bring himself to travel more than a couple miles.

Circling vultures cast shadows on the soil, and the sun beat down on his dehydrated body without mercy. The wide brim of his hat was useless today. Thankfully, he wouldn't be outside for long. He never was. He climbed the two steps to the saloon and pushed through its swinging doors, welcoming the familiar space.

As usual, he was one of the only patrons at that morning hour. The dark wooden sanctuary, with its dim gaslight and dusty drawn curtains, had become a cherished prison, chaining him to his one escape from years of grief. The only thing that made him forget the past he'd thrown away long ago—whiskey.

By the time Gabriel reached the counter, the bartender placed a full glass on the surface. "Kicked out again, huh?"

"And two dollars poorer," Gabriel groaned.

"This one's on me."

"Good man, but I won't let my misfortune become yours." With a brief nod, Gabriel placed a few coins on the bar and brought the glass to his favored table at the back of the room.

The old bartender was about the only person Gabriel didn't mind sharing the occasional word. As for all the others, conversing had become something he tried his best to avoid at all costs, and it was better that way, for everyone's sake.

He despised most of Creekwood's inhabitants, just as much as they despised him.

* * *

Ellie stood inside the post office, her heart sinking as the postmaster shook his head.

"I'm sorry, Miss Baker, but this facility doesn't employ women. Never has, never will." He plunked his elbows on the counter between them and leaned forward. "You'd be better off tryin' your luck at one of the shops or hotels in town."

"But I have tried them," Ellie said, aware of the stares she'd been receiving from the handful of people inside. Lowering her voice, she added, "I've tried almost all of them, and somehow, every position seems to be filled."

The balding man gave a half-hearted smile. "I wish there was somethin' I could do, but I can't. I'm sorry."

She sighed. "I understand. Thank you."

Her third rejection today. Not wishing to appear desperate, Ellie kept the disappointment from her face until after she'd left the small wooden building. Her stomach twisted with hunger pangs as she picked her way down the front steps and onto the muddy street. How many hours had it been since she'd eaten her last can of beans? She couldn't remember. Food was one necessity Papa's debts had made it hard for her to come by—almost impossible.

But moving to Creekwood had been a good idea. A town this size had to have more opportunities than her tiny hometown of Black Hawk. Something would turn up soon. It must. Gazing down rows of buildings surrounding her on either side, she refused to let the new start she'd imagined fade into a distant fantasy.

"Miss Baker!" A voice called out behind her.

Ellie stopped in her tracks and spun around, praying the postmaster had somehow changed his mind. But she saw someone else entirely. A tall, slender man in a black hat and suit leapt over the steps to catch up with her. His shiny black hair hung past his prominent cheekbones, tapering all the way down to his sharp, pointed chin.

She gripped her gray skirt as he drew near.

As the man's dark eyes swept over Ellie, he gave a small chuckle. "My, my, but you look like you've seen a ghost. I'm sorry to have startled you. I assure you that was not my intention."

His voice was smooth, and judging by the quality of his clean-cut suit, he probably worked for a profitable business. He removed his hat and placed it against his chest.

"Please, allow me to introduce myself," he said. "My name is Jasper Cogs. I was in the post office when I overheard you inquiring about a job. You're new in town, I imagine."

"Yes, sir, quite new."

He nodded as if understanding her burden. "Creekwood can be a tough place to break into, especially when about every business around is family-owned and operated. No one wants to risk hiring new blood when they've got trusted relatives to work for them instead." A polished grin stretched across his sharp face. "But I'd like to think of myself as a fair employer . . . and if you'd care to apply, I happen to have one position available at The Inn, right now."

A position at an inn? A spark of promise ignited inside her.

The scent of tobacco and peppermint invaded her nostrils as Mr. Cogs took another step toward her. The man was intimidating, mysterious, and mesmerizing, all at the same time.

"I don't have much—any experience," she stammered.

"Not necessary." He placed his hat back on his head. "You're trainable just like everybody else, aren't you? Experience has to begin somewhere."

Her stomach growled, taunting her.

"My establishment houses people from all over this fine country. There's hardly a slow season, and I guarantee you'll make more money than if you were to work anywhere else in this town. Much more, Miss Baker."

Her mouth almost fell open. She tried to wrap her head around the offer, but everything was happening so quickly that she could barely make sense of it.

"I greatly appreciate the offer, Mr. Cogs—" She smiled to be polite. "Might I have time to think about it?"

"Please, call me 'Jasper.'" Mr. Cogs gave a kind smile. "Though I can't promise the position won't be filled quickly, you're more than welcome to stop by before making any decisions. The Inn is the only white building on Federal Street. You can't miss it." He bowed at the waist, his long fingers tipping his hat. "Have a pleasant evening, Miss Baker."

Ellie dipped her head. "Thank you, sir. Thank you very much."

She watched him start to walk off, yet he hadn't taken more than six steps in the opposite direction when he spun back to face her again. "Oh, Miss Baker, I forgot to ask. You wouldn't by chance be related to a Mr. Samuel Baker, would you?"

The sound of Papa's name sent a painful jolt through her chest.

"You . . . knew my father?"

"So you are his daughter. Imagine that." His eyes turned soft and he smiled. "Oh yes, I knew Samuel very well. We met several years ago, when he first stopped by Creekwood after a long cattle drive. He enjoyed his visit so much that he made The Inn his lodging of choice every time during his runs."

Ellie stared, speechless. She knew Papa had always liked passing through Creekwood—which fueled her decision to move here instead of Denver, Colorado Springs, or another big town after Mama died—but she never would have imagined him frequenting the place so often that he'd befriend someone. There were suddenly so many questions she wanted to ask Jasper, yet her voice was locked somewhere deep inside her throat.

"I was sorry to hear what happened to him." His prominent features grew even more sympathetic. "Such a terrible accident that was . . . and with his own herd, too."

The reminder was like a kick to her stomach. Even at the age of twenty-three, the pain of losing Papa six years ago felt raw as ever. Now she could only dream of happier times, of warm childhood days spent with her parents at their ranch, and of a blue-eyed boy who'd been her best friend for five unforgettable years. So many memories she could never get back.

She trembled. That life was forever ago now, and every day since then she'd hoped to miss it all a little less.

When Ellie returned home, the sun had just begun kissing the mountain peaks. She shut the door to her shack and pressed her back against it, the harsh realities of loneliness haunting the silence around her. Unpacked crates and tattered furniture cluttered the cramped room, making the space appear even smaller. Someday she'd escape the cruel reminder of Papa's debts once and for all. The merciless collectors had stripped her of everything, including the several acres she'd forever call home. Her family's white ranch house, their fertile soil and prized livestock—all gone to the state.

She gripped the door handle, desperate for fresh air.

A gentle breeze struck her face the moment she stepped outside, causing her tangled hair to brush against the bare flesh of her neck. The late afternoon chill penetrated her clothing as she walked along the side of the house, studying the weathered wooden panels that were the outer walls. They were plagued with jagged splinters, and a spider had taken residence in a space beside one of the window panes where it sat very still, waiting for the next meal to fly into its intricate web.

Turning her attention to the endless horizon of grassy plains and distant mountains, she thought long and hard. Each time she considered accepting the job, Papa's words would repeat in her head. *"Being naive can cost you everything, Ellie. Trust no one but yourself."*

Maybe if Papa knew what his debts had done to her, if he knew about Jasper Cogs, then he'd tell her otherwise. She was so hungry and so desperate. With no experience, who could say when another opportunity would come around? There would be no harm in simply going to Jasper's inn and seeing whether she'd be interested. This could be her chance to make a new life for herself, entirely on her own. And she was too impatient to wait until morning.

  She stuffed her blue floral blouse into her skirt, snatched her shawl from inside the shack, and headed out the door.

  The sun had disappeared, taking the day's heat with it. She walked swiftly, arms folded tightly across her chest. At first the sounds of her breathing and dirt crunching beneath her shoes cut the evening's silence. Then the faint commotion of civilization grew louder as she neared the town. Once the buildings came into view, she headed straight for Federal Street.

  Ellie passed a loud saloon with swinging doors and a few patrons smoking on the stoop. They stared as she walked by; she averted her gaze until they were well behind her. Creekwood certainly seemed different at night. A hotel was connected to the saloon, followed by the bank, general store, livery and the mercantile. Two men riding by on horses gave her a holler and a whistle. Her quick gait turned into a full-on sprint.

  Building after building flew past as her legs pushed further, until the large white structure she'd been searching finally appeared. It stood two stories, with thin white curtains dancing between red shutters upstairs.

She'd never been to this part of town. After catching her breath and composing herself, she climbed the steps to the front porch. A wooden sign was mounted by the door, the words "The Inn" carved into it. Judging by the laughter and upbeat piano tunes inside, business was good. She let out a breath, wondering what sort of task he had in store for her. If she worked hard enough, a front desk position might become available. Determination swelled within her, and she balled her hand into a fist and rapped on the door.

It swung open in seconds, bringing Ellie face-to-face with a voluptuous redhead draped in revealing clothing. The sassy smile the woman had been wearing turned into a scowl.

Leaning against the frame, she glared. "Can I help you?"

"I'm sorry . . . I must have the wrong—"

"Scarlet!" Jasper broke in and pushed past her. "Stop pestering her. I swear, not a single bone in your body has any damn manners."

When his coal-colored eyes found Ellie, his lips curved into a grin. He stepped out onto the porch. "Please excuse Scarlet. She can be downright rude with other women, especially the pretty ones."

He shot Scarlet a strange smile, and she rolled her eyes before storming back into the building. "I knew you'd come around, Miss Baker." Coolness crept back into his expression. "Please, let me show you inside."

Ellie didn't want to stay, but before she could move, Jasper had one hand on her back and was escorting her through the doorway.

The room inside bubbled over with life. Several men drank and smoked at the bar, while others sat at tables with scantily clad women clinging to their laps. Some stood by the piano, laughing wildly as they swayed to the hearty music. Crimson velvet settees lined the walls, while a couple of poker tables—both occupied—sat toward the back of the room.

Ellie bit her lip, a terrible feeling knotting inside her. The Inn's identity had become very clear from the moment she entered the building, and now she was deep inside—part of it all.

"Don't stare, Ellie," her mama's voice echoed in her head. *"Count your blessings for the good life you have."*

She snapped from her daze when Jasper's liquid voice trickled back into her ears. "So what do you think, dove?"

"I'm sorry, but I can't work here. You have the wrong girl." She attempted to free herself from his hold, but the man stood calmly, maintaining his firm grip on her.

"Give me one night to change your mind. You need the money, don't you?"

"I'd rather starve than be a . . ." She shook her head. "Please let me go."

Jasper drew in a long breath. "I doubt you mean that. This can all be very overwhelming at first for a girl like you, Miss Baker.

But I can assure you that all you need is a little more convincing. Please, won't you step into my office for a moment?"

His clutch grew forceful as he began guiding her toward a small door beneath the stairs.

She tensed, feeling her uneasiness give way to anger. "Nothing you can say will convince me. Now let me go or I'll cause a scene."

"I only want to talk. After that, you're free to decide whether you'd like to leave."

He pulled open the door and dragged her inside a dark, musty room with a small oil lamp burning in the corner.

"I did hope you would have obliged easily. Now you leave me no choice but to tell you the truth," he said, pulling a key from his pocket and locking the door from the inside. "Please, take a seat."

A primitive warning sounded in her brain. When Jasper turned back to face her, his eyes looked even darker.

"Take a seat," he repeated, more firmly.

Terror shot through her veins. Each increasing heartbeat quaked her body as she slowly lowered herself into the leather chair behind the man's desk.

He removed a silver case from his coat pocket, pulled out a cigarette and lit it. "Do you know how I first met your father, Ellie?"

She swallowed, gripping the arms of the chair tightly.

Jasper took in a long drag, clearly savoring the tobacco taste as he began pacing toward her.

"He was a patron of mine many years ago, back when my establishment was new. It was early summer, and he'd stopped by, offering a large sum to bed the best girl I had. Being a man of my word, I let my beloved sister, Charlotte, take him in for the night."

The floor creaked beneath his boots as he drew closer. "She and I ran this place at the time, and we weren't afraid to get our hands dirty when it came to The Inn's success. Charlotte herself had taken on a small number of customers." A cluster of ashes sprinkled to the floor as he tapped the cigarette.

"She was a real beauty. After just one time with her, your father was hooked. He returned every couple of weeks to bed her again and again. Hell, the man paid us so much that I'd kept everyone else from Charlotte . . ." He stared off, his face hardening. "Until the end of that summer, when I found her in her room, stone-dead. The doc told me she'd tried giving herself an abortion. Of course, I knew who was responsible." Ellie could feel herself shrinking under his cold stare. He stopped directly in front of her and leaned down. "You see, dove, your father is the reason my big sister is dead."

No! The poisonous words stabbed into her like rattlesnake fangs, and her paralyzed lungs struggled for a gulp of air. How dare he say something so terrible, so unimaginable . . .

"That isn't true. You're lying," she rasped.

"Lying?" Jasper scoffed and took in another drag. "What would I possibly gain from lying to you?"

She gritted her teeth, unable to control the rising panic any longer. "I don't know, but the man you just spoke about was not my—"

"I'm sure it must be hard finding out your father wasn't the man you thought he was, and you have my sympathy. However, Samuel Baker owes me a great debt. I took care of him, and he repaid me by taking my only sister's life. Something I can never get back. Business has never been the same since Charlotte's death."

He doused his cigarette in an empty glass on his desk before turning back to her with arms folded. With the venom still deep inside her chest, Ellie could barely move. All she could think about was Papa, and how the image of him had shattered all around her like broken glass. Then she felt the cold stab of betrayal. Her eyes flooded with moisture, and her throat felt parched.

"I . . . apologize on my father's behalf," she managed to choke out. "But I have no money to give you. Our land was taken away, and his debts drained the remaining funds. I wish I had something to offer, but I just don't."

Jasper didn't appear phased by her words. He stood silent, cold, with a devilish grin stretching across his thin face. "Oh, but I think you have something to offer, Miss Baker."

His eyes swept her body, targeting her like a ravenous predator.

She gasped, finally regaining motion and springing from her seat. "No, I could never! I was raised with integrity and values—"

He barked a mocking laugh. "Values? Your own father fucked a whore behind your mother's back."

Without thinking, she slapped him hard across the face. He reached up and grasped her by the neck, towering over her and pushing her backward. She let out a cry and struggled to free herself, but was no match for the man's strength. His grip tightened. She scrambled for air as he pinned her to the wall.

"Now, why'd you have to go do a thing like that, Cherry? Are you trying to get me heated?"

"No," she gasped.

"You can blame your son of a bitch father for putting you in this situation, 'cause you're gonna work for me whether you like it or not. You're all alone now, and there's no one coming for you. You're prettier than Charlotte was, and will bring in good money."

He tore her from the wall and forced her onto the desk, where he held her arms down and climbed on top of her.

"What are you doing?" she shrieked as he began unbuttoning his trousers.

"Breaking you in. Gotta test what I got so I can sell you right."

Panic rioted within her, so hard that she felt like vomiting. She prayed with all her might that this was some sort of nightmare.

"No! Help! Someone help!" She fought and cried out until her lungs burned.

Jasper rolled his eyes. "Do you think anyone can hear you above all the racket in there? The more you relax, the easier this will be. Hold still, girl!"

Refusing surrender, she struggled desperately, despite her exhausted muscles.

"Enough!" He pulled a revolver from his belt and pointed it between her eyes. "I don't want to have to use this, but so help me I will. Now, are you going to behave yourself?" She stared into the black, hollow tube of death and fell completely still.

He slid the gun back into his belt. "Good girl."

Tears streamed down her cheeks and she began to tremble. "Please, I'm begging you, don't do this."

"I have to," he said, without a trace of warmth. "This is all about business, and I'm a business man."

She flinched as he shoved up her skirt and stripped off her bloomers.

Chapter Two

The brass bed frame creaked beneath Gabriel's weight as he sat up and rolled a cigarette. It was uncommon for him to smoke unless the occasion called for it, which he recently found to be the case more often than not.

"He doesn't know you're here, does he?" the mousy harlot beside him asked. She lifted her gaunt, naked body into a seated position and ran a hand through her raggedy hair.

Gabriel shook his head, the butt dangling from his lips. "No, and does it look like I give a damn?"

"Well it's your hide, not mine. I already got what I needed." She shot him a sultry look and reached for his crotch.

He pushed her hand away, in no mood for her playful antics this time. "That's enough." He handed her the cigarette, threw his legs over the edge of the bed and wobbled to his feet. He reached for his flask on the side table, and poured the strong bourbon down his throat as if it were water.

"Tell me, mister, are you ever sober, or did you come out of your mama full as a tick?" she carped, before sucking in a long drag.

He wiped his mouth and reached for his discarded trousers. "I don't pay you to ask me personal questions, you know that."

The room tilted as he pulled up his pants. His fingers struggled to close the buttons of his shirt, and he felt a stab of anger when he realized he'd left one extra button hole at the bottom. It wasn't worth the effort to do it over again.

The scrawny harlot rolled her charcoal-smeared eyes and shook her head. "I know, I know. Such a damn mystery." She tossed him his vest. "One of these days, I'm gonna find out your name and your story."

"I doubt that. I don't remember it myself." Well, at least he didn't when he was drunk. Someday, maybe he'd wake up and forget about the family, wealth and career he once had. Better yet, maybe he wouldn't wake up at all.

"If you come back to bed, I'll help you figure it out." She licked the base of the cigarette and leaned against the headboard. "Don't you wanna hear me scream your name for once while you fuck me?"

He grimaced, disgusted with himself. Brothels and whores—who the hell had he become? "You have plenty of other customers to do that with."

Saying nothing else, he shrugged on his dirt-stained coat, stuffed the flask into the side pocket and left the small room.

The prying questions had irritated him to no end. Irritation—an emotion which often superseded the rest. True, he couldn't remember the last time he'd been sober, but what of it? Drink served as a barrier, one that allowed escape from both his past, and his present reality, for as long as he wanted. And he wanted it always.

He trudged down a few steps, then stopped. With one hand clutching the banister to steady himself, he observed the crowded brothel, unable to keep from scowling at the buffoons parading before him. All liars, cheaters and dirty dealers, yet he was the one who seemed closest to having a bounty on his head.

His vision blurring, he scanned the room for Cogs—the bastard who'd kicked him out that morning—whom he hated as much as the devil himself. Despite Gabriel's sense of loathing, he was in no mood for a brawl if he could avoid it. But the greasy maggot was nowhere in sight, and the bar looked so damn tempting.

Christ. Tugging down the brim of his hat, Gabriel's clouded judgment decided on taking the risk.

* * *

"Tight little virgin," Jasper panted as he pulled up his trousers. "That's gonna be popular around here. Looks like 'Ol Jasper's back in business."

Ellie lay silently on the desk, still shivering, stripped of every emotion but shame. Her mind felt numb, and her body hurt in ways she'd never experienced. Such deep, nauseating pain. But he remained cold. With an expressionless face, he lit another hand-rolled cigarette.

"Get yourself together and come back out. You're no longer a 'cherry,' so no respectable man's ever gonna touch you now. You've no choice but to work for me. I'll take care of you here, and it's not like you've got much else anyway." He patted her cheek as if she were a small child. Then he sauntered to the door and unlocked it before turning back around. "And don't even think about running from me, dove, because I'll find you. No matter where you get to, I'll find you."

He pulled open the side of his coat, revealing his weapon once more before leaving the room.

Every limb cried out as she sat up slowly and wiped her tear-drenched face with trembling hands. She looked down at her blood-stained petticoat, overtaken with a sense of worthlessness. She was numb. Everything in her life had officially been taken from her, leaving nothing but the shattered memories of a false past.

Looking around the empty room, she wondered if the hollow end of Jasper's pistol didn't seem so bad after all. If this was what was to become of her, she might as well be dead.

She drew her knees into her chest, buried her face in her arms and sobbed. It was the only thing that made sense. The sound of someone's laughter boomed just outside the door, snapping her out of her daze, reminding her that Jasper would be back. She couldn't face him again. She took deep breaths until she felt strong enough to lift her head.

Ellie battled against weakness as she pulled on her bloomers, straightened her skirt, and crept out the door. The boisterous room remained oblivious, the commotion continuing as if nothing had happened. Her eyes immediately found Jasper. Leaning against the bar, he was talking to a well-dressed man. His gaze caught and held hers.

Though he stood calmly, his stare burned dark and threatening.

"Here ya go honey, you look like you could use one of these."

Ellie turned to find a woman offering one of two whiskey shots. The sight of the copper-colored alcohol made her stomach churn more than it already had. Her body cried for rest, and her mind had all but shut down as she struggled to acknowledge the woman standing beside her.

"I don't drink," she muttered.

The woman shook her head as if she'd seen the expression a million times before. "Listen, the only way you're gonna survive here is to end the modesty. Now take it, will ya?"

Without waiting for answer, she forced the drink into Ellie's hand. The woman effortlessly tossed her own shot back before slamming the glass down onto a nearby table.

"All right, your turn. I promise it'll help you relax." She rested a hand on either side of her cinched waist and stared at Ellie without blinking an eye.

Ellie looked at the woman, then the drink. Perhaps the alcohol would ease the terrible ache between her legs. She only hesitated a moment before putting the glass to her lips and throwing her head back just as the woman had done. The alcohol burned as it coursed down her throat, and she coughed violently. Her lungs struggled for a clean breath.

"Don't worry, it'll get better each time you do it." The woman chuckled and gave her back a few hard pats. "So I take it you're the new girl. What's your name, sweetheart?"

"Ellie Bak—, just Ellie," she choked.

"All right, 'Just Ellie,' you can call me Rebecca, but I don't go by that here. Here I'm Belle. None of us goes by our real names . . . Keeps us from having future trouble with the clientele, you know?"

Ellie lifted her head, really noticing Rebecca for the first time. Her curled, corn-colored hair was piled on top of her head in a tangled mess, and her breasts were nearly pouring out of her restricting corset. Her sunken cheeks and dark circles below her tired eyes made it nearly impossible to guess her age. A faded bruise hugged the left side of her jaw, sending a chill down Ellie's spine.

"You know—" Rebecca tilted her head and ran her eyes over Ellie. "You look a lot like a girl who used to work here a long time ago. You've got her same figure and hair color, but personally, I think you're complexion's much prettier than hers ever was. Poor thing looked dragged out more often than not."

Lowering her gaze, Ellie traced a finger around the rim of her glass. She could feel the whiskey beginning to warm her veins and, to her surprise, she welcomed the feeling.

"What happened to her?" she asked, trying to mask the tremble in her voice. She braced herself for an answer she feared.

"She was Jasper's sister, actually," Rebecca said with a shrug. "I'm the only one here who's worked for her. Shows how ancient I am. She'd always been more like a whore than madam, on account of her loving attention a little too much. See, there was this one man who kept coming by for her, and she'd fallen hard for him."

Ellie's heart began to pound. "What was the man's name?"

"Samuel Baker, why?"

So it was true about Papa. *Oh God, it's all true.*

"No reason," Ellie faltered, feeling vomit creep up her throat.

Rebecca eyed her a moment before continuing. "Anyway, as luck would have it, he knocked her up. He threatened to never see her again unless she got rid of the kid. She asked us not to tell Jasper for fear of him killing the man, but in the end, she was the one who ended up dead. That prussic acid is hard to dose correctly. It was tragic as all hell."

Papa, how could you! Ellie bit her lip to prevent it from trembling. She'd forgiven his debts, she'd forgiven him for leaving her and mama too soon, but she would never forgive this. A cold, angry shiver ran down her spine at the thought of his heartless betrayal. The man who'd raised her had been one big lie; she might deserve to work at The Inn after all.

Rebecca put a bony arm around Ellie's tense shoulders. "Don't worry, it ain't that awful here. You'll get used to it soon enough, and the pay is something real nice. You'd be surprised at the kinds of johns coming in here. Some are rich, some are poor. Some are strangers, while others are—"

A loud crash cut her off.

"I thought I told you to never show your face in here again after what happened this morning!" Jasper's voice bellowed. Ellie glanced up to find him holding a man by the collar and dragging him toward the door. "You destroyed my property, you drunk, deadbeat bastard!"

"You know that wasn't my fault," the man slurred, tearing himself from Jasper's grip.

Jasper stabbed a long finger into the man's chest. "You threw a customer onto one of my brand new poker tables right before my eyes. Every time you're in here, there seems to be some kind of trouble."

"There wouldn't have been any trouble if they'd just left me alone like I asked." The man took a step toward Jasper. "I don't start fights, but I'll damn well finish them."

Jasper snatched the man's shirt with both hands, coming face-to-face with him. "Is that a challenge, son?"

The man chuckled. "Someone like you is hardly a challenge."

Ellie didn't know who the drunk stranger was, but she found herself silently wishing he'd beat Jasper to a pulp in front of everyone.

But when Jasper released his grip, the Marshal approached and decked the man square in the jaw. He stumbled backward until he hit the front door, then sunk to the floor. When he lifted his head, all Ellie could make out was an unwashed face with long shabby hair and a neglected beard.

"Now I don't want any more trouble from you, hear?" the Marshal growled. "I'm here to enjoy my time off, and don't want to have to be putting you in a jail cell tonight. This is Cog's establishment, so if he wants you out, you're out. I reckon you pull those horns in real quick and get lost if you know what's best for you."

The man put a hand to his swollen jaw and glared at the Marshal. "Are you going to help me up?"

He yelped when the Marshal gave him a hard kick instead. A few customers nearby laughed and remarked at the entertainment.

"Some law," he muttered. Without another word, he lifted himself up and trudged out the door, letting it slam behind him.

But the poor drunkard left his hat behind. Ellie left Rebecca's side and crept over to where the brawl had broken out. Slowly, she picked up the weathered old buckskin hat. Every scratch, tear and mark damaging the surface seemed to hold its own tragic story.

"I forgot my hat."

The voice made her jump, and she looked up to meet the eyes of the man who'd just stormed out. Now that he stood before her, he was close enough to get a better look. He was taller than he'd seemed earlier, and despite his neglected appearance, his eyes were a vibrant, almost familiar shade of blue. Too familiar, in fact.

Unsure of what to say and not wishing to further upset him, she extended her arms and silently offered the hat. His gaze never left hers as he took it from her hands. He placed the hat on his head and said "Thank you," then backed away and trudged out the building again.

Jasper grasped the arm of a thin brunette and yanked her from the stairs. Ellie didn't need to hear his words to know the girl was in trouble for associating with that man. Jasper's eyes burned as his lips moved swiftly, taking care not to cause any more of a scene in his establishment. When the harlot nodded, he flung her back into the rambunctious crowd. Ellie's stomach dropped when he aimed his gaze her way, his eyes narrow and black. "You stay away from that man, you hear?" He marched to where she stood, frozen. "I swear if I catch him in here again I'll—"

"Careful choosing those next words around me, Cogs," the Marshal chimed in, picking the crud from beneath his nails.

Ellie turned to the Marshal, still too afraid to look at the man who had ruined her—who now owned her. "Who is he?"

"The town drunk these days," the Marshal replied. "There's lots of stories about him, but nobody knows who he is for sure. He won't tell his name to a single soul. He's got a small camp just outside of town, and he barely talks to anyone unless he chooses to."

Jasper scowled and walked away, and the Marshal's gaze swept over her slowly. "Tell you what, beauty," he said, his mouth curving into a lustful smile. "There's something else I can tell you about him, something only I know. But it comes at a small price."

She shivered as he took her by the arm and closed in.

He gave the room a visual sweep, then turned back to her. "A friend of mine used to live over in Black Hawk years ago. Says the drunkard spent a lot of time as a kid there, and had a father as rich as they come. Wealthy Easterners."

Ellie clamped down on the inside of her cheek, confining a gasp. The Marshal's words tore into a hidden vault of memories inside her mind faster than a bolt of lightning. Images and flashbacks flooded her, so quickly that her knees nearly gave out. No wonder he'd seemed familiar . . . because she knew exactly who he was.

Gabriel Peterson.

The boy she'd grown up with for five years, the boy who often visited her dreams. When they first met, he'd been nine-years-old and she was only four. His father was a wealthy railroad tycoon, and their family's temporary home had sat just beyond her own family's land. With Gabriel's father away on business often, his mother allowed them to play for hours, regardless of their social differences.

Her heart warmed with memories of skipping home with dirt on her dress and scrapes on her knees. For a second, she almost forgot the very room she was standing in.

Then came the one September she'd remember forever—when Gabriel's family left town on the Transcontinental Railroad and never returned. It was enough to devastate her nine-year-old heart for years. They'd managed to write to one another a handful of times, but eventually, the letters stopped.

"Snap out of it, girl." Jasper's voice cut through her reverie. "This is Mr. James. He hails all the way from New York and requests your services for the evening."

The Marshal released her arm as Jasper motioned to the young, well-dressed man beside him, the same man she'd seen him speaking with earlier at the bar.

Mr. James' youthful, clean-shaven face donned an awkward smile. "I hear that you're the best girl here, Miss Lucy. You're certainly the most beautiful."

"You heard right, Mr. James." Jasper turned to Ellie. He grinned, but his eyes looked dangerous. "Why don't you take this fine gentleman upstairs, Lucy?" Leaning into her ear, he added, "You're new name is Lucy, and your room is the last door on the right. I'm taking it easy on you tonight, so you'd better give the man what he wants and give it good." His fingernails dug into her flesh as he clutched her arm. "You've got no reason to hold back. If I hear so much as a negative word from him, you're going to deal with me."

The feel of his hot, foul breath against her skin made her stomach lurch. She wanted to cry, but it would do her no good. If only she were strong enough to hit him and run.

Avoiding Jasper's glare, she forced a smile and took Mr. James by the hand. "Right this way, sir." She escorted him up the stairs, down the hall, and to the very last room.

It was the longest walk of her life.

* * *

The morning sun stretched its piercing rays through the cracks of the curtains, rousing her from a restless sleep. As her eyes drifted open, she could only wish to be back inside her pathetic shack, waking from a long nightmare. She rolled onto her back. Every aching muscle cried out as a cruel reminder that last night had all been real.

Mr. James stood beside the vanity, buttoning up his shirt. Heat flooded her face. She thought he'd left. Yanking the quilt on top of her, she held her breath.

"Thanks for last night, darling," he said, looking into the mirror and patting down his blond locks. He snatched the soiled male safe he'd worn while inside her from the dresser and searched the room. "Wastebasket?"

Ellie said nothing. She prayed for him to leave.

"Ah, here we are." His footsteps echoed throughout the room as he walked to the pail beside the closet and tossed the filthy rubber inside.

Embarrassment froze her on her back. She'd never shared her bed with a man in her life, and trembled at the thought of what mortifying deeds she'd engaged in with a complete stranger. It pained her more to know she had no choice in the matter. But she remembered little of last night, and that she could be thankful for.

Once fully dressed, Mr. James sauntered towards her and stripped the quilts off to expose her naked, shivering body. She closed her eyes and gritted her teeth as he put an unfamiliar hand on one breast and his mouth on another. Several agonizing seconds seemed to pass before he finally pulled away and went to the door.

"I'll see you when I'm back in town," he said.

He couldn't have shut the door fast enough. Ellie grabbed the blankets and pulled them over her head, shielding herself from the outside world for as long as she could.

"Breakfast! Come and get it!"

A woman's voice shot up from the first floor, loud enough to creep into Ellie's dreams and wake her. Her heavy eyes begged to close again, and she wondered how long it had been since she'd fallen back asleep. Not nearly long enough.

Worse than her burning eyes was her growling stomach, urging her to leave the haunting bedroom and eat whatever waited downstairs. This time, after a day of no food, hunger took the upper hand on sleep. She threw on her wrinkled dress and crept quietly down the stairs and into the kitchen.

The room was oddly cheery, with white painted walls and a sunny window, with small plants lining the sill. A cook kneaded dough and sifted flour for biscuits, while several pots and pans filled with hot food rested on the stovetop.

Ellie glanced at the table, her breath catching once she saw Jasper at the head. Fear trickled down her spine. He looked up from his plate for just a moment before returning to his meal, awarding her with a slight twinge of relief. Rebecca, Scarlet and three other harlots she hadn't met filled the remaining seats.

Rebecca rose from the table. "I was wondering if you were gonna come down or not. Here, I'll fix you a plate." She ambled to the stovetop and began loading a spare dish.

"Thank you." Ellie sank into an empty chair. The hefty woman beside her smiled with a mouth full of food.

"Jasper was just tellin' us about you," she said in a thick, Irish accent. "Ellie, is it? I'm Mattie, and this here's Lydia." She motioned to the girl Jasper had reprimanded the previous night. "That there is Bertha," she continued, pointing to the aloof brunette at the other end of the table. "She's deaf, so don't bother sayin' nothin' to her. That's Scarlet—"

"We've met," Scarlet said, without glancing from her plate.

"—and still upstairs is Chenoa. She's an Indian girl and don't speak much English, but she sure can pleasure a john or two."

"Here you go, hun." Rebecca set Ellie's plate down in front of her, while Mattie inhaled another heaping spoonful of porridge.

Compared to what had been in her cupboards, the sight of the rolls, bacon, eggs and porridge made Ellie's mouth water. As she lifted her fork, Jasper took one last swig of coffee and rose from his seat.

"I'm going to the bank and a few other places," he said, while pulling his hat and coat off the rack. "Becky, take Ellie into town and buy her a better dress and undergarments."

Ellie tried not to cringe as he turned his attention to her. "You listen to everything she says, understood? Don't be leaving her side for any reason."

She nodded, barely able to look at him. Terrible, cruel, frightnening man. An undeniable sense of ease seemed to pass over everyone once he'd left, and she cleared every delicious scrap from her dish in minutes.

"Hell, you just ate like you were never gonna see food again." Lydia stared at her while pouring generous amounts of whiskey into her own coffee cup.

"Shut up and let the poor girl eat how she likes," Rebecca snapped. She turned to Ellie and grinned. "Just don't end up lookin' like this one over here."

Rebecca shoved Mattie playfully, and Mattie placed a hand on her full-figured waist and glared. "My fat arse can pleasure a man ten times better than your dreary old bones ever could."

"Old bones? You could be my grandmother!" Rebecca snatched the whiskey from Lydia and drank straight from the bottle.

Scarlet shot up and slammed her hands down on the table. "I can't believe I'm forced to listen to this hogwash every damn day! You all should have been torn out of your mothers' filthy wombs and thrown to the dogs."

With an awful moan, she flung her plate into the wash basin and stormed out of the kitchen.

"You just got your back up 'cause Jasper's got a new favorite!" Rebecca called after her, clinking glasses with Mattie.

Lydia rose and moved to wash her plate in the basin. Ellie gathered Mattie and Rebecca's plates along with her own and followed. Perhaps she should ask about Gabriel Peterson. If anything could take her mind off the hell she'd been thrown into, it was the thought of speaking to him again after so many years.

"I'll wash, and you dry." Lydia tossed her a rag and a plate without so much as looking up.

Ellie began wiping down the dented tin. She swirled the rag in repeated circles, prolonging the time she had with each dish. "That man you were with last night—"

"Which one?" Lydia glanced over her shoulder and smirked.

"The one you got in trouble for seeing." She slid the dish into the cupboard a moment before Lydia handed her a second plate. "Do you know anything about him?"

"What's it to you?"

"Nothing. It's just that I think I know him is all."

Lydia ceased her washing and turned to face her.

"That's impossible. Nobody knows him, not even me. And I've been servicing him long enough to ought to know something." She wiped the dry end of her arm across her forehead. "He's like a stone wall, that one, and he ain't allowed back here on account of all the fights he's gotten into, breakin' tables and chairs and what not. Jasper was blowin' up about it when he saw him here last night. I shouldn't have let him in but . . ."

She shrugged her shoulders, shook her head and returned to washing.

"It's just that he's too damn good lookin' to say no to. All you have to do is stare into those eyes and you're a goner. I really gotta quit this time though, 'cause Jasper said he'd smack some sense into me if I ever did it again. My advice would be to stay far away from that man."

Ellie nodded and asked no more questions.

No one seemed to know much about the man apart from disliking him, and from the way he'd been talked about, she wondered if she might end up disliking him, too. No, she dashed that thought away and placed the rest of the dried plates in the cabinet.

Later, as she walked the muddy street beside Rebecca, she wondered how she might approach Peterson were she to see him again. The main drag stirred with five times the amount of people as last night, and the judgmental glares seemed to follow them everywhere. She struggled to keep pace with Rebecca, who appeared indifferent to the negative attention thrown their way. Ellie wished she could ignore it too, because it felt horrible.

Rebecca led her into a shop that had a fancy sign hanging above its display window. Exotic garments and fabrics lined the shelves in complete color coordination.

"Ah, my Belle," the silver-haired man behind the counter said with a grin.

Rebecca matched his smile's liveliness. "Mornin', Joe."

"Well, it is now." Leaning forward, he rested his hands on the counter and made eyes at Ellie. "And who's your friend?"

"She's Lucy. New girl." Rebecca took Ellie by the arm and gave her a nudge.

"Ah, very nice." He took a step back and gestured around the store. "Welcome to my humble shop, Miss Lucy. All the new stuff is over there by the window. You ladies let me know if you need help finding anything."

"Thanks, Joe."

Rebecca dragged Ellie toward the newly displayed items. "Joe's a customer of mine and I'm a customer of his," she whispered once they were out of earshot. "He takes care of me as long as I don't shop on the days his wife's here."

"He's married?" The same bitterness Ellie had felt the night before crept into the pit of her stomach.

"Oh, honey, a lot of them are married. What makes you think that blond gent you serviced last night wasn't married? When the master's away, the dogs will play."

Ellie said nothing else. Several minutes later, Rebecca had proven her fashion skills, choosing a violet taffeta dress with matching petticoat, corset and bloomers. Joe threw in two complimentary pairs of stockings, along with a nice pat on Rebecca's behind as they left the shop.

"All this dress needs now is to be altered to feature your best assets," Rebecca said, playfully pinching at Ellie's side.

Ellie flinched, ashamed at the annoyance she was beginning to feel at the woman's unconventional hospitality. The garment's neckline was already lower than anything she'd worn before. She didn't want to show off her body, and she certainly didn't want another strange man to touch her in any way.

"Can't we just leave it the way it is?" she asked.

"Trust me, Ellie, I know what I'm doing," Rebecca assured her. "Now, I need to visit the general store real quick for some perfume before we head back."

Something caught in Ellie's peripheral vision and she turned. As if on cue, Gabriel Peterson shuffled into the saloon across the street—just beyond her reach. The thought of speaking to him so soon dulled the pain in her chest. She held her breath, knowing a quick decision had to be made.

"If it's all right with you, I might head on back. My stomach isn't well at all." Her fingertips felt numb and she prayed the excuse was convincing enough.

"How bad is it?" Rebecca hesitated. "Jasper said you weren't to be leaving my side."

"He won't find out unless either of us sees him, which I'm sure we both can avoid."

The thought of finding Jasper inside the saloon sent a cold chill up the back of her neck. He wouldn't be in there when he had his own bar, would he?

Rebecca looked around. "All right, I'll hold on to the clothes and meet you back at home. Don't be goin' nowhere else."

Ellie nodded, making sure Rebecca had fully entered the store before she darted to the saloon and pushed through its swinging doors. Inside, thick clouds of smoke smothered her lungs, and she couldn't help but cough while her eyes adjusted to the dim light. Six men lounging at the bar greeted her with intimidating stares, while others lifted their heads from private table conversations to get a glimpse of the racket.

She covered her mouth, noticing the attention she'd drawn. The urge to flee welled up inside her, freezing her in place and erasing her reason for being there.

"Can I help you with somethin', miss?" Curiosity coated the bartender's voice. He stared in the same way his customers did.

"No, no thank you, I was just looking for—" She caught sight of Gabriel sitting alone in the far corner. He looked like a posed statue, resting his head in one hand and holding a half-empty bottle in the other. "Him."

The bartender's bewildered gaze bounced back and forth between her and the man. "You sure, miss? Nobody ever looks for him."

"Yes, I'm sure."

With a deep breath she shook out her hands, gathered whatever remaining courage she had, and slowly inched toward the man. She was thankful when most of the patrons had returned to their conversations, drowning out the awkward sound of her approaching footsteps.

Nerves wreaked havoc on her stomach as she drew closer, and she tried to ignore his rugged, intimidating appearance as he sat alone in the shadows. He looked nothing like the privileged boy she remembered. He could have been a completely different man. She let out the breath she'd been holding. When she reached him, he didn't blink an eye at her presence.

"Sir?" Her voice cracked the moment it left her throat.

He didn't respond.

She decided to try something different. "Mr. Peterson?"

"Mr. Peterson . . . was my father," he mumbled.

At least it was progress, and—she bit back a gasp. Had he just confirmed what she'd hoped? The heat of excitement tingled throughout her body, but if she wanted to learn more, she needed to keep talking.

"Gabriel, then?" Saying his name again felt like a dream. She probably hadn't said it since she was nine. "I was wondering if I'd be able to speak with you for a moment."

The disheveled man finally raised his head. He squinted up at her as if attempting to focus a distorted view. The beauty of his eyes—even glazed over—rendered her speechless. She knew in an instant they were the same. Her own Gabriel Peterson, sitting before her now, an outright mess.

"What did you call me?" His voice was rich and deep.

He was roostered for sure, but now might be her only chance to speak with him.

"Last night at The Inn . . . when I gave you back your hat. I thought you looked familiar, and then I realized—" Her botched words embarrassed her. Thank goodness he was drunk. Clearing her throat, she tried to relax and speak again. "I believe we may know each other."

He leaned back in his chair and tilted his head to the side as if it would help him get a better view of her. "You have the wrong man. I've never seen you before in my life." He sniffed and took a swig from his bottle.

"Then how do I know your name?"

"You don't," he grumbled.

"Yes, I do." She took a deep breath. This wasn't going to be easy. "And I meant when we were young. Your family had a home on the land beside mine, many years ago in Black Hawk. My name is Ellie Baker. Do you remember me at all?"

A moment slipped by, then he turned his head and took another swig. "Everything about my past is erased, gone. I couldn't remember you if I tried. Now I suggest you forget, too, and don't bother me again."

Defeat. With the way he was now, any more effort would prove useless. A tree would have been easier to talk to.

"Fine, I won't." She scowled, resisting the urge to shake some sense into him, before turning and storming out the doors.

Once outside, she knew she should go back to The Inn, but the ache in her chest prevented her from traveling any further. Gabriel Peterson was the only remaining piece of her past, and he hadn't the slightest idea who she was. Either that, or he denied it. Even worse was the thought of what a drunken disaster he'd become.

She sunk down on the stoop and buried her face in her hands, watching the dust dance around her feet in the breeze.

"Miss Elaine Baker?"

The deep seated voice was followed by two large leather boots appearing on the ground in front of her. She looked up, meeting eyes with the Sheriff.

"Yes, sir," she answered softly.

The large man smiled and tipped his hat in a friendly fashion. "I assumed it was you, seeing as I know all the folks in this town. Never seen you before, so I thought I'd try my luck."

The man reached into the pocket of his long leather duster and pulled out a sealed envelope. "This letter came to me this morning, along with the instructions to give it to you personally. I thought I'd be searching for days."

Ellie dug her fingernails into her palms to be sure she wasn't dreaming. As far as she knew, she'd paid all the bill collectors by the skin of her teeth, and had no living relatives she knew of. Who would send her a letter now? And in Creekwood?

Anxiety ravaged her as the Sheriff handed her the envelope, and she tore it open.

Dear Elaine,

I write to you with sympathy. I recently received the news regarding your mother Anne's death, and I imagine you're unmarried and living alone now. Your mother was the first cousin of my late wife, which binds us as family. For that reason, I insist you come to New Hampshire to live at my estate under my care. Arrangements are being made for a private coach to take you to Denver, where you will board the railroad bound for New England. I look forward to meeting you soon.

Regards,

H. Westgate

She rose to her feet and closed the letter, tears pricking the back of her eyes. She'd somehow been thrown a saving grace. She didn't know who H. Westgate was, nor did she care. Her heart wanted to burst at the promise of no longer being alone in the world, of moving far away from a shattered, uncertain life. For the first time in weeks, a smile stretched across her face.

The Sheriff tilted his head. "I take it this is good news for you."

"Yes, yes it is." She wiped a rogue tear while letting out a small laugh.

"I'm glad—" He pulled off his hat and dragged a hand across his brow. "Because I heard this note has gone through a lot of trouble to find you. Now my instructions were to send this coach your way, so where's home for you, miss?"

"Is there any telling when it might arrive?"

"Doesn't say."

If only she knew. Ellie bit her bottom lip to keep it from trembling. *Think of a place, fast. Any place other than—*

"Well?" he inquired.

"The Inn," she blurted, wishing she could snatch the words in the air and pull them back into her mouth.

The stunned Sheriff looked her once over. "Are you sure?"

"Yes, I'm sure."

He gave a nod. "Well, all right then."

"Please though, not during the evening hours. Late morning or midday is best."

Jasper would be out during the day, which now served as her best chance at escape. Here the Law was standing directly in front of her, and she couldn't bring herself to confess what the man had done. With no proof, Jasper would be free to lie through his teeth and punish her once the questions were through.

She didn't know how many more men he'd throw at her, how many more sleepless nights she'd endure, or how she would ever forget she'd seen Gabriel Peterson.

The only thing she did know was that somewhere, a coach was on its way.

Chapter Three

Ten days and still no coach.

Ellie sat on a settee, the last of her hope fleeting as a man sucked on the nape of her neck. Thanks to Jasper's advertising, the past few days had brought her twice as many customers as the other girls with little time in between. Her once virginal body had transformed into a sore, abused and tired vessel. Every second spent at The Inn stole a larger piece of her soul.

"I'm gonna get a drink. Be right back, don't you move." The foul-smelling patron stood and adjusted the crotch of his trousers before ambling toward the bar.

His absence pulled her from her daydreaming, and she put a hand to the raw space on her neck where his unwelcome lips had been.

"That fella's left one hell of a mark there. I've got a salve that can help," Lydia said as she approached. She claimed the unoccupied space beside Ellie.

"Thank you."

Lydia reached over and wiped the smeared makeup beneath Ellie's eyes. "You must be tired as all hell, even if your pockets aren't."

Ellie sighed. She hadn't realized it at the time, but she'd been spoiled by her first customer, Mr. James. He'd been the only one to use a rubber. The only one who hadn't treated her like a discarded rag doll. Now every day held the risk of pregnancy, which struck more fear into her heart than Jasper's wrath. The girls had told stories of what had happened to those unfortunate women who'd found themselves with child. Unless a wealthy man was involved, it almost always turned out bleak.

Lydia removed a small tin box from her pocket and opened the lid. Her fingers smeared the ointment around before dabbing at Ellie's bruised neck. "Anyone good enough to remember?"

Ellie gripped her forearms and hunched forward. "I don't pay attention to anything but wanting it to be over."

"That's because you're lettin' the men control you," Lydia stated, placing the top back on the tin. "They're only supposed to think they've got power, but the truth is you're not their puppet." Pride settled beneath her tone. "You've got the skills to finish 'em off and keep 'em comin' back again and again, which is far more than their wives are able to do."

Thoughts of Mama came to mind. She'd loved Papa with all her heart and worked so hard for him. Why wasn't she enough? Ellie would never know the reason, let alone understand it. But she didn't have to anymore.

Her naive, sheltered eyes had been opened to the foul, untrustworthy world where even the most adored man in her life had betrayed her. One thing was for certain; she would make sure the same thing never happened to her. She'd shut her heart away from the filth of men for as long as she lived. No matter what.

Suddenly, the idea of moving across the country felt like a cruel joke. Yes, Mama was from the East, but she'd never mentioned an H. Westgate before. The unfamiliar name was probably a hoax created by Jasper himself, testing her will to leave.

And had she passed his test? A life at The Inn would surely spare her from love and heartbreak, and perhaps one day, she might even become as free spirited as the other girls there. Jasper's rough morning visits to her room might even become tolerable. The money in her pocket would grow until she could find a way out.

Oh God, what am I thinking?

"Ellie." The voice made her flinch.

Mattie stood before her, her small eyes surveying the room before she leaned in to whisper, "There's a man outside asking for you. He ain't a customer. He wouldn't let me see his face, but he promised he meant no harm. He's waitin' out there now."

"A man?"

Mattie didn't answer.

The coach. It had to be the coach.

Ellie trembled from the inside out. Her body shivered beneath her clothes, yet her palms grew damp. She'd been wrong. Her ride had arrived, after dark, and she was unprepared. The racing of her heart made her head light, and she sprang from her seat, unsure of exactly what to do next.

"Thank you, Mattie," she whispered.

She glanced at the bar. The sloppy man who'd fancied her neck sat on a stool, cuddling Scarlet on his knee. That ought to keep him distracted for the next few minutes. But where was Jasper? She searched the crowded counter until she finally found him, immersed in conversation with a blond businessman. If she acted casual, he'd be too busy to notice.

"I'll be right back."

She slithered through the room with as much stealth as she could muster, her eyes fixed on Jasper the entire time. Each step toward the door dragged on longer than the one before, until finally, her fingers touched the handle. The door creaked open. She slipped outside and into the chilly darkness.

It wasn't until the door closed behind her that she found she hadn't been breathing the whole time. Standing on the dimly lit porch, she peered out into the moonless night.

"Hello? Is anyone there?" Her chest shook from the endless thrashing of her heart. Boot steps crunched on top of soil, and a dark male figure rounded the corner of the building. He approached steadily, trudging up the two steps leading to the porch where she stood, motionless. When the hanging lantern's light illuminated his face, she gasped at the sight of Gabriel Peterson.

The man had made an effort to groom himself, tying his wavy brown hair back. A few shorter strands dangled beside his face, now scrubbed clean of excess filth. He'd trimmed his beard, too, enough to reveal a hint of the strong jaw line beneath. Much less intimidating.

"I remember . . ." Remorse coated his tone, while a shaking hand pulled his hat from his head. "I remember you."

Ellie blinked. Those three words were the best thing she'd heard in ages. Part of her wanted to wrap her arms around him, but with fourteen years between now and their last hug, she stood her ground.

"Do you?" she asked, folding her arms.

"Of course." A look of shame crossed his face. "How could I not?"

"You denied it that day in the saloon. You were rude, uncaring and didn't seem to—"

"I know. And I don't expect your forgiveness, but I'd still like to apologize." He glanced up at the night sky before returning his gaze to her. "I'm sorry. I'd been drinking . . . and I wasn't myself. Please know that I'm not usually that way." He gave a humorless chuckle and shook his head. "Lord, who am I kidding. I suppose I've been *that* way for quite some time now."

Now that he wasn't slurring, the way his sober speech flowed off his tongue sounded very different than the other men in town. Aside from being much deeper, it was still the well-bred voice of privilege she remembered so well.

"I see," she said, surprised she wasn't more upset with him than she actually was.

"Well, I—" he cleared his throat. An awkwardness radiated from him, the way it would after years of social neglect. "I assume you still go by Ellie. If there's one thing I remember, it was your getting very upset at being called Elaine."

Yes! How strange—an unmistakable feeling of warmth spread beneath her ribs at the sound of him speaking her name. Well, he *did* remember that much.

She nodded. "Yes, I still go by Ellie. And you're still Gabriel, aren't you?" She lost the battle to remain serious, and allowed herself to smirk. "I only ask because you denied that, too."

He seemed to return the grin with little effort. "Forgive me. You can't imagine how strange it is hearing your name spoken aloud after so long."

She tilted her head, confused as to why he'd keep his name a secret. But she didn't pry.

Gabriel drew in a deep breath, as if breathing were difficult, and folded his arms tight across his chest. Despite the chilly evening, a dusting of perspiration on his forehead glistened in the lantern's light. He was struggling, and she didn't like seeing him this way. Still, if her presence was all it took to keep him sober, then perhaps one day she'd be able to break him from the bottle entirely.

This time, she heard the name *Lucy* called out from inside. It was Jasper's voice.

Gabriel's grin faded. "Please tell me if I'm being too forward, but I never would have imagined . . . finding you at a place like this."

Her chest cramped. Every part of her suffered at the decision to keep the truth from him . . . at least for now. Jasper always had a gun in his belt, and after fourteen years of separation, she couldn't imagine losing Gabriel now that she'd found him again.

"And I never would have imagined you this way, either," she retorted, clenching her jaw to prevent herself from asking for more too soon.

"You're right." He leaned back against one of the porch posts. "We certainly aren't children anymore, and sometimes life can be . . . difficult." Jasper's calling stabbed her ears again, only closer and more agitated this time. Gabriel lifted his head toward the sound, his eyes shadowed with hatred. "I only hope that snake hasn't hurt you in any way. If he has, then I might be inclined to do something about it."

Ellie let out a quiet breath. "I have to go back inside." Though she wanted nothing more than to stay. But if they were caught, it would be the end. "Will you meet me in the alley between the hardware store and the tailor tomorrow morning? I'd love to speak with you again."

His lips curved slightly. "Eleven o'clock?"

"I'll be there."

"I will, too. Now go back inside before I have to see that boss man of yours. Goodnight, Ellie." He placed his hat back on his head and descended the steps, disappearing into the darkness.

"Goodnight," she whispered into the empty space, closing her eyes and melting with joy.

The front door swung open and she jumped.

"Ellie! I've been calling you, dammit." Jasper's eyes burned with suspicion as he looked around the porch. "Was someone else out here with you?"

"No, sir," she rasped. "The smoke made me dizzy and I needed some fresh air."

She didn't blink as he glared at her.

"Are you lying to me?" he asked, tracing cold fingers along her jaw.

"No."

Her cheeks ached beneath his hand as he gripped her face. "No, what?"

"No, sir."

"Good." He covered her lips with his cigarette-tasting mouth and kissed her hard. "Now that you've had your fresh air, get the hell back to work."

He jerked opened the door and pushed her from behind, sending her back into the room.

* * *

Four o'clock in the morning, and Gabriel hadn't slept a wink. He snapped the case of his watch shut and dropped it beside his cot, his overheated body trembling beneath a sweat-drenched blanket. God, he felt terrible.

It might have been years since he'd practiced, but the physician in him still knew exactly what was happening to his deprived body. Any moron with a brain would know. He cursed out loud at his own recklessness. Each passing minute of withdrawal felt worse than the one before, and his mind battled between praying for death and reminding him that he wasn't going to die. He clutched his stomach as hard waves of nausea overtook him, while his head pounded without mercy. Every part of him struggled to resist opening his flask and tasting what his body craved.

Then he remembered the willow bark in his bag. His useless arms shook beneath his dead weight as he strained to lift himself up. Once he had a hold of his bearings, he snatched up the leather satchel at the foot of his cot and began digging. He breathed a sigh of relief as he pulled out the small wad of paper he'd been searching for and unfolded it, revealing a few pieces of the natural pain killer. He threw them in his mouth, chewing and sucking the bitter juices in hopes that it might ease his aching head.

He was suddenly tired. Tired of scraping by, and tired of running from the good life he'd left behind. As if the physical misery weren't enough, his mind—no longer clouded by liquor—struggled under the burden of regret. His patients, his friends, and most importantly his family, all believed him dead. It was unacceptable. He should have returned long ago. So much wasted time, but maybe it wasn't too late.

With his elbows balanced on his knees, he dropped his head into his hands and reminded himself to breathe as his stomach twisted. He needed better thoughts to comfort him, and quick.

The way Ellie Baker had looked standing on the lamp-lit porch was a welcome distraction. After fourteen years, he never would have imagined seeing her angelic face again.

Her features looked the same as he remembered, and to his delight, the familiar batch of freckles on the bridge of her nose had carried into adulthood. They'd always been his favorite part of her face. As for her body, now *that* had changed a great deal since he'd last seen her, and in ways that made his trousers tighten around his crotch. Young Ellie Baker was now very much a grown woman, whose rich raven hair, emerald eyes and tantalizing curves could make any man's thoughts turn inappropriate.

Christ, and she was a harlot.

She didn't look like any he'd seen before, that he was sure of. Her soft, youthful face showed no signs of the harsh wear resulting from that lifestyle. She'd been reluctant to answer his questions pertaining to her line of work, and he thirsted to know the reason why. Something didn't seem right, not when he recalled hazy images of the pigtailed rancher's daughter he used to play hide-and-seek with. Whatever the reason, he'd be sure to find out and convince her to leave that place—and the worthless man she worked for.

He owed her that much after what she'd unknowingly done for him. While the rest of the town turned their heads, Ellie Baker had the courage to seek him out and actually talk to him. Until she'd forced him to remember, he'd forgotten what it felt like to engage in civil conversation with another person. He still had a life, and he was wasting it.

Cold chills replaced the burning of his body, and he laid his head on the moist cot. He pulled the thick wool blankets back over his shivering torso and shut his eyes, praying for sleep to find him. He didn't know how he'd endure the torture for much longer, but he had no damn choice in the matter.

He'd made up his mind.

* * *

Ellie awoke with a headache. One too many nips of whiskey had proven a brainless mistake, even if it did help her forget the man in her bed. She pressed a palm to her forehead, sat up, and looked at the clock resting on the bedside table.

Ten twenty-five.

That gave her just enough time to wash up, dress, and dash to the meeting place. The thought of seeing her old friend again instantly outweighed the sickness she felt, and a newfound sense of purpose was quickly replacing the gloom.

As she threw her legs over the side of the bed, a strong hand clasped around her wrist.

"Hold it, where do you think you're goin', missy?"

Darn, she'd been too preoccupied to notice that her customer from last night never left. He gave a yellow-toothed smile that made her stomach churn.

"I got a piss-proud erection that only your tight little snatch can take care of."

Frustration boiled her blood. "Your time is long up, mister. You never paid to spend the night."

"I only got one thing that's long and up, and it ain't my time. I'll pay that dark-haired fella as soon as I'm done, I swear it. Now come here, girl." He slapped a calloused hand onto her bare shoulder and pulled her back towards him. She cringed, knowing she'd no choice but to oblige when it came to Jasper's profits.

By the time the man left it was five past eleven. She'd be late, but she hurried to dress in the hopes that Gabriel had waited. Her clumsy fingers only seemed to tousle her hair more as she made an effort to fix it while conjuring up questions for him.

She would try to find out why his family had left Black Hawk for good. Had he missed her as much as she'd missed him? Most importantly, she'd ask what had brought him to Creekwood, and hopefully learn the reasons behind the heartbreaking life he now led. Somehow, some way, she had to help him out of it.

She glanced into the mirror one last time. Her old skirt and blouse, hidden away in the drawer for days, made her look like her old self again. A tiny spark of something resembling optimism kindled inside her. But when she turned the knob and swung the door open, she nearly collided with Jasper.

His expression was bland, but his eyes held danger. Something told her he hadn't come for one of his occasional morning visits. She backed away as he slowly paced toward her and shut the door.

"Ellie dearest, how nice to see you." His gaze swept her dress, and he gave a mocking smile. "And looking so incredibly *plain* all the while."

She shuddered as his heels tapped against the floorboards. "I don't think you know why I'm here, do you?" he asked calmly.

Her mind began to race, and she wondered if the yellow-toothed rancher hadn't paid him after all, or if he'd somehow got wind of Gabriel's visit the previous night. Either way, she was destined for punishment.

"No, sir," she stammered, her voice barely above a whisper.

Folding his arms, he barked a sarcastic chuckle. "Are you sure? Why don't you go over to the window and look down. Tell me what you see, hmmm?"

She hesitated for a moment, then crept over to the single, half-opened window and peered between the white curtains. A coach with four horses was parked directly in front of the building.

Her stomach dropped.

The letter had been real. And Jasper had found out.

"It's funny, that thing pulled up just as I was leaving to go to town. The driver asked me for you. Now why would he do that, Ellie?"

"I don't know."

Her only chance to get away dangled before her like bait on a hook, and she'd never be able to touch it.

"Oh, yes you do," Jasper said. He reached out and fingered a loose strand of her hair. "And to think that if I'd left just a few minutes earlier, you'd have been long gone by the time I returned. Funny how things work out, isn't it? So, you were planning on going somewhere without telling me about it?"

She couldn't breathe.

"No . . ."

"Well, it sure looks that way to me."

He shrugged off his coat and hung it on the hook behind the door. This was no ordinary offense. He must have something terrible in store for her. Something painful. She attempted to regain control of her fear, but it was impossible.

"There must be some mistake." As a last resort, she made a desperate effort to lie. "Who would send a coach for me? By all means, tell him to leave." Her legs wobbled beneath her as she crossed to Jasper and took his hand. "I want to stay here with you . . . I like it here."

His other hand reached up to caress her cheek. The room began to spin. She took deep breaths in fear of collapsing and never waking again.

"You're a terrible little liar, Ellie Baker." He pulled her letter from his jacket pocket. "This is why I search my girls' rooms. Like hell you weren't getting on that coach. Remember what I said about you running away from me? I thought I'd made myself clear."

"Please, Jasper, I'll never hide anything from you again." She gripped his coat with both hands. "You have my word!"

He shook his head. "I'm afraid that's not good enough. I have to make sure by teaching you a lesson you won't soon forget."

She bolted for the door. Jasper charged, snatching her by the hair and whipping her to the floor. He yanked her up, and she cried out when he struck a hard blow to her face. Her body hit the wall so hard that it knocked the breath from her lungs.

"Go ahead and cry all you want to, but the girls know better than to stand up to me. And I locked the front door, so your damn driver can't help you, either!"

He smacked Ellie again before hurling her to the bed and mounting her. His chilly hand covered her mouth, silencing her cries as he pulled a knife from his boot.

"Now, what should I do that'll teach you a lesson but won't affect business?" he said, as he held the knife over her trembling body. "Aha. You could easily do without one of your pretty little toes."

He pulled the gun from his belt and pointed it at her face in the same way he'd done the night he ruined her. She flinched as he ripped into the bottom of her stocking with the knife, exposing her left foot.

"Eenie, meenie, miney . . ." He tapped the tip of the blade playfully over each digit, enjoying himself. "Moe . . ." He stopped at her fourth toe and looked her dead in the eye. "Perfect. In case you were wondering, my dear, this is going to hurt," he snickered. "A lot."

Ellie squeezed her eyes shut and gripped the bed sheets. She waited for the painful sting of the first cut, but instead, she felt Jasper's heavy body being torn from hers. Her eyes shot open to find Gabriel pinning him to the back wall.

He decked Jasper hard enough to shatter his nose. "So you like hurting women, do you, Cogs?"

"How dare you," Jasper spat through blood cascading down his lips. He headbutted Gabriel, sending him backward, and stripping him of control.

The two men broke into a full-on brawl, slamming against walls and furniture, while thrashing about the small bedroom. Ellie reached out and clutched Jasper's knife from where he'd dropped it on the bed.

Gabriel threw a punch to Jasper's gut, followed by a swift knee to his groin. Jasper swung a fist, which met Gabriel's jaw with a hard smack. Gabriel blocked the second swing and decked Jasper back, sending him crashing into the bed's footboard.

The shudder of Jasper's body colliding with brass made Ellie shriek, and within moments Gabriel had tackled her boss to the floor. She sprung to the bed's edge for a better view. As she clutched the brass posts, it dawned on her that Jasper still had a weapon beneath his belt.

"Gun . . . he has a gun!" she cried.

Her warning came too late. Jasper had pulled his Colt revolver and was attempting to aim, while Gabriel tried to wrestle the weapon from his hand. Their grunts filled the room, and neither dared give in. Ellie gripped the knife tighter as Gabriel's arms began to shake from holding Jasper off. Oh, God, she couldn't take it anymore, and she couldn't watch Gabriel die.

She had to do something!

Ignoring her terror, she leapt from the bed and plunged the knife deep into the back of Jasper's thigh. He screamed, dropping his guard long enough for Gabriel to knock him unconscious and hurl him to the floor.

Ellie fell backward, her heart pummeling her chest.

Gabriel rushed to her, breathless. "Are you all right?"

"I think so." She looked up at him, her thoughts a blur.

"Thank you for what you did." He peered back at Jasper one more time before returning his gaze to her. "Does anything hurt or feel broken? I was . . . *am* a doctor."

He placed a gentle hand on her swollen cheek, then proceeded to search the rest of her body for places of pain. Her pounding heart began to relax as his hands slid from her shoulders to her wrists, from her ribs to her hips, and from her thighs to her ankles.

"No, n—nothing's broken." Her voice struggled past the tightness in her throat. "How did you get in?"

"The window," he said. "When I didn't see you in town this morning, I grew worried. The Ellie Baker I once knew would have never missed an opportunity to visit with me."

He winked in an attempt to make light of the situation. She appreciated it.

"I came here and saw a coach sitting outside. The driver told me he'd been waiting for you, which is when we both heard your screams coming from upstairs. He boosted me up the wall and I climbed in through the window."

"I can't thank you enough," she whispered. The tears began to form, but she prayed she could compose herself long enough to see him off.

"I'm so sorry this happened to you." His nostrils flared, and he shook his head as he surveyed her battered face. "Dammit, I wish I'd gotten to you sooner."

"What the hell's going on in there?" a male voice thundered from the hall.

Gabriel lifted her up off the floor, cradling her in his solid arms. "I'm getting you out of here."

She gripped him tightly, resting her face in his dirty, sweaty shirt as they headed for the door. She exhaled against his chest, the feeling of safety wrapping around her the first time in days.

He ceased walking, and she lifted her head to see a burly, shirtless man with unfastened trousers standing just beyond the doorframe. A smaller, thinner man no older than twenty stood behind him.

"How could I have thought this would be easy?" Gabriel grumbled, bringing her back into the room and lowering her onto the bed.

He turned and stormed over to the door.

"Everything is under control here, gentlemen. I'd highly recommend returning to your rooms if you don't want any trouble."

Both men observed Jasper's limp body before turning their attention to where she sat.

"I'm afraid that ain't possible. We're involved now, see," said the man with no shirt as he cracked his dirty knuckles.

The younger man spit. "You shouldn't have done what you did, fella."

Gabriel pushed up his sleeves. "You can leave now, or I can go through you. Your choice."

Ellie shuddered as the shirtless man ogled her with a mocking smirk. "I'm sure that whatever Cogs was gonna do to her, the whore deserved it."

Gabriel swung his fist, bashing the big man square in the jaw and sending him backward into the hall. The younger man joined in the scuffle, leaving her alone inside the room. Feet shuffled, the walls shook and curses blared. Gabriel must have been worn out from his first fight. How he could he possibly manage taking on two more men?

She spotted Jasper's gun beside his unconscious body. She rushed to the Colt, wrapped her fingers around the warm handle, and picked it up. But how did one fire a gun? If it meant defending her friend's life, she'd do it any way she had to.

She'd taken but one step when the disturbing racket suddenly ceased, and she fingered the trigger while aiming at the door frame. Her stomach twisted with anticipation. Footsteps drew closer and she squared herself off, ready to fire. Gabriel rounded the corner with no one trailing behind him.

Dropping the weapon, she ran to him. He took her hand while catching his breath. He led her into the hall, where they stepped carefully over the two unconscious men before trudging down the stairs and rushing outside.

He lifted her into the coach, slapped a few bills into the driver's hand and shut the door. "Make sure her ride is as smooth as possible," he instructed. Reaching through the window, he wiped the blood from her bottom lip. "You're safe now."

Instead of relief, Ellie felt nothing but sorrow. Fourteen years apart, and she hadn't even spent a day with Gabriel Peterson. Now they would part ways again—most likely forever.

"Please, come with me!" she begged.

He shook his head. "I can't, Ellie. I have my own life to repair. You reminded me of that."

She nodded, barely able to make sense of what was happening.

"You just go wherever you're headed and don't look back, understood?"

"Yes."

A single tear rolled down her swollen cheek. It was all her drained eyes had left to give. Gabriel parted his lips as if to say more, but Jasper hollered from somewhere inside, calling out her name like a madman.

"Go, now!" Gabriel pounded the side of the coach twice.

Ellie clutched the window frame as the driver cracked the whip and the vehicle began rolling forward. "Thank you, Gabriel."

His lips curved into somber smile. "Until we meet again, Miss Baker."

"Goodbye," she said softly. She mourned their short-lived reunion more than she ever would have imagined.

When the coach had passed him by, she leaned out the window, and watched his silhouette become smaller until she could no longer see him.

She buried her face in her hands and prayed he would be all right.

Chapter Four
New Hampshire

"Nearly there, miss," the carriage driver called over his shoulder.

Ellie lifted her head from the carriage window and yawned. After roughly two weeks of travel, the man's words flowed like music to her ears. She stretched her cramped neck as the vehicle's wooden wheels rolled from soil to gravel, and gave silent thanks that the long journey had finally reached its end. But she shouldn't complain. The spring weather had been mostly forgiving along the way, and she'd found the trains fairly uncomplicated to board once she'd asked for help. Best of all, the wounds on her face had sufficient time to heal before she encountered new faces.

As the carriage rolled on, the narrow, lonely road gave way to house-lined streets, and finally, to a wide, two-lane thoroughfare in the heart of a busy town. The wheels bumped along the cobblestone as buildings drifted past, all of them nicer than anywhere else she'd ever seen.

Part of her hoped this would be home. The way everything rested in a valley, surrounded by forested mountains and clear rivers, reminded her of a fairytale.

The carriage rounded another turn, speeding past numerous homes and into rolling hills. Houses sat fewer and farther between now, all much larger and more elaborate than their downtown cousins. Just past a thicket of dogwoods, they turned through an iron gate at least eight feet tall.

Her pulse increased.

They had arrived.

With her head against the door, she shut her eyes and let out a nervous breath. Two weeks ago, she'd attributed her doubt in this place to Jasper's trickery. Now she was moments away from meeting the distant relative who had brought her across the nation with just a word.

Thank heaven no one could see how she gawked as they rolled down a long drive lined with perfectly trimmed hedges. Moments later, the estate grounds opened into full view, stretching for acres around an enormous house with wide roofs extending towards the heavens. She'd never seen a castle before, but surely they must look a lot like this.

White columns stretched three-stories-high in pairs, on either side of the wide entry. Thick flowered vines climbed the mansion's stone walls and curved around its massive windows. Blooming rose bushes wove colorful patterns in the center of the driveway.

The carriage coasted to its final stop and the driver opened the door. Undeniable feelings of nervousness accompanied Ellie as her feet made contact with solid ground. Tilting her head back, she marveled at the new and intimidating fortress she would now call home.

When the driver marched up the steps leading to the portico, she tried to follow, but her frozen knees made walking difficult. So she straightened out her skirt instead, watching as he lifted one of the heavy brass knockers and rapped three times.

When the door opened, a well-dressed butler, accompanied by two large dogs, stepped outside. He frowned when the animals bounded out from behind him, both whining anxiously and wagging their tails with excitement. Ellie grinned as they went straight to her and danced around her legs in circles.

"Zeus, Charles, inside at once!"

The dogs hesitated upon the command, until a clap of his hands sent them rushing back into the house. As the man eyed Ellie with a stony expression, she became aware of the plain clothing she wore. She felt like a beacon, and not in a good way.

"I've arrived with Miss Elaine Baker," the driver announced.

"Yes, of course." The man bowed at the waist. "Wait here, please."

He spun around and strutted back inside, returning moments later with a young maid in a green dress, white cap and apron.

Her gaze settled on Ellie and she grinned. "Good afternoon, Miss Baker," she said with a curtsy. "My name is Mary, and I'll be showing you to your room while Mr. Hanlon tends to your things." She glanced at the stiff butler on the steps before gesturing for Ellie to follow.

Ellie swallowed, embarrassment welling up inside her. Leaning close to Mary, she whispered, "I don't . . . have any things."

"Oh." The maid paused for a moment, yet still smiled. "Well, no matter. Mr. Westgate has taken the liberty of purchasing a few welcoming gifts for you. I've already put them in your room."

Ellie's mouth nearly fell open. "Oh, no, he didn't have to do that."

"As lovely as your ensemble is, Miss Baker, I don't think Mr. Westgate would be too thrilled if you wore it to dinner."

"Still, that was too kind of him."

How was this happening to her? Abused one minute, then pampered the next? As she followed the maid toward the steps and took in the overwhelming scenery around her, she'd never felt more grateful.

They reached the top of the portico, and Mary extended an arm inside. "This way, miss."

Just when Ellie thought the house couldn't get any more splendid, she stepped through the gaping doorframe and into an utterly mesmerizing interior. Expensive rugs created patterns of color across the marble floors, and tastefully papered walls displayed the finest oil paintings and tapestries. Each room they passed appeared more elegant than the last, with plush armchairs, tall fireplaces, and intricately patterned curtains framing the sparkling windows.

She kept close to Mary as they ascended one of two carpeted staircases that curved like a horseshoe into the entrance hall. They turned left at the top, which led to a wide hall with a cream-colored chair rail and blue floral wallpaper. When they reached the third door from the end, Mary came to a halt.

"This is your room." She turned the knob and opened the door.

Ellie stepped into a space larger than her entire shack in Creekwood. The bedroom's decor reflected the good taste of the rest of the house, with pink and yellow tea rose wallpaper that glistened under the light of four bright windows. A fireplace stretched halfway up the wall between two plush arm chairs, and beautiful custom furniture filled the remainder of the room.

"It's like a dream," she whispered.

"Yes, it's my favorite," the maid answered, before disappearing into the washroom.

Running a hand down the hand-carved bedpost, Ellie gaped at the sky blue satin dress displayed atop the covers. She'd only seen dresses that beautiful in catalogues and shop windows. Never in her wildest dreams had she ever imagined wearing one. She moved closer, brushing her fingertips over the cream-lace collar as Mary reappeared.

"I've drawn you a warm bath, and I'll return in two hours to dress you for dinner. You'll meet the family then." She pointed to a tasseled rope dangling beside the bed. "Don't hesitate to ring for me if you need anything else."

"The family?"

"Yes, of course." Mary tilted her head. "Surely you didn't think the master of the house lived alone."

"I'm not sure what I thought," Ellie admitted.

"It's all right, miss. You're tired. I'll leave you to rest."

"Thank you, Mary."

The maid nodded with a brief curtsy, then shut the door behind her.

Despite Ellie's scattered nerves, the warm, lavender-scented bath was a welcoming sight. She slipped into the clawfoot tub, unable to remember the last time she'd experienced water so soothing. The soap felt like rich velvet against her skin as she washed away the dirt and grime of the past few weeks. But no matter how hard she scrubbed, she'd never reach the deep places that needed cleansing the most. She would never wash away Jasper Cogs.

Once clean, she threw her naked body onto the large, cloud-like bed, stretching as far as her tired limbs would allow. She let out a much-felt sigh. Her mind reeled with anticipation, but her body felt heavy, and her eyes burned for rest. She needed to close them, if only for a few minutes. Those few minutes eventually gave way to sleep.

A rapping on the bedroom door jostled her awake. Her head felt like it weighed a hundred pounds as she lifted it from the pillow.

"Miss Baker?" Mary spoke from the hallway.

She'd overslept! "Just a minute!"

She flew out of bed, smacking her knee on the post as she stumbled about. Ignoring the searing pain, she raced to the mirror and ran uncoordinated fingers through her damp, tangled hair and pinned it back into a low bun. She reached for her old clothes. Her eyes latched onto the brand new gown that still lay on the bed. Luckily, she hadn't rolled on it during her nap. She held up the complicated pieces of clothing, completely unaware as how to even begin putting them on. Then, she remembered Mary's offered assistance.

"Mary? Come in!" she called out.

The door flew open and Mary darted inside, shaking her head. "I told you I'd dress you, miss. Believe me, these fancy garments are the farthest thing from simple."

Mary worked swiftly with every piece of the ensemble, tugging corset strings and fastening hooks and buttons with impressive speed. Ellie could barely breathe once fully dressed. They raced down the stairs and through the halls, until they finally reached the dining room. The Westgate family sat at a large, well-adorned table.

Their heads turned upon her entry.

At the end sat a dark-haired man with graying temples, deep brown eyes and a thick, curled mustache. He stood, along with the boy beside him.

"At last, here she is," he announced with a proper grin. "Welcome, Elaine. We're so pleased to finally have you here with us." Adjusting his eyeglasses, he gestured to the upholstered mahogany chair beside him. "Have a seat, my dear."

"Thank you, sir." She dipped her head, praying she wouldn't collapse right there at the table as she lowered herself into the chair.

Her winded lungs battled for breath against her restrictive corset. The man and boy lowered themselves back into their seats, while the delicate young woman sitting across from her gave a polite smile.

"Allow me to introduce myself," the man said. "I'm Henry Westgate. This is my daughter Jane and my son John." He gestured to the young woman and the dark-haired boy, a spitting image of his father.

"It's wonderful to finally meet you." Jane beamed. "That dress suits you very well. Blue is certainly one of your best colors."

"It's the loveliest thing I've ever worn, thank you very much," Ellie replied, squeezing her hands together in her lap. She didn't know what to do with them, and could only hope she didn't look as nervous on the outside as she felt inside.

Mr. Westgate sipped from his water glass and set it down on the table. "The pleasure is mine, my dear. And Jane is right" —his friendly gaze swept over her— "You do look marvelous."

The door swung outward and five servants entered the room. A steaming bowl of creamy asparagus soup was placed in front of each person. Hanlon lowered a basket of warm bread onto the center of the table, and proceeded to pour wine from a crystal container into each gold-rimmed glass. Each glass, apart from John's . . .

The boy frowned. "Father, I'm sixteen years old. All the other boys in school have been drinking since age nine. Why can't I have just a glass?"

His father puckered his brow and raised his soup spoon. "I don't care if those boys have been drinking since infancy. I'm the head of this household, and I say you wait until you're eighteen.

Holding one's liquor requires the responsibility and level headedness of a grown man."

Ellie twisted the napkin in her lap as she thought of Gabriel. She'd learned firsthand what the effects of alcohol could do to a man—even a grown one—and never cared to see it again. Bless him for having tried his hardest to abstain for her. She'd be forever grateful for his effort, but her concern for his well-being still unsettled her. If only she knew where he was, what he was doing, and most of all, if he were safe.

"Yes, sir." John's shoulders sank in submission.

"However," Mr. Westgate cleared his throat, "as far as I'm concerned, Elaine's arrival marks this evening as a special occasion." He grinned as he brought the spoon to his lips. "Therefore, just for tonight, I'll allow it."

"Thank you, Father." John's dark eyes sparkled as Hanlon filled his glass with the deep red drink.

Ellie looked down at her soup. The delicious scents of butter, asparagus and pepper tantalized her nose. Now that good food sat in front of her, the challenge of maintaining etiquette during conversation had commenced. But she'd try her best. Jane plucked a specific spoon from her sea of silverware. Ellie took care to mimic the young woman's example, move-for-move.

"I'd hoped and prayed you'd be here in time for my wedding, Elaine," Jane said with another genuine smile. "I can't tell you how delighted I am."

Ellie accidentally slurped a hot spoonful, and fought to keep the pain from showing on her face. "Oh, congratulations, Jane. When will you be getting married?"

"I'll be marrying Mr. Matthew Tiller in two weeks time." The girl's eyes danced as she gently stirred her soup.

"The finest match I've ever seen." Mr. Westgate sipped from his wineglass and lifted it high into the air. "In fact, I propose a toast. To Jane's marriage and Elaine's arrival, new beginnings for all."

"To new beginnings for all," his children replied in unison.

Ellie raised her glass along with them, surveying the contented faces of her newly acquired kin. An orphan no longer. She'd nearly forgotten what it felt like to be part of a family. Already, the thought of being included in the Westgate's plans caused something warm to seep into her chest.

Light conversation accompanied the remainder of the first course. Once everyone's bowls were cleared, the same servants returned carrying china loaded with steaming food. Roast turkey with fluffy dressing, along with seasoned boiled potatoes and creamed spinach, had been generously portioned onto every plate. Silver bowls brimming with soft butter and an assortment of jams were placed on the table, and a fresh batch of warm rolls replaced the previous one.

She'd never seen a feast so remarkable, and the moment she tasted it, the urge to dig in like a starved animal almost overcame her. Still, she paid detailed attention to the family's dining etiquette, cutting into one small piece at a time and dabbing at the corners of her mouth with her monogrammed napkin. By the time dessert ended, Mr. Westgate firmly insisted she turn in early during her first night at the house.

But she couldn't sleep. Especially once she'd opened the armoire and seen the generously stocked shelves of clothing inside. It was too much, even if Mr. Westgate saw money as no object. Why was the man being so kind to her? She didn't deserve kindness. She stood before the bedroom mirror, gazing at herself in a brand new nightgown, barely recognizing the reflection staring back. The sight of herself in the white cotton almost made her forget how naked she'd been in the clutches of hungry strangers. She looked almost virginal.

But no amount of expensive clothing could fix the damage done. A cold, hard truth. And when the time came for her to marry, everyone would know it, including the Westgates. How would she explain herself after leaving no stain upon the bridal bed?

The thought sickened her. She climbed into bed and fell back against the pillows.

A faint tapping came from the door.

"Are you awake, Elaine?" Jane's soft voice asked from the other side.

Ellie lifted herself up, almost feeling as if she were hearing an old friend. Something about the girl exuded comfort. "Yes, Jane, come in."

The door inched opened and Jane tiptoed inside, wearing a similar nightgown. She smiled warmly, her strawberry blonde curls bouncing across her back as she bounded toward the bed.

"I thought I'd pay you a visit to be sure you were all right," she whispered. "I know how unsettling change can be, especially when you're sleeping in a brand new place far away."

Ellie grinned, savoring the natural kindness like a breath of fresh air. "That's very kind, thank you. The good thing about traveling is that it makes it much easier to fall asleep no matter where you are."

"You're completely right, and I'll leave you to get some rest." Jane dipped her head and began to turn, yet stopped once she settled eyes on Ellie's hair. "Oh, that braid is beautiful. Will you teach me how to make one?"

Ellie arched an eyebrow and pulled the dark rope of woven hair over her shoulder. "What, a simple braid? You were never—" But of course Jane's mother was deceased, so maybe she had no one to teach her.

Jane shook her head. "Mother was far too busy for such things when I was small. The nannies and maids have always fixed my hair."

How could something so simple have been kept from Jane her entire life? Ellie felt her eyes go wide. There hadn't been a day when Mama didn't spend time with her, teaching her things like braids, cooking, gardening and sewing clothes.

"It's very easy, just follow my lead." She slid the ribbon off the end and unraveled the braid.

She showed Jane how to separate her hair into three sections, weaving them into one another in a specific pattern. Three attempts later and Jane had finally gotten it right.

"Oh, thank you, Elaine! I've had many braids in my life, but this one is my favorite because I made it myself," she said, admiring her work in the mirror.

"That's always when you appreciate things most." Ellie watched her proud pupil laugh and twirl about the room. "But please, call me Ellie."

Jane's hazel eyes lit above raised cheekbones. "Is that what you're used to being called?"

"Yes, since I was small."

"Then from now on, we will all call you Ellie," she proclaimed. Optimistic and vibrant, she couldn't have been more different than the girls at the brothel. "Tomorrow I can give you a painting lesson if you'd like. I've become quite good at landscapes."

"I'd like that very much."

Jane twirled around and glanced at the clock resting on the fireplace mantle. "Goodness, it's late. Time to leave you to get some rest."

Ellie nodded, finding she already missed the girl as she frisked to the door and twisted the knob. Jane slipped into the dark hall, popping her head back inside the small opening.

"I've always wanted a sister," she whispered. "Goodnight, Ellie."

Ellie grinned. "Goodnight, Jane."

She doused the gas lamp beside the bed and slid beneath the warm sheets, thankful sleep was beginning to find her. She had plenty of time to worry about fitting into upper class society tomorrow. After less than a day with her new family, she knew she'd been blessed. And she'd work her hardest to gain their approval—no matter how intimidating she found them.

The Westgates were all she had now, and she would try to hide her shameful secret for as long as possible.

* * *

The rusted hinges of the front door rasped as Gabriel pushed it open, fighting against the pile of unopened letters that sat just beneath the post slot. Four years later and the lock still held, allowing his spare key to work once he'd blown off the debris. Thank God he'd somehow remembered its hiding place beneath the veranda.

As he stepped over the neglected mail and into the dark foyer with a lantern in hand, he waited for a sense of familiarity. He was home, but it certainly didn't feel that way. Hell, he'd been surprised to find the house still remained in his possession after so long. His jaw clenched at the cold reality of it now being the only possession to his name.

Extending the lantern into the parlor, he expelled a breath of relief. Not only had his furniture remained, but someone had taken the time to cover each piece with white sheets. He must have his uncle to thank for that. Even in limited visibility, he could still make out the layer of dust settled over everything, and a mass of cobwebs hugged the nooks and crannies. It was a hell of a mess.

"At least I've arrived before the mice," he muttered.

He dragged a hand along the walls of the hallway as he crept past each room, taking in their abandoned, ghostlike state. When he reached his old examination room, he stopped. A wooden examining table sat in the center. Various shelves holding spoiled medicine bottles and tools; three chairs and a coat rack sat untouched, as if frozen in time. He let himself smirk as he gripped the doorframe. Finally, he felt at home.

He missed the time he'd spent there, treating many of his neighbors and friends. Those who hadn't deserved to be left behind. There must have been at least one new doctor to come about during his absence, and a regretful bitterness turned his stomach at the thought of what he'd lost. Reestablishing his practice wouldn't be easy, but damn if he'd succumb to defeat.

The staircase groaned beneath his footsteps as he made the ascent to his old bedroom. The settled dust covering his bed glistened like gray snow in the dim light. He placed the lantern on the bedside table, shielded his face with one arm, and pulled the protective sheet off in one swift motion. When he leaned forward to pound the remaining grime from the bare mattress, his toe struck something solid.

What the hell?

He dropped to his knees and slid an unfamiliar wooden box out from beneath the bed. The hinged lid squeaked as he lifted it open, revealing a generous pile of personal pictures and portraits that someone must have tucked away. He reached over and snatched the lantern from the table, placing it near the photos for better visibility as he began rummaging through the box.

The first few images he pulled were of himself during various years of aging, followed by a photo of his parents cradling him as an infant at his christening. He hadn't seen that one in years, and chuckled at the sight of himself in the long white dress and bonnet, pouting but completely unable to protest at his tender age.

His father stood stoic as always, while his mother's gaze seemed to reach out through the photograph as he studied her graceful features. Even in black and white, he could almost see the deep blue irises that he'd been fortunate enough to inherit. It felt like only yesterday he'd seen his reflection inside her eyes.

His chest grew tight, and he tossed the image away. He dropped his face into his hands. Overwhelming regret and self-loathing consumed him, and he fought with himself to regain his strength . . . to let things go in order to move on.

For God's sake, pull yourself together.

Gabriel drew in a breath and lifted his head. He had to continue, to push himself into facing more of the past. His eyes darted away as he lifted the next picture from atop the pile, and he swallowed hard before peering at it.

The photo wasn't of his parents, but instead of a young woman he'd wronged just as much as his family. A pretty little thing, only fifteen when the picture was taken, with corkscrew curls and a perfect up-turned nose in the center of her doll-like face. She looked like the very definition of innocence, and her name was Emily Tuttle. He was supposed to marry her.

"Oh, Emily," he found himself saying aloud. "I'm sorry."

Regardless of their nine-year age difference, he couldn't help but feel a hard knock of guilt for disappearing on the girl he'd been matched with since the day of her birth. Once longstanding friends and business partners, their fathers traveled the states together while surveying railroad progression. But their families only came together on special occasions, leaving Emily much more of a stranger than a fiancée.

As Gabriel dropped the photo back into the box, the thought of a very different young woman invaded his mind without invitation. He'd known Ellie Baker for nearly the same amount of time as he'd known Emily, yet she couldn't have felt less like a stranger. The image of her beautiful face, bruised and battered when he'd last seen her, still haunted his thoughts. If only their parting moments hadn't been so rushed. Part of him wished she knew just how much she'd done for him in such little time.

Her familiar innocence, her courage in seeking him out, the way her voluptuous breasts sat high above her slender waist—everything about her intrigued him. No other woman had come close to doing that, especially those a man of his upbringing should never have slept with. Ellie made him remember, she made him feel.

And much as he wished to deny it, he couldn't help but wonder if she'd had that effect on dozens of men before him. How many more men would share her bed? Hopefully none, if the place she'd gone to was better than where she'd been.

Gabriel groaned and kicked off his boots. Creekwood didn't matter anymore, and it was high time he reclaimed his old life. He threw himself onto the bed and stared at the ceiling, inwardly sorting through every daunting matter he needed to address.

First thing in the morning, he would acquire a horse, visit the Tuttle's estate, and apologize to Emily. If she were smart, she'd want nothing to do with him. He had little to offer a woman of her status. Or any woman, for that matter. Emily's social graces and handsome dowry were enough to make every man in New Hampshire think him a fool for not pursuing her. But he'd rather be damned to hell than incapable of providing for his wife. Besides, no girl came close to deserving a wretch like him.

But the weight of responsibility still encased him like a lead blanket. Everything his family had achieved over a century was gone because of him. A brainless, irredeemable mistake on his part. And he vowed to work even harder because of it.

Gabriel rolled to his side, dreading the moment he'd face his uncle most of all. The man had been like a second father, his children like Gabriel's siblings. Even in his drunkest state, not a day went by when he hadn't missed his family to the point of pain. What could he possibly say to them now?

Coming back from the dead before the whole town would prove insignificant when compared to the task of confronting those he loved most.

Chapter Five

Ellie breathed in the musty aroma of fresh grass as she climbed the tallest hill in front of the mansion. The sun beamed brightly though scattered clouds, the wildflowers sprinkled the hills with vibrant color, and the birds tweeted their merry songs of spring. She shut her eyes and sighed. How she'd missed taking afternoon walks.

She'd barely released another breath when a horse whinnied somewhere beyond the hill. Her eyelids shot open. She listened for it again.

There it was, a second time! Lifting her skirts, she dashed to the hilltop where her sight settled on an impressive stable several yards off. Her heart danced and she darted forward. She almost tripped from her downhill momentum as she sprinted toward the open doors.

The moment she reached them, she saw seven thoroughbreds resting in well-maintained stalls. A red-headed groom, appearing no older than eighteen, swept the floor with his back to her. Surely he wouldn't mind her being there for just a few minutes. She tiptoed to the chestnut-colored mare in the first stall and stroked her velvety nose, relishing the long-forgotten feeling. So soft, so warm, so—the mare jerked her head back, a burst of hot air snorting from her nostrils.

"Sorry, girl," Ellie whispered. "That's my favorite part of your sweet face. I used to pet my own horses on their noses, too."

"Like horses, do you?"

She spun around to find the groom leaning on his broomstick, staring at her. Perhaps she should have introduced herself before barging right in. When he grinned, her embarrassment eased up a little.

"Her name's Patriot," he said, gesturing to the mare. "Mr. Westgate's somewhat of an American history enthusiast." The young man approached and gave the mare's head a scratch. "Want to give her a treat?"

Ellie nodded. "May I?"

He pulled a large carrot from his apron pocket and placed it in her hand. With her palm held flat, she raised the treat to the mare's mouth and Patriot eagerly accepted. Such a loud, comical crunch a horse's molars made when eating carrots or apples. Ellie rubbed the flat space between Patriot's eyes and smiled.

"This is incredible," she said. "I had no idea there were stables on the grounds."

The groom offered Patriot another carrot. "But of course. Do you ride?"

"I've ridden since I was able to walk." She strolled down the line of stalls, savoring the familiar fragrance of straw and manure, something only a horse enthusiast would enjoy. "My father and I used to race our horses all the time."

"Side saddle?"

"Never. The only way to really ride is with one leg in each stirrup."

He chuckled. "That won't be allowed here. Mr. Westgate wouldn't think it very lady-like to ride the way men do."

"Then I guess I'll just have to ride that way in private." When she turned to smirk at him, his face grew redder than a ripe tomato.

"You must be the mysterious cousin from out West everyone's been talking about," he said. "The name's Timothy O'Hare." He extended a calloused hand. "You can call me Tim for short."

"Ellie Baker," she replied, shaking hands.

"Do you want to ride? I promise to keep mum about it."

She bit her lip and glanced around, knowing she could never resist. It felt like ages since she'd last sat atop her favorite animal's back. "All right . . . but just a short one."

Tim's olive-colored eyes lit. "Bully! I'll saddle up Lincoln for you. He's a friendly gelding who loves a good ride." He rushed into the small tack room, returning moments later with a riding crop in hand.

Ellie couldn't help but admire his enthusiasm. "Thank you Tim, but I'm from the land of cowboys and Indians. All's I need are my bare hands and a set of reins."

"Suit yourself, ma'am." The boy shrugged and turned back. He fetched Lincoln from his stall and strapped an expensive-looking saddle onto his back. The rich leather was nothing like the simple western saddles she'd been used to, but it was still a place to sit nonetheless.

"Need help mounting him?" he asked, as he finished adjusting the chocolate-colored horse's bridle.

He gaped when she slipped her right foot into the stirrup, grabbed hold of the saddle, and hoisted herself up. "I'll be back in a half hour," she said.

Clicking her tongue, she nudged the animal gently with her heels. Tim hadn't been kidding about Lincoln loving a good ride, because the gesture was all it took to send him cantering off. She felt like a mere feather atop the muscular power of the thoroughbred animal as his outstretched hooves pounded the earth with increasing speed. If she explored the rest of the estate on horseback, then she'd cover much more ground.

She passed a large carriage house, followed by a winery, and then a greenhouse surrounded by several vegetable gardens. Shortly after that, a fishing pond, complete with a wooden footbridge that connected the path on either side of the water.

Fallen strands of hair began whipping into her eyes and around her shoulders, blowing every which way, as she veered Lincoln into a shaded canopy of trees. For the first time in ages, she felt completely free. All worry and uncertainty dissolved as her hands gripped the reins and she sank deeper into the saddle. She put her trust in the animal beneath her as they flew through the woods, combined as one.

"The first one to reach the old tree stump gets an extra slice of cake tonight!" Papa's voice rang clear in her mind, and when she turned her head toward the trees flying past, she could almost see him galloping along beside her. He leaned forward and laughed, just as he'd done every time they'd raced. "You always beat me, didn't you, my Ellie Bear?"

Please, go away. Her stomach wrenched and she averted her eyes, changing the horse's direction until they'd reached a clearing. When she looked around again, Papa was gone. She pulled back on the reins and slowed Lincoln to a halt. The emotions wreaking havoc inside her had to be tamed.

She took in the breathtaking countryside surrounding her, its endless meadows tempting enough to distract anyone from deepest woe. Somewhere between here and the woods, the estate's parameters must have ended. Before her sat another expanse perfect for riding. But the sun settled lower in the sky now, her signal to turn back. How could she just yet?

She scratched Lincoln's black mane, staring at the Eden ahead of them. Then, she urged him on, and they flew into the dell if only for a moment.

Thanks to Mary's dressing skills, she'd somehow miraculously arrived at the table in time for dinner. She should have known a mere half hour on the back of a horse wouldn't suffice her appetite. Bless Tim for waiting for her. The evening meal had come and gone quickly, followed by a simple painting lesson from Jane. Ellie found she enjoyed mixing colors more than she'd anticipated.

Now, as she sat in bed grazing the text of a romantic novel, she could barely keep Papa from her mind. His face, his smile, his laugh, everything about him made her angry now. And it hurt her to feel this way. She sat still and wished the pain away, yet nothing but chills and emptiness accompanied her.

A small knock came from the bedroom door.

"Ellie?" Jane's voice was a welcome relief.

Ellie dropped her book onto the bedside table. "Come in, Jane."

The girl rushed into the room and pounced onto the other side of the bed, her hazel eyes sparkling with mischief.

"Look what I have." She unfolded the cloth in her hand and revealed two round chocolate candies. "I snuck them from the kitchen when no one was looking. They're supposed to be for tomorrow."

"Why, thank you, clever girl." Ellie took one of the delicious-looking morsels and popped it into her mouth, savoring the coconut on her tongue. She studied Jane's expression as they chewed in silence. "Jane, how old are you?"

"A lady never reveals her age." Jane held a hand to her mouth, hiding the remaining bits of chewed chocolate from view. She lifted her chin with a dainty little grin. "But if you must know, I'm twenty."

Ellie shifted and tucked her legs beneath herself. "Are you happy you're getting married?"

"Oh yes. I've dreamt of it since I was a young girl, haven't you?"

"Yes, yes, of course."

It wasn't a lie. She had wanted to get married since the moment she met a boy for the first time—one who'd made a lasting impression on her until the very day he left years ago. And somehow, seeing him again in his disheveled state had only strengthened that impression. Yet as far as marriage was concerned, she wanted nothing to do with it.

Jane dipped her head. "Ellie . . . I hope you don't mind me asking this, but" —she smoothed a hand over the bed sheets— "Why aren't *you* married yet?"

"When I was nineteen, my mother became sick. We could no longer afford ranch hands, so I had to care for her and run things on my own." Ellie shrugged, remembering how long and hard Mama had battled her illness. The woman had stayed strong until the very end. "During those three long years . . . marriage was the last thing on my mind."

"I can't imagine the hardship." With a somber smile, Jane touched her hand. "You're a kind soul, Ellie. You deserve a wonderful gentleman like Matthew. Your turn will come soon enough."

Ellie tried not to wince. "Do you love Matthew?" She hoped the question wasn't out-of-place.

Jane drew her knees into her chest as a splash of pink crept across her cheeks. "I would hope so after being arranged since infancy. It isn't a love that a husband and wife share, but I know that someday it will be."

Ellie found herself hoping it too, with every fiber of her being. Jane was so pleasant, so sure of people's character. She didn't deserve to be hurt, to have her faith in humanity shaken . . .

"Wait a minute, do you hear that?" Jane asked, her fair brow creasing.

"Hear what?" Ellie hadn't heard any sound. Only when they both fell silent did she hear the faint, muffled voices of two angry men.

"There it is again!" Jane left the bed and rushed to the window that looked down on the front end of the house. "What on earth is going on out there?"

"Can you see who they are?"

"Well, I know one of them is father and—" Jane pressed her forehead to the glass and squinted for a better view through the darkness. "And the other . . . Oh, it's too difficult."

"Don't give up yet." Ellie doused the kerosene lamp beside the bed in hopes that visibility would improve.

Jane looked again, and no more than five seconds passed before she tumbled to the floor with a hand clasped over her mouth. Her expression changed dramatically. Tears filled her eyes and began spilling over her cheeks. "It's my cousin," she whimpered. "He's . . . he's alive. Oh, he's alive!"

Ellie ran to Jane, scooted beside her and rubbed a hand up and down her back. "There, there, it's all right. What cousin, Jane?"

"He's supposed to be—" Jane shook her head. "Something terrible happened to him years ago, and we all thought him dead.

But God, he's alive, and"—her voice shook and she pressed her palms to her eyes—"And why does Father sound so angry with him now? Oh, I'd give anything to run out there!"

The distressed girl was barely making sense, but still, Ellie refrained from delving any deeper. For now, she'd help Jane in any way she could. "Why don't we eavesdrop on their conversation for a minute? With the lights doused, they won't be able to see us."

Jane sniffled, and then nodded. She wiped her cheeks and composed herself before springing back to the window. Ellie helped her lift the pane, and they crouched down to listen.

"So that's it then?" A rich, familiar voice growled. "After all we've been through, you would abandon your own flesh and blood without so much as listen——"

"How dare you accuse me of abandonment! Do you honestly expect me to forgive you after the countless grief and agony you've put me through?" Mr. Westgate's voice countered.

"Uncle, if you would just listen to me."

"There's nothing left to hear. You're disgraceful! You let her die—"

"Something I have to live with every single day."

"And then you—" Mr. Westgate's voice quaked with raw pain. "You killed yourself for the last four years! Four years, and you never had the decency to return. How much grief can you put one man through? A man who loved you like a son, Gabriel. How much?"

Ellie's legs gave out. An invisible stomach punch sent her to the floor.

"Oh, no, now you're the one down!" Jane reached for her. "Are you all right?"

Ellie took hold of Jane's arm, certain she'd been imagining things. The angry voices had stopped, and she peered out the window to find Mr. Westgate returning inside while the other man stormed away. Her teeth dug into her thumbnail. Should she ask, or leave the subject of the strange coincidence alone?

Rising to her feet, Jane straightened out her nightgown. "You mustn't mention a word of this to Father. He'll be even more furious if he finds out we listened."

Ellie couldn't hold it in. "Your cousin's name is Gabriel?"

"Yes."

She swallowed. She'd heard that part correctly then. Still, there must be hundreds of men with that particular name, and her Gabriel was still far off in Colorado. Wasn't he?

"Gabriel *what*?" she asked, grasping the fabric of her own gown as she stood.

A look of confusion washed over Jane's face and she arched a light eyebrow. "You mean his surname?"

"Please, Jane," Ellie whispered, certain her desperate expression was baffling the girl even more.

"Peterson."

The name thundered in her ears, and her mouth almost dropped to the floor.

Jane grasped her shoulders and gave her a shake. "Ellie, what is it? You're frightening me."

But Ellie couldn't answer.

Her legs regained feeling. She sprung up and dashed from the bedroom, bursts of energy pushing her faster and faster. Within moments she'd cleared the staircase, and the two heavy front doors seemed light as cardboard when she yanked them open. She darted out into the moonlit darkness, soaring over the portico steps and ignoring the rough gravel on her bare feet as she bolted down the drive.

"Gabriel, wait, come back!" she called out into the night. "Gabriel! Gabriel Peterson!"

The crunching beneath her strides invaded the crisp silence. Only when she realized just how far she'd gone without an answer did she stop shouting.

"Please, come back," she panted, slowing her pace.

The rush had worn off and she coasted to a halt. Something resembling mortification took over. Was she really standing outside, shouting in her nightgown like a complete lunatic? She folded her arms and turned back for the house, prepared to face Jane and praying Mr. Westgate hadn't heard her.

Horse hooves stirred the gravel behind her. Her nerves returned. With her arms still encasing her chest, she spun around to watch as the animal and rider came into view. Her heart pounded and she backed into one of the burning gas lamps lining the drive, stopping once her spine touched the iron post.

A moment ago she'd been shouting Gabriel's name to the heavens, and now she stood tongue-tied with a knotted stomach. The silhouetted figure dismounted and slowly crept closer until he stood just outside the pool of light.

"My God," he whispered.

With one more step, the lamp was on him. The wind shot from her lungs the moment she looked upon his completely unrecognizable face.

Neatly parted brown waves, brushed back off his forehead, replaced his long mess of hair. A clean shave had revealed a smooth, flawless face, and his pristine clothing looked tailored just for his frame. The only thing that hadn't changed was the brilliant blue of his eyes that sparkled in the lamp's radiance. A transformation unlike any other she'd seen. Her knees buckled at the realization of how breathtaking he was.

They stared at one another, neither uttering a word as the chirps of the evening insects marked off the passing seconds.

Gabriel finally cleared his throat and gave his head a quick jolt, as if returning to reality. "Ellie Baker. Forgive me . . . but I can't seem to make sense of what I'm seeing."

"Neither can I." She realized her mouth still hung open, so she snapped it shut. "What on earth are you doing here?"

"I should be asking you the same thing," he said, a look of astonishment all over his face. "That day I put you in the coach . . . this was the place you were going?"

"Yes!" She flinched and covered her mouth. Remembering to whisper was proving difficult. "I live here now."

"You live here now," he repeated, raising a dark eyebrow.

"Mr. Westgate sent the coach for me. His late wife was Mama's cousin."

He slapped a hand on his head and took another step towards her. "Of all the places in this entire country . . ."

"And you—" she darted her eyes to be sure they were alone. "You're Henry Westgate's nephew?"

Something unsettling, wounded, showed on his face. "He told you about me, did he?"

"Yes . . . er, no. Jane did."

"Ah, well that would be me." He sighed and rubbed the back of his neck. "But I'm not sure I still hold the title of 'nephew' in his eyes any longer. Who knew coming back from the dead would be so difficult?"

He grinned, but there was little humor behind the smile. Though his unguarded nature was something very different than the rough facade she'd seen in Creekwood, part of her hoped this was the real Gabriel standing before her.

"It must be a lot for him to take in. Give it some time and things will turn out all right."

"I suppose I knew he wouldn't be standing before me with open arms, and I could never blame him after—" He stopped, and his lips curled into a smirk as his gaze swept across her from head-to-toe. "Are you . . . wearing a nightgown?"

Oh my God. She looked down at her thin white garment, her cheeks suddenly burning. With no denying the obvious, she might as well acknowledge it. Gripping the back of her neck, she grinned.

"It seems to appear that way, doesn't it?"

He folded his arms and began to chuckle, which might have annoyed her if it weren't the first time she'd ever seen him laugh—or the loveliest sound she'd ever heard.

"If only Henry could see you now," he said. "Outside in the middle of the night, alone in a man's presence, and wearing nothing but a nightgown. You could be burned at the stake for something like that out here."

"Forgive me for not taking the time to think about what I was wearing when I made the split decision to run after you." She batted her eyelashes and pretended to fan herself. "I suppose I'm not accustomed to the rules of upper class society yet."

He barked another laugh. "Well, I'm glad you did. And please, promise me you won't change into one of those pretentious aristocratic women who are all the same." He wagged a finger at her. "Stay just the way you are."

She narrowed her eyes. "The way I am?"

"A compliment, Ellie."

"Oh, well, thank you, and I—" Her blood ran hot and she bit the inside of her cheek, unsure of how to react to the flattery. At The Inn, compliments had only been given in vulgar terms. "I suppose I should go back inside now." It was the only sentence she could think of, and she wished she hadn't said it.

"Yes, you probably should. But before you do, an old patient of mine is throwing me a bit of a welcome home party at his house tomorrow night. You wouldn't be interested in coming as my guest, would you?"

The thought of being in a fancy room surrounded by privileged strangers was enough to make her cringe. She'd never attended a party in her entire life. Nor could she ever pass for a frilly, aristocratic socialite. "May I think about it?"

"If you'd like, but you'll need to tell me in the next few seconds, seeing as that's how long we have until we part ways."

He smiled a dashing smile as if it were bait. She rolled her eyes, unable to keep from giggling like a child at the smart remark. Then, as quickly as it came, his grin faded.

"Lord," he cocked his head to the side, studying her face. "This entire time, I've been too distracted to ask you how you are."

Ellie tucked a windblown strand of hair behind her ear. She'd almost forgotten how terrible she'd looked and felt the last time he'd seen her. "Never better, thanks to you."

"You've healed perfectly. I'm so glad."

"I don't know how I'll ever be able to repay you for what you did that day."

"Come to the party tomorrow, and your debt will be paid."

"Well that's not very fair."

"I'll be the judge of that." He pulled a pencil and small wad of paper from his coat pocket and scribbled down a set of directions with an address. "Give this to your coachman and he'll know where to go. Be there at seven o' clock sharp."

She glanced down at the hieroglyphic-like drawings and his chicken scratch handwriting. How anyone could expect to interpret such a mess was beyond her. "Your uncle will hang me if he finds out about this, and I'd like to enjoy my time alive a little longer."

"Come now, you're more clever than that, Miss Baker." He eyed her in a way that made her grin. "Besides, I can't be the only one pleased that our paths have crossed again." With a dip of his head, backed away. "I'll see you tomorrow night."

Not a single protesting word came to her as she watched him mount his horse and ride off. Part of her expected to wake tomorrow morning to find this was all a dream. Here she thought she'd never see Gabriel Peterson again. Now, he'd come back into her life, due to a coincidence she couldn't even begin to understand. But she was grateful. No, beyond grateful.

If only she didn't have to slink behind Mr. Westgate's back so soon. Her entire being was filled with guilt and anticipation as she returned to the house.

Chapter Six

The next day, Ellie strolled though the estate's main garden beside Mr. Westgate. With the sun high in the sky, and the carefully planted flowers in full bloom, the sight resembled a spectacular watercolor painting. Fountains trickled in the center of a small courtyard, benches rested beneath blossomed trees, and stone footpaths wove themselves between foliage and trellises. Angelic statues, their marble sparkling in the sun, added peaceful contrast to all the greenery. The air churned with the aromas of plants, roses and flowers. Oh, so many flowers.

She resisted the urge to reach out and touch them. "I could spend forever here."

"You're welcome to it whenever you like, Ellie." Mr. Westgate looked at her and grinned. "Jane mentioned you would rather be called by that name."

She smiled back at him. "If it's all right with you, sir."

"Of course it is."

At this moment, it was hard to imagine Mr. Westgate sounding as angry as he'd been the previous night. She couldn't imagine what it must feel like to see a loved one after years of presuming him dead. But she couldn't imagine being in Gabriel's position, either. She certainly didn't care to hear such affliction in their voices ever again. Whatever feud sat between them, she hoped it wouldn't last long.

"You probably have a hundred questions for me regarding your mother." Mr. Westgate tilted his chin up toward the sky. "I wish I possessed the knowledge to answer them all, but the truth is I knew little about her. By the time I'd met Helen, Anne had already gone West."

Ellie clasped her hands, her eyes wandering between the rose bushes. "It's all right. I'm just thankful to be here. But I do wonder why my mother never mentioned Helen."

"I don't believe they were on the best terms when your mother left for Colorado," Mr. Westgate said. "Helen was two years younger than Anne, but that never affected their close bond growing up. Their mothers were sisters."

"What happened?"

"From what I understand, Anne met your father at a county fair when she was eighteen. He'd worked a small booth with maps and pamphlets advertising the idea of The New Frontier, and she'd succumbed to his sense of adventure before you could say Jack Robinson. Naturally, Helen didn't approve of the scandal. Once your mother eloped with Samuel, the family cut her off."

Ellie tried to picture her simple mama in lavish gowns, with everything she'd ever wanted right at her disposal. Wanting for nothing. How could she have given it up for a man she barely knew? A man who later betrayed her? At one time, Ellie might have thought it romantic, but now, it angered her.

"Then . . . how did you know about me?" she asked.

Mr. Westgate glanced at her, his hard eyes softening. "Your mother had written a long letter to Helen when she was ill. She mentioned you in it, along with the heartbreak she felt at leaving you penniless and alone. Little did she know that Helen had passed several years before, so I read the letter, and stopped at nothing to find you."

Ellie's heart ached. Even on her deathbed, Mama had still managed to put herself last. She hadn't deserved to worry like that, not when she was so sick. And the courage it must have taken to write such a letter—Ellie wished she'd known about it. A terrible sadness filled her, and she couldn't bring herself to ask any more about Mama during the remainder of the walk.

An hour later, as she sat in bed with a lunch tray perched on her lap, Ellie refused to think about anything. Not about her parents, not about her past, and certainly not about the party tonight. Of course she wanted to spend more time with Gabriel. But how was she supposed to learn anything personal about him in public? She thirsted for secrets, not cocktails and spirits.

She'd just bitten into a cucumber sandwich when an urgent rapping rattled the door.

"Ellie, it's Jane. Are you in there?"

She dropped the sandwich. She'd known this moment would come, and washed down the food in her mouth with a gulp of lemonade. "Come in," she said, pushing the tray toward her feet.

The door swung open, and Jane scurried into the room like a mouse after cheese. Her eyes brimmed with questions while her lips frowned in disapproval.

"What on earth were you doing running out of the house last night? I saw you out the window. I thought you'd gone mad when I watched you disappear down the drive."

"I'm sorry, Jane. I didn't mean to scare you."

Jane crawled onto the bed. "Well, what then?"

Ellie slipped from the bed and went to the door, opening it just wide enough for her head to peer through. She surveyed the empty hall, listened for sounds and gently shut the door. "If I tell you, you must promise not to say a word to anyone else."

"I promise."

She climbed onto the mattress and pulled the sheets up to her neck. She explained everything regarding her and Gabriel, from their childhood friendship, to reuniting in Creekwood years later. When it came to details about the state she'd found him in, she skipped around them. It wasn't her place to tell. She skipped around the brothel part, too.

Jane sat upright on the bed, her eyes enormous. Ellie dropped her shoulders and leaned back against the sea of pillows. "Now you know why I had to run after him last night."

Jane raised her fingertips to her lips, a smile taking form. "Incredible. This sort of thing never happens. It must be fate, Ellie."

"I won't deny that it's very strange—" Ellie gazed out the far window. "And somehow, amidst our conversation, he asked me to be his guest at a party tonight."

"A party?" Jane's smile disappeared. "With no chaperone? Ellie, that's clearly out of the question. Father would never let you go."

"You're right. I guess I'm not going, then." Ellie rolled onto her stomach, burying her face in the plush, goose feathered pillow. She was glad for the excuse. Surely Gabriel would understand if she'd suddenly taken ill or something.

"But you didn't let me finish," Jane said. "William Carroll's annual dinner party is tonight. Father never misses it, and usually doesn't return until almost sunrise."

Wonderful . . .

Ellie lifted her head. Jane's elated expression only made her more nervous. For once, she actually wished the circumstances hadn't been in her favor. There must be a better way to repay Gabriel than attending some outlandish party. Countless strangers would be there. Watching her!

"No, Jane, really, I've made up my mind."

"But you must go and tell Gabriel how much I've missed him. He needs to know that I'm not upset with him the way that Father is. He needs to know that he's still loved." Distress crept into Jane's voice. "You're new here, far braver than I, and could most likely get away with it. Besides, it's not my place to tell a soul."

Ellie narrowed her eyes at the subtle trickery. Withstanding guilt had never been one of her strong points.

"All right." She sighed. "How do I make my escape?"

* * *

Several hours later, Ellie peered out the open carriage door and recoiled. This mansion might even be bigger than the Westgate's. Turning back now didn't seem like such a bad idea. If the colossal house and cluster of parked carriages weren't intimidating enough, she was late. No arriving carriages trundled up the illuminated stone drive, and no guests milled about the entrance.

She clutched the door handle to pull it shut, but Tim's interfering hand stopped her. His apprehensive expression only added to the humor of his ill-fitting coachman's uniform.

"What are you doing?" he asked through gritted teeth.

"I've changed my mind. Let's leave." Her grip on the handle remained determined as she tried to tug it toward her. No success.

"Do you have any idea what I went through to get this rig? And I'm sure you didn't fail to notice the length of the ride. We might as well be in a different town."

She let go and slid her bottom farther down the black leather seat. "You go in then."

He yanked the door open, a smug look on his freckled face. "Miss Ellie, if you don't exit this carriage right now, I'll tell Mr. Westgate that you rode his horse like a Western for three whole hours."

"You wouldn't."

He bounced his eyebrows twice, seemingly pleased with himself.

She glared back at him, jumbled up her skirts and slid down the seat. Her heel caught the long silk when she attempted stepping down unassisted. In the span of a blink, Tim caught her by the forearm and steadied her.

Jane's lavender gown, with its white lace trim and beaded bustle, sat heavily on her frame. Mary had drawn her corset tighter than usual, thanks to Jane's insistence that it was the 'manner in which all ladies dressed for parties.'" Pounds of elaborate fabric smothered her from head-to-toe.

"I'll be right out here waiting for you." Tim tugged on his hat and climbed back into the driver's seat.

She couldn't help but smirk at the cheeky boy. "I promise I won't be long."

"Where have I heard that before?" He cracked the reins and took off, surrendering her to her own devices.

With one last tug on her evening gloves, she walked up the steps to where a well-dressed servant stood. He directed her through the open doors. Well, at least she'd managed to make it inside. A handful of guests mingled about the foyer, and she froze in place once she heard effervescent music and laughter resounding from down the hall.

A matriarchal voice spoke from beside her. "Good evening."

Ellie turned, meeting the eyes of a plump, middle-aged woman with feathers ornamenting her outlandish mass of orange hair.

"I am Mrs. Tuttle, lady of the house and hostess of this evening's event." The woman folded her hands and gave Ellie a glance over.

"Oh, good evening," Ellie said with an awkward curtsy. Hopefully it would suffice as a proper greeting.

"Your name, my dear?" The woman looked confused, yet she remained polite.

"Ellie Baker. It's nice to meet you, ma'am."

"Pleasure." Mrs. Tuttle offered a gloved hand, and she gripped it with a small shake. She must have done wrong, because the gesture only seemed to disgruntle the woman. "Yes, well . . . you must have been escorted by one of my guests—" the woman elongated her neck to peer at the empty space behind Ellie. "And just where is your chaperone this evening, my dear?"

Ellie could feel her tongue swelling inside her mouth. "My chaperone?"

"Yes, of course." Mrs. Tuttle glared, unamused.

"I . . . well . . ."

No words would come, and the woman's outward expression grew more impatient with each passing second. Ellie's face began to heat and she swallowed hard. Suppose she were to turn and dash out of the house right this very sec—

"Cousin Bertie is her chaperone, Mrs. Tuttle."

Both their heads snapped to find Gabriel ambling towards them with a proper smile. Impeccably groomed, he donned a black tailcoat, slacks and waistcoat with a white cravat. A pair of white gloves completed the ensemble, suiting him for the role of dashing gentleman without question.

"Miss Baker." He bowed in Ellie's direction, then stared at her as if to say, "play along."

She curtsied, unsure of whether he expected her to speak or not.

"You know this woman, Gabriel?" The woman's lips stretched into a thin grin, as if she were struggling to contain her shock.

"I do, madam," he said, appearing almost at ease. "Miss Baker is my aunt's second cousin from Colorado. She's residing with my uncle at his estate, and I'd like to see her engage in some social activity . . . under cousin Bertie's watchful eye, of course."

His radiant smile and genial charm would make any woman believe the fabricated words.

"Oh?" Mrs. Tuttle arched a red eyebrow, assessing Ellie like a prospector would appraise fool's gold. "Isn't that wonderful. And how long will you be in town, my dear?"

Ellie opened her mouth, yet found herself looking to Gabriel to save her. But he simply grinned, a slight tilt of his head serving as indication that he didn't intend to speak anytime soon. She'd have to fend for herself.

Smiling gracefully, she lifted her chin. "Indefinitely, ma'am."

It was a start, and Mrs. Tuttle's suspicion finally melted into something warmer. "Well in that case, welcome to New Hampshire, Miss Baker. I do hope you take advantage of all the treasures our fine state has to offer."

"I'll be sure to, thank you."

"And we must have you over to dine with us so we may know you better. I insist."

Ellie gave a polite nod, perplexed as to why she'd been questioned one moment and invited to dinner the next. She knew such a forward invitation wasn't custom in high society. She also knew Gabriel had something—no, everything to do with it.

Mrs. Tuttle's attention shifted to an elderly couple entering the foyer. "Oh, it seems a hostess' duty is never complete. Show her to the ballroom, Gabriel. I do hope you find the evening enjoyable, Miss Baker."

Gabriel bowed and Ellie curtsied. After a slow, regal dip of her head, Mrs. Tuttle rushed off to greet her arriving guests. Ellie released the breath she'd been holding, thankful she wasn't the last to arrive after all.

"Shall we?" Gabriel asked, offering his arm.

She took it reluctantly. If only they could spend the rest of the evening in the quiet foyer instead.

As they turned a corner leading to the main room, she attempted to still her steps. Yet his obvious determination in pulling her alongside him won the battle.

"You look very nice this evening," he muttered, keeping his attention forward.

She huffed, ignoring his sly attempt at masking what had just happened. "Cousin Bertie?"

"You're late."

"That's beside the point."

"Is it? And just what would you have done if I hadn't found you at that exact moment?"

"I would have left, and been better off for it."

She felt his arm tense beneath her hand.

"I'm sorry," he whispered, hauling her along with wide strides. "I failed to mention that an unmarried woman isn't allowed to attend a party without a chaperone. The only way a man can chaperone a woman, aside from being married to her, is if there's a close family relation."

"If I didn't know any better, I'd say you purposely failed to mention that."

He turned to her with a gratified smile. She shook her head, suddenly despising him. The music grew louder as they rounded another corner, and he stopped once they'd approached two glass-paneled doors. A sea of glittering, colorful gowns and black evening suits crowded the other side. Everything looked so expensive.

Everyone looked so frenetic. As if sensing her disinclination, his free hand took hold of her upper arm.

"I already feel like a complete fool" —she attempted to break free of his grasp— "and now a ballroom? I don't dance . . . I can't dance."

He didn't let her go. "You have a broken toe, then."

"That is absurd."

"I need you here with me, Ellie," he pressed, nearly sounding vulnerable. "This is the first time I've been to an event like this in years, and believe it or not, I'm just as intimidated as you are."

Intimidated? She'd never believe him if it weren't for the subtle hint of nerves beneath his tone. He practically dragged her into the lively room. When they cleared the doors, his gaze darted to the left, and he grinned as if acknowledging someone far off in the crowd. Heck, he did a much better job of masking his jitters than she did.

The crystal chandeliers and ornate candelabras lining the white moulded walls bathed the room in a rich glow. A five-piece string orchestra played passionate, expressive music in the corner, while several men and women glided and whirled about the polished wooden floor. Cloth-covered tables near the entryway flaunted savory morsels, enticing those not dancing to indulge themselves.

"My father's cousin is over there." Gabriel said, indicating the far end of the room. "She's agreed to take you on as a formality this evening. You don't have to worry about her speaking to Henry, even if she does remember you tomorrow. She's a bit wallpapered by now."

Ellie found herself tightening her grip as they approached. It wasn't the tipsy, gray-haired cousin Bertie she worried about, but the group of intimidating young debutantes with whom she stood. "Who are *they*? Do I have to speak with them?"

"You act as if I'm cutting your arm off. It's good for you to start meeting women your own age around here."

A knot formed in the pit of her stomach, especially when they drew too close for her to protest opposition without anyone else hearing. He released her arm, resigning her to the prying eyes of at least seven well-bred women.

"Cousin Bertie. Ladies." He bowed at the waist. "I'd like to introduce you to Miss Elaine Baker."

She didn't miss the subtle smirk on his lips as he said her full name. He probably relished how it irritated her. And toying with her in public, where she couldn't pull away and cause a scene? All the more infuriating.

"So this is the young woman you've been telling me about, Gabriel," Bertie said with a slight stutter. She extended the hand that wasn't holding her champagne glass and cupped Ellie's chin. "A true beauty if I've ever seen one. Your mother must have been absolutely stunning."

Ellie liked this woman. "She was, thank you, ma'am."

"I'd be eternally grateful if you would all make her feel welcome," Gabriel said. Nearly every one of the women blushed and giggled at his attention. She wanted to roll her eyes, but she didn't. He glanced toward the dance floor and looked back at her. "Will you be all right if I leave your side for a few minutes?"

Now he was leaving her? She leered at him through a fake smile, wishing her eyes would burn right through his skull. "Where are you going?"

"I have to dance this one," he whispered, enfolding her in his lavender scent as he leaned in, and away from surrounding ears. "I promise I'll come right back."

"Fine." If only she didn't owe him her life. Nonetheless, she'd have to get him back for leaving her to her own devices with a group she probably had little in common with—and who would see right through her.

After one more polite bow, he turned on his heel and made his way back through the ballroom. She watched him stop at the side of a portly man and three girls, the eldest of them strikingly beautiful. They smiled and moved their mouths as if they'd known him for years.

"Where did you say you were from?" the young woman nearest her inquired.

Ellie's gaze remained on the conversation unfolding across the room. "Colorado."

"That Transcontinental Railroad is a blessing, I say," Bertie tipped her head back and poured the small remainder of her drink into her mouth. "To think of all the blood, sweat and tears put into such an incredible feat. My dear cousin Patrick saw it first-hand."

"Have you ever visited the shore?" another woman asked, while fluttering her fan.

"Not yet," Ellie answered. But she longed to see the ocean someday, to touch the water and feel the sand . . .

Gabriel was leading the elegant young woman onto the dance floor, and Ellie hadn't expected to feel a twinge of sickness at the sight. They must know each other very well. But what did that matter? She'd simply have to get used to sharing the attention of her old friend, even if he did seem to be getting along fine without her company, and even if it meant occasionally being stranded with complete strangers.

He blended so perfectly with the other dancing guests as they twirled in graceful formation about the floor. How anyone could retain so many steps after years without practicing baffled her. It would take her more than a lifetime to learn a single dance, let alone remember it. She found herself so immersed in the thought that she barely noticed the tall man approaching her until he cleared his throat.

"May I have the honor of dancing the next set with you?" he asked.

She looked for Cousin Bertie, only to find her halfway across the room in search of more refreshments. This man was patiently awaiting an answer. What would Jane say in this situation?

"I regret to decline, sir. I have an injured toe that gives me pain to dance upon." She could have slapped herself for using the ridiculous broken toe bit.

"I'm sorry to hear that. I do hope it feels better soon."

The man bowed politely and moved on.

A small victory, but enough to make her grin inside. Perhaps proper etiquette wouldn't be as hard as she thought, though fancy words would always feel strange on her tongue.

"A broken toe, how dreadful. Such unfortunate timing to attend a dance." The girl with the fan gave a sympathetic shake of her head.

"Abigail, you mustn't make her feel worse," whispered the tawny-haired woman on her right. "She can't help it, for goodness sake." She turned to Ellie. "You'll have to excuse Abigail. My name is Rosalie Maxwell, and this is Meredith George, Catherine Higgins, and Samantha Carter." She gestured to each of the ladies in the circle, most of whom were barely paying attention.

"Pleasure." Ellie curtsied. "And who's the young woman dancing with Mr. Peterson?"

"Why that's Emily Tuttle of course, eldest daughter of this evening's host and hostess," Rosalie answered at a volume louder than Ellie would have liked.

"Is she friends with him?" She fingered the lace at her neckline, trying her best to appear aloof.

"Friends? Oh no, they've been matched for years."

"Such a lucky girl she is." Rosalie sighed. "I doubt there's a woman on earth who wouldn't fancy that man's attention. Thank heaven he's safely returned to us."

Ellie forced a smile. "Oh, yes, thank heaven."

What has Gabriel been telling everyone? No doubt he served as quite the prize in town—probably even the state. Young, smart, handsome, even she couldn't deny his charm. This man seemed completely opposite from the broken soul she'd come across not too long ago. Something told her she was the only one who knew it.

She couldn't blame him for wanting to hide such a thing. Aside from those five years they'd shared in Black Hawk, this was Gabriel's entire world. Why should he want to ruin his reputation by admitting to the degrading life he'd led?

Her gaze returned to the handsome couple on the dance floor. Miss Tuttle possessed a certain dignity that few others in the room could match. The flowers and pearls atop her head swayed in tandem with her light brown curls as she pranced around the ballroom with her equally attractive partner. A perfect match.

Ellie bit back a sigh. Gabriel's marriage plans probably went as far back as their tree-climbing days in Black Hawk. Back when time hadn't existed. Back when her innocent, childish heart had called him hers. But God, they were adults now, which is why heaven only knew why seeing him in the arms of another woman bothered her so much.

Chapter Seven

When the longest set in the world finally ended, Gabriel's body burned beneath his clothing. He'd forgotten how quickly the feet were supposed to move on the dance floor, and the cool night air seemed to be calling his name now. But he kept his steps uniform while escorting Emily back to her family.

"I just love the gallop, it's always so much fun." Emily patted his arm. "But surely you practiced every step before you arrived tonight."

He gave a small chuckle. "Only about a hundred times."

"Is that all? I would have assumed at least one hundred and fifty." She stopped beside her two younger sisters. Emily curtsied and he bestowed a quick kiss to her gloved hand. "Honestly, even if this party weren't in your honor, you'd still be the envy of every gentleman here."

"Ah, but that's because he has you beside him," her father gloated. He clapped a hand onto Gabriel's shoulder. "It's so nice to see you back where you belong, dear boy."

"It's good to be back, sir. I look forward to many more dances in the future." Gabriel managed a smile, despite his gut clenching at the undeserved adoration.

Mrs. Tuttle's boisterous pink ensemble caught his eye, and he twisted to find her whisking toward them with a visage just burning for chitchat. He should escape now while he still could. It wouldn't be long until the woman mentioned Ellie to everyone else. Introducing Miss Baker to the entire Tuttle family wasn't something he felt prepared to do just yet. Or ever, really. Damn, he really should have thought this through.

He grinned at Mr. Tuttle and his two daughters. "Ladies, sir, if you'll excuse me for a moment." Without waiting for an answer, he turned and began walking back to Miss Baker.

What a cad he'd been for leaving her behind. In his defense, he hadn't expected her to arrive half an hour late, and had promised Emily a dance only after assuming Ellie wouldn't show. Thank God he'd gone to the foyer to escape the masses when he did.

With her tightly pinned black curls and that fanciful silk gown—which hugged all the right curves—he almost hadn't recognized her. He'd thought her attractive then. But now, as she smiled and conversed with Cousin Bertie and a cluster of debutantes, he could see how her natural beauty outshone those around her ten-fold. He wasn't the only man to notice, either. Aside from those eyeing her from a safe distance, he'd watched three brave gentlemen approach her during the set. A tiny hint of satisfaction had settled inside him when she'd denied every one.

He approached the group. "Thank you for looking after her, ladies."

He tried not to smirk when everyone but Bertie nearly jumped out of their skin.

"Think nothing of it," Cousin Bertie half-chirped, half-slurred. "Miss Baker is simply a delight. Don't tell anyone, but I've been secretly educating her on the mechanics behind railroad function." She turned to him, her face bright with humor. "Who would have ever imagined your old Cousin Bertie knowing more on the subject than you, my dear?"

He brushed the comment off, knowing she meant no harm by it.

"Yes, I had a marvelous time getting to know these lovely ladies." Ellie turned to him, her open fan held beneath large, green eyes. Her tone held a note of mockery; oddly, it almost roused him. "But I do believe I'm in need of some fresh air."

He raised an eyebrow. "Shall we step out onto the patio, then?"

He offered his hand, and she proceeded to give it a hard, angry squeeze as they left the group. Was this an attempt at causing him discomfort? Adorable. His digits curled around hers, bringing an abrupt end to her effort as they stepped into the long-awaited air.

The further they walked toward the expansive lawn, the more the droning music faded into a mere background hum. Several guests stood around the patio, mingling in small groups, or flirting off in the shadows. The evening breeze felt so good on his face and neck. He wished he could remove his gloves, feel just a little more of it against his bare flesh.

"It's funny, you seem a natural socialite despite your so-called nerves," she said.

He let his smile show, appreciating her honesty. "If you're upset with me for leaving you with those women, I only did it with the intention of your making friends."

"On the contrary, I'm glad you did." She freed her hand and moved toward the thick stone rail. "Otherwise, who knows when I would have learned about Miss Tuttle."

He should be paying attention, but with the full moon's light pouring down her backside, he couldn't. Damn, he wished he didn't find her so appealing—so intoxicating. The last thing he needed was to be discovered in a state of arousal in public.

"I see." He freed himself from the tempting view by joining her side. "I'd forgotten that I left you with the most chat-savvy women in the room."

She turned to him and glared. "Were you just not going to tell me, then? You lied and said an old patient was throwing a party, not your fiancée's family."

"I never lied to you," he corrected her, resting his elbows on the stone. "Mr. Tuttle had been a patient of mine years ago when he contracted the stomach flu. And Emily isn't my fiancée. It's more of . . . an agreement."

Or at least he assumed so. He didn't know what to call their status anymore, now that Emily's family had welcomed him back like the prodigal son. Yesterday, when he'd stepped through their doorway to apologize, when he'd seen the joyful tears on their faces, his plan of telling the truth had somehow slipped away from him.

Still, looking up at the night sky, he found a hint of amusement at Ellie's chiding. She couldn't be jealous. Harlots always shared several men between them at a time, so why would Ellie get herself all worked up over the subject of Emily? Whatever the reason, it flattered him.

"You never would have said yes to coming if I'd told you all of it."

"Of course not."

"Well, there you are." He glanced at her, and she looked away with the worst attempt at feigned anger he'd ever seen. If they weren't near others, then he might be inclined to reach out and turn her pouty little face back toward him. "And of course I was going to tell you about Emily. This is but the second time you and I have spoken since meeting again, and as I recall, the circumstances were far from appropriate the first time. You in your nightgown, and me cast from my uncle's property gave me little reason to speak of personal details then and there. You must understand that, Ellie."

God, he hated the patronizing resonance of his tone. He didn't want to sound like her father. Her cherry lips pursed, and her gaze darted from side-to-side as if attempting to summon a quick rebuttal. But the fire in her eyes finally dimmed and, to his relief, she faced him with no anger left on that sharp tongue of hers.

"I suppose . . . you have a point," she mumbled.

"Our families matched Emily and me a long time ago, but our age difference kept us from marrying right away. When I left, she was still only fifteen."

She tilted her head in a teasing manner. "How fortunate for you that her family has so graciously accepted you back after vanishing for so long."

"Yes, well—" He lowered his voice, wary of listening ears. "I might have stretched the truth relating to my absence a bit."

"Stretched? Now it's getting interesting."

He found himself staring at her perfectly shaped mouth. "Why does it seem you enjoy torturing me, Miss Baker?"

"Oh heavens, the last time I really tortured you was when I put ants down your britches."

"Ha!" The little spitfire had done that to him, hadn't she? "Yes, and as I recall they bit me all over and I itched for days."

She stood upright, plunked her hands on her hips and smirked. "Well you deserved it, because you'd tricked me into eating a disgusting mud pie the day before."

"I was proud of that mud pie, too. It took me countless minutes to make, using only the finest Colorado soil and rarest of weeds."

"I believe there was at least one worm, too."

She lifted a gloved hand to her mouth and trembled with repressed laughter. He folded his arms and chuckled, a sense of warmth permeating his body. Pleasant memories, now there was something he'd forgotten all about. And he liked seeing her happy.

"Despite your obvious reservations—" He cleared his throat, allowing all the laughs to leave his system. "I'd like to thank you for coming tonight. You're the only one here who's seen me at my worst, which is why your company keeps me . . ." He searched for the right word. "Grounded. Furthermore, I'd never admit to being terrified if it weren't true."

Something resembling pity showed in her gaze, the last thing that he wanted.

"Yes," she said softly. "But you couldn't be more different now, and I mean that in the best way possible." She looked up at him as if he were some sort of puzzle she had to solve. "Don't be so hard on yourself. Act or not, you're much better at blending in than I."

He sighed and held out his arm. "Thank you, but that's only because I've had more practice. Now I suggest we return inside to continue yours."

"Must we?"

"I'm afraid so."

She slid her arm through his like a key in a lock, and they made their way back through the doors leading to the ballroom. A waltz began to play, his favorite dance. Suddenly, he had a devilish idea. If he were to bring her far enough onto the floor without her noticing, she'd have no choice but to partake in the set and learn to waltz. He'd teach her the same way he'd taught Jane at her tenth birthday party.

"Jane misses you a great deal," Ellie said.

Christ, was she reading his thoughts? "Does she really?"

"Oh yes, she made me promise to tell you that in person. She really cares, you know. She's the kindest girl I've ever met."

His heart ached. "She's always been that way, too. And John?"

"He's sweet, but a quiet one. I honestly haven't had the chance to know him yet."

"You'll learn he's not as quiet as you think. He's a remarkable boy." God, but John was barely a boy anymore. Gabriel breathed into the tightness of his chest.

Then he felt a hard tug on his arm.

"We're on the dance floor," she whispered, clutching him tighter.

The plan had worked better than he'd expected. He'd almost forgotten about it himself after talking about his cousins. He mock-glanced at the couples around them and fabricated a look of surprise. "It does seem that way, doesn't it?" Peering down at her terrified face, he shrugged. "I suppose there's only one thing to do in this situation . . ."

"Gabriel, no. I told you I can't dan—"

"Come now, it's only the waltz. It's the simplest dance there is."

"I don't care how simple it is. Please don't."

Her face went pale and she looked as though she'd be sick. He pushed back a twinge of guilt, reminding himself how overly dramatic she could be. It was just a dance for God's sake, and she'd have to learn the steps eventually.

"Trust me." He pried his arm from her grip and squared himself off to face her. Reaching around her waist, he grasped the small of her back and pulled her firmly towards him. Even a statue would have felt more limber. "Left hand on my shoulder."

Her eyes bore hatred into his as she lifted a tense, rigid arm and clutched the spot.

"Very good. Now the right arm is out, and the hands are clasped." His left hand took up her right, and he lifted both their arms, holding them straight out to one side. "There, now we have our starting position."

"I hope you're enjoying yourself," she muttered.

"And I hope you're listening. Begin by stepping back with your left foot, then out with your right." Slowly, he followed through with the movement. She took his lead and obeyed with surprisingly little resistance. His signal to continue. "Perfect. Now, right foot forward and out with your left."

"It forms a box," she said as they completed the motion.

He grinned. "Exactly. All right, let's go again. One—two—three—two—two—three—three—two—three . . ."

Her eyes fluttered shut as she listened to his counts and followed the steps. A few more rounds and she had the knack of it, thankfully sparing his toes from any mistakes. All that protesting for naught.

Her eyelids opened, and he stopped counting aloud when he saw how intensely she looked up at him. Her grip on his shoulder relaxed. The corners of her lips curved into an angelic smile. "I don't believe it. I'm actually doing this, aren't I?"

"You are, Miss Baker," he replied, trying to ignore his spiking pulse.

She surveyed the crowd and bit her lip, drawing his attention back to that inviting part of her face. "But what happens if the men I turned down see me dancing with you?"

"I'd imagine they may never ask you to dance again." He locked eyes with a gentleman two couples away and received a subtle glare. Part of him enjoyed it. "I hope you aren't too devastated."

She giggled, glancing up at him for a split second before returning her focus to his shoulder. "In that case, I suppose I should thank you for this lesson."

"Oh, I wouldn't thank me just yet. Not until you've conquered the tricky part. Now, follow my lead." He began turning their bodies and she gasped. Her feet fumbled, but he kept his grip firm on her as he continued in pace with the music. "It's the same as before, only traveling now. See how everyone else is doing it? Just count it out in your head."

"This is impossible," she protested.

"Don't think about the steps, just stay in rhythm with me," he said, ignoring the occasional pinch atop his toes as she struggled to keep up.

Somehow, she must have understood him, because her erratic trips and jerking gradually lessened until they finally moved in tandem. Not perfect, but progress, regardless of whether she had the right footwork.

"Well done." Once he sensed she'd relaxed enough, he began weaving them through the sea of other couples.

Friendly smiles from those he hadn't seen in years greeted him in passing. He grinned back, his jaw tense as stone. Everyone now believed the lie he'd told the Tuttles, and it was already eating away at him. Some acted as though he'd never left, while others pitied him like a neglected puppy. In the gutter one minute, and dancing amidst an elaborate soiree the next—with so many people.

The room suddenly grew warm. He felt the close presence of watchful eyes, and the waltz music faded into a blur of mismatched chords. Bright spots clouded his vision. His stomach churned, warning him of what would follow if he didn't snap out of it.

"Are you feeling all right?"

He looked down to find Ellie staring at him with a crinkled brow. Then he noticed he'd stopped dancing entirely. Dammit, this can't continue. His very reputation relied on his getting a hold of himself. Pretending shouldn't be this difficult.

As he looked down at her concerned face, a critical thought struck him. He had to tell someone—no, he had to tell her everything. He'd never move on if his past remained locked up inside him. Who could he trust more than the girl with whom he shared nursery rhymes and ghost stories? The woman who had her own dark secret to hide from society?

"I'm fine," he muttered, keeping his voice low and his mouth stiff. "But I'd like to ask you something very improper."

She rolled her eyes, reminding him of who he was speaking to. The song drifted to an end and the room applauded, signaling a perfect opportunity.

"Would you be willing to come to my house tomorrow?" he asked through the racket. "You can ask me as many questions as you'd like, and I promise to answer them all truthfully."

She clapped along, eyes sparking with intrigue. "You'll tell me anything?"

"Anything and everything."

"Then how could I refuse?" She smiled gracefully, keeping her attention on the orchestra like a natural little actress.

The foxtrot began.

"Good, let's meet at one o' clock," he said. "My house is a five-minute ride from the estate. You still ride, don't you?"

She placed a hand to her chest in mock insult as she took his arm to leave the floor. "Now you insult me, Mr. Peterson."

He chuckled. The sickness began leaving his stomach, and the tension in his muscles finally eased up a little. But his pulse, he feared, wouldn't slow for the rest of the evening.

He had Miss Baker to thank for that.

Chapter Eight

"I need a horse," Ellie panted.

Tim glanced up from his sandwich with a mouthful of meat. "Miss Ellie?"

"Please, I'll explain later." She gripped her tightly bound midsection and struggled for air, regretting the decision to sprint all the way from the mansion to the stables.

It was half past two and she still hadn't left for Gabriel's house, thanks to a surprise piano lesson from Jane at noon. But after all the girl had done for Ellie last night—letting her in through the billiard room window when she'd arrived home late—she'd no choice but to oblige. Besides, Jane didn't know a thing about today. Despite her approval of the party, she'd most likely protest the idea of visiting a man's home alone, regardless of whom he was. Thankfully, Ellie didn't have to sneak around. Jane had gone to meet her fiancé in town after the lesson.

Tim swallowed his food and rushed toward the stalls. "Maybe one of these days you'll ask me to do something that won't risk my employment."

"I'd take all the blame," she said with a small laugh.

Within minutes, Tim led Lincoln out to her completely saddled, and she said a quick prayer of thanks that he'd paired her with this particular gelding again.

"Will you at least tell me where you're going this time?" he asked as he helped her mount.

Gritting her teeth, she took the reins into her hands. She considered Tim a friend and felt just as guilty hiding her plans from him as she did from Jane. But she couldn't tell him, so she urged the horse to canter instead. "I'll be back before sundown!" she shouted over her shoulder.

Recalling Gabriel's directions, she followed the trail through the woods until she reached the familiar clearing on the other side. Lincoln flew through the open span of grass just as he'd done two days before, his happy grunts and head-tossing sure signs he enjoyed the ride as much as she.

She cut through the trees, eventually emerging onto a quiet road. They reached a fork and, with a gentle tug on the reins, she guided Lincoln to the right. Houses came few and far between at first, but soon lined the streets. She searched address numbers, ignoring the curious stares from residents in their backyards, their eyes wide at the sight of her riding astride.

They skirted a stone wall netted with vines until they arrived at an iron gate that divided the barrier. The number 317 peeped out from behind the greenery. A squeak, like a wheel in need of oiling, ushered the approach of a man pushing a wheelbarrow across the lawn.

"Excuse me, sir," Ellie called.

"Yes, ma'am?" he said, looking up from his work.

"Is this where Mr. Peterson lives?"

"It is." He drew an arm across his tanned, perspiring brow. "Are you here to see the doctor?"

She nodded. "Yes, if he has the time, of course."

The man sauntered to the gate and pulled it open. "He's always got time when it comes to his patients."

"Thank you." She returned his smile and tapped her heels on Lincoln's sides, coaxing him up the driveway.

Her breath caught when she saw the white, three-story home with pointed roofs. A stone path leading to the front porch curved through newly planted flowers and shrubs, and a wide veranda wrapped around the side of the house.

To her, it was perfect.

"I can bring him to the carriage house for you. That's where the doctor keeps his horse."

She glanced over her shoulder to where a boy no older than eight approached. His small hand reached up and gave Lincoln's side a pat.

"I promise to take good care of him. It's my job," he said with an endearing seriousness.

She slid from the saddle, resisting the urge to tousle his ash-colored hair as she handed him the reins. "Well, thank you very much, that would be wonderful."

"What's his name?"

"Lincoln."

"Oh, like the president. That's a nice name. The doctor's horse is called Roger. I'm not sure why."

She laughed. "And what's your name?"

"Harry Newton, what's yours?"

"I'm Ellie." She leaned forward and extended a hand. "It's nice to meet you, Harry."

The boy blushed and shook it. "Hello."

"Now—" She gazed at him playfully while scratching the horse's mane. "The only thing I ask is that the person who handles Lincoln here must love animals."

He did a little jump. "That's me! I love animals!"

She placed a hand on his bony shoulder. "In that case, I wouldn't put my trust in anyone else."

"You won't be disappointed. Harry is the best animal caretaker in the state," Gabriel's voice broke in.

She whipped around to find him leaning on a veranda post, casually clad in a gray waistcoat, with shirt sleeves pushed up past his elbows. The crooked smile he wore suggested he'd been listening the entire time.

"I'm not really the best, am I, sir?" Harry asked with wide eyes.

"Do you think I'd let just anyone handle my prized horse?"

"I suppose not . . ."

Gabriel slapped a hand atop his head with a feigned look of shock. "Come on, son, where's your confidence? Roger likes you better than me!"

Harry puffed out his chest and lifted his chin to stand tall. "I mean no, sir! I'm the best there is!"

"That's more like it. Now go introduce Lincoln to Roger, and be sure to tell me what they say to one another later."

Harry nodded diligently. With a smile stretching from ear-to-ear, he led Lincoln toward the back of the house and disappeared. Gabriel winked when Ellie caught his eye. A certain nervousness gripped her. Such a look could have melted steel.

"You certainly know how to make a boy's entire year," she said, moving to join him on the porch.

"Ben's been up since sunrise restoring my neglected grounds to their original state. Poor Harry had to come along with his father. It didn't sit well with me to see him so bored all day."

She folded her arms, unable to deny the warmth she felt at seeing the man interacting with the child. "So, you gave him something to do that he'd enjoy."

"Once I noticed his love for animals, the decision of dubbing him as Roger's official caretaker wasn't hard. Don't be fooled by his age. He takes the job very seriously."

"I can see that he does."

Gabriel stepped away from the post and raised his arms above his head in a stretch. She found herself outwardly staring at all the places where his clothing clung to hard muscle. Her heart leapt into her throat when he caught her looking. She didn't dare look at him again until she'd climbed the three steps to where he stood. But now, the question of how to greet him almost froze her in place. Until this moment, all their encounters had happened amid chaos.

"Won't you come in, Miss Baker?" he said, pulling the newly painted door open.

On the wall beside it, a metal nameplate bore the words, G. Peterson, Physician. "You really are a doctor, aren't you?" she said, tracing the words with her finger.

He jerked his head back. "Was that a question? Have they begun already?"

"I believe they have."

"You certainly don't waste any time."

She shrugged. "Thanks to my tardiness, we don't have much left."

"True." He glanced at the nameplate. "Yes, I'm really a doctor."

"Had you always wanted to be one?"

"From the day I first had a tongue depressor shoved into my mouth."

She glared at him, completely unsatisfied.

"I'm being serious," he said with a trace of laughter. "I'd been fascinated by medicine ever since I was a boy, and would often bury myself in whatever relevant books I could find in my father's library. It wasn't long after the war broke out when I learned the effects of life-saving surgery and became determined to join the medical practice."

"You must have started training shortly after Colorado." A cold shiver spread over her as she remembered. She'd thought she'd die on that awful day he left, and her parents barely knew what to do when she didn't stop crying during those following weeks.

"Yes, I was fifteen. A physician's apprentice for three years, then I went on to study at Harvard for three more years," he stated as if under oath. "Does that answer suit you?"

"It does, thank you." She raised her chin, satisfied for now. "I must say I'm very impressed. I've never been friends with a doctor before."

"Well, now you are," he said. "Though I won't feel like much of one until my practice is dusted off and rebuilt."

She strolled past him and into the hall. "Oh I doubt you'll have a hard time after the way people adored you last night. Pretty soon, they'll be breaking down your door just to have you treat them for a single sneeze."

"If you're referring to the women in town, then you're right, I'm entirely adored. After all, who could blame them?" He gestured grandly to his physique as he followed her inside and shut the door. A joke in his opinion, but darn if he wasn't right.

"I could easily blame them for adoring such arrogance."

He folded his arms and leaned a shoulder against the green papered wall. "If I didn't know any better, Miss Baker, I'd say you were jealous of the female attention that's been bestowed on me."

"Jealous?" Oh, how she wanted to shake that smug look right off his all-too-perfect face. She'd have to retaliate for that one. "Why on earth would I be jealous when I had numerous gentlemen practically falling at my feet for a dance?" She settled her fingertips on her lips, debating whether to continue. Why not? "Others couldn't take their eyes off me all night."

He smirked, surrender written all over his gaze. Success. She'd beaten him at his little game. Although, she wished she hadn't sounded like the harlot he thought she was while doing it.

"You're absolutely right, and I'm happy for you. Every man in his right mind should have asked you to dance." He spoke in a casual way, catching her off guard. "Now why don't you have a seat in there, and I'll join you shortly."

He gestured to the parlor on her left and backed away, victorious.

She hid her grin behind a glower until he disappeared into another room. Should she be enjoying their gentle sparring this much? She hoped so as she stepped into the bright parlor illuminated by four bare windows. Though much cozier than the Westgate's parlor, the space lacked any hint of a feminine touch. In fact, the only decor was a collection of framed photographs placed haphazardly about the room.

She examined them one-by-one. When her gaze settled on a photo of Gabriel's parents, she stopped. Statuesque and proper, they looked exactly the same as she remembered. The round-faced baby perched on Victoria Peterson's lap wore a pout that could only be the result of fussing moments earlier. Poor little Gabriel, so small, adorable and helpless.

Images of Patrick Peterson only skimmed the edges of Ellie's memory. His age and closed-off nature stood out most. At least twenty years his wife's senior, the Transcontinental Railroad's expansion had led him away on business more often than not. But

Victoria couldn't have been more opposite. She'd always been kind and personable, treating women like Mama as no less than her equal.

"You'll have to excuse the mess."

Ellie jumped at the sound of Gabriel's voice. She whipped around to find him staring at her. He gripped a silver tray, fully stocked with hot tea, small cakes and cookies.

"You do like sweets, don't you?" he asked warily.

"Oh, yes . . . of course I do." Her fluster eased off, and she lowered herself into the nearest armchair.

He continued into the room. "Good. For a minute, I was afraid I was going to have to check your pulse." The tray clanked against the table as he set it down beside her. Then he began pouring two cups of steaming black tea. "As I was saying, I've yet to uncover several things that have been packed away." He glanced at the naked windows. "Curtains, for example."

"Who packed everything in the first place?"

"My uncle would be my first guess. Sugar?"

"Just cream, thank you." She folded her hands in her lap and peered around the room again. "If he thought you were dead, then I wonder why he didn't sell this house."

He added cream to both drinks. "I've wondered that, too, which leads me to believe that somewhere inside him, he still clung to the idea that I was alive."

She took her teacup from his hands. "Well, if that's true, then he'll most certainly forgive you."

"I'll toast to that."

They raised their cups and clinked. Their eyes met as they sipped the hot liquid against the lull of the room. A warm, cheery silence. He tossed two cookies into his mouth and collapsed onto the chair opposite the table. She tried to stifle a chuckle, pressing against her lips as she reached for her own cookie.

"I don't recommend two at a time," he mumbled with a very full mouth. Amusement flickered in his eyes. "Moisture seems to expand them."

That did it. She burst out laughing and handed him his cup. "It's so good to see the old Gabriel again. I was afraid he'd gone off and disappeared."

He chuckled. "Are you calling me a boy?"

"Didn't anyone teach you to swallow before you speak?"

"Touché." He slurped his tea. "And what about Ellie Bear? She must still be around somewhere."

Her body stiffened. The sound of her old nickname cracked like thunder in her ears. Papa had first called her that, and for years, she'd introduced herself as "Ellie Bear" to everyone she met. Somehow, Gabriel's remembering was comfort amidst a vexing memory.

She looked away while swirling the cookie in her tea. "I wish I could say she was, but I'm not so sure anymore. I haven't felt her in a very long time."

"I didn't mean to upset you."

Of course he hadn't, because he didn't know what Papa had done. Part of her wished she'd remained ignorant to the whole thing.

Then she wouldn't have to feel this shadow across her heart. All focus left her gaze, and she stared blankly at the wall. "Things can change so quickly, can't they? If only we could be children again, when life was simple."

"Was it simple, or were we too young to know any different?" he asked softly. "I remember my father always saying there can be no progress without change. And change doesn't necessarily represent a bad thing. Whether a human or a nation, the difficult times are what make you stronger in the end."

Ellie bit into her cookie, regretting the decision of soaking it once she felt the soggy mush sloshing inside her mouth. "Do you truly believe that?"

A somber smile graced his lips. "I must, or else I'm liable to go mad."

"Is that why you didn't touch a drop of alcohol last night?" Oh, God! She cringed. How could she say something so forward without thinking? Her breath quickened, her cheeks became warm; she wished she could take it back. "I'm so sorry. Please, don't feel you have to answer that. Actually . . . don't say anything."

He stared at her, his left eyebrow raising a fraction. "Ellie, when I invited you here, I was prepared to answer everything you might throw at me."

"Yes, but that was completely out-of-line —"

"I put the bottle down the day I sought you out to apologize. See? I honestly don't mind."

His voice held no hostility. When he lifted the porcelain to his lips and sipped, she suddenly noticed how steady his hands were. The hands of a surgeon. He truly had recovered. A thrill rushed through her, and it took everything not to reach across the tiny table between them and touch his arm. Instead, she settled against the back of her chair and gave a shallow nod.

"I hated who—no, what I had become . . . but I couldn't bring myself to escape it either." He looked at her fondly. "Not until I remembered you. The way I'd spoken to you and cast you off like . . . like you were the dirt beneath my boot. I didn't know myself anymore. I wasn't raised to speak to a woman, or anyone for that matter, with such degradation and hostility. So I forced myself into sobriety and decided to reclaim my life, no matter how difficult." His gaze darted sideways and his lips parted as if to say more, but he seemed to keep himself from voicing it.

She stayed silent, yet offered him a smile.

"There were moments when I thought the withdrawal would kill me, especially during the trip East." He shook his head. "Hearing imaginary gunshots in my stagecoach, breaking into cold sweats in my train car, vomiting into—I'll spare you the gruesome details."

"I don't mind at all, and I'm very proud of you. I'm sure it wasn't easy." She tossed him a cookie, which he hurled right into his mouth.

"It wasn't, but it had to be done. Now throw one into the air and I'll catch it."

"Can you still do that?"

A boyish smile broke across his face as he shifted to face her. "We'll see in a moment, won't we?"

She plucked the smallest morsel from the dish. "Ready?"

"Pull."

Angling her wrist, she pitched the cookie high. He jerked sideways before catching it in his mouth with astounding accuracy.

"Hooray!" She clapped like some sort of giddy school girl.

He cast his arms out to the side and gave a triumphant bow. "I haven't attempted that in years. Those cookies are dangerous."

"These are, too." She snatched a small pastry and attempted to shove the entire thing in her mouth . . . yet failed miserably. A drop of red jam splattered onto her chest before she could stop it from spilling down her chin.

He laughed, deep, warm and rich. He pulled a handkerchief from his waistcoat pocket and handed it to her. "I see you're still a mess as always."

"That definitely hasn't changed." She dabbed at the stain, wondering if her cheeks weren't redder than the jam itself.

When she looked back up, she noticed the parlor's light and shadows had shifted. Who knew how much time they had left? Even if the fun and games could last an eternity, what she'd come for was answers.

"It's a quarter past four."

Her head swung back to see him holding up his pocket watch. "You were concerned about the hour, weren't you?"

"Yes," she admitted, hearing the disappointment in her own voice.

His cup and saucer clinked against the tray as he placed it on the table between them. "Go ahead then, ask me what you've been wanting to."

She stared at him. "But—"

"Go ahead."

The air seemed dense, and she gripped her cup with both hands. His own hands were clasped so hard that his fingertips turned white. He sat tall in a display of anticipation. What might she do to him if she brought up the past? But that was whole the reason he'd invited her over in the first place, wasn't it? He wanted to tell her everything.

"All right—" She shifted in her seat. "What brought you back to Colorado, and why?"

"My father's death," he answered quickly. Then he raked a hand through his thick brown hair and shook his head. "No, what I meant to say was it all began with my father's death. He'd locked the only copy of his will in a safe at our Chicago home. Moments before he died, he bestowed me with the title of executor."

When he glanced at her to be sure she was following, she gave a reassuring nod.

"So I made a decision. Once I retrieved the document, I'd sell the house in Chicago. With my father gone and my mother aging, we had little use for several properties, and I certainly didn't need all of them. I assured my mother that I'd handle everything, but she insisted on coming along to sort through our belongings herself."

He rubbed his hands together, entwined his fingers and placed them to his lips. The line of his mouth tightened a fraction more. She found herself motionless, watching every inch of his face as if he were lit dynamite.

"She was so stubborn about it that I finally gave in. I figured it was better than enduring her wrath were I to auction off some priceless family heirloom." Releasing a heavy sigh, he leaned forward and rested his elbows on his thighs. "It took us weeks to sort through everything in the house, and once it was over, I could breathe a little easier. That lasted all but five minutes."

His expression changed, darkened.

"On a cold night in March, I woke to several screams. I ran into the hallway and there was smoke everywhere . . . like some sort of hellish nightmare. The servants were panicked. My eyes and throat burned. I opened a downstairs window and helped them all out before sprinting back up for my mother."

"God in heaven," she whispered.

He stared ahead, eyes lost in thought. "I remember feeling a hint of relief when I noticed the smoke had barely begun filling her side of the hall. I figured she'd be fine. I figured I'd carry her out, and to hell with the house." His voice hardened. "But when I found her, she was still in her bed, and there was . . ."

He shut his eyes and sank his head into his hands. She battled the urge to reach out and clutch his knee.

"You don't have to continue," she said softly.

"Yes, I do." He rose from his chair and paced the room with wide, determined strides. "Someone had shot her. There was blood everywhere. I fell to my knees . . . I'd never felt so helpless, so broken." He paused, his face bleak with sorrow. "I don't know how long I'd been sitting there when I felt the bite of a bullet and everything went black."

"Oh . . ." She stared across at him, her heart pounding.

"I came to in a hospital, with a bandage around my chest and several nurses hovering over me. They told me the bullet just missed my heart and I was lucky to be alive, thanks to a bad shot in poor visibility." Bitterness edged his words. "But I didn't feel lucky at all. The anger I felt at my life being spared, the guilt I suffered for not being there to save my mother, it was simply unbearable."

Ellie shut her eyes and dipped her head. Sharp, tiny breaths were all she could manage as Gabriel's anguish radiated across her chest like a fresh wound. She knew all too well what it felt like to be stripped of both parents, yet their shared loss brought her little comfort. Instead, the more she looked at him, the more she wanted to take his pain away.

"I'm so sorry, Gabriel," she murmured.

He stopped at the fireplace and turned to her. "How's that for a heroic tale?"

"And you never saw who shot you?"

"No."

She cast her eyes downward. "You saved so many others . . . how could you have known your house had been purposely set on fire? That there was a gunman inside?"

"Not a gunman. An assassin." He ground the word out between his teeth. "I learned that the moment I found my father's will had been stolen."

"But, who would steal a will?"

"Someone who wanted to destroy every part of my family name until there was nothing left. Someone clever and wealthy enough to have others carry out their dirty work." One hand clutched the mantle while the other rested on his hip. "The Boston police eventually found the man who'd shot us. They killed him on the spot during an assault.

"They sent my mother's body back to New Hampshire, while I sat useless in a Chicago hospital bed, day-after-day. By the time they released me, I'd completely lost myself. I couldn't eat, I barely slept and I never spoke. I was consumed with grief, and after that I—"

"You never returned home," she said, finishing his sentence.

"I was young and selfish," he answered in a low, tormented voice. "I didn't think about going back to claim my family's wealth, and I didn't know how I'd face my uncle after failing to save his sister. So I headed West, where I kept my identity a secret while discovering the numbing effects of alcohol. Creekwood was the final stop on my path to self destruction."

She placed her teacup atop the tray, a blunt question suddenly wracking her mind—one that left a bitter taste in her mouth before even asking. "Part of that self destruction was frequenting The Inn, wasn't it?"

His eyes pierced the distance between them. "Do you judge me for it?"

"No."

"Liar."

"I couldn't judge you, even if I wanted to."

"Why not?"

"You're so quick to forget where I was, what I've done . . ." A shiver ran through her. "I'm damaged, used, and it's only a matter of time before everyone knows it."

The lines on his face softened. "I am quick to forget it, because you know I don't care about that."

"But others will, once they find out." Her skin felt tender and cold, as if she were in Jasper's office all over again. The memory of each lustful, violent grab was almost enough to stop her heart from beating. She rattled her head. "I never would have chosen that existence, or set foot in that place, unless . . . unless my very life depended on it."

He dropped his hand from the mantle and stared. "What do you mean?"

She met his gaze, losing herself in a sea of blue for a moment. Tears blinded her eyes and swelled her throat. The last thing she wanted to do right now was cry, yet it seemed the first thing on her emotional agenda. "I had no choice—" she rasped.

Admitting everything now would bring it all back, would make it all real again. She'd only just found happiness in this new place. A hot tear rolled down her cheek and she covered her face with her hands. Within seconds, she felt her arms being pulled down. Gabriel kneeled before her. His stare was serious, his expression stone.

"Tell me what happened to you," he demanded.

"I can't..."

"Ellie." His gaze didn't waver and his bare hands remained attached to her sleeved arms. She looked down at them, finding herself wishing there was no barrier of fabric between them. Her head snapped at the unconventional thought, and she pulled her arms away.

"What time is it?" she asked, wiping her fingertips beneath her eyes.

"I won't let you change the subject."

"Gabriel, please, I have to leave at five o'clock." She looked out the window and bit her lip, dreading the hour more than she welcomed the excuse.

"Good Lord, woman." He yanked his watch fob from his pocket and popped the case open. "Nearly half past five. Why didn't you tell me that sooner?"

Panic struck her. She sprang from her seat. "Oh, mercy, I'm late. No one can know I was here!"

He stuffed the watch back into his pocket. "They won't find out. I'll grab your horse and meet you out front." He bolted from the room and she followed suit, turning for the front door while he went the back way.

Leaping over veranda steps, she raced outside with a pounding heart. She could have slapped herself for neglecting the time. Now, she might have betrayed Jane's trust and disgraced the entire family. She clenched her fists as Gabriel appeared from behind the house with Lincoln in tow.

"Do you know your way back?" His brows drew together, his eyes roaming her face. "Will you be all right on your own?"

God, she hated that she'd cried in front of him—again.

"Yes, I'll be fine." She shoved her foot in the stirrup and hoisted herself up.

He handed her the reins and stepped back. "Impressive."

She looked down at him, relieved by his lack of malice toward her unconventional nature. "I always thought fondly of your mother. I couldn't be sorrier for what happened to her, and . . . I truly appreciate your telling me everything today."

She wished she could express how much his confession had meant to her. He trusted her, above everyone else, with what he held closest to his chest. No one had ever confided in her like that. Perhaps someday, she might find the courage to trust him—as long as it didn't involve her heart.

"I appreciate your listening. Now, get going." His voice held a faint tremor, as though some emotion had touched him.

She exchanged a warm smile with him. Then, she urged Lincoln forward and they cantered down the drive. The beautiful house vanished behind her.

She clutched the reins with numb hands, dreading what might await her at home.

Chapter Nine

"Can I enter through here?" Ellie half-spoke, half-whispered.

The startled cook dropped the garbage in her hands and jerked her head up. Her bewildered eyes darted to the open service door, then back to Ellie.

"Wouldn't the front door suit you better, miss?" she asked, snatching up the fallen pail.

Ellie wrung her fingers while the woman poured the day's waste into the ground. "Not today. Please?"

The stout cook lifted her head. Quizzically, she took in Ellie's windblown hair and wrinkled dress. After a brief look around, she nodded toward the door. "I didn't see nothin'."

"Thank you, ma'am."

Ellie breathed a sigh of relief, creeping down the wooden stairs leading into the kitchen. She moved fast and kept her head low as she breezed through the galley, only interrupting the work of those who caught sight of her. The savory aromas of a rich dinner being prepared made her mouth water. It smelled like roast beef and sweet potatoes. Delicious.

She tiptoed through the halls and up the secondary staircase. The upstairs hallways resembled an elegant, yet inconvenient maze as she rounded corners and crept through unfamiliar corridors. She really had to start learning to navigate this house.

When she finally reached the hall leading to her bedroom door, her nerves slackened.

Almost there without being discovered. She rushed for the handle, pulled it open, and flew back at the sight of Mary inside.

"Miss Ellie!" The maid rushed to her with fret on her brow.

"Oh God, does anyone know I was gone?"

"No, miss. Everyone arrived home less than an hour ago. I came upstairs to dress you, but you weren't here. I didn't know what to do."

"Please, don't tell a soul." Ellie prayed that placing her fate in Mary's silence would be better than some fruitless excuse.

"It's not my business," Mary murmured. "But there are guests downstairs, and we'd best get you ready as quickly as possible."

Bless the girl.

Mary took her by the arm and shut the door.

Several minutes later, Ellie rushed back into the hall sporting neatly pinned hair and a new dress glued to her frame. A pair of stiff new shoes pinched her feet, and she wished she were nimble enough to slide down the banister instead of descending the steps one at a time. She paused just outside the formal sitting room where the family's chatter rang out, and took a moment to gather herself before facing everyone.

If Gabriel's somber face and heart-wrenching story remained in the forefront of her mind, she'd never be able to play the part she needed to now. Closing her eyes, she dashed all thoughts of their conversation away. There'd be time to absorb it later.

She entered the room. Within seconds, every male was on his feet to greet her.

"Ah, Ellie," Mr. Westgate extended a welcoming arm her way. "I'm glad you could join us, my dear."

Ellie summoned a smile as she faced the two unfamiliar men. One appeared slightly older than Mr. Westgate, while the other looked closer to Gabriel's age.

"Good evening," she said with a curtsy.

"A pleasure, my dear," the older man replied.

"Ellie, this is Mr. Jackson Tiller, and his youngest son, Mr. Matthew Tiller." Mr. Westgate gestured to the gentlemen, one at a time.

She remembered the name. "Oh yes, Jane's fiancé."

"I take it you've heard of me." Matthew Tiller offered an arresting smile. "It's very nice to meet you, Miss Baker."

He had a fresh, light look about him, with sandy blond hair and a well-groomed mustache. A seemingly perfect match for Jane, yet a man just the same. Ellie dipped her head, disguising her conflicting emotions with another smile.

"The pleasure is mine, Mr. Tiller," she said. "Jane speaks very highly of you."

A glint of pride touched his face. He glanced at Jane, who in turn blushed at his attention. "I can assure you it's not as highly as I speak of her. And please, call me 'Matthew.' We're to be family, after all."

"Come sit with me, Ellie." Jane patted the space beside her on the robin's egg-blue settee.

Ellie ambled toward Jane, studying her expression with a shivering jumble of nerves. Mr. Westgate appeared completely oblivious to her absence, and she could only pray the same went for Jane. The moment her bottom touched the cushion, the men reclaimed their seats, and then continued conversation amongst themselves.

"I feel terrible for leaving you alone all day," Jane whispered, giving her hand a gentle squeeze. "We weren't supposed to be out for so long, and I'd love to take you shopping tomorrow to make up for it."

Ellie squeezed back, relieved. By some miracle, she had a reprieve. For the first time since sneaking into the house, she relaxed.

"I'd love to, Jane."

"Miss Baker, Henry tells me you hail all the way from Colorado, is that so?" Matthew's father inquired, while Hanlon topped off his scotch.

She sat a little taller. "Yes, sir. Have you been?"

"Would you believe I've traveled the entire world and have yet to go West? The closest I've gotten was the day I decided to invest in oil."

"It's very different from here." She folded her hands in her lap. "Both states are beautiful, but Colorado is far more harsh and unpredictable."

Matthew smirked and raised his scotch glass to his lips. "Sounds like New York."

A symphony of chuckles floated through the room.

"New York indeed. I imagine the Wild West was given its name for a reason," Mr. Tiller said. "It's chock-full of large beasts, rocky mountains, Indians, rough terrain—"

"Cattle," Matthew broke in.

Mr. Tiller chortled and leaned back in his chair. "Oh yes, you'll certainly find me running the other way when I cross paths with a Devon."

Matthew teetered his glass. "On the contrary, sir, I'm sure Miss Baker will agree that cattle can be as dangerous as bison."

Ellie could feel her lips wanting to break from their complacent smile as all eyes shifted to her. Her heart squeezed inside her chest. It took everything in her not to say something spiteful. But despite the sting of the comment, she reminded herself that Matthew was oblivious to the way Papa died. Same went for everyone else. She'd no right to resent him for a harmless question—no matter how much she wanted to.

"He's right, stampedes are no laughing matter," Mr. Westgate stated before she could answer. As if sensing her discomfort, he added "Now, I believe a lighter subject is in order, gentlemen. For the sake of the ladies."

Hanlon stepped into the room. "Ladies and gentlemen, dinner is served."

Ellie didn't know who she could have kissed first, Mr. Westgate, or his old butler.

* * *

The next morning, the clip clop of horse hooves and crisp smell of Spring temporarily distracted Ellie from thoughts of last night. She'd tried contributing to conversation at dinner, but between memories of Papa's death, thoughts of arranged marriages—or any marriages for that matter—and simply feeling awkward, she'd found it difficult.

The carriage took a sharp turn, churning the rich breakfast in her stomach. A few minutes later, she looked across the gently swaying vehicle to where Jane sat, smiling radiantly.

"So, what did you think of Matthew?" Jane asked, her pitch higher than usual. "I've been just itching to ask you."

He'd better not break your heart. "He seems perfect for you, Jane. I couldn't believe how much he knew about geography and art. He's kind, and very smart."

"And . . . do you think him handsome?"

"Very handsome," Ellie said. She took in the fiery vibrance of Jane's hazel eyes before adding, "But I didn't have to tell you that, did I?"

A vivid pink colored Jane's cheeks and she leaned forward. "Oh Ellie, sometimes I find myself thinking very unwholesome thoughts. As a proper woman, I know I'm not supposed to, but I can't help it, for heaven's sake. Have you ever . . . thought about your wedding night?"

"All the time." Ellie wished she meant it in the way Jane thought.

"I do, too. Sometimes, a simple, innocent look from Matthew is all it takes for me to . . ."

"To what?"

"I don't know . . . to *feel* things," Jane whispered. "Things a woman notices when she's in the presence of a man she admires. All sorts of things I can't begin to explain." She squeezed the closed parasol on her lap and sighed.

Ellie gazed out the window, watching the fleeting scenery, and wishing she knew what Jane meant. It couldn't be the same experience she'd gotten from the men who'd paid for her. While they thrusted and groaned, she'd felt nothing but anger and emptiness. Women weren't meant to experience such pleasure—*that* she'd learned first hand. But she could never dash Jane's hopes.

"I'm sure you won't be disappointed on your wedding night." She prayed the words rang true. The innocent, wide eyed girl didn't deserve Ellie's same fate.

Jane grinned. "Well, when your day comes, I'll be sure let you know what you have to look forward to."

"What will I do without you? Why must you leave me so soon?" Ellie gave a playful frown, despite the twinge of loss she truly felt.

Jane's glowing, youthful happiness faded. "Oh honestly, none of that. I'll only be a twenty-minute carriage ride away, and you had better pay me visits as often as you can."

"I promise to visit so often that you'll find me obnoxious."

They shared a laugh as the first cluster of buildings drifted by, signaling the start of downtown. Ellie inwardly smiled at the thought of spending the entire day in Jane's company. She'd never done fun, girlish things with anyone but Mama. Slingshots and sword fights with tree branches had always taken precedent over dolls and bows.

When the carriage slowed to a halt, they were escorted out the door and into a bustling scene. Aside from storefronts lining the cobblestone streets, clusters of well-stocked merchant carts filled the vacant spaces between. Buggies and carriages whirled by. People appeared to be everywhere, haggling with vendors, walking with their dogs and floating in and out of stone buildings.

Ellie slipped her reticule onto her wrist, unsure of where to look with all the visual stimulation surrounding her. "Where do we even begin?"

"Just leave that to me," Jane said. "I'm an expert on the women's sport of shopping."

She took Ellie's hand and pulled her into a large building with the word *Emporium* painted on its glass display window. The inside went on for miles, and each turn flaunted shops selling everything from perfume to gardening tools.

Nearly two hours later, they emerged onto the shaded street, toting several parcels of every shape and size. Ellie had never seen anyone shop like Jane. The girl not only had an eye for luxurious items, but for bargains, too. Almost everything they'd purchased was either discounted, or had something extra thrown in for free.

"You were incredible in there," Ellie said, switching a few packages from one hand to the other. "Is this how everyone shops in the East?"

"Heavens, no. When I was a girl, I learned a thing or two from watching my nannies dicker with the shopkeepers. Father would be appalled if he knew how I haggled." Jane's eyes scanned the streets and she smirked. "But we have larger problems at the moment. It seems you've officially been spotted in public."

"What does that mean?"

"It means you should prepare yourself for an endless line of suitors. Don't look now, but several gentlemen are glancing your way."

Ellie's stomach clenched. Well, how could she not look? Subtly, she took in her surroundings, noticing the sea of male eyes that focused solely on her. The newfound, unwanted attention was overwhelming. "Oh, my. I suddenly feel inclined to flee."

A corner of Jane's mouth tilted upward. "I couldn't agree with you more. Let's go to the sweetshop and escape these prying eyes."

They stopped at the carriage first, where the coachman took up their packages and stacked them neatly inside. Ellie focused on the shop windows as she followed Jane to a side street tucked away from the boisterous crowds. The small bell above the sweetshop's door dinged when they entered. Aromas of chocolate, citrus and sugar filled the air.

"Afternoon, ladies. What can I bring you today?" the aproned clerk asked as they approached the long marble counter.

They claimed two vacant red stools.

"Lemonade, please," Jane said politely.

"And for you, miss?"

"I'll have the same," Ellie replied, rolling her ankles below the counter.

Jane let out a long sigh. "It feels so nice to sit down. My feet always ache after shopping. How are yours faring?"

"They'd be better if I were barefoot."

"Shopping without shoes?" Jane giggled. "A very unsanitary idea."

The clerk returned with two pale yellow beverages and set them down in exchange for the coins Jane gave him. Inside each drink—three beautiful cubes of ice. They cracked and popped as Ellie lifted her glass to her lips and took a sip. Of all the luxuries she'd been introduced to, the constant access to ice never ceased to amaze her. She relished the cold, thirst-quenching goodness. The shop's bell chimed again.

"Mr. Fowler?"

She almost dropped her glass at Gabriel's voice. An odd ripple of excitement rushed through her, but subsided the moment she saw Jane's shaken expression. The dear girl looked as white as a sheet. Slowly, they twisted in their stools to face outward.

Gabriel stood beside the door, shaking the hand of a bald, portly gentleman.

"Lord in heaven, of all the people to find me in here." The man's tone thundered above the handful of other voices inside. When Gabriel glanced at the butcher's package in the man's hand, the man's round face donned a guilty smile. "Our cook is unwell, but the Missus had her heart set on brisket for dinner tonight."

"Mr. Fowler." Gabriel folded his arms, eyeing him with a speculative expression. "You expect me to believe that your wife, the same wife who pesters you about your gout, would want you to partake in a steak dinner?"

A nervous laugh floated up from the man's throat. "Partaking? Who said anything about partaking?"

"It's been less than three hours since I prescribed you a strict diet, and you're already trying to stray."

"All right, you've caught me red-handed," the man admitted, leaning on his cane. He held up a fat finger. "But in my defense, I was planning on one last night of indulging before starting your regimen tomorrow."

"I suppose I'll have to trust your word on that, sir."

"I won't disappoint you, Doctor."

"Good. Now may I suggest you leave this shop before you're tempted any further." Gabriel placed a hand on the man's shoulder and pulled open the door.

"Oh, fine." Mr. Fowler's face crinkled with defeat, yet he offered a cordial handshake before making his exit.

"I'll see you in two weeks, Mr. Fowler!" Gabriel called out after him. Ellie froze as he shifted his attention from the doorway to the counter. "I thought I felt someone watching—" His eyes found Jane and his face turned to tenderness. He slid his tall hat from his head. "Jane . . ."

With a small cry, Jane sprung from her seat and flew into his arms. He lifted her tiny body, twirled her around, and set her back down.

"Oh, cousin! My dear cousin," she cried out. "How I've missed you!"

"Sweet Jane, I—I can't believe my eyes," he said, his voice shaking with emotion. He dragged a hand down his face and took a step back, taking her in from head-to-toe. "Just look at you. When did you become a woman?"

She drew her brows together, pretending to study his face. "It must have been around the same time you grew so old!"

They shared a laugh, and he wrapped his arms around her again. "God, I've missed you."

"I've so much to tell you. I'm . . . getting married soon."

He released her. "What?"

"To Matthew Tiller, in a little over a week." She took his hands. "I wish you could come. There's nothing I'd want more."

"But, it's too soon." He searched her face. "You can't be getting married. Not yet."

"I'm twenty years old, Cousin."

"Lord. I've missed everything, haven't I?"

"None of that matters. I couldn't be more grateful to have you here at this moment, alive and well."

His broad shoulders heaved as he sighed. "I'm so sorry for leaving you."

"Come now," she said with a small smile. "I'm sure Ellie is bored with all our sentiment."

Ellie tried to quell the tingling in her limbs as he looked at her. The remorse behind his blue eyes vanished, leaving something much lighter in its wake. His smile reached out across the few feet between them, warming her. "I see you've told Jane we know each other."

She nodded, awkwardly.

He bowed his head. "Miss Baker, always a pleasure."

"Good afternoon." She felt so ridiculous for blushing. The way he affected her had nothing to do with reason.

The shop's bell chimed again, and Emily Tuttle floated in with her mother, like little snowflakes in the breeze.

"Well, there you are," Emily said, her gaze settling on Gabriel. "I was afraid we'd lost you when you wandered off. Honestly, I've never seen anyone unable to stand in a candle shop for ten minutes." Her melodic, high-pitched voice was nearly piercing. The assortment of frills, lace and ruffles accenting her puce pink dress trumped every other garment in the room.

"I didn't mean to worry you." He placed his hat back on his head. "I became a bit sidetracked when I found my cousin."

"Miss Jane Westgate." The heavy lashes shadowing Emily's rosy cheeks flew up, and she sped over to join them. "Why, it's been simply ages. I read all about your engagement in the papers. I offer my heartfelt congratulations and best wishes to you and Mr. Tiller."

Jane must have been confused, yet she politely smiled and dipped her head. "Thank you, Miss Tuttle. It's no nice to see you again. How is your family?"

"Very well, thank you, my dear," Mrs. Tuttle cut in. She took her daughter's hand, turning to Gabriel. "It's always a delight crossing paths with friends and family when one is about. We won't interfere a moment longer."

The pair scuttled off toward a display of confections and candies.

Ellie sat back, puzzled by Gabriel's abrupt change in character. She could practically see every muscle tensing beneath his frock coat—as if he were changing into some type of soldier right before her eyes. Something told her he wasn't planning on acknowledging her in Emily's presence. And that irritated her in the worst way.

She finished the last drops of lemonade, slid from her stool and marched over to where he stood. "Jane and I had a wonderful time shopping today. She took me to The Emporium."

His mouth spread into a thin, awkward smile. "Did she? That's nice."

"It's definitely a far cry from the general store."

"Yes, it is."

"Gabriel, which do you prefer, peppermint or licorice?" Emily reappeared, slipping herself between them. She turned to Ellie with an artificial look of surprise. "Oh, good afternoon. I don't believe we've met."

Jane placed a hand on Ellie's arm. "Miss Tuttle, this is my good friend Ellie Baker," she said without missing a beat. "Ellie, this is Miss Emily Tuttle."

Ellie looked at Gabriel. His eyes flashed a gentle but firm warning. No, she wouldn't play along this time. "It's nice to finally meet you, Miss Tuttle—" She heard her voice, stifled and unnatural. "I'm so sorry I didn't have the chance to make your acquaintance the other evening at your party."

"The party?" Emily's head tilted with an exaggerated smile. Then, something in her mind must have clicked. "Oh, of course, Miss Baker. I thought you looked familiar. You're the girl from Colorado." She slipped a possessive hand through Gabriel's arm and peered up at him. "How on earth do you two know each other?"

His jaw remained clamped, his back straight as a pole. Ellie felt her annoyance increase. Was this how things would be if he married? Would he start ignoring her little-by-little, until she existed as much as a unicorn or mermaid? Lying may suit him, but she'd be damned if she'd sacrifice their friendship for society's sake.

"Yes, Gabriel. How *do* we know each other?" she asked, boldly meeting his eyes.

The line of his mouth tightened a fraction more. They stared at each other across a sudden ringing silence. Then, he turned to Emily with a bland half-smile.

"Miss Baker is my aunt's second cousin. We've only just met."

The nerve! Ellie's breath burned in her throat. Startled hurt turned into blinding rage. "That's right. He's little more than a stranger to me," she muttered, drilling her glare into him. "A pompous, arrogant stranger!"

"Ellie!" Jane exclaimed in horror.

People began staring. The blood rushed to Ellie's temples, and a shudder of humiliation pounded into her. "I'm sorry, Jane. I seem to have forgotten my place."

She tore her eyes from him and stormed for the door. The bell almost ripped from the frame when she yanked it open and slammed it behind her. Clenching her skirts in her fists, she ran down the street to the Westgate carriage and jumped inside. She scooted down the seat, an awful bitterness assailing her.

"Ellie!" Jane climbed onto the space beside her, breathless. "Would you be so kind as to explain what in heaven's name you were thinking back there?"

"I didn't mean to embarrass you."

"Well, you did," she said in a disapproving tone. "You can't behave that way in public. Not unless you fancy disgracing yourself and everyone with whom you associate."

With a gentle jolt, the carriage started rolling.

Ellie settled against the back cushion, her temper deflating. "But I suppose Gabriel's behavior was completely acceptable. He acted as though I didn't exist, and I couldn't stand it."

"That's not true."

"Yes, it is. You saw the way he changed."

"Whatever his reason, I'm certain it was to protect you."

"Or himself," Ellie muttered.

Jane sighed and folded her hands in her lap. "Ellie, my cousin has been part of this society nearly all his life. He knows the rules. If he'd admitted to your deep history together, however innocent it may be, suspicions would soon arise. Especially if he's still pursuing things with Miss Tuttle." Her fine eyebrows slanted in a frown. "Although, every part of me prays he isn't. They have so little in common."

Ellie flicked an imaginary speck of dirt from her skirt. "I don't know. I guess I'd hoped he would have been—"

"What? Different than the rest of us?"

The hurt in Jane's voice was like a dagger to the heart. Suddenly, Ellie felt guilty and selfish. Jane had shown her nothing but kindness since the day she'd arrived, and Ellie still had the nerve to throw out a harsh judgment. One she didn't really mean.

Jane looked down at her hands. "I can only imagine the adjustments you had to make in coming here. Things in New Hampshire might not be the same as they were in Colorado, but if you would just give us a chance . . . then you'll see this life has a lot to offer, too."

They sat in lonely silence, watching the buildings drift past. Ellie's thoughts had become a bitter battle. Why should it matter how Gabriel acted towards her in public? It wasn't as if she were jealous. Oh no, Gabriel Peterson could easily be the *last* person she'd ever want to marry. His compelling presence, strikingly handsome face and smooth voice, gave him no exemption from the nature of betrayal that all men possessed. Why should she ever risk opening her heart to him, only to have it crumble to pieces someday? His friendship mattered far too much for that. Friendship was consistent. Friendship was safe.

Now, if she could just stop the heat from rushing to her ears whenever he smiled at her.

The taste of iron flooded her mouth as she bit hard into her cheek, trying to feel anything other than the knot in her stomach during the quiet ride home.

When the carriage pulled up to the portico, Jane hopped out and rushed through the front doors. Ellie chased after her, desperate to apologize. But when she passed the parlor, Mr. Westgate's voice pulled her to a stop.

"Ellie, there you are," he beckoned. "Come in here a moment, would you?"

She flinched. So close to going by unnoticed; the apology would have to wait. She entered the room, where Mr. Westgate and a tall, middle-aged man stood to greet her. Despite his older years, he was quite attractive. Dark eyes sat high above a prominent nose and square-set jaw, and uniform mutton chop sideburns framed his granite expression. Without the slightest trace of a smile, he bowed.

"This is Magnus Cain, a dear old friend of mine." Mr. Westgate said. "Magnus, this is Miss Ellie Baker."

"Pleased to meet you, sir." She dipped her head cordially.

"Good evening," Mr. Cain replied, dull and listless.

She tugged on her sleeve, hoping for a speedy dismissal.

"How was your day in town with Jane?" Mr. Westgate asked.

She disguised her restlessness with an even wider smile. "Very eventful, thank you."

"Marvelous. I'm so happy to see the two of you getting along so well. Magnus and I have had quite the boring afternoon discussing rifles and bear traps."

Ellie stole another glance at Mr. Cain. He stood with slightly stooped shoulders as he studied the face of his pocket watch. Even so, he towered over Mr. Westgate by nearly a foot. An uncomfortable silence stirred the air. Then, Mr. Cain placed the watch back into his pocket and shifted his gaze to her. She caught the subtle intrigue in his eyes as they darted over her figure. Her stomach clenched.

"Do you hunt, Mr. Cain?" she asked quickly.

"Yes, I enjoy it very much." His mellow baritone was one of the thickest she'd heard.

"What do you enjoy most about it?"

"The capture, of course."

"Really?" She cleared her throat. "I'd imagine the thrill of the chase to be more exhilarating."

"I agree, Ellie," Mr. Westgate said.

"That's all very well," Mr. Cain answered, his fingertips stroking his chin. "But there's nothing quite like studying your quarry up close. Seeing a beautiful creature completely surrender at your hands."

A shiver trickled down her spine. Like many of her customers, Mr. Cain seemed to enjoy power. The next time this man came around, she must remember to avoid him at all costs.

Mr. Westgate chortled. "I doubt there's room for another pair of antlers or stuffed beast anywhere in your entire house."

"What happens if the creature escapes and runs away?" Ellie asked, part of her fervent to challenge him. "Do you try again, or go after another one?"

Mr. Cain released a low chuckle, as if sincerely amused. "Miss Baker, nothing has ever gotten away from me, and I assure you nothing ever will."

A small chill ran down her spine at the familiar words. Even if Mr. Cain meant nothing more than the hunt, the memory of Jasper's voice came back to her. *Don't even think about running from me, dove, because I'll find you. No matter where you go, I'll find you.* God, but he could never find her here, could he? She began to shake as fearful images entered her mind. The things he would do to her if he ever—

"Are you feeling all right, my dear?"

Mr. Westgate stared at her with fatherly concern.

"Suddenly I'm not sure. I think I may need to lie down," she said, trying to keep her heart still.

"By all means, you're excused for the rest of the evening. I'll have a dinner tray sent to your room. Jane will check in on you later."

"Thank you, sir."

Mr. Cain displayed the first grin she'd seen on him yet. "It's been an absolute pleasure meeting you, Miss Baker. I hope you feel better soon."

"Good evening." She hurried into the hall, where she sprinted up to her room and locked the door behind her.

A terrible uneasiness filled her, followed by an even more terrifying realization. Jasper *had* found her. Maybe not physically, but in her doubts, her fears, in any man showing interest—and he would never let her go.

She threw herself into bed and pulled the covers over her head, shutting herself away from the world for the rest of the night.

Chapter Ten

Four weeks later, Ellie flew through the open fields atop Lincoln's back. She cheered aloud as they cleared the broken fence separating the tall grass from the road, savoring the rush of being airborne, if just for a moment. It might take a carriage twenty minutes from Jane's house to the estate, but the sturdy gelding always completed the trip in a mere seven. With the sun peeking in-and-out of dark clouds all day, she could use the extra time. The weather would soon take a turn for the worse, but thankfully, home was near.

Part of her still expected to see Jane at the dinner table, or hear her soft knock on the bedroom door late at night. She missed their evening visits, chatting about life and girlish nonsense. But Jane's wedding had come and gone quicker than a Colorado dust storm. An intimate ceremony at the church, followed by an elegant reception in the estate's main garden was nothing short of what someone would expect from the Westgates. And Jane had looked beautiful, with her creamy complexion matching the fabric of her Parisian gown and her rosy cheeks radiating bliss. Even Matthew had grown on Ellie, especially when she'd watched the way he doted on his new wife.

When they reached the meadow halfway between the estate grounds and Gabriel's street, she kept herself from looking at the farthest set of trees. She'd done so well today. For once, she hadn't thought about him at all. After the chilly way he'd acted toward her in the sweetshop, she didn't want to. Avoiding the heart of town was the best way to be sure she wouldn't run into him again. But his face still lingered around the edges of her mind.

By the time she returned to the stables, Tim had gone off somewhere, so she unsaddled Lincoln herself before tucking him in his stall with a pile of fresh hay. Hanlon and the dogs greeted her as she entered the house. She gave both animals a nice belly-rub, and then headed toward the staircase for a long-awaited bath.

"Miss Baker."

The voice stopped her cold in her tracks. She spun around.

"I was afraid you might catch the storm," Mr. Cain said, emerging from the hall on her left.

She held her breath and glanced around for Hanlon, but the butler had gone. For once, she was grateful she looked an absolute mess. "The skies have spared me today." She stretched her lips into a close-mouthed grin. "Are you here visiting Mr. Westgate?"

"Yes. We're discussing boring business matters, I'm afraid." He let out a single, stoic chuckle. "I decided to greet you at my own discretion."

"That's very kind of you, sir. But you didn't have to abandon your conversation for me." She inwardly kicked herself for entering through the front doors.

"Think nothing of it. Henry had to leave the room for a moment anyhow." His toothy grin made her think of a crocodile she'd seen in a book once.

"I see." She swallowed hard, trying to think up an excuse. "I apologize for sounding impolite, Mr. Cain, but I've had a very tiring day. Is there something you wish to speak to me about?"

"To ask you, actually."

"Of course."

"I won't keep you long, Miss Baker. I'd simply like to request permission to call on you from time-to-time."

"Why?" she blurted without thinking.

"Well, I—" He gave an awkward cough. "I'd simply like the opportunity to become better acquainted. I've spoken with Henry, and he seemed to encourage the idea of your socializing more."

"*No,*" she wanted to cry out. Those insinuating words, "better acquainted," conjured up old fears and uncertainties. If only she could somehow deny him without embarrassing Mr. Westgate. Maybe she could make herself extremely unappealing. Yes, so unappealing that Mr. Cain would want nothing to do with her after a couple visits. It stood as a simple, yet effective plan—the only one she could think of.

"Oh. Then . . . you have my permission, sir," she said, screaming on the inside.

The man raised his thick, dark brows with satisfaction. "Marvelous. I'll take my leave now. Good evening, Miss Baker. I hope to see you soon." He bowed and disappeared down the hall, leaving behind a chilly wake.

Ellie clutched her stomach, feeling as though she were suffocating. The tight knot within her begged for release. She had to get out, and fast. She looked to the grand staircase on her left, then to the large front doors on her right. With the voice of reason far from her mind, she raced to the doors and tore them open.

Freedom! She darted into the twilight and raced all the way to the stables, ignoring the cast of clouds obscuring the scattered stars. The horses grunted in alarm as she slipped through the back door and lit one of the lanterns. She crept past each stall, the light reflecting off the eyes of each hoofed resident. When she reached Lincoln's stall, he approached for a pat.

"Hello there, beautiful boy," she whispered. "Ready for another ride?"

He nickered as she scratched along his jaw, more than eager to stretch his legs again. Restless, just like her. She tacked him up and rode toward town.

God, she was out of her mind—but she felt so alive at the same time. Even the still warning in the air couldn't turn her back now. She gripped the reins hard, the idea of spending another minute in Mr. Cain's uncomfortable presence spurring her on. He'd never have her. No man would.

Stay calm, you're getting ahead of yourself.

The busy streets of town had all but shut down after dark. Only straggling shoppers hurrying to their carriages and merchants locking up their stores remained. She tethered Lincoln to the nearest hitching post and headed for the lit windows of a brick building. The sign overhead read *Grady's Alehouse*. Going inside would surely be the most reckless thing she'd ever done, but *reckless* was exactly how she felt right now. A drink sounded like the best thing in the world.

Tugging the sides of her bonnet down over her face, she trudged up the steps and into the smoke-filled bar. Several top-hatted patrons glared in confusion as she brushed past them and made her way to the counter with bold strides. Any other day they might have bothered her, but tonight, she was in no mood to be reckoned with. She placed her hands on the counter and cleared her throat for attention.

"Can I help you, miss?" the bartender asked.

"I'd like a drink, please."

"A drink?" He stared, complete surprise on his face.

She found herself becoming more irritated with each mumble and snicker surrounding her. "Yes, a drink."

"I'm afraid that isn't possible, miss. Women aren't allowed inside this establishment."

"Where else am I supposed to go?"

"How's about home?" the bearded man beside her said with a note of mockery. "No respectable woman ever shows her face in a bar."

Those standing nearby began to chuckle. Her mood veered sharply to anger. Insolent pigs, all of them. She turned to the man and gestured to the quarter-filled glass sitting before him. "What is your drink of choice this evening?"

He stalled for a moment, glancing at the others with a smug look. "Bourbon."

"Fine." She snatched up the glass, threw it back, and slammed it down on the counter before the man could generate a reaction. She squeezed her eyes shut. Her throat struggled to keep from rejecting the putrid drink as it burned its way down to her stomach.

Those watching fell silent.

"A respectable woman," she rasped through the strong, smoky taste in her mouth. "You must know there's no such thing, gentlemen."

She lifted her chin, trudged past the stunned customers and pushed through the door without looking back. Surely, she'd gone mad. A flash of lightning ripped across the black sky as she hurried back to Lincoln on trembling legs.

"What have I done?" she muttered, her blood pounding.

Sparse drops of rain tapped at her face as she yanked the reins free from their tethered knot. That's twice she'd made a public spectacle of herself in town. At this rate, she'd disgrace the family much faster than a husband discovering she wasn't a virgin ever would. Her head felt foggy and she longed for her bed. Never again would she do something so careless.

She crawled onto Lincoln's back and guided him down the road. They'd only just cleared the buildings when the skies opened, sending down buckets of heavy rain. Thunder cracked and lightning flashed. She squinted, barely able to see a few feet in front of her as she turned her mount in what she prayed was the right direction. But the farther they went, the less-familiar things became. Pretty soon, thick woods had them surrounded on both sides.

Crack! A bolt of lightning struck a nearby tree. Lincoln reared back on his hind legs as the entire thing went crashing onto the road in front of them. She steered the frightened animal into the woods, where the thick foliage provided a slight means of shelter from the pummeling rain.

Darkness closed in around her, the sporadic flashes of lightning her only source of light. She dismounted and led Lincoln beside a tall spruce, where she huddled close to his wet hair and prayed the storm wouldn't last the night. With the rain came the cold, and with the cold came sickness.

"Ellie!"

She thought she heard her name against a rumble of thunder.

"Ellie Baker! Ellie!" the distant voice called again, more clear and urgent than the last time.

She hadn't imagined it. Mr. Westgate must have discovered her missing and sent out a search party. Despite the heap of trouble in store for her, she'd much rather face it in warm clothes than be stuck in the storm any longer. Cupping her hands around her mouth, she called out, "I'm over here!"

"Ellie!" The voice had grown faint, as if it were traveling in the opposite direction.

She hoisted herself back into the saddle and urged Lincoln toward the sound. "Wait, don't leave! I'm over here!" Wet branches smacked against her face as she rode deeper into the dark woods. "I'm over here!"

"I hear you, don't stop shouting!" the voice hollered back, closer and clear as a bell.

She yanked Lincoln to a stop, her stomach cinching. God, why did it have to be *him*? Why did she have to call out so frantically like some damsel in distress? When she turned to flee, a low-hanging branch caught her in the neck. Pain ravaged her body as her ribs crashed against the hard roots of a tree, while her palms met muddy pine needles.

A strong hand slid beneath her arm while the other went under her knees. She looked up to see Gabriel staring at her. A wave of frustration hit her, and oddly, relief.

"Are you hurt?" he asked.

Embarrassment ruled over pain. "I'm fine. Now please put me down."

He jerked his head back, eyes wide. "Bourbon on the breath. Interesting."

Impressive. "You've no room to say a word about it."

"That's the thanks I get for saving you a second time?"

No, he deserved far more thanks, and she'd have been happy to give it to him if he didn't bother the heck out of her. Shunning her one minute, then to her rescue the next.

"I didn't need saving." She ignored the ache in her ribs as she squirmed to free herself.

"Are you sure?" He peered out into the downpour. "Because I don't think I imagined you calling out so desperately."

"I didn't know it was *you* until now."

"And you're disappointed."

Somehow, the opposite. But she nodded, turning her face away.

He set her down and raked both hands through his wet hair. "I suppose that means you're still angry with me."

"How did you even know I was here?" she said over a crack of thunder.

"I was with the pharmacist when I saw you riding by in a frenzy. Only an idiot would have let you go off like that. What in God's name were you doing alone in town at night?"

"Nothing." She looked away and climbed back into the saddle. "I appreciate your concern, but as I said before, I don't need saving."

He snatched the reins before she had the chance to pull them up. She groaned in protest, watching him hop back on his horse with them secured in his fist.

"The temperature is dropping, and whether you like it or not, I'm not leaving you to catch your death. I know a place where we can wait out the storm."

When he veered his mount left, she'd no choice but to oblige. The heavy rain didn't let up a bit as they rode deeper into the woods. Eventually, they reached a clearing with a small, dark structure sitting in the middle. She stirred uneasily at the sight of the abandoned shack, with broken windows and a deteriorating stone chimney. Something out of an old ghost story.

They tied the horses under the attached lean-to before approaching the shack's entrance. Gabriel jiggled the rusty knob, throwing his shoulder against the door with no success.

"Stand back," he said.

She did as he ordered. After a quick count to three, he struck a blow to the wood with his riding boot. The door flew inward as the latch ripped loose. She folded her arms across her chilled body and watched him step inside, awaiting his signal for her to join. When he reappeared in the frame, she breathed a little easier.

"It's safe."

She lifted her skirts and followed him into the dark, musty space.

"Feel around for any wood to make a fire," he said from somewhere to her left. "The longer we're without warmth, the worse off we'll be."

Extending her arms into the pitch black, she began feeling along the base of the wall. Spider webs kissed her fingertips. She gritted her teeth, reminding herself not to squeal if she came across a dead mouse or two.

"Anything?" he asked.

"Not y—yet." Something hard grazed the side of her foot. Reaching down, she touched what felt like a small stack of logs covered in cobwebs. "Wait . . . I think I feel something!"

He shuffled his way to the pile. "Well done. I found some kindling materials too. Hopefully, this should be enough."

She listened to him load the wood into the fireplace. After several minutes of twig snapping, shuffling feet and paper tearing, the spark of a match ignited the darkness. He lowered the small flame to the tinder, blowing lightly until the blaze had grown strong enough to burn on its own. A dim fire flickered inside the hearth, illuminating the shack's interior inch-by-inch as it grew steadily.

He squatted beside the flames, his classically handsome profile highlighted in a golden-orange glow. Ellie curled her toes inside her wet shoes. Maybe she didn't feel things the way Jane did, but she knew a striking man when she saw one.

He stood and began removing his coat. "Take off as much wet clothing as you can. It isn't good for us to stay in so many layers."

As if alone in his own bedroom, he went on to remove his waistcoat and unbutton his shirt. She stood motionless, blank, and unable to look away as he continued to undress in front of the fire. This wasn't the first time a man had disrobed in front of her, yet for some reason, she found her eyes latching onto Gabriel's flesh like a magnet.

He turned to her and she jumped. "Ellie, did you hear what I said? You don't want hypothermia settling in."

"Yes, sorry," she answered, forgetting all animosity toward him. In fact, all of her thoughts and feelings had turned to mush. Slowly, she unbuttoned and pulled off her shoes. She reached for the back of her dress with trembling hands, struggling against the confinement of her tight sleeves. The seams at her shoulders allowed for little movement. Where was Mary when she needed her? "I . . . can't," she stammered.

His mouth quirked with humor. "Such complicated things you women wear. Here, let me help you."

She pulled her sodden hair over her shoulder as he walked up behind her. One-by-one, he unfastened the fabric buttons of her bodice. A strange sensation spread across her body at his nearness. His warm breath brushing against the back of her neck made her senses spin.

When he finished, he began sliding the garment forward, over her shoulders and down her arms until she brought her hands to her chest to stop it from coming off. Something felt different. Suddenly, she found herself extremely conscious of her own body.

"What are you doing?" he asked.

"I'm feeling a bit . . . modest," she said, pretending not to be affected by any of this.

"Modest? The same girl who ran outside in her nightgown?"

She shrugged. "It's silly, I know."

"You're aware that I've seen the human anatomy many times, aren't you?"

She nodded.

He stepped away from her back and walked around to face her. "Then I trust you're able to set aside modesty for good health."

She nodded again, swallowing the extra moisture inside her mouth while her eyes found the floor. Was she was losing her mind? Undressing shouldn't be this complex.

"I promise I won't look. How's that?" He turned his back to her and moved away.

"That helps, thank you." She slid the bodice off and unhooked her corset, while he began hanging their clothing beside the fully ablaze fire.

She unfastened her sopping skirts, letting them drop to the floor before removing her petticoat and stockings. In the end, nothing but her bloomers and thin camisole covered her. Squeezing the water from her hair, she looked up to find Gabriel shirtless. Her mouth dropped open.

The combination of flickering light and shadows stretching across the contours of his back made him look so powerful. Even in the dim light, his defined muscle showed. She could barely breathe as she watched him move about.

"That should do it," he said, once all the clothing was either suspended or laid flat by the hearth. He sat down in front of the flames, his back to her still. "Ellie?"

"Y—yes?"

"What are you doing? Come over here where it's warm."

She crept to him on tiptoes as he prodded the flames carefully with a long scrap of wood. When her bottom touched the warm floor, she couldn't deny how nice the fire felt.

Keeping her eyes on the dancing flames, she finally started to relax. She let out a long, heavy sigh. Heat engulfed her face and body in a way that could lull her to sleep. Neither of them spoke—the crackling flames and rain pummeling the roof were the only sounds for several moments.

Gabriel cleared his throat. "Despite the circumstances, it's nice seeing you again."

"Is it? That's surprising. I could have sworn you preferred me invisible these days." She winced at her own jab, yet remembered why she was still angry with him.

"You're the one who's been avoiding me."

"Oh, really?"

"Yes, really," he said with quiet emphasis. "I've been to town every day these last weeks for the sole purpose of running into you again."

"Hopefully to apologize." She hugged her knees, somewhat relieved he hadn't chosen to rid himself of her just yet.

"Ellie." He let out a long, frustrated sigh. "I'm sorry for upsetting you that day, but you must understand that I was only trying to—"

"I don't understand why we can't admit to being old friends. It shouldn't matter how long we've known each other, or that we're the opposite sex. You've come so far since Creekwood ... Why must you play two different parts now? What are you so afraid of?"

"I'm not afraid of anything. My family name came with a reputation to uphold. We must all do what society requires of us, plain and simple."

She groaned. "That's the worst response I've ever heard."

"You don't know a thing about this life, Ellie."

"And you don't know a thing about living!" She snatched the stick from his hand and began poking violently at the hearth. "Forgive me for struggling with the fact that I must lie to complete strangers about our friendship. You on the other hand seem to be having little difficulty. Perhaps I'm being too sensitive."

One of the logs slipped from its position atop the rest. It fell with a *thud*, sending a jumble of sparks and embers flying every which way.

"Now look what you've done. Give me that." He reached over and seized her wrist.

"No!" She fought back as he tried to pry the stick from her hand.

Their eyes met. Something intense flickered in his gaze. His eyes traveled down to her lips, then to her shoulders, then her breasts. She shivered at feel of his bare hand on her naked wrist. Quickly, she surrendered the stick.

"Ugh, you're impossible," she grumbled, burying her face in her knees.

"As are you, my dear. But even so, I'm sorry for leading you to think so ill of me."

She lifted her head from the cradle of her arms and focused on the smoldering logs. The way he'd looked at her moments ago—that desirous way—she couldn't tear the image from her mind. Why hadn't it angered her? Why hadn't she wanted to slap him?

"Our friendship means just as much to me as it does you," he continued. "Maybe even more. But that doesn't change the fact that this is your home now. We're no longer out West in the land of gunslingers and saloons. These people don't think the way you do. They'll eat you alive before you have time to react." His voice held a sharp edge. "They notice every word, every move, every breath . . . and I'll be damned if you're judged and branded just for associating with me in public."

An invisible rope wrapped tight around her chest. "I'm already judged and branded."

"You deserve another chance, for God's sake. Now allow yourself to have one."

He was right. Suppose she were still Jasper's property? Suppose she still walked the muddy streets of Creekwood, while dodging looks of hatred from the women whose husbands she took to bed? Not many people got a fresh start in life the way she had. She'd been lucky, no, blessed. If she wanted to move on, she'd have to try her hardest to forget those ten agonizing days.

"All right, I understand," she forced herself to say. "You deserve a second chance as much as I do, so I'll do you the honor of playing this little game for as long as you need."

"Don't think I enjoy one minute of it." He chuckled. "Part of me would love to see everyone's reaction upon discovering I was best friends with an attractive, eligible woman."

"Attractive?" She was glad the semidarkness hid the flush in her cheeks.

Several men, including Jasper himself, had called her attractive. Insatiable lust and greed had driven their every filthy touch. But the words coming from Gabriel's lips gave her a different feeling entirely. A tingling started at her fingertips, spreading warmth throughout her insides. For the first time, she accepted it as a genuine compliment.

"I was grateful when you gave me a reason not to look at you," he said matter-of-factly.

Ellie drew her knees closer to her body. "I thought you said you were accustomed to the human anatomy."

"I am, but that doesn't mean I'm blind to beauty. I have a pulse just like everyone else."

"If that's a polite way of saying you have the natural urges of the male sex, then you . . . you disgust me."

"I never said that."

"But you must be thinking it." She heard the bitterness in her own voice, yet chose to ignore it. "Why else would you have taken care of those urges several times at The Inn, just like every other disgraceful man? No doubt you saw plenty of anatomy there—"

"If you *must* know, I went there to feel the slightest hint of anything that would remind me I still had a pulse." The force of his seething reply caught her off guard. "I'm not proud of who I was or what I've done, and I'd appreciate it if you'd cease the accusations. You don't see me giving you grief for your time spent at that place. Time I doubt you're proud of."

"How dare you!" She shot to her feet and stormed to one of the windows. Ribbons of rain cascading down the glass splashed angrily inside the broken left pane. She bit the tip of her thumb until it throbbed like her pride.

"I'm sorry," he said, after a long silence. "I shouldn't have said that. It was wrong of me to take my shame out on you." She heard him rise, but she kept her back to him. When he spoke again, his voice was tender, almost a murmur. "The moment before you left my house, you were about to tell me something important. I've thought about it ever since."

"I don't know what you're talking about," she lied.

He began walking toward her. "Yes, you do. Why were you at that brothel, Ellie?"

"It doesn't matter anymore . . ."

"It matters to me." He stopped just behind her. "Very much."

Crack! A blast of thunder crashed nearby as lightning struck. The shed shook so hard that she leapt backward, falling straight into his arms. She cried out as caught her. He pulled her into his bare chest, cradling her back with one arm, while holding her head with the other.

When Ellie opened her eyes, she found herself pressed against his solid, warm body. Something inside her longed to stay there, to feel his chest rise and fall against her cheek forever.

Wait a minute, what was she thinking? She twisted in his arms and tried to get free, but his hand remained locked on the small of her back. Slowly, he lifted her chin to meet his face. Passion burned in his eyes.

"Please—" was all she managed to whisper before his lips touched hers.

He kissed her for a soft moment, gently covering her mouth. Her pulse skittered and a delightful shiver ran through her body. Then he pulled away, all too quickly.

"Forgive me," he muttered, his sweet breath warming her face.

She swallowed, every inch of her craving more. "No . . . don't stop."

He captured her mouth again, a little rougher this time. She settled into him, enjoying the feeling of his arms around her as he held her close. Her hands explored the smooth skin of his back, the firm muscle beneath her fingertips. When she opened her mouth wider, he slipped his tongue inside, deepening the kiss. She whimpered. Never before had the taste of coffee and mint been so delicious. His movements were determined, exploratory, and she matched each thrust of his tongue with hers until they danced in perfect unison.

A wonderfully new sensation rushed through her body, but her mind was too numb to make sense of it. Instinct drove her every move. When she pressed her hips against him, he let out a deep groan. The hardness of his arousal dug into her as his large hands slid down her waist and gripped her bottom. As shiver of delight ran through her, and she claimed his bottom lip like some sort of depraved animal.

He pulled his mouth from hers, breathing heavily, searching her face. The hearth's light reflected in his blue gaze, creating the perfect combination of fire and ice as they glistened with desire. At this moment, she'd let him do anything to her. She pressed her lips to his, wordlessly giving him permission to continue.

An abrupt voice came from outside the cabin. Her heart lurched, and they tore away from each other just as two policemen burst through the door. Holding up vivid lanterns, they squinted.

"What in God's name?" one of them barked, observing their sparse amount of clothing. His brow furrowed as his eyes flew from Gabriel to her. "Has he hurt you, miss?"

"Not at all, sir," she said, crossing her arms over the thin fabric covering her breasts. God, her head was spinning madly. "We were caught in the storm and needed shelter."

Gabriel angled his body away to shield his erection. "She's right. I assure you our indecency is for no reason other than avoiding hypothermia."

The second officer raised a lantern to Gabriel's face. "Doctor Peterson?"

"Good evening, officers."

"I don't doubt your precautions, Doctor—" The first officer paced to the fireplace and examined their drying garments. "And I'm sure your uncle will be pleased to know that Miss Baker was in good hands." He looked between them. "But I'm curious . . . How did this happen?"

Ellie glanced at her companion, who seemed at a sudden loss for words. She felt the weight of the interrogation smothering her like a thick layer of tar. "It's my fault," she blurted. "I was heading home when the storm began and I got lost. If Doctor Peterson hadn't found me freezing in the woods, I don't know what might have happened." She may as well exaggerate a little.

"Miss Baker." The officer shook his head. "I realize you're new here, and I'm not sure what made you decide that going out alone and after dark was a good idea, but might I suggest you refrain from ever doing so again."

"Yes, sir." She dipped her head, relieved the man didn't pry. If she had to tell them about the bar incident, she might as well bypass home and head straight for the asylum.

"And since Mr. Westgate so generously continues to fund our department—" The officer continued. "We'll keep the details regarding this evening off-record for his sake." He snatched Gabriel's trousers off the floor and handed them to him. "Lucky for all of us, the worst of the storm seems to be over. We can move on as soon as you dress yourselves."

Thank God. Both their lives could have been ruined, and all because of one foolish mistake. The relief she felt almost made her forget her trembling limbs and her tingling lips.

Several minutes later she sat atop Lincoln's back, wearing her slightly damp clothing. The pounding rain had let up into a mere drizzle, but not before turning the dirt roads into sloshing mud. She thought it best to ride side-saddle in the policemen's presence, even if it meant struggling to keep her balance with every bump and dip along the way. The air had grown calm, yet her mind remained restless at the feeling of Gabriel's presence just behind her.

She couldn't believe he'd kissed her. And somehow, she'd kissed him back—*Willingly!*

Her own driving need shocked her. There must be a plausible explanation as to why she'd done such a thing. Maybe the lightning had scared her senseless, but that still didn't explain why everything about being in his arms felt so right. And those lips, both soft and strong as he'd kissed her hard. Just thinking about it left her weak and confused.

When Gabriel rode up beside her, she hesitated before glancing at his profile. Only now did she notice the waves in his tousled hair from the increased humidity. The shadow of stubble hugging his jaw line made him all the more handsome, and she couldn't help but wonder if he was aware of his unmatched looks. Then she studied the flat, unreadable expression on his face. Perhaps he already regretted kissing her. What had made him decide to do it in the first place?

They reached the road leading to the estate, which gave her something else to think on. Within minutes she'd be thrust back into reality and punishment. The officers assumed Mr. Westgate was on good terms with his nephew. Best to keep it that way.

She turned to Gabriel, mouthing the words *"go home"* as they made the final turn up the drive. He shook his head, mouthed *"no,"* and led his mount ahead of her.

Damn him. She frowned and swallowed past the dryness in her throat.

If Mr. Westgate were already upset with her for running away, surely seeing Gabriel bring her home would blow his lid clean off.

Chapter Eleven

Ellie pulled up the reins and dismounted near the mansion's entrance. Her feet had barely touched gravel when Hanlon appeared in the doorway, seizing the dogs by their collars as they yelped and lunged to greet her. Mr. Westgate brushed past him, charging down the steps like an enraged bull. God only knew the fighting words about to spew from her guardian's mouth.

The first officer tipped his hat. "Good morning, sir."

"Gentlemen," Mr. Westgate said, sharp and quick. The gravel crunched beneath his shoes as he approached. "Thank you for bringing her home safely."

"By the time we got to her, she was already in good hands. You're nephew here saved her from the storm. Found them shelter for the night, too."

Gabriel dismounted. He looked Mr. Westgate dead in the eye. "It's good to see you, Uncle."

Mr. Westgate said nothing, only blinked. He pulled several bills from his coat pocket and offered them to the second officer. "I thank you for your services, gentlemen. We won't take up any more of your time. I can handle matters from here."

The policeman held up a hand in refusal. "That won't be necessary, sir. Our job is to serve the citizens of this community, and that's precisely what we've done. We're happy to see Miss Baker home."

"Thank you, officers," Gabriel said.

How could he be so calm? Ellie tried to open her mouth to show her thanks, yet her tongue felt paralyzed. In fact, almost everything did. Now that Mr. Westgate had officially seen them together, things would become much more complicated. As the two lawmen rode off, she could only breathe in quick, shallow gasps.

"Now—" Mr. Westgate pushed back the sides of his morning coat as he clamped his hands on his hips. His gaze darted from Gabriel to her, then back again. "*What* is the meaning of this nonsense? What are you doing here?"

"I was in town when I saw a woman in distress, and I followed her to make sure she wasn't in danger," Gabriel answered. "You saw the storm last night. Our only option was to find shelter and wait it out. Since when is it such a crime to care about others?"

Mr. Westgate's jaw flexed. "I would say never, were it anyone other than you. But you made it very clear how much you cared about others four years ago. All you've ever seemed to give a damn about is yourself."

"I've always cared, Uncle," Gabriel said, barely masking the hurt in his voice.

"You have a terrible way of showing it."

"No worse than your way of *not* showing forgiveness."

Gabriel caught and held her gaze for a moment, just long enough for her to see every ounce of regret in his eyes. There must be something she could do to help. She forced herself to speak on his behalf—to put him in a good light, even if it meant darkness for her.

"I made the regrettable decision of going for a ride last night," she declared, feeling her voice crack at the end. "It was beyond foolish. I don't know what might have happened, had this man not come along and found me lost in the woods. He's the reason I'm safe and in one piece."

Mr. Westgate turned to her with a brutally disappointed stare. "Go inside, Ellie. We'll discuss your frivolous actions later."

She wanted to speak again, yet no words would come. This wasn't her business. Gabriel and Mr. Westgate would have to sort things out on their own. A soft orange glow filtered through the indigo sky, signaling the start of a new day. Exhaustion hit her so hard that her nerves throbbed.

She inclined her head and turned to leave, keeping her eyes away from the man who'd kissed her passionately moments ago. If she looked at him, she'd be reminded of every intimate touch they'd shared while she stood in his bare arms. She didn't know how to feel about what had happened between them.

After a warm bath, she hid in her room, the heavy bedclothes pulled all the way up to her chin, with the thick curtains drawn tightly. Her eyelids felt like hundred-pound weights, but every time she let them close, unsettling images flashed through the darkness. The appalled patrons at the bar. The storm. The kiss—*Oh, the kiss.*

She flipped to her stomach and clutched the cool underside of her pillow. All this time, she'd been so certain she'd never feel an ounce of desire towards a man. Yet now she was nearly writhing at the thought of being touched again—by her good friend, nonetheless! She'd experienced plenty of kisses and caresses at that terrible brothel. Why should Gabriel's hands have felt any different?

Don't be ridiculous. His firm, gentle touch—so powerful, so intoxicating, so male—and that sense of familiarity, couldn't have been *more* different. Perhaps that's why she'd kissed him back. Never before had she wanted something so badly. But such a mistake couldn't happen again.

His association with the flawless Miss Tuttle was reason enough. Things had been fine the way they were. They'd only just begun enjoying their rekindled friendship, so why did he have to complicate things by kissing her? Why did every man want more? Clenching her teeth, she repressed the moan at the base of her throat.

The sooner they could agree on their mistake and return to normal, the better. But who knew when she might see him again? Her anxious nerves would have to wait. She shut her eyes, recalling once more the smoldering passion that had swept her body.

His lips were the last thought to cross her mind before she surrendered to sleep.

* * *

Gabriel sat in the Tuttle's parlor, gripping the handle of his tea cup so hard he thought he might break it. His bulky frame overwhelmed the small pink armchair in which he sat, making him feel like a giant in a doll's house. Bouncing his left leg up and down rapidly seemed the only way to curb his sense of restlessness.

Everyone else appeared perfectly content on that cloudy morning. Mr. Tuttle rested in the armchair across from him, while Mrs. Tuttle sat perched on the settee with their fat white cat purring in her lap. Emily played the pianoforte as her obedient sister turned the pages of her sheet music. As much as Gabriel enjoyed listening to Mozart's Andante Grazioso, he could barely pay attention today.

He sipped his tea, wondering what in God's name he was doing. A complete lack of sleep only seemed to increase the pangs of guilt eating away at him as he struggled to focus on the present. Yet Ellie had consumed his thoughts ever since he'd ridden away from her hours ago.

He couldn't believe he'd kissed her. It wasn't like him to act on impulse, but in that moment, the choice had seemed obvious. Her incomparable lips, the curve of her back, the way her full breasts pressed against his chest as he tasted her; he'd grow hard in his chair if he weren't careful. But as much as he craved to have Ellie in his bed, what drew him was far beyond her physique. She calmed and excited him at the same time. She made him feel *alive* inside. They shared a connection unlike any other he'd experienced.

An unwelcome thought entered his mind, twisting the pit of his stomach with spasms of jealousy. How many men had helped themselves to her? Those bastards at The Inn didn't deserve to breathe the same air, let alone touch her soft, angelic skin. But she must have grown numb to it over time. Hell, she'd probably returned his kiss out of sheer pity.

It didn't matter, because it shouldn't have happened. It had been nice and fun, but it was finished. He needed to focus on restoring his practice, on building a respectable life and fixing his strained relationship with his uncle. Nowhere among those things did the pursuit of romance fit in, especially with a woman in Henry's care.

A light applause fluttered across the room, snapping him out of his reverie. Emily had finished her piece.

"Bravo! You've mastered Monsieur Mozart, my dear," her mother praised.

Emily slid from the bench and curtsied. "Thank you, everyone. I might be skilled at Mozart, but my expertise could never compare to Sarah's on a Schumann sonata."

Mrs. Tuttle waved her hand in a gesture of dismissal. "Such humble children I've raised. Never doubt your exquisite talents, Emily, especially in the company of gentlemen."

"Gentlemen?" Emily's perfect eyebrows raised in amusement. "It's only Father and Gabriel."

Gabriel felt a ripple of mirth. He'd always enjoyed her wicked sense of humor, despite how much it offended her parents. When she turned to him, he could tell she thirsted for a compliment. Thankfully, she hadn't noticed how aloof he'd been during her playing.

Say something, dammit. "Your mother is right," he said. "The notes couldn't have sounded better had they come from Mozart himself."

"Hear, hear," Mr. Tuttle added.

"Thank you, *gentlemen.*" Emily smiled and sat beside her mother. The overblown compliment must have sufficed.

Emily took her tea from the servant's tray. She truly was a sophisticated treasure. If only he felt something more for her. Anyone privileged enough to receive her hand should be ecstatic, and four years ago, he wouldn't have dared question whether she was right for him. Had someone told him where he'd be today, he might have laughed.

A middle class liar, that pretty much summed it up. He'd taken advantage of the Tuttle's hospitality after his uncle's rejection. He hadn't needed to go into detail about "the terrible case of memory loss" that had kept him away for so long. No one questioned him—perhaps one advantage of being a physician. But the contrived story was far from the pitiful truth.

Sarah claimed the bench and began playing Bach's Minuet in G. The servant offered more tea and Gabriel declined politely, attempting to mask a yawn all the while. It had been almost an entire day since he'd last slept. His eyes burned and he longed for his bed. But this visit had been arranged since yesterday, and he couldn't be rude.

"You look exhausted, dear boy," Mr. Tuttle said. "Have you not been resting well?"

He must have looked worse than he felt. "Not lately, unfortunately."

Mrs. Tuttle placed a hand on her large bosom. "That will never do. A lack of sleep ages the face, you know. As fond as I am of doctors, I'll never understand the appeal of staying up all night making house calls and studying medical journals."

House calls. Thank God for her assumption. "I assure you we enjoy it, ma'am."

"Let the man do what he wants, Penelope," her husband grumbled. "If he'd wanted to go into the railroad business, he'd have followed in his father's footsteps long ago."

Gabriel brought his cup to his lips, ignoring the subtle jab. People had been judging him since the day he first told his father about his chosen career path. He debated mentioning the subject of Harvard, but decided against it. A discussion like that required a lot more sleep and preparation.

A handful of letters from his alma mater had been among the pile of mail festering at his door. The medical school had written to him, requesting his presence as a guest lecturer on the subjects of anatomy and physiology, clinical surgery, obstetrics and a slew of others. The first letter was dated three months ago, and the last he'd received only yesterday. He'd best keep the subject—and his excitement—to himself until he received further details.

"How are you finding the new competition since your return?" Mr. Tuttle asked, stuffing his pipe with fresh tobacco. "Dr. Chaucer has been here for three years now, and I'd imagine he's well established. Dr. Brown is much older than you, with more experience under his belt."

"Experience isn't solely based upon age, Mr. Tuttle." Gabriel smirked, impressed by the man's unyielding efforts to sway him out of practice. "The world of medicine is always changing, and breakthroughs are discovered on a daily basis. Seasoned doctors are often too set in their ways to give these new methods a try."

Mr. Tuttle lit the tobacco and puffed on his pipe. "Nonsense. You can always teach an old dog new tricks."

"Gabriel, when can we expect your family for dinner?" Emily asked innocently.

The question made his chest constrict. He gulped down his chilly tea, and to his shame, found himself wishing it were spiked with whiskey.

"Emily," her mother chided. "That's Gabriel's personal business. I'm sure he'll tell us when things are sorted out."

Emily gave a small shrug. "His cousin appeared perfectly amiable when we crossed paths three weeks ago."

"Ah, yes, Jane was a dear as always. And Miss Baker . . . such a *lovely* young lady she is." Mrs. Tuttle's eyes darted to the side.

Gabriel almost winced at the memory. "About that day in the sweetshop, Mrs. Tuttle—" He cleared his throat. "I sincerely apologize for Miss Baker's behavior. She was in no condition to be out and about while recovering from a high fever. I can assure you she's a very pleasant woman."

Stop lying, dammit. The fibs seemed to slip from his mouth like sand through a sieve.

Yet this time, the words weren't meant to safeguard himself. Ellie deserved a new life free of scorn, and he'd do whatever was necessary to protect her dangling reputation. God, she appeared so strong at times, and at others like a frightened fawn. His gut knew something wasn't right. No matter how much she tried to avoid his questions, he'd find out her story.

A smile stretched across Mrs. Tuttle's plump, cherry-colored face. "Really? Oh, the poor girl. I knew something must have been amiss that day."

"How refreshing," Emily said, with a little less bounce in her voice than before. "I do hope she's feeling better."

"You know, Emily," Mrs. Tuttle placed a hand on her daughter's arm, "I think you should spend more time with those young ladies. A girl your age can never have too many friends." Her eyes flickered and grew large. "In fact, you should seek their help with the wedding arrangements. I'm sure they'd be delighted, wouldn't they, Gabriel?"

Wedding?

He tried to stop the tea from reaching the back of his throat, but it was too late. His lungs spasmed. He pounded a fist to his chest and coughed violently.

"Merciful heavens!" Emily rushed to him. She slapped his back several times, which seemed to do more damage than good.

Sarah stopped playing and gasped.

"Are you all right, my dear?" Mrs. Tuttle asked.

Mr. Tuttle leaned back in his chair and chuckled. "Inhaling one's drink. I despise it when that happens to me."

Gabriel sucked in several breaths between coughs. Finally, the air returned to his aching lungs. He cleared his throat, wiped the tears from his face and looked up.

"I'm fine," he rasped. "Thank you."

The Tuttles had never mentioned marriage, and after losing his fortune, part of him had hoped they wouldn't. But he should have seen this coming. He'd enjoyed their hospitality so much that he'd forgotten their loyalty to his family. They expected him to propose. Marriage plans had already gone into effect—those that could possibly include Jane and Ellie.

His throat might be clear, but he was still choking.

Chapter Twelve

Sunday morning could not have felt hotter. Ellie swore her legs would melt inside her skirts as she stood in the churchyard surrounded by the Westgates, Tillers and the Maxwells. She'd met Barnaby and Clara Maxwell at Jane's wedding, and had liked them ever since. Despite owning the largest funeral businesses in the Northeast, they smiled more than anyone else she knew. Their twelve-year-old twin girls stood beside them, exchanging secrets, while their older sister Rosalie seemed eager to take part in the group conversation.

Ellie fluttered her fan in front of her face until her wrist ached. She savored every bit of the warm breeze against her cheeks. Darn New England's humid air.

But even with the heat, she could breathe a little easier now that Mr. Cain had left the group. He'd sat several pews behind her during church, and aside from exchanging a few polite formalities with her, he'd mostly spoken to Mr. Westgate after the service. She didn't want to give Mr. Cain the wrong impression by chatting with him in public, not after he'd called on her three times during the past two weeks. But she'd fully deserved those two weeks of confinement, even when they included his visits. Today marked the last day of her punishment.

Mr. Maxwell cracked a light joke, and she laughed lightly while stealing a peek at young John Westgate. She'd seen him glance over his shoulder more than once during conversation, to where three boys and two girls his age mingled in the graveyard. One of the girls, a blonde, would look back at him in a way that made his cheeks turn red. Ellie remembered giving that expression of fondness all too well. She'd first done it years ago at the tender age of nine.

It had been early summer, just as it was now. She'd been standing on the bank of a stream, learning how to skip stones from her fourteen-year-old counterpart. Her best friend had physically matured during the past year, but her innocent young mind couldn't seem to understand the changes happening to him.

His lanky, boyish physique had turned into something stronger, and his once-familiar voice fluctuated between his usual tone and a much deeper one. She tried not to giggle when it cracked occasionally, afraid she might embarrass him.

But she'd studied the way his muscles strained as he heaved the stones across the water one-by-one, sending them skipping several times before they finally sank to the bottom. A feeling very different than friendship had stirred deep inside her that day. Looking back, she couldn't help but wonder whether Gabriel had noticed the way she'd admired him during their last summer together.

She shifted from foot-to-foot. Why did her thoughts always end up finding him? Because his wonderful mouth had awoken something inside her body that she could never forget? *No, because he's your friend, and you care about him,* she told herself. Oh, how she wanted to hate him for kissing her. So typically male to assume control without considering how she might feel about the situation—no matter how magnificent it was.

"What did you make of Pastor Wilke's sermon, Elaine?" Mrs. Maxwell asked.

Ellie batted her fan more slowly, thankful for the distraction. But what was the sermon about? Oh yes, forgiveness. She should have remembered that, seeing as she'd watched Mr. Westgate the entire time, praying the pastor's words would reach him in some way.

"I found it to be very insightful." She'd try her own, subtle approach at getting through to him. "Forgiveness is something mankind has struggled with throughout the ages. I only hope that we'll be able to look past our own grudges someday and live in harmony. Life is too short after all."

"Hear, hear!" Mr. Tiller said. He turned to John. "What about you, son? You've been quiet as a church mouse all morning."

Matthew planted a hand on John's shoulder. "If I was sixteen and had to listen to boring adult conversation, I'd be, too."

Ellie chewed her lip as the group chortled. Matthew had set the stage for the perfect opportunity to speak on John's behalf. If she didn't try to help him now, she'd regret it the rest of the day. "I agree with Matthew. Since John has been such a good sport, may he visit with his friends over there?" She gestured toward the graveyard.

Everyone fell silent, turning their heads in the direction she pointed to. John stiffened, his chocolate eyes darting back and forth with slight panic.

"I don't see why not," Mr. Tiller said. "Sunday is a day of leisure after all."

Mr. Maxwell chuckled. "Why don't we let the boy's father decide, Gregory."

"Please, Father," Jane beseeched. She turned to smile at her mortified brother. "John deserves to have a little fun once in a while."

Mr. Westgate eyed his daughter with fond skepticism. Jane had mentioned her powers of persuasion before when it came to her father. When the corner of his mustache lifted with a small grin, Ellie didn't doubt Jane was right.

"Speak up, son," Mr. Westgate said. "Is that what you want? To visit with your—" He stared at the graveyard, watching the middle-class youths roughhousing in the distance. "Friends?"

Keeping his head low, John replied, "Yes, sir."

"All right then," his father said atop a sigh. "I'll allow it, but you must come home in Matthew and Jane's carriage when they bring Ellie back from lunch. You be sure to listen to their instructions on where to meet them."

"Thank you, sir." John struggled to control the elation on his face as he turned to Matthew.

"Three o' clock, on the dot. We'll meet you at the fountain in the town square." Matthew gave his back a double pat. "Now go on!"

John nodded eagerly. He flashed Ellie a smile of thanks before running off. An invisible ribbon of warmth wrapped around her heart. At least there was one thing she hadn't made a complete mess of.

Two hours later, after a lunch of chilled soup and baked cod, Matthew looked at his pocket watch and winced. "Well, that's unfortunate."

"What is?" Ellie asked, dabbing the corner of her lips with her napkin. She'd never had fish before moving to New England, but now, she could barely imagine a life without the light, flaky taste. She'd eat it for every meal if she could.

"It's five past three," he said with a chuckle. "I was so wrapped up in conversation that I failed to check the time. Poor John must be wondering where we are."

Jane rested a hand atop his arm. "Oh heavens, we're all guilty. But John has never been the most punctual boy, and I doubt he's changed his habits today."

"I'll walk to the town square right now and find him," Ellie offered.

"Would you mind?" Matthew asked, twisting one end of his sandy-colored mustache. "We'll settle the bill, fetch the carriage, and meet you east of the fountain."

Ellie rose from her seat and placed her napkin on the table. "Not to worry. I'll see you both shortly."

If only lunch hadn't passed so quickly. She could always count on relaxed, lighthearted conversation in Jane and Matthew's company. Not that she didn't respect the proper etiquette required in Mr. Westgate's presence, but she treasured her time spent with those her age like a breath of fresh air.

Fortunately, The Painted Shanty restaurant sat two short blocks from the town square. She found the large mermaid fountain within minutes, but the closer she came to it, the more she noticed John's absence. It was a quarter past the hour, and a twinge of fret twisted the pit of her stomach. Where was he? Fidgeting her fingers at her sides, she searched the crowded square for any sign of him.

She froze when she spotted him on a bench just outside the park's entrance. He sat with his upper body slouched forward and his head hanging low. Something wasn't right. She rushed to him, fret turning to fright. When he glanced up to greet her, her stomach lurched. His cheek was bruised, his jaw swollen, but worst of all, a large gash stretched clear across his forehead.

"My God, John. What happened to you?" she cried out, kneeling before him.

"Please don't cause a scene. That's my sister's job," he muttered, apparently not too injured to tease.

She pulled a handkerchief from her reticule and dabbed at his freshly bleeding forehead. Her head felt light and, not wanting to faint in public anytime soon, she kept her eyes off the terrible wound. Such a lovely time for a weak constitution.

"That isn't funny," she said. "And I'm not going to make a scene. Tell me what happened."

"I don't remember."

"Hogwash." She reached out and lifted his chin. "You tell me now."

He looked away, then down. "Promise you won't say anything to anyone?"

"I promise."

"Not a soul."

"Yes, John. I promise."

"There's this girl. Claire Banks." His face lit at her name.

"Was she the pretty blonde in the church yard?" Ellie folded the handkerchief and pressed it onto the wound. "Hold that there and keep pressure on it."

He obeyed. "Yes. I'm afraid I love her."

"Love? Are you even old enough to know what love is?"

"Of course I'm old enough."

She didn't dare question the emotion behind his voice. Given his current state, she decided it best to appease his infatuation. "You're right, I apologize," she said calmly. "But I still don't understand what led to all this."

"Well, Lucas Wade fancies her too. He said he's going to marry her someday, and that I should stay away from her unless I want trouble. He said she belongs to him."

She stood and plunked her hands on her hips. "That's absurd. Claire doesn't belong to anyone, because a woman isn't property. Don't you ever forget that, John."

"I know that, but Lucas doesn't." He shrugged. "I tried telling him to leave her alone, and when he saw her holding my hand, he picked a fight. I must have looked like such a coward running away after the first few punches. I wouldn't be surprised if she never speaks to me again."

The tears forming in his eyes tugged at her heartstrings. Just because she was afraid of love didn't mean John or anyone else should be. She sat beside him and put an arm around his back. "Come now. I'm sure Claire appreciates your standing up for her, and there's nothing wrong with avoiding a fight. If she has any sense, she'll speak to you."

He dragged the back of his sleeve across one eye. "What makes you so sure?"

"Because any young lady would be lucky to receive your attention." She gave him a small shake. "Just promise me you'll try solving your problems with words from now on."

He gave a small grin. "I will."

Jane and Matthew's carriage pulled up on the opposite end of the square. Ellie reached out and removed the handkerchief from John's forehead. Bloody, torn flesh stared her dead in the eye. The wound looked much deeper than she'd originally thought.

John winced, observing her face. "It's bad, isn't it? What am I going to do?"

"I think . . . I think you need medical attention," she stammered, fighting a wave of nausea.

"There's a pharmacy just down the street. They've got ointment and bandages."

When he lifted his bare fingers to touch the gash, she smacked his hand away. "No, John, that won't be enough. Besides, the pharmacy is closed on Sundays. You have to see a doctor." She knew only one doctor in town, and swallowed hard at the thought of seeing him again.

"But—"

"Come on." She pressed the handkerchief back on the wound and helped John up.

They walked toward the carriage, ignoring the handful of stares from those who caught sight of them. After two long weeks of obsessing over that kiss, the chance to speak with Gabriel had been handed to her on a silver platter. She'd spent hours planning what to say to him, yet still felt unprepared. Who knows how he'd react to her dropping in on a Sunday unannounced—and with John, no less? She brushed away her doubt and tried seeing the positive side. With Mr. Westgate nowhere near reconciling with his nephew, it was high time the cousins reunited.

Once the driver had helped them into the carriage, Jane and Matthew greeted them in horror.

Matthew's mouth fell open. "Good God in Heaven!"

"Oh, my brother!" Jane gasped. "What happened to you?"

"We were climbing trees. I was halfway to the top when I slipped and fell on a branch down below," John answered quickly.

Jane pressed a palm to her lips. "You fell? How could you have done something so dangerous! Suppose you had broken your neck!"

Ellie gripped the velvet seat, wishing she hadn't promised her silence to John. She hated lying. "I saw the tree, Jane. It wasn't terribly high, but the cut on his forehead looks too serious to heal on its own. I'm afraid he needs medical attention, and quickly." She took Jane's hand, trying her best to communicate with her eyes. "Can you think of any doctors nearby?"

"Well, yes . . ." Jane paused for a moment, dropping her gaze. She understood. "There's one I can think of."

"Davis, Chaucer or Brown?" Matthew asked.

She wriggled in her seat a little. "Someone new, actually. Would you mind telling Grey to turn onto Mason street, dear?" Matthew's brow furrowed. Ellie tensed as Jane leaned forward and added, "Please darling, I'll explain everything later."

Uncertainty crept further into his expression. He turned to John, noting the completely blood-soaked handkerchief on his forehead. "Very well, but you must tell me what's going on here." Leaning half his body out the window, he called out to the coachman. "Take the next left, Grey."

The carriage turned at the fork in the road.

"Where are we going?" John asked, switching the hand that clutched his forehead.

"To see the doctor." Ellie gave her best solacing grin, but her stomach fluttered and her mouth felt dry.

Five minutes later, they slowed to a stop beside the familiar stone wall covered in vines. She peered out at the iron gate. It was slightly open this time. When Jane touched her arm, she jumped.

"You take John inside," Jane said. "We'll follow shortly, once I've had a chat with Matthew."

Ellie took a deep breath. "All right. Come along, John."

Grey opened the door and helped her down. She shook out her skirts, watching John's every move as he stepped out of the carriage and surveyed the area. Folding his arms, he skirted along the wall until he reached the entrance.

"Wait a minute," he said. He pushed away the overgrown vines, revealing the cast iron address plate with the number 317. He turned to her and took a step back. "I know this place, but I don't understand. Nobody lives here."

All her nervousness slipped back to grip her. "Suppose I told you someone did? Someone who misses you very much. Now it's your turn to keep a secret for me."

"But . . ." A shadow of alarm touched his face. "But he's—"

"Very much alive."

She took his free hand and led him through the gate. Neither of them uttered a word as they went up the driveway, and she found herself clutching him even tighter once they'd reached the house at the end. With a fresh coat of white paint, it looked even prettier than before. She'd forgotten how much she loved it. But as they climbed the wooden steps leading to the veranda, she remembered who lived just inside those doors.

"This c-cant be true," John stammered, freeing his hand. "My schoolmates told me he was back, but I didn't believe them. Father would have said something about it immediately. If this is your and Jane's idea of a joke, then—"

"It's not a joke, John." She took him by the shoulders and squared off to face him. "Jane and I would never tease you that way. But your injuries are important, and I wanted this to be your first option. If you're not ready, I promise we'll go somewhere else. You decide."

He looked at the front door, hesitation draped all over his bruised face. At first she thought he might take off in the opposite direction like a startled jackrabbit. But slowly, the strain in his brow lessened, and his shoulders relaxed into something closer to normal posture.

"No," he said. "I'd like to go in."

She reached for the doorknob and twisted. Unlocked. The door creaked as she inched it open. They stepped into the vacant hall with its dark wood trim and green wallpaper. It smelled more lived-in than last time—more like him. She pressed forward slowly, peering into each room and finding them empty. Maybe he wasn't home.

She heard a muffled chuckle come from somewhere down the hall. She glanced back to find John still standing near the entrance, his eyes wide as dinner plates. A pang of guilt gnawed at her. She'd make sure to give him a long explanation about everything this evening. Trying her best to be quiet, she tiptoed toward the farthest door and pressed her ear to the wood.

"What a mess," a man said. "You'd think I'd know where to tread lightly by now."

"No one's immune to accidents, Ben," Gabriel answered, his voice deep and clear. "I'm just glad you got away fast enough. If any more had stung you . . . Well it could have been much worse."

"It's fine. You can say it, Doc. I'd be dead."

"For God's sake, don't mention that to your family. Now go home and take care of yourself. I doubt things will get worse, but see me immediately if they do."

"I appreciate it, sir. Thank you very much."

The door swung inward and Ellie lurched forward, colliding with the ointment-covered groundskeeper.

"Whoa!" Ben caught and steadied her. "I'm sorry, miss. I had no idea you were standing there."

"No, no. It's my fault," she said, trying not to wince at the sight of his red, swollen neck. The poor man looked awful. "Are you all right?"

He shrugged. "It looks worse that it feels. I was trimming a tree out back when I disturbed a bee hive. The darned things got me good, but Dr. Peterson was nice enough to fix me up."

"You'd better not be scaring off my patients, Ben." Gabriel chuckled as he appeared in the doorframe with his sleeves rolled up, toweling off his hands. When he saw her, his brows shot up in surprise. The corners of his mouth curved into an attractive grin. "Well, hello there."

She would not let herself blush. "Hello."

Ben put on his gray cap and scooted past her. "Sorry again for startling you, miss. I'll see you Wednesday, Doc."

"Take care, Ben," Gabriel said.

She swallowed when he took a step closer.

"I was beginning to wonder when I'd see you again." He tilted his head. "You're not ill, are you?"

Everything about his nearness made her knees darn near buckle. The sunlight spilling through the window onto his coffee-colored hair, the contour of his forearm muscles as he reached up and clutched the doorframe, the way his deep-blue eyes searched her face—it all brought her mind back to their stormy night together. The one night she had to forget.

"I'm very well, thank you. But I've brought someone who needs your help."

She turned to John, summoning him with a hand motion. He began creeping forward, but stopped the moment Gabriel stepped out into the hall. Their eyes met. They stared at one another, blinking with bewilderment.

"Good God," Gabriel said. "John?"

John's dark eyes showed the dullness of disbelief. His once-timid expression hardened into something more resentful. Perhaps he truly wasn't ready for this moment.

"I don't understand," he muttered, the hurt in his voice resonating like a low bell. "You're dead. You're . . . supposed to be dead."

Gabriel moved toward him slowly, as if he were approaching a wild stallion. "I know. You have every right to think that. But I promise I can explain everything."

"Explain what, exactly? How you abandoned us? How you came back without telling me? This is a load of horse shit," he grumbled, turning to storm away.

"What did you say?" Gabriel shot after him. He snatched John by the shoulder before he could make it a few feet. "Listen, I don't care how angry you are with me. That does not give you reason to spit out profanity in a woman's presence. Don't you ever speak like that again, understood?"

"Let go of me! You're not my father!" John used both hands to fight back, the bloody handkerchief stuck to his forehead. He hurled a fist at Gabriel, but Gabriel caught it mid-swing.

"I never said I was," Gabriel growled, twisting John's arm behind his back and pinning him to the wall. "But that doesn't mean I'll sit by and let you make a fool of yourself. You're far better than that."

"How do you know what I'm better than? You barely know me anymore!"

"I know you enough."

"Boys, stop," Ellie shouted.

She flinched as John slammed his heel down on Gabriel's toe. Gabriel groaned and released his grip, but tackled his younger cousin to the ground seconds later. "I know you're not as stubborn as your father, and you'll listen to what I have to say before you fly off the handle."

"I can't breathe. You're crushing me!" John yowled.

Gabriel flipped him onto his back, pinning his wrists to the floor. "I'll let you go if you promise to stop this nonsense and act civilized."

"I'm not the one who disappeared on my family." Tears spilled John's down his cheeks. "Do you know how long I stared out the attic window, waiting for you? Three months!

"You were the closest thing I had to a brother. Nothing bad was supposed to happen to you, ever." John wept like a small boy. "Father was furious when he caught me. He said I had to accept that you were gone and never coming back. I hated him for it, too, until the day I heard him crying in his office. I knew I had to be strong for him. I had to let you die."

A long, tense silence enveloped the hall. Gabriel released his grip and dropped to the floor. "There's nothing I can say to make up for what I've done . . ."

"No, there isn't." John propped himself onto his elbows. "But you can still bloody apologize, just like I'm about to." He wiped his eyes and looked at Ellie. "I'm sorry for the language I used earlier, Ellie. I never should have said something like that, and if you'd like to wash my mouth out with soap, I'll go quietly."

A little tenderness had finally returned to his expression. Ellie folded her arms and nodded, trying to convey an ease she didn't necessarily feel just yet. "It's all right. Let this first time be a warning."

"Yes, ma'am." He looked at Gabriel. "Your turn."

"My *turn*?" Gabriel stared blankly for a moment. Then, in a somewhat broken voice he said "Do you really think it's that easy, John? When I look at you, all I'm reminded of is the time I'll never get back. The time I wasted because of something I thought I couldn't deal with years ago. The choices I made . . . the way that I handled things . . ." He shook his head, battling back emotion. "I should have brought you comfort, but I let you grieve, instead. I'll live with that regret every day."

John released a ragged breath. "And . . . ?"

"And I'd sooner die than hurt you or anyone else again," Gabriel said, rising to his feet. "I'm sorry, John. I'm so very sorry."

"You should be, you big oaf." John extended his hand. Gabriel clasped it tightly, yanked up the young man and pulled him into a firm embrace. It took but a moment for John to wrap his arms around him and bury his face in Gabriel's shoulder.

The tension in the air dissolved completely. Ellie felt a warm glow flowing through her as she watched four years of sorrow turn into an outpouring of love. She wouldn't trade seeing such a moment for anything in the world.

"Afternoon, Peterson. Welcome back." Matthew slipped in through the front door, severing the reunion.

"Thank you, Mr. Tiller," Gabriel said, releasing John. He approached Matthew and shook his hand. "You seem very well. I offer my warmest congratulations on your marriage. Jane has never looked happier."

A suggestion of wariness darkened Matthew's eyes.

"Where is Jane?" Ellie asked quickly.

"She's waiting in the carriage," Matthew answered in a strange, impersonal tone.

The cold look on his face disturbed her. It didn't suit him at all. Neither did the awkward way he stood with both hands clasped behind his back. Jane knew so little about Creekwood, but she must have said enough in the carriage to set him off. Perhaps it was the part about sneaking behind Mr. Westgate's back. Ellie couldn't blame him for that, because she despised it, too.

"Anyway—" Matthew cleared his throat. "I came to see how things were going, but it appears nothing's happened yet."

Gabriel grimaced. "Lord, I'm sorry, John. Let's have a look." He went to the boy and gave the handkerchief a gentle tug. It didn't budge. "It's stuck on there pretty well. The dried blood might as well be glue."

"How long will this take? Jane and I have dinner plans this evening."

Gabriel kept his focus on John's forehead. "Not to worry. I would be happy to take John and Miss Baker home after I finish addressing John's wound."

Matthew tapped his fingers on the hat in his hands. He clearly hated the idea. Ellie wasn't sure she liked it either, but what other choice did she have? If she wanted Gabriel's friendship, she'd have to learn to spend time with him again eventually. When Matthew met her eyes to read her reaction, she tried easing his doubts with a subtle smile.

"Fine," he said tersely. "Fix John up, and then it's straight home after that. I'd prefer staying away from trouble if at all possible."

Gabriel nodded. "You have my word."

Matthew thanked him, then said his goodbyes. Ellie closed her eyes, relieved and terrified at the sense of ease she felt once the door was shut.

Chapter Thirteen

"This is going to open the wound all over again, so don't worry if it starts to bleed a lot," Gabriel said, as he began peeling the handkerchief from John's forehead.

Ellie fidgeted with a loose button on her bodice, trying to focus on John, while pretending to be anywhere but the examination room. She didn't want to see his forehead bleed again. The potent smell of pharmaceuticals, the terrifying surgical tools, and the human skeleton in the corner only added to her uneasiness. But she refused to humiliate herself by showing weakness. She wasn't some damsel in distress Gabriel could save, then snatch up and kiss whenever he pleased. And she'd tell him that, too—soon, hopefully.

Gabriel dabbed at the fresh blood with a swab. "May I ask how this happened?"

"A girl," John said with a shrug.

"A girl did this to you? She must have been a monster."

Ellie raised her eyes long enough to see Gabriel wink at her. Her breath hitched. The button she'd been toying with now dangled by a single thread, so she tore it off and clutched it tightly in her fist. She forbade herself to move on to the next one. But God, how she wanted to.

John flinched as his cousin tore another section of handkerchief away. "You know what I meant."

"Of course I do." Gabriel snipped off a piece of blood-soaked fabric and dropped it onto a metal tray beside him. "You found yourself in the middle of a brutal fist fight over a pretty girl. But let me ask you this: Does she make you stumble? Does she knock the very breath from your lungs when she so much as looks at you?"

"Yes, all that and more."

"Then the fight was worth it. And get ready, because the feeling only gets worse when you're older."

What? The knots in Ellie's stomach grew tighter. *That statement couldn't have had anything to do with her, could it? Surely it couldn't...*

"I beg your pardon?" she asked.

"It's true, Ellie. You haven't a clue about your power," John said. "Pretty women are like sirens luring unsuspecting sailors to their demise."

"Why, thank you for the compliment, John." She placed her gloved hands on the plush leather table and leaned into him. "But I'm curious. What exactly is man's demise? Matrimony?"

"Of course," he answered matter-of-factly.

Gabriel threw back his head and let out a great peal of laughter. In spite of herself, she couldn't help but join in. Getting to know John better had been one of the only good things to come from her two-week punishment. His cleverness, his wit, his deceptively large heart—she couldn't imagine life without him.

With one final tug, Gabriel removed the remainder of the handkerchief. He studied the large gash without touching it. "You were smart in coming here. This laceration is deep and definitely needs to be stitched."

"I had a feeling . . ." She glanced at the raw, bloody mess for just a moment too long.

A terrible mistake. Her palms grew damp, her skin felt cold. Then her head started spinning, and she fought to control the nausea creeping into her throat. Spots closed in, brighter and brighter until she felt Gabriel's strong arms cradling her like an infant. Her reaction must have been worse than she'd thought.

His muffled voice kept fading in and out. Plush cushions met her head as he lowered her onto something soft, and within moments, Gabriel had a glass of liquid pressed to her lips. She gulped down the lemonade. His blurry outline slowly returned to focus, his compelling eyes looking down at her with concern.

"There you are, Ellie Bear. You've come back to me." His rich voice coated her like warm honey as he wiped the beads of cold sweat from her forehead.

"What happened? Where's John?" She blinked repeatedly, taking in the sunny parlor.

"He's still on the table." Kneeling beside her, Gabriel slipped off her glove and turned her wrist up to face the ceiling. "You fainted. Nothing to be ashamed of."

He placed three fingers firmly on her pulse. The contact sent a rush of something pleasant through her. She wondered if he felt it, too. "That's easy for you to say."

"Many people lose consciousness at the sight of blood. You should have told me if it bothered you."

Physician or not, the more she noted his calm demeanor, the more her frustration grew. So much for not showing weakness. Lying on the settee, barely able to lift her head—she must look about as weak as a kitten. This situation was exactly what she didn't want. How could she possibly forget their kiss with him kneeling so close?

"Silly me. I wasn't aware I had to tell you every little detail about myself," she muttered, freeing her arm from his hold.

"You're agitated. You need to rest." He extended an open palm. "Now, may I please have your wrist back?"

"Don't tell me what I need. I'm perfectly fine." Her arms shook as she struggled to lift herself into a sitting position. If the room would just hold still, things would be a lot simpler.

He rose up, slapped one hand on the back of the settee and the other on the arm rest behind her head, preventing her from making another move. "In this situation, I *am* telling you what you need. I'm the doctor, you're the patient. You're going to listen to me."

His delicious breath warmed her face, and the sweet smell of his skin overwhelmed her senses. She forced herself to lie back down in order to escape it.

"Thank you," he said in that familiar, authoritative tone she so despised. "Am I able to back away and trust you won't try that again?"

"Ugh, I'm not a child," she grumbled, snatching a pillow from behind her head and covering her face.

"Says the woman with a pillow over her head." He lowered himself onto the small space of cushion beside her. "Ellie, you can't deny that you revert to child-like behavior every time you disagree with me."

"You're the only one I happen to disagree with."

"Doubtful. You know what I think? I think you chose to be sheltered for a little too long."

The scoundrel! She ripped the cushion from her face and flung it at him. "How dare you make that assumption."

"I've no choice but to make assumptions, because you haven't told me anything at all."

"Why do you feel so entitled to know?"

"We spent five years together, for God's sake. I've opened up to you. I thought I at least mattered enough for you to . . ." He shook his head, clamping his mouth shut.

She darted her eyes, shriveling a little at his frustrated expression. The commotion inside her mind kept her from arguing rationally, and she wished for just a moment of clarity.

"You're right," he said, rising to stand. "Forgive me. You don't owe me anything."

"Yes, I do." She pressed her head back against the pillows, searching for a memory. "I had a brother once. He died when I was a baby."

Gabriel's eyes grew large and he knelt back down. Honestly, she didn't know how he put up with her. After all he'd shared with her, why was she so reluctant to do the same? Because that might make her feel even closer to him, and she didn't know if she could handle closer.

Shutting her eyes, she recalled her childhood; the time when her parents were alive, when the crisp breeze flowed through the valley and tousled her hair—when Jasper Cogs had never existed. Then she imagined Gabriel as that blue-eyed, scrawny boy with sun-kissed cheeks and dirt beneath his fingernails. Telling that boy everything had been so easy. Surely she could do it again.

Keeping her eyes shut, she summoned a deep breath and said, "His name was Walter. He'd gotten terrible pneumonia at just three years of age. A year later, my parents lost another child to stillbirth. They called her Martha. My mother couldn't have any more children after that. So they did everything in their power to protect me for as long as they could."

She opened her eyes. Gabriel clasped his hands and pressed them gently against his lips. Such a beautiful, impressive specimen he'd grown into.

"In answer to your question—" She stared up at the ceiling, glad her dizziness was almost gone. "Yes, I was sheltered, for far too long."

"I'm sorry your family had to endure such loss," he said sincerely. "No one should have to bury a child, but it happens frequently."

"Are you satisfied, then?"

His eyes shot wide. "Satisfied? You act as though I'm heartless."

"You wanted to know something about me, so I told you."

"But I don't wish to hear it at the cost of your distress, no matter how much I appreciate your finally sharing something with me."

An ounce of comfort crept into her soul. She'd never spoken to anyone about Walter and Martha, yet somehow, sharing something so private with Gabriel almost felt nice. She folded her arms, knowing her walls were crumbling. He must have seen through her bluff, too, because his eyes held a trace of humor as he rose to stand.

"I'd best see to John. I don't want that wound—" He winced. "I mean, small scratch of his exposed any longer." He took the glass of lemonade from the side table and handed it to her. "Finish drinking this, and stay here until I'm through stitching him up."

She shivered as he reached out and tucked a loose strand of hair behind her ear. His fingers burned hot against her skin, and the same confusing feelings she'd experienced in the cabin crashed her body again. She allowed a grin to spread up her cheeks.

"You should smile more often. It suits you better," he said, just before turning to leave the room.

Oh, no! He wouldn't have the upper hand this time. Someone had to acknowledge their ridiculous kiss, and if he wasn't planning to do it, she certainly would. Now might be her only chance to admit the mistake and move on.

"Wait. There's something we must discuss."

He paused just inside the door and turned to her. "Ellie, if this is about the—"

"Yes. The other night." She could barely look at him. Digging deep for the rest of her voice, she said, "That kiss . . . in the cabin. It meant nothing."

Two weeks of preparation, and all she could say were two short sentences? Speaking the words aloud had proven a lot harder than she'd anticipated. She took a sip of lemonade, ready to tell him how she wished things to return to normal, or whatever sort of normal there'd been between them, anyway.

"Of course it meant nothing," he said, his nonchalant tone slicing through her.

So he *had* regretted it. For some reason, hearing the exact same words from his mouth stung—painfully. Had they sounded that harsh when she'd said them? An agreement was what she'd wanted, wasn't it? She had as much intention of coming between Gabriel and Emily Tuttle as she did marrying at all.

"Well then—" She twisted the glass in her hand. "I'm glad we agree."

He gave his shirt collar a small tug, and she watched his Adam's apple slide up and down his throat with a heavy swallow. "Of course. Will that be all?"

"Yes." She'd expected her voice to be of normal volume, but it came out choked, instead.

He turned on his heel and strode out the door, his heavy footsteps echoing down the hall. She waited for a sense of relief, but it never came.

* * *

Gabriel looked back over his shoulder, watching his uncle's estate grow smaller, until it finally disappeared behind the tree line. Whether he'd set foot inside that house ever again seemed more of a distant thought than a hopeful reality. With the gray sky darkening by the minute, the early evening set the tone for his somber mood. He gave the reins a firm crack, urging Roger to increase his pace before the skies opened up.

As the buggy bounced down the road, he tried pushing Ellie from his thoughts. But damn if her little mind games didn't drive him mad. He'd purposely sat John in the middle of his two-seater when he'd taken them home, afraid the wind might blow her jasmine scent into his nostrils, or that her warm body squeezed against his would arouse every part of him. Most of all, he did it to avoid conversing with her.

She'd given him the cold shoulder the entire way, and had only spoken in short sentences if John asked her a question. When he'd offered his hand to escort her down from the buggy, she'd refused to take it. And she'd barely thanked him before leading John back up to the house in a hurry. Why was she so angry with him?

He'd planned on apologizing for kissing her, but it had skipped his mind the moment he saw her standing in his hallway, her big green eyes drinking him up in a way that made his pulse spike. Want, risk, lust—all for him. He could never have prepared for the abrupt way she'd yank him down from his cloud minutes later, after finally opening up to him, no less.

Droplets of rain began tapping against the black canvas above his head. They grew heavier, but the absence of thunder and lightning made the ride home tolerable. Perhaps he shouldn't have answered her so brutally. He'd only meant to counterattack her own biting words.

It meant nothing.

True, he'd kissed her on impulse—one he'd wanted to act upon since the night of the Tuttle's party—but he never would have put it like that. It had meant a little something, whether he'd wanted it to or not. He knew it meant something to Ellie, too. The tiny line between her eyebrows—the same look she'd given him as a child when she'd kept something from him—told him as much.

She could have resisted him. Sex was something very ordinary to her, after all. But the way she'd whimpered and melted into his body had seemed . . . innocent, as if she were feeling every touch like it was her first. She couldn't have been that good an actress.

He rested a foot atop the buggy's dash rail, plagued by thoughts of what the Tuttles expected of him. Propose to Emily, marry her and inherit her father's empire—despite the love they didn't share. Something so practiced, so common.

So damn difficult.

He didn't want handouts. He wanted to make his own way, even if it meant sacrificing his social status. Clenching his jaw, he stared at the intersection ahead. The right turn he'd make toward home was fast-approaching, but he had other plans today. He dropped his foot and sat tall, tightening his grip on the leather reins. Determination filled the pit of his stomach as he guided Roger past the turn and continued down the road.

"Hell with it," he muttered.

Since Gabriel's return, he'd avoided making the trip to his father's attorney. He'd wanted time to settle in, to establish himself a little, before pursuing the criminal who had ruined his life. Gabriel knew that quest could take months, even years, and he refused to be left with a bunch of empty yesterdays. But no one knew more about Gabriel's father than his lawyer.

Gabriel veered the buggy down a secluded street lined with thick pines. The giant gray house waiting at the end of the road only added to the day's gloom. Stone gargoyles peered menacingly over corners of the roof, while neglected foliage crept up sides of walls and over a broken birdbath in the center of the driveway. No wonder he'd been afraid of visiting with his father as a small boy. Even now, the property looked haunted.

He parked, walked up the steps and pounded the heavy lion's-head knocker against the door. When it opened, a familiar woman stood in the frame. A pair of round spectacles perched atop the bridge of her beak-like nose, and her dark hair stretched back in a tight bun. Thin lips pursed as she looked him over.

"May I help you?" She spoke in the same, monotonous way he remembered.

"It's nice to see you again, Mrs. Belding." He removed his hat. "You probably don't remember me, but my name is Gabriel Peterson. I'm Patrick Peterson's son."

She removed her spectacles and polished them on her dark skirt, then placed them back on her nose and squinted her beady eyes. He never recalled the housekeeper looking particularly young—or feminine, for that matter. Seeing her now, with only the addition of a few more wrinkles, the question of her age baffled him even more.

"Yes, of course, Mr. Peterson." She wore a dull, lifeless expression. "What can I do for you?"

Conversation and warmth had never been one of her strong points. Gabriel found it relieving for a change. He raked a hand through his damp hair and opened his mouth to answer, but before he could, the man he'd come to see appeared behind Mrs. Belding.

"I'll have no solicitors on my property. Away with you," he said, with a dismissive gesture of his hand. He took the door from Mrs. Belding and slammed it shut in Gabriel's face.

Gabriel called, "I am not a solicitor, sir. I am the son of your late client!"

The door lurched back open. His father's lawyer stood in the frame, pale-faced and wide-eyed, as if he'd been slapped across the face.

"Mr. Cain, sir." Gabriel bowed at the waist. "You look well."

Cain didn't blink. "So the rumors were true. You really are alive . . ."

"Yes."

"I—I'm absolutely stunned. You're just now paying this old man a visit?" Cain grabbed Gabriel's shoulder and led him inside. "Please, come in. Come in!"

The drawn parlor curtains made the late afternoon hour seem like midnight. Countless animal heads and antlers still covered the walls. Mrs. Belding lit the lamps while Cain poured himself a glass of liquor at a small bar. Gabriel lowered himself into a stiff, uncomfortable armchair made of zebra skin. The room smelled faintly of death.

Cain held up one of his crystal decanters and gestured to it. "Scotch?"

"No, thank you," Gabriel said, giving his cravat a loosening tug. Stuffed, mounted wildlife stared at him from all corners.

With a glass in one hand, Cain gripped the chair beside Gabriel and dragged it to a position across from him. The leather upholstery creaked beneath his weight as he lowered himself into the seat. "Forgive my unconventional reaction upon seeing you. I felt as though I were—"

"Seeing a ghost. No need to apologize. I've grown accustomed to it, actually."

The man nodded, swirling his glass around in circles. "Your father's funeral was hard enough, but nothing could have prepared me for news of you and your mother's deaths months later. Such a devastating year that was."

"I should have come back."

"Then may I ask . . ." Cain paused and shifted uneasily in his chair. "Gabriel, I've known you since you were no taller than the back of my chair. I hope you don't mind my asking why you didn't."

Gabriel swallowed. *Don't lie, dammit. Don't lie.* "Youth. Cowardice. Shame?" He held his breath, while every muscle in his body tensed at the truth. Three words, but at least he'd said them.

To his surprise, Cain's expression softened. "Your honesty is refreshing. We've all done things of which we're not proud, and some of us take longer to learn from our mistakes than others. What's most important is that we never make those mistakes again."

"Lord, not in a million years." Gabriel relaxed into his chair. Aside from spending time with Ellie, he hadn't felt this light in a while.

Cain sipped his scotch. "It's odd. Your uncle never mentioned your return. I had to hear it on the streets, which is why I barely believed it."

Gabriel diverted the soreness in his chest by drumming his thumbs atop the chair's arm. He'd almost forgotten that Magnus and Henry were not only good friends, but old schoolmates as well. "I'm afraid my uncle's having a hard time forgiving me. We're not on the best terms at the moment."

"I dreaded that much," Cain said. "But chin up, dear boy. I'm sure whatever lies between you will be resolved in the end."

Gabriel managed a pathetic grin. If he spoke, the doubt in his own voice would disappoint himself.

"Well then." Cain took another sip of scotch before placing his glass down beside him. "As much as I'd like to think you've paid me a visit out of sheer fondness, I'm certain that isn't the case. Is there something else you came to discuss?"

"Yes, there is." Gabriel leaned forward, clasping his hands together. "As I'm sure you already know, my father's last will and testament was stolen."

Cain nodded. "After the incident, I wondered if a distant relative were intent on forging the document. I looked into it, but came away with nothing."

"Then you must also know that the man they found in Boston was not the one behind all this."

"Fred Vickers, wasn't it? I had never heard that name before in my life."

"Whomever Vickers worked for hated my father enough to destroy my family. You knew my father's business and personal life better than anyone else. I need your help, sir."

Cain stroked his sleek mutton chops and furrowed his well-groomed eyebrows. "Patrick was a powerful man. He made several . . . questionable choices to get ahead in life. It was no secret he had many enemies."

"I want to know why, and I want to know whom," Gabriel said. "When I find them, they'll regret nothing more than the mistake of leaving me alive."

Cain shook his head. "I don't doubt the revenge you must be seeking after losing your mother. But something like this requires extensive time and investigation—"

"I'm willing to compensate you in whatever way I can."

"Dear boy, it would be harder than finding a needle in a haystack."

"Mr. Cain." Gabriel shot to his feet, sending his chair back so fast that the legs scraped the floor. "I'll be damned if I sit by any longer while someone lives and breathes with my mother's blood on his hands. I know it won't be easy, but I have to try. With all due respect, I can do this with or without your help, sir."

Cain withdrew from his chair and sighed. "You have the same tenacity as your father. I don't know how useful I'll be, but I'm willing to help you in any way I can. Patrick wasn't just a client. He was a dear friend."

Cain extended his hand.

Gabriel clasped it tightly. "Thank you, sir. I truly appreciate it."

"Search through your father's personal items, if you have any. I'll take a look at my files and see what I can find."

"I'll start tonight," Gabriel declared. His mother had given him several boxes of his father's documents after his death. She'd been too grief-stricken to sort through them herself, so Gabriel claimed that responsibility. He didn't have time to look through them before traveling to Illinois, so he'd stashed them away in the attic. With any luck, his father's papers were still there.

With four years against him, time was of the essence.

Chapter Fourteen

The bright red curtain closed off the opera stage, followed by thunderous applause.

"That was it?" Ellie searched her companions' faces, baffled by their reserved expressions. "How are we supposed to know what happens?"

Everyone inside the private box laughed. Jane leaned over and placed a gloved hand on her forearm. "It's only intermission, Ellie."

"That means the show is halfway through, my dear," Westgate added with a chuckle.

"Oh." Ellie flushed miserably, twisting her colorful program into a crinkled mess. Darn it, did she always have to be so obvious about her upbringing? It was bad enough she hadn't even heard of the opera until she'd met the Westgates.

Matthew rose from his chair and stretched out his back. "I could tell you right now how it ends, if you'd like. I've seen Le Nozze di Figaro at least a half a dozen times."

"Don't ruin it for her, dearest," Jane said, as she placed her opera glasses back into their monogrammed case. "Surely you remember your first time at the opera and how special it was."

Laughter floated up from his throat. "I fell asleep. But my parents couldn't have expected much more from a six-year-old." He grinned at Ellie. "You're very lucky. I wish my first experience had been at an age where I could appreciate it."

Ellie imagined she'd love the show at any age. The magnificent costumes, the realistic sets and the breathtaking voices had brought her to tears at least twice during the first half, regardless of whether she understood Italian. No wonder the upper class fancied the theater so much.

Westgate stood and glanced down at the orchestra level. "Those of us who desire refreshments should act quickly. Everyone is migrating toward the lobby with purpose."

Ellie gathered her reticule and followed Jane, Westgate and Matthew through the short hall to the second level of the lobby. Resting a hand atop the wooden balcony rail, she watched a sea of patrons swarming below. So many colorful dresses glistening beneath the crystal-beaded chandeliers. To them, tonight was probably just an ordinary evening.

When Ellie turned back, she realized the others had already begun descending the staircase. She'd lose them in the dense crowd if she didn't hurry. Step-by-step, she scurried down the carpeted staircase as quickly as she could without drawing attention. Once she felt confident enough to lift her eyes without rolling an ankle, she looked up from her feet and saw Gabriel standing near one of the marble pillars.

She gripped the railing. Her heart shot into her throat as she tripped on the hem of her dress. What was he doing here?

Her mind revoked the question once she spotted Miss Tuttle beside him. In fact, the entire Tuttle family hovered around them, along with a handful of others Ellie didn't recognize. Gabriel looked divine in his crisp cutaway jacket, and Emily wore her lace-trimmed gown better than a fairy tale princess. They looked exquisite together. Too exquisite.

An unpleasant feeling attacked the pit of Ellie's stomach, as she tore her eyes away. She didn't dare look at them again throughout the rest of intermission. When the warning bell sounded, Matthew had barely begun telling his favorite fishing story.

"Drat," he said. "I suppose I'll have to continue later."

"Nonsense, the suspense will do me in if I'm forced to wait." Westgate sipped his port and turned to Jane. "You ladies hurry back so Ellie doesn't miss the opening. Matthew and I will join you after we finish up in the lounge."

Jane smiled and took Ellie's hand. Ellie stayed close as they slipped through the scurrying patrons heading every which way to reclaim their seats. Thankfully, she didn't see Gabriel or the Tuttles anywhere. Perhaps they'd returned to the theatre sometime before the warning bell. When she spotted the ladies' washroom at the opposite end of the lobby, she stopped scouring the crowd. She'd never make it through an entire second act after a full glass of champagne.

Slowing her pace she released Jane's hand. "You go on ahead, Jane. I'll join you in a moment."

"Is everything all right?" Jane asked with concern.

Ellie chewed her lip, her eyes darting toward the washroom once more.

Jane sighed, tilting her chin in disapproval. "Ellie, if a lady can wait until she's home to use the washroom, then she should most definitely wait."

"I'll only be a moment." Ellie knew that wasn't the answer Jane had expected to hear, and she also knew that far more men had entered the gentlemen's washroom than women entered their own. But she had little choice.

"Fine." With a stoic grin taking the sting out of her disappointed eyes, Jane gave a small nod, and turned to ascend the staircase.

Maneuvering against the crowd felt like a complicated dance, with two side-shuffles here, and a step back there. Ellie kept her focus down, avoiding inevitable stares as she approached the deserted washroom. Public ladies' rooms must only exist as a cruel attempt to challenge a woman's willpower and mock her. Well, Ellie's fear of judgment had run off tonight.

By the time she stepped out, the lobby had grown so quiet that her footsteps echoed from all corners. Behind closed theater doors, the orchestra began playing and a soprano started her song. The second act had started without her.

She peered around the black-and-white tiled lobby, taking note of any who might see if she made a run for it. Only a few ushers remained, along with bartenders polishing glassware and a handful of straggling patrons. Yanking up her skirts past her ankles, she dashed for the staircase. She climbed the steps two-at-a-time, tugging on the railing for momentum, until she'd reached the very top.

"Miss Baker." The rich, distinctive voice seeped through her.

She froze. Her heart pitched when she turned to see Gabriel gazing at her from the bottom of the staircase. "Oh. Good evening," she said.

"Good evening?" He began ascending the steps. "Judging by the look on your face, I have reason to believe you feel otherwise."

Heavens, had he appeared out of nowhere? Two ushers turned their heads and gave her a quick glance. She squeezed the green satin of her skirt, clenched her teeth and struggled to catch her breath. "Well . . . what kind of expression did you expect when you surprised me?"

"The look of thrill and utter delight, of course."

Her pulse hammered in her ears as he stopped on the step below. The way his starched white shirt collar stood out against his slightly bronzed skin made it difficult not to stare.

"I'll try harder next time," she said. "I suppose you spotted me during inter . . . inter . . ."

"Intermission?" A grin inched across the right side of his face.

Damn that stupid, crooked smile.

"You're not the only one with sharp eyes, Miss Baker." He rested a hand on the carved cherub atop the banister. "From where I'm seated on the mezzanine level, I have a clear view of the

Westgate family box. I saw you long before you noticed me in the lobby."

So he *had* noticed her. "Honestly, why must everything be a competition with men?"

"Because it's more fun that way."

His gaze fell to her neck for a second, and she thought she detected a flicker of desire in his eyes. She really should move. Standing one step above him almost put their lips at the same level. The strength of her yearning was unsettling, especially when she remembered his response—*"Of course it meant nothing"*—just days ago.

He glanced toward the theater doors, his grin fading a little. "Forgive me. I just realized I'm keeping you from your first opera."

"How do you know it's my first opera?"

He quirked an eyebrow. "Do you really want me to answer that?"

"No, I don't," she said, grimacing playfully.

When his gentle laugh rippled through her, she couldn't keep herself from giggling, too. There was something so warm and contagious about his happiness. She wondered how much he shared that same marvelous laugh with Emily Tuttle. Ellie fingered a long, slender bead at her low neckline, pretending she didn't feel an ache in her breast at the thought.

"Anyway—" He cleared his throat. "If I had not said hello to you, I would have regretted it all night."

She found that somewhat satisfying. "I'm glad you did."

"May I escort you to your box, madam?" he asked, offering his arm.

"You may." She slipped her hand through the gap, breathing in his scent of clove and spices as she fell into step beside him.

The urge to apologize for her behavior days ago pressed hard on her mind. She shouldn't have blamed Gabriel for agreeing with her when the person she'd truly been upset with was herself. She hadn't expected to feel such disappointment when he agreed to friendship, at never feeling him touch her again the way he had in the cabin. The very depth of her feelings had shocked her to the point of fear.

"I'm sorry for acting a fool the other day," she said, wishing this didn't feel so awkward. "It was childish and uncalled for, especially when you were kind enough to attend to John."

"All is well, I assure you," he replied lightly.

They stopped just shy of the black velvet curtain that closed off the hallway. She withdrew her arm and stepped in front of him. "Will you please acknowledge my apology? You don't know how awful I've felt these last few days."

"All right, all right." He held up his hands in surrender. "If it will ease your mind, then I acknowledge and accept your apology."

There, that was settled . . . hopefully. "Thank you."

"My pleasure. How is John, by the way?"

"Healing very well, thanks to you. I was planning on sending for the family physician tomorrow to remove the stitches."

His eyebrows rose. "They haven't come out yet?"

"Well, no, I—" She didn't like the way he was looking at her. "I thought you said it would take a week for the wound to heal." Hadn't he? Perhaps she should have been less busy resenting him and busier paying attention to his instructions.

"Dear God." He placed a hand on his hip and dragged the other down over his mouth. "I said five days, Miss Baker. Five days. The face heals much faster than the rest of the body. Those sutures should have come out yesterday."

She clapped a hand to her cheek. It was one thing taking her own risks, but to let someone else pay for her mistakes? She'd never forgive herself if John's forehead suffered permanent damage. "Oh, no. What should I do?"

"Tomorrow is Sunday. Doctor Davis doesn't practice on Sundays," he said. "But I can help you. Bring John to Jane's house at nine o' clock tomorrow morning and I'll be there with my bag."

She took an abrupt step toward him, restraining herself from rejoicing and wrapping her arms around him. "Oh, thank you. Thank you."

He narrowed his eyes, genuinely amused by her reaction. "My pleasure. Be sure to dress as lightly as you can tomorrow, because John, Jane and I have a surprise for you afterward."

Her body stiffened. "A surprise? What are you talking about?"

"Can't tell, but I promise it's better than the time I blindfolded you and cracked an egg over your head."

"But . . . how did you—"

"It's already been arranged. I'm sure Jane will tell you at some point tonight. We originally planned to leave at nine-thirty, so you'll have to let her know that John's stitches will cause a bit of a delay." He bowed like a gentleman, yet shot her a roguish wink. "Good evening, Miss Baker. I'll be seeing you bright and early."

She backed toward the curtain completely tongue-tied, watching him turn the corner and disappear. Did that really just happen?

Once back in her seat, she found herself glancing at Jane every few seconds. How could she be expected to pay attention to the show after such an unpredictable tease? When Henry and Matthew re-joined them, the task of waiting to hear about this so-called surprise became even harder.

She borrowed Jane's opera glasses and searched the dark mezzanine until she spotted Gabriel. He sat very still, his thoughts possibly far away. Even as Emily placed her hand on his, his face remained a mask of stone.

Ellie both dreaded and yearned for tomorrow. She'd been caught off-guard by the vibrancy of his voice when he'd mentioned the surprise. Clearly he held their friendship in high esteem, and she'd show him she could do the same without becoming some breathless girl of eighteen. Maybe she should start by not staring at him so much.

She put down the viewing glasses, averted her eyes and repeated the word *friend* in her head until the show was over.

* * *

Despite the late hour, the humid July evening smothered Gabriel like a thick blanket as he walked beside Emily in the Tuttle's main garden. He swiped a hand across his perspiring forehead, thankful for the chance to speak with her alone. Until now, a slew of social events, doting family members and chaperones had made privacy impossible. But after one too many drinks at the opera, Tuttle had finally allotted them some time together.

The nature of their relationship had weighed heavily on Gabriel's heart since the morning after he'd kissed Ellie—the same morning he'd heard the word "wedding" come from Mrs. Tuttle's mouth. For once, he needed to be honest. The dark cloud of his financial future couldn't sway his mind, nor could his late parents' wishes. In his heart, he knew he could never marry Emily. Life had changed him. She needed to know how far he'd fallen from what she required of a husband. He just prayed to God he wouldn't hurt her in the process.

"The woman portraying the Countess was much better than the one who played her last time," Emily chirped as she took his arm. "Who was your favorite character tonight?"

He looked up at the crescent moon in the cloudless sky. "Figaro will always be my favorite."

She laughed. "Such a boring, predictable choice."

"How can he be boring if the entire opera was named after him?"

"That's exactly *why* he's boring."

He glanced down at her, allowing himself to chuckle. Truthfully, he'd always enjoyed their light-hearted banter. But a life with Emily demanded far more than an exchange of witty remarks, and that he could no longer give her.

"Emily." He slowed his pace a little. "I need to speak with you about something very important."

"What a coincidence. I've been meaning to speak with you about something, as well." She smiled up at him, her wide, turquoise eyes sparkling with news. The happy look sent a spiked club through his conscience.

"After you," he said.

"What do you think of the South?"

He stopped walking. "The South," he repeated, just in case he hadn't heard correctly..

"Yes. Virginia to be exact." She let go of his arm and strolled toward the lilac shrubs. "You see, it's always been a dream of Papa's to live in the Southern countryside, closer to his factories. Now that he's retired from railroads, he and Mother are moving this fall in hopes of a milder winter." She spun around to face him. "It would simply devastate me to have to live so far from them and my sisters."

"Emily, I—"

"You needn't worry about a thing. I spoke to Father, and he wants to purchase us a house in Richmond as a gift. A Virginia wedding sounds divine, doesn't it? Mother has plenty of family there, too. Just think of all the lavish Southern dinner parties we'd host over the years!"

Her words came a-mile-a-minute. Gabriel did everything in his power to not remove his jacket and yank his tie loose as he lowered himself onto a stone bench. "Despite your father's incredible generosity, I could never allow him to do that."

"Why not?"

"Because I can't accept favors I don't deserve." He rested his palms on the rough stone. "I also can't sit by and watch you not be provided for in the manner in which you're accustomed to."

"Don't be silly." She brushed him off with a flick of her wrist and claimed the seat beside him. "Besides, Father would be insulted if you didn't accept. He'd gladly put you in charge of at least one of his factories . . . and you could still practice medicine on the side, if you wish."

He tensed, hearing the forced brightness in her tone. He took up her dainty hand and looked her straight in the eyes. "Do you really want to marry me, Emily?"

"Of course I do."

The candidness in her voice was disheartening. She was still so young, so full of life, that he wanted to give her the chance to experience it. How could she really know what she wanted when it had been chosen for her at birth?

"Tell me why," he said.

Confusion touched her pale face. "Because you're the most handsome, eligible bachelor in the entire Northeast. Because we would make the perfect couple, and because—"

"And because it's what our parents wanted for us."

"Yes, but . . . we're a very fine match, Gabriel." The pitch of her voice began to rise, and she drew her brows together in a frown. "Everyone can see that."

Damn, he felt terrible. Perhaps he couldn't avoid hurting her now, yet he saw no other way to save her from countless years of unhappiness down the road. He had to convince her that everything about their being together was wrong. "They see what they wish to see, Emily. That's how society is. But the truth is we barely know each other, and you haven't been given the chance to look elsewhere."

He rose to his feet and sighed. The nine years between them made him feel more like a protective older brother than a fiancée. She deserved a wealthy man, someone who ached to be near her always, to relish in fancy gatherings and to listen to every bit of nonsense she prattled over. A man who gave her no less than one hundred percent of his affection. A man who thought of her as much as he was beginning to think of—

Christ.

Ellie. Even the thought of her name warmed him. He feared he'd never tire of her jesting quips, her awkward social skills or the way her freckled little nose crinkled when she looked at him in defiance. None of her flaws mattered. In fact, they only increased the attraction he felt.

He had almost tripped over his own feet when he saw her at the opera house, atop the lobby staircase in her mint-colored gown, which contrasted perfectly against her pitch-black hair and rosy lips. When she'd blushed, the vivid scarlet in her cheeks had spread down her bare neck and across her exposed collarbone. He'd never seen her quite so naked in a public setting, which led him to imagine what it might have felt like to press his lips to the forbidden area.

"I don't have to look elsewhere. That's the beauty of an arrangement," Emily said, snapping him from his delusion. Her russet-colored curls danced in the evening breeze as she pouted with discontent.

He tried to lighten her mood by plucking a small purple lilac from beside the bench and tucking it beneath her comb. "You deserve a man who can provide you with everything you desire, and more. You know I can't do that anymore. There are many others far better-qualified than I."

She met his gaze as if to reassure him. "Your esteemed family name and fine character is reason enough for our contract. Father will keep your financial secret safe from society until you inherit his fortune."

Fine character, indeed. His character had been anything but fine around Emily's family. "At one time, I very well might have been the right man for you." He knelt down before her, careful not to soil his trousers by balancing on the balls of his feet. "But Emily,

I'm very different than before, and it pains me to admit that I . . . haven't been completely honest with you."

"What do you mean?" she asked, her eyes narrowing.

He held her gaze, intent on being truthful no matter what the outcome. "I've never really cared for extravagant parties or the opera. Furthermore, business has always bored me. Medicine is, and always will be, my passion, my career. The woman I marry must support and accept that." He searched for the simplest way to say the hardest part. "I . . . never lost my memory after the accident. The truth is, the moment I left the hospital, I ran."

She blinked. "You ran?"

"My mother died before I could save her. I was too afraid to face my family, and too grief-stricken to see her buried. So I disappeared . . . from everything and everyone." He gripped his knees, digging his thumbs into his muscles until he felt pain. "I drank heavily, gambled, lived as a vagabond and did several other things I'm ashamed to admit. Many of those things are far too unwholesome for your innocent ears to hear. I've been to Hell and back, and I could never forgive myself if I deceived your family a moment longer."

Her mouth slipped open. A vast silence echoed between them, broken only by the chirping of crickets. There must have been dozens, and each and every chirp sounded like the word "bastard." A chorus of "bastard, bastard," mocking him.

Emily rose from her seat as if propelled by an explosive force. Her nostrils flared and her vibrant eyes bore into his like a warrior's spear. He barely had time to stand before her delicate right hand slapped his face.

"I deserved that," he said, pressing a palm to his cheek.

"I cannot believe you lied to me!" she spat. "How dare you subject my family to scandal, you . . . you . . ." She clenched her fists and began pacing back and forth. "And to think I might have married a scoundrel like you!"

"I would never have let things get that far, which is why I needed to speak with you." He curbed the defensiveness in his tone and tried keeping his voice down. The last thing they needed was another pair of ears listening in.

"Oh, that's rich!" Sarcasm drenched her voice as she threw up her arms. "How very considerate of you to confess to your deceit before we married. You know, this could have all been avoided had you just come back like any decent man would have!"

The words bit, despite how much he deserved them. He didn't try to stop her as she stormed off into a maze of hedges and disappeared. He pressed his back against the trunk of a white birch, sliding down until he landed hard on his rump. *To hell with it*, he thought of dirtying his clothes. With his legs sprawled out in front of him, he tossed his head back and braced himself for the worst of the evening—when he'd tell the Tuttles the truth.

No more lies, no more stories. Only consequences remained, those he had no choice but to accept.

Minutes later, at the sound of Emily's returning footsteps, he lifted his head. Her silhouette emerged from the tall hedges, and when she drew closer, he could see her hostility had abated a great deal. His knees cracked as he stood and brushed the dirt from his bottom.

"Thank you for giving me a moment," she said as she approached.

He bowed his head. "Of course."

"After stepping away, I was able to come to a sense of clarity." She folded her hands in a composed manner. "It was selfish of you to mislead my family about your absence, but it was also selfish of me to react in the manner that I did."

"You were never selfish."

"Don't flatter," she said, sounding years beyond her age. "Your mother was someone I admired deeply. In some regards, I looked up to her even more than my own. When I think about the way you lost her—" She shook her head and took a small step towards him. "Well . . . it's far more than I would ever care to endure. I can't imagine the pain you went through."

A tightness formed in Gabriel's chest. He couldn't bring himself to appreciate her understanding, when he knew she owed him nothing. Yet in the way she spoke, he could almost feel a thin veil of comfort drape over his shoulders.

"But what you did afterward is unforgivable." Her voice hardened and her bottom lip began to quiver. "You deserted everything and everyone, including your family fortune, on purpose. Had you truly seen a future in us as I did, then you might have chosen otherwise."

"I'm so sorry it had to be this way, Emily," he said softly.

She lifted her chin and met his eyes. "I am, too. But you're right. You're no longer the man for me, just as I'm no longer the woman for you. Therefore, I . . . fully support the decision to end our arrangement."

He cupped her cheek. "You are a treasure."

"Please, Gabriel." A single tear cascaded down her cheek and she turned away from him. "I can't bear to have you touch me, now that I know how soiled your hands are."

"I understand." His fingers curled into a fist and he lowered his arm to his side.

She dropped her lashes as if trying to hide the hurt—as if attempting to erase every detail she'd planned concerning their future together. Then she took a deep breath, wiped a finger beneath her eyes and glanced at him. "I suppose we should tell Mother and Papa as soon as possible."

Gabriel nodded. "They're going to hear everything, just as they should have several weeks ago." He offered his arm unconsciously before remembering her earlier statement and withdrawing.

The silent walk back to the mansion seemed to take decades, while each step filled him with more dread. He stared at the glowing windows ahead, bracing himself for the looks he'd receive, the words he might hear, and the possibility of the Tuttles exposing his lie to the rest of society. It could very well ruin him. But he'd gotten himself into this mess, and somehow, he'd get himself back out again. Nothing mattered now but the truth.

The truth, and the promise of seeing Ellie Baker tomorrow.

Chapter Fifteen

"Can I bring you anything else, miss?" Jane's maid asked, reaching for Ellie's empty breakfast plate.

Ellie dabbed at the corners of her mouth and placed her napkin on the dish. "No thank you, Libby. The biscuits were especially delicious."

When Libby started clearing the plates and silverware, Ellie's restless hands fluttered in her lap. The change from simplicity to luxury hadn't come without its obstacles, particularly when it came to servants doing all the dressing and household chores. She found it a constant struggle to keep from offering her assistance.

"I'm so pleased you enjoyed everything, Ellie," Jane said, as another servant refilled her coffee cup. "Don't tell Father, but I think my cook might be better than Beatrice herself."

Ellie grinned. "She's certainly talented. But your family's cook lets me in through the kitchen and saves me midnight snacks, so I wouldn't feel right casting her aside".

"More coffee, miss?" the servant offered.

"Yes, please." Ellie watched the steaming liquid fill her cup in a graceful stream. The aromas of vanilla and cinnamon danced around her nose as she brought it to her lips and sipped.

Her gaze darted to the hall. It must have been twenty minutes or so since Gabriel had taken John into the study. "Do you think they're almost finished in there?"

Jane poured her own cream. "I should hope so. Then again, I don't know the amount of time required to remove sutures."

"Neither do I." Ellie blew on her coffee, unable to keep herself from looking toward the hallway a second time. With her hands gripping the porcelain tightly, she took another sip.

Jane stared. She tilted her head with an all-too-knowing smile, one that belonged somewhere between dignity and playful suspicion. "Dear girl. If I didn't know any better, I'd say you're beginning to succumb to certain feelings for my cousin."

Ellie lowered her cup. "Gabriel? Oh, never."

"He's quite handsome, is he not?"

"I . . . hadn't noticed." Ellie stirred endless circles with her teaspoon, attempting to hide her flustered expression. "We're old friends, Jane. That's all."

"Is it really all?" Jane narrowed her eyes. "I'm not as naive as you think, you know. I've noticed the way you look at him when he's around. How your eyes light up at his name. And why shouldn't they? Tell me, what is so horrible in admitting it?"

Ellie traced an imaginary pattern on the tablecloth, searching for an answer that wouldn't sound nearly as bad as *I refuse to trust any man because my father betrayed my mother, and I was raped.* Something general, perhaps. "Your imagination must be getting the better of you. He's practically an engaged man. And have you forgotten that your father hates him?"

"Father does not hate him," Jane was quick to say. She set her cup back onto its gold-rimmed saucer and folded her hands in her lap. "He wouldn't have built such a cage around himself if that were true. He's different now that Gabriel is back . . . I can see the pain trapped behind his eyes. One can act irrational when one's afraid of being hurt again. I only wish I knew how to mend things between them."

Ellie nodded. She knew all about acting irrationally, especially when it came to matters of forgiveness. But she wished for Gabriel and Mr. Westgate's reconciliation too, for the family's sake, much more than her own. She despised Jane and John having to sneak around, watching Matthew turn cold and skeptical in Gabriel's presence, and listening to Mr. Westgate feign indifference when she knew he still cared.

"As long as we keep our spirits up, things will turn out just fine." The words barely sounded convincing. She placed the teaspoon on her saucer, eager to change the subject before it returned to Gabriel. "Tell me more about married life, Jane. Is it everything you hoped it would be?"

Jane's eyes lit. "I'm so glad you asked." She dismissed the servants, then waited until they left the room before continuing. "I knew it would be a delight running my own home, but I never would have imagined how . . . *delectable* a few other things could be . . ." Her smile broadened as her cheeks filled with color. "Oh, Ellie. The marriage bed is the best part of all."

"Mrs. Tiller" —Ellie laughed— "how very unexpected of you."

Jane held a hand to her cheek, giggling with embarrassment. "I know it's incredibly improper of me to say, but to truly please a man is unlike anything else in the world."

Ellie fought to remain jovial as her lungs grew tight. She *had* pleased several men, done what each of them had forced her to do, and had sworn she'd rather die than be fondled by one of them ever again. The lust, the pain, the routine of it all—she'd thought nothing could change her mind. Until Gabriel had touched her. And touched her, and touched her . . .

"I do hope there's nothing wrong with me."

Jane's voice broke through her daydreaming.

"Not at all." Ellie reached across the table and patted her wrist. "You should congratulate yourself on being one of the few women with a husband who's adequate in the bedroom."

They shared another heartfelt laugh. How refreshing that dear Jane had found happiness between the bed sheets. Perhaps pleasure—though Ellie might never experience it—truly could exist for a woman.

"It's moments like these that make me wish we could have spent more time together," Jane said with a sigh. "I hope you haven't grown any less fond of me now that I'm married."

"Are you joking?" Ellie rose from her chair and draped her arms around Jane's shoulders from behind. "Even if you'd married a pirate and lived on a ship, you'd still be dearer to me than you'll ever know."

Jane reached up and clutched her. "I feel the same way about you. I told you I'd always wanted a sister, and as far as I'm concerned, you're the most incredible one in the world."

The warm words wrapped around Ellie's heart, yet she couldn't help but wonder if Jane would feel the same way were she to learn about Creekwood. And what about Henry, Matthew and John? Ellie shivered. They must never know.

The sound of a door shutting, followed by a pair of heavy footsteps, echoed throughout the hallway.

"Finished at last," Jane proclaimed, springing from her seat. "And it only took half a century."

It could have taken an entire century if it meant that John's flesh weren't permanently damaged. When the boy strolled into the breakfast room seconds later—with his chin held high and a newly bandaged forehead—Ellie felt slight relief.

Jane rushed to him, brushing his dark hair back with one hand, while straightening his collar. "How did it go?"

"I handled it without a single flinch," John said. He gestured to the bandage. "But I'll have to wear this stupid thing for another few days."

"That *stupid thing* is protecting you from infection and the elements." Gabriel stepped through the doorframe and brushed past him. "By all means, take it off if you'd rather have a gruesome scar for the rest of your life."

"No!" Ellie and Jane shrieked in unison.

Jane snatched her brother's chin. "Don't you dare. You're far too handsome for something like that."

"I'm not so sure." Pursing his lips, John looked at her smugly. "Women love a man with a battle wound. Just think of the stories I could tell."

Gabriel dropped his black medical bag onto a vacant dining chair and poured himself a cup of coffee. "That's called lying, you know." He held the cup to his lips and glared at his cousin. "Don't think I wouldn't tell everyone the truth about your negligence."

"A hypocritical remark coming from you."

Jane's jaw dropped. "John Henry Westgate!"

In that moment, Ellie understood the reason behind their lengthy time in the study. Gabriel must have told John the truth—or most of it—about his absence. He was making progress. If only she possessed the same strength.

"I didn't mean it," John said, smugness turning to shame.

Gabriel sipped his coffee, gripping the back of the chair so hard with his other hand that his knuckles turned white. "No, he's right." He turned to John with a defeated grin. "You're right, you little . . . You're lucky there are women present, otherwise I could think of several words to use."

"In that case—" John extended a hand. "Would an apology do, sir?"

Gabriel spat in his palm before returning the shake.

John's face crinkled in disgust. "Ugh, that's foul play!"

"No, that's how a proper bargain is made."

"A bargain, not a truce," John grumbled, wiping his hand on the leg of his gray knickerbockers. He tilted his head. "But I don't blame you for forgetting, Gabe. I know it's been eons since you were my age."

Gabriel folded his arms, a dark brow arching high. "Are we making old man jokes, then? In that case, I revoke my acceptance of your apology and plan to retaliate."

"What?" John's chocolate eyes went wide. "When?"

Gabriel shrugged. "When you least expect it, of course."

"That's not fair."

"Oh, isn't it?"

Ellie rolled her eyes, eager to end their banter before it escalated into full-on horseplay. "All right, you two. That is quite enough of that."

"Ha!" Gabriel slapped a hand onto his midsection. "Well listen to you, Miss Baker."

"'That is *quite* enough of that!'" John emulated her tone, feigning a feminine pose. "My, how the debutantes and matrons have already influenced you."

She felt the heat of embarrassment warming her ears. *The hellions.* She could burst into laughter and wring both their necks at the same time.

"Don't listen to them, Ellie." Jane placed a reassuring hand on Ellie's shoulder and turned to glare at her male nemeses. "Honestly, sometimes I feel as though I'm dealing with children."

"We only tease out of sheer affection," Gabriel said. Then he smiled, and she swore she could see every one of his perfectly lined teeth.

Damn the man for being the closest thing to divinity she'd ever laid eyes on. Suddenly, the sun filtering through the glass windows felt much warmer on her back, and the increased drumming of her heart clamored all the way up to her ears.

Jane's butler entered the room—a welcome distraction.

"This afternoon's provisions, madam," he announced, displaying the large woven basket in his hands.

"How wonderful!" Jane lifted one corner of the lid and inspected the contents. "Thank you very much, Roberts. You may put this in the carriage."

Ellie watched Roberts bow and make his exit. Finally, some sort of clue. "A picnic?"

"Yes, a picnic," Gabriel said. "But that's all you'll know until we reach our destination."

"Can't you tell me just a little—"

"Shhh." His index finger sliced through the air, silencing her. "Not another word about it." He looked at Jane, who nodded with slight difficulty.

Ellie held up her hands in surrender. "Oh, all right."

She could have tugged at Jane just enough to get another clue, but that wouldn't have been very fair to Gabriel. He exuded a boyish kind of excitement today; something in his step appeared lighter, and his eyes shone with a refreshed vibrance. Seeing him so happy tickled her heart. She could never take that away, so she sat back in silence.

But darn, how she wished she knew where they were going.

* * *

Gabriel struggled to stay awake during the slow, lengthy carriage ride. The gentle swaying—back and forth, back and forth—soothed him like a babe in a rocking chair. He rubbed the space between his eyes, willing the two cups of coffee he'd gulped down to take effect before he started drooling.

The previous night had gone on longer than he'd anticipated, and his voice still felt raw from all his talking in the Tuttle's parlor. But he'd owed them every detail regarding the past four years, no matter how long it took to explain. In the end, they'd bestowed little forgiveness—yet they'd agreed not to expose him, out of respect and loyalty to his parents. It was more than he deserved, but his heart still sank at the thought of losing the Tuttles' friendship. Perhaps someday, by the grace of God, he might hear from them again.

"Is this really necessary?" Ellie asked with a frown. "I feel ridiculous. How much farther is this place?" She looked so adorable in the blindfold fashioned from his cravat, that everything inside him ached to silence her with a hard kiss.

Hell, he wanted to do more than that. He'd cover every inch of those soft, parted lips with his mouth again, tasting her sweetness as she whimpered against him. He shifted in his seat, trying not to grow hard. A carriage ride with his beloved cousins was hardly the place for inappropriate thoughts.

"If you complain again, I'll have to cover your ears and gag you, too," he said, careful to keep the humor from his tone.

Jane drew her lips inward to repress a giggle as the carriage turned down another road.

"You never should have agreed to being blindfolded in the first place," John said smugly. "I would have refused."

Gabriel gave his shin a swift kick. "If you'd refused, then you wouldn't have come along. It's called a surprise, John."

"I know what a surprise is." John kicked him back with force. "Surprise!"

"Why you little . . . That was much harder than when I did it!"

Ellie groaned and threw her hands atop her hat. "Oh, please, don't start again. I'd much rather listen to the horses clopping than you two rough-housing."

Gabriel grinned, baffled as to how her dramatic pout could win him over so easily. But if she was sport enough to endure a lengthy carriage ride without sight, the least he could do was control the urge to brawl with John—no matter how fun.

Leaning forward, he extended a hand out to his cousin. He silently mouthed the word *"temporary"* just before saying, "Truce?"

John spat in his hand and smacked it against Gabriel's with a triumphant smile. "Truce."

Damn. An impressive trick. "Well played, Cousin. Well played."

Gabriel debated getting him back, but white flecks circling high above snagged his attention before he could think of a retaliation. Five seagulls soared overhead—the signal that they were nearing their destination. He hushed all conversation inside the carriage.

"All right, Miss Baker," he said. "We're almost there. Can you guess where we're headed?"

"A park?" she asked.

"No."

"A carnival?"

"Try again."

"Maine?"

"Be serious."

She sat back with defeat and leaned her head against the window. "You aren't making this easy."

"Hold on," he said, as the secluded beach he'd known since boyhood crept into view. The carriage stopped beside the narrow path, now masked by tall, rapidly growing grass. "This should be easy now. Use your senses."

As if on cue, the seabirds began their distinctive squawking. She turned her face toward the window. "I smell—" Her little nostrils flared as she took in a deep sniff. "I smell salty air. And I hear birds . . . and rushing water." She placed three fingers to her bottom lip and jumped in her seat. "Oh! It's the ocean, isn't it?"

"Yes!" He reached out and pulled off her blindfold as Jane and John burst into applause.

Before he could say another word, Ellie had half her body out the window, exclaiming words of pure joy. The white crested waves, the golden-brown sand, the rocky coastline, it was all so new to her. And hell, after four landlocked years, it could have easily been new to him, too. He wouldn't have traded anything for this moment.

"I don't believe it." She pulled herself back inside, dashing a tear from her cheek. "This is the best surprise anyone has ever given me. I can't thank you all enough."

She wrapped her arms around Jane, then John. When she turned to Gabriel, the hesitation behind her eyes gnawed at his heartstrings.

"You're most welcome, darling," Jane said as the coachman opened the door. "But this was all Gabriel's idea, you know. You should really be thanking him." She gathered her parasol and reticule. "Out we go, brother," she ordered John with a flick of her wrist.

Had Gabriel blinked, he might have missed the interesting way she smiled at Ellie just before leaving the carriage. But his curiosity vanished the second he found himself alone with her. The combination of tears and the sun's light made her eyes sparkle like precious emeralds, and when she looked at him, he saw his reflection. Her cheeks flushed pink with excitement, and her cranberry-colored lips stretched into a smile that weakened him.

He'd be a fool to think he didn't feel something deeper than friendship for her. If only he knew what to do about it. The odds in his life weren't exactly stacked in his favor.

"You planned all this for me?" She offered him his cravat. "I . . . don't know what to say."

Her warm, gloveless fingers touched his as he took the neckband. So subtle—so arousing. "You don't have to say anything. The look on your face is all the thanks I require."

"I've dreamt of what the ocean would look like since I can remember. And now that I'm here, it's everything I'd imagined and more." When she gazed out the window, her smile lost some of its sparkle. "I don't deserve this."

He shook his head. "If I'd brought you all the way to the Parthenon, you would have deserved it."

Tiny worry lines formed between her eyebrows. "Why are you always so nice to me? All I do is run my mouth off around you. Those words I said to you in your parlor were just—"

"I seem to remember your apologizing at the opera and forcing me to accept. Honestly, Ellie, I've forgotten all about it."

"I suppose I haven't." She looked down at her hands as she folded them. "You were good enough to doctor both John and myself that day, and the way I mentioned our . . . our—" She cleared her throat awkwardly.

"Kiss?"

"Yes. It was tactless, and the manner in which I behaved afterward was even more uncalled for. It tortures my thoughts day and night."

Tortures? Now it was getting interesting.

He leaned back against the velvet seat, eager to learn more. "There must be a reason why you still pine over it. From my experience, the times when I feel the most consumed by guilt are . . ." He debated testing her, fully aware that the repercussions could be explosive. Yet he decided to try his luck. "When I've lied to someone."

Her eyes snapped up from her hands to his face, her expression the exact one he'd hoped for. She resembled a child with her hand caught in the cookie jar and no place to run. There was no denying it. Somewhere, deep inside her guarded heart, she felt something more for him.

"But then again—" He shrugged. "I'm only referring to myself."

"Of course. Thank you for the insight, Doctor," she answered quickly.

Not wanting to probe the woman he cared for any longer, Gabriel slid across the seat and hopped from the carriage. "Well, *that is quite enough of that*," he said, hoping to draw out a smile by imitating her earlier words. "The shore is calling your name, Miss Baker."

He offered his hand.

She lifted her light blue and cream skirts while clutching his open palm. "You are terrible."

He coiled his fingers around hers. A delicious smirk settled on her lips as he helped her down. She radiated a vitality that drew him like a magnet. Such an attraction would be perilous.

Several minutes later—after everyone's shoes had come off—he stood back, watching her stare out at the vast Atlantic, with Jane by her side. The ocean wind blew their dresses to the left, creating a picture-perfect image, worthy of an artist's canvas.

"I can't believe you spent five years together," John said, coming up beside him. "Do you know how rare that is, to see her again? To have her here?"

Gabriel didn't break his gaze from her backside. "Don't make me regret telling you that."

"I like her . . . a lot. She's different." John shoved his hands into the pockets of his knickerbockers and kicked the sand with his bare feet. "And pretty, too. I've seen your boring behavior around women before. You don't act that way around her."

"No, I don't."

"I know you're pursuing things with Miss Tuttle, and Father has disowned you until the turn of the century. But have you ever considered . . ."

Gabriel eyed him. "Considered what?"

"Never mind," John said with a shrug. "I only meant that women can complicate things, I guess."

"When did you grow so old?" Gabriel clapped a hand on John's shoulder. "It's going to be much harder pulling the wool over your eyes, isn't it?"

John grinned. "I'd say impossible."

Gabriel chuckled. Speaking to John as a friend instead of a kid brother was going to take some getting used to. But he welcomed the change, and the idea of taking part in the boy's promising future. He'd damn well be there in whatever way he could. The same went for Jane.

"What are you fellas doing back there?" Ellie called out.

When he turned to see both women staring, he hollered, "Admiring the view!"

Ellie pulled the sides of her hat down over her face, turning a bright shade of pink.

Jane shook her head as if she were decades older than all of them. "I think it's time for lunch."

Chapter Sixteen

Ellie stared at the last strawberry frosted cookie on the empty dessert plate, trying to convince herself that she didn't want it. The oysters and sandwiches had been filling enough, not to mention the other two cookies she'd already helped herself to. But when Jane offered her the dish, she realized how intensely she must have been eyeing it. She turned to Gabriel and John, who both insisted they were full.

Waste not, want not. But the moment she popped the sugar-sweet morsel into her mouth, Gabriel feigned an appalled look. "I was going to eat that."

Damn him. She pressed a hand to her mouth to keep the crumbs from spilling out as she hurled her napkin at him.

He chuckled, tossing the napkin into the basket. "Everything was delicious, Jane. You and your staff have outdone yourselves."

"Thank you, sister," John added. He attempted to mimic Gabriel's napkin toss, but overshot the basket entirely.

Ellie picked up the cloth and dropped it inside. "Yes, thank you, Jane. Thank you all for this unforgettable day."

"Nothing warms my heart more than spending time with my beloved family," Jane said. "Hopefully, someday soon . . . Father might be able to join us, too."

A short silence followed. Jane smiled tentatively, smoothing her hand over the floral, hand-stitched quilt on which they sat. She looked out at the ocean and sighed. "I've been considering whether to tell you all something today, but I suppose now is as good a time as any." When she turned back to face them, something bittersweet shone in her eyes. "This may be the last time I go on an outing like this for a while. I haven't said a word to Matthew yet, because if he knew . . . then he might not have let me venture out today in my condition."

Ellie froze, shock flying through her.

"Condition?" Gabriel jerked forward, his eyes growing wider than she'd ever seen them. "My God, Jane. Jane!" He grasped Jane's hand and kissed her cheek.

"I'm going to be an uncle!" John exclaimed, throwing his arms in the air.

Ellie tried moving, but somehow, she couldn't. The news still blared in her ears—loud enough to turn the roaring waves pounding the rocks into mere whispers. *A baby?* But it seemed only yesterday Jane had gotten married! Instead of dying down, the winds of change were increasing at an exponential rate. She swallowed hard and bit back tears, recalling the time Jane had told her how Mrs. Westgate had died.

She'd been delivering her third child—a boy, who would have been fourteen had he survived—when she'd suffered fatal complications. The thought of Jane's life being taken in the same way surpassed unbearable. Then Ellie thought of the trials her own mother suffered with Martha. A flash of terrible worry ripped through her.

She watched Jane, now nestled between John and Gabriel, and tried calming her pounding heart. The past wouldn't have its dark hold on her this time. Children played a crucial part in marriage, and in life. Jane wasn't going anywhere—she'd better not. Everything would be fine. No, it would be wonderful.

Swallowing all doubts, Ellie put on an elated smile, wrapped her arms around Jane and joined in the celebration.

By the time she found herself strolling along the ocean with Gabriel, the sun was pleasant, warm against her skin. She hadn't protested when he'd insisted she see more of the beach. She wanted to take in every sight, smell and touch until her senses overflowed. Guilt attached itself to the relief she felt when Jane and John chose to stay behind. She loved them like siblings, yet a senseless excitement stirred within her at the idea of spending time alone with Gabriel.

White, fluffy clouds decorated the bright sky, while the sound of waves lapping the vacant beach soothed her ears. She peered down at their toes sinking into the wet sand, each step inviting childhood memories of playing in the fresh Colorado mud after a rainstorm.

Only, she didn't have to worry about wearing long, expensive dresses back then. The ground would ruin her hem in a matter of minutes if she didn't do something. Keeping her steps in pace, she gathered the fabric into her hands.

"Jane was just sixteen when I left," Gabriel said in a dull, troubled voice. "Now, she's going to be a mother. I can't seem to grasp it. I'm going to worry about her even more."

His distress ate away at her like rust on a railroad spike. Somewhere beneath his calm exterior, she knew thoughts of his aunt vexed his mind.

"Jane is a grown woman. A married one . . ." She looked out at the horizon where the ocean touched sky. "I know it must be strange, but think of all the joy and excitement a baby will bring. Something so wonderful might even . . ." She paused, choosing her words carefully. "*Help* things."

"Your positivity is refreshing."

He glanced down at her. When she saw the resignation in his eyes, she dropped her skirts and stopped abruptly. "I think you should speak to your uncle again."

"Do you?" He halted his strides and raised a dark eyebrow. The way his features tensed—as if fighting off a smile—confused her. The expression conveyed either amusement or sincerity, but she couldn't make out which. Perhaps it was because she stood so close to him.

She summoned her sternest expression. "Please, don't ever stop trying. No matter what."

He lowered his head toward hers, sweeping her away in his azure eyes, which seemed even bluer with the ocean as their background. Warm, familiar feelings coursed through her body, and she looked away in an effort to impose control upon herself. But he reached out and took her chin, turning her back to face him.

"I won't stop." he said, his voice low and husky. "I promise."

He had her again, and again she didn't want to break free. The inside of her mouth grew wet as she focused on the perfect spot between his bottom lip and his chin. Part of her wanted nothing more than to stand on her toes and kiss him deeply.

When he released her, she fought back a shiver. Casually, he offered his arm. The idea of touching him was so tempting that she re-gathered her skirts in an effort to resist the invitation.

"I'm afraid I can't," she said, sounding more disappointed than she'd hoped. "I need both hands to keep my dress from soiling."

He cocked his head to one side and took a step back, his eyes sweeping over her. "I thought I told you to dress light, madam."

"This *is* light." She narrowed her eyes, faking smugness. "I apologize for not packing the appropriate beachwear when I hadn't the slightest clue as to our destination."

It wasn't fair that he could roll up his trousers carelessly and wear nothing but a thin white shirt—which distracted her every time it clung to his solid frame in the ocean breeze.

"Lucky for you, I can fix that problem." He pulled the cravat he'd used as her blindfold from the back of his trousers. She should have known better than to think something so simple could deter him. He knelt to a squat and swiveled his index finger in a circular motion. "Turn around, please."

She did so, thankful that he couldn't see her grin as she released the fabric from the cradle of her hands. Her toes wriggled and dug into the cool sand as he tugged at her from behind. Suppose he were to reach a little further and caress her bare ankle? Gooseflesh spread down the back of her neck at the fantasy.

"There we are," he said as he stood. "How does that feel?"

She twirled around once, feeling the awkward weight of the bulge behind her. "A little strange, but much better, thank you."

"At least your hands are free for more important things, now." He offered his arm once again. "Shall we continue properly this time?"

So much for resisting him. Ellie chewed her lip as she took his arm. She fought hard to ignore the closeness of their bodies and the delicious smell of his cologne as she fell into step beside him.

"So—" When he glanced at her, one corner of his mouth lifted into a grin. "How are things?"

She wanted to laugh at his attempt at idle prattle. "Let's see. I've been socializing with women my own age, I'm becoming quite good at card games, and I'm slowly adjusting to riding side-saddle. Every day, the transition into this new world seems to become a bit more—"

"Bearable."

"I was going to say easier." She shrugged. "But I don't think I'll ever become completely used to it. I've always preferred simplicity."

"Something we've always had in common."

In the short silence that followed, she debated mentioning Mr. Cain. The man had started sending her flowers and gifts, yet only rarely did he grace her with his physical presence. When he did, she found she appreciated the chaperone rule more that she'd ever thought possible. Little did Mr. Cain know that his polite facade and handsome features could never win her over. And those starved *looks* he gave her . . .

But she didn't owe Gabriel any explanations. She didn't. She wasn't his—Emily Tuttle was. Any man could freely pursue her—and fail—without his approval.

"And you?" Ellie glanced up at his profile, entranced by the attractive curve of his jaw as he stared ahead. "I hope you've gained more patients, because if I had my say about it, the entire town would be giving you their business."

"Then I suggest we find you a false beard and a good wig, and have you run for city council." Appreciation lightened his voice, and the heavy sigh that followed suggested he hadn't heard supportive words in a while.

She laughed as they both stepped over a twisted piece of driftwood. "If I dressed as a man, I'd much rather be a lawyer than a politician."

His arm tensed beneath her hand. "Lord, that reminds me. I spoke with my father's lawyer. He's agreed to help me track down the person responsible for destroying my family."

"That's wonderful. I have all the faith in the world that you'll find him," she said. With every fiber of her being, she hoped her words rang true. "Please, tell me if I can help in any way."

"Are you any good at sorting through papers? I have several boxes in my study, all filled with my father's bills, letters, contracts, and God knows what else. I just need one of them to hold some sort of—"

"Yes!" she screeched. He was asking *her* to assist with the possible capture of a criminal? It would prove a welcome change from the lady-in-training routine Mr. Westgate had her practicing nowadays. "I mean, I'd be happy to sort through them at your earliest convenience."

"Would you? I couldn't tell." He smiled at her. She smiled back with ease, not realizing she'd given the crook of his arm an affectionate squeeze, until he noticed.

She dropped her hands and looked away. "I'm sorry."

"For what?" he asked. "Really, Ellie, I assumed we were closer than that."

Her stomach fluttered and her heart flopped in her chest like a fish out-of-water. He was right, they *were* closer than that—much closer. That was the problem. Ever since she'd told him that their passionate kiss meant nothing, she found herself obsessing over the thought of him touching her again. Even worse, she sensed he knew it, too.

It was as if her mind enjoyed playing tricks on her, making her want what she'd pushed away. But in her heart, she feared she'd always wanted him. She wanted him badly.

"That felt a little improper. Etiquette must be getting the best of me," she fibbed. "Perhaps I'm spending too much time with the ladies of the elite class."

He stopped dead in his tracks, took her by the arm and pulled her back. "Good God. If you ever become like them, I'll have something to say about it."

"But I thought you fancied that type of woman." She arched a brow. "You are marrying one, after all."

Oh dear. She'd no right to judge him, even if her reasons were solely due to the fact that she knew him better than anyone else. But the few times she'd seen him in Emily Tuttle's presence made her feel as uncomfortable as he appeared. He became serious, dull and snobbish, suffocating little-by-little as society's puppet. That was never him, even before he'd lost everything.

She squinted and peered up at him, dreading his reaction. But his eyes were calm—so calm, that she wondered whether he'd heard what she'd said.

His gaze fell to a fallen tree trunk at the forest's edge, and he raked his hands through his hair. "May we sit for a moment?"

She nodded. She would have given anything to read his thoughts. Taking the lead, she lowered herself onto the thick piece of eroded wood, nearly snagging her sleeve on a jagged limb while she sat. He claimed the spot beside her, leaving more of a gap between them than she cared for.

He took in a slow, steady breath. "Ellie, about Emily Tuttle and me—"

Harsh crowing interrupted him. Ellie turned toward the sound, to where a band of large sea birds plunged into the water in a perfectly orchestrated show. "What are those?"

"Gannets," he grunted in a voice of frustration. "Obnoxious feathered things. They must have found a school of fish."

She'd never seen anything quite so unique. The birds were like perfectly designed machines, folding their wings back and diving like bullets.

"They're fascinating. Tell me more about them."

"Notice how they're mostly brown in color?"

"Yes."

"When they fully mature, they become white with black-tipped wings. They nest on cliffs and can dive up to thirty feet."

Is there anything the man wasn't good at? "You're quite the bird enthusiast."

"Not really." He chuckled. "Our butler taught me about them when I was a boy. Now there was a man who shared a true passion for all things avian."

"I'm glad you paid attention. Otherwise, I would know nothing about those Gabbots."

"Gannets."

"I knew that." She lifted her chin into the air. "I was only testing you."

"Of course you were." He kicked a heap of sand at her feet.

When she gawked at him, he stared back, eyes glistening with challenge. With a flick of her foot, she sent a load of sand splashing against his trousers. He retaliated, but she quickly evened the score by getting at him once more. His eyes burned with mischief, and he smiled that smile she could look at all day. They were suddenly children again. She gloried briefly in the shared moment.

All too quickly his smile faded, and he shifted his body to face her. "Ellie, what I was saying before . . . about Emily Tuttle and me . . ." Steadiness deepened his gaze. "We spoke last night after the opera. I told her the truth, and I wanted to tell you that our arrangement has been called off."

Called off? She was both astonished and ashamed at the relief she felt, especially when she knew Gabriel had regretted hurting Emily. It showed in his expression. "She didn't like what you had to say, did she?"

He shrugged matter-of-factly. "In her position, would you?"

"I can't say that I would. But thankfully, I'm not in her position."

"No. You aren't. Though sometimes—" He leaned toward her slightly. "I find myself wondering what your position actually is."

His bold, intimidating presence brought every one of her limbs to tingle. She noticed that his neck—along with the bare space of his chest where the top buttons of his shirt were undone—had received an attractive splash of tan. Astonishing how that one, exposed space brought back images of his half-naked frame pressed against hers clear as day.

She picked at a stripped piece of bark. "It certainly isn't to marry . . . especially for love."

"Interesting. A normal person would say the opposite, you know."

The bark chipped, and she dropped the broken piece into the sand. "Maybe I'm not a normal person."

"I see," he said. "After my mother died, I'd often think of how unbearable it would be to lose someone else I loved. That fear was part of the reason I never came back." He shook his head. "But a life alone is no life at all, is it? Love is in our nature."

"Romantic love isn't. Why would anyone want to give her heart away, only to have it stepped on and broken into a million pieces?"

He stood and plucked a flat, smooth stone from the sand. "I'm sure you have plenty reason to think that, but it's hardly true."

"Yes, it is."

"No, it isn't." There was an edge to his voice. "And it's a terrible way to think."

"Not when you've been through what I have," she grumbled. "I have to protect myself. You haven't a clue what I've seen—"

"Then for pity's sake, Ellie, tell me!" He threw his arms out and trudged toward the ocean. He heaved the stone into the water just as he'd done years ago, and it skipped across the surface several times before finally sinking.

God, but he was right. The man had grown up with her, saved her life twice, and spilled his own grievances without fear of judgment. It had been her turn for a while now. He deserved to know about Jasper and Papa.

"Gabriel, wait!"

She knew she'd shot after him too fast when the tie at the back of her skirts came undone. Her feet caught the loose fabric and she plunged into the sand, head first. A pair of strong hands lifted her up. She froze with mortification as Gabriel brushed the tiny granules from her chin.

"Are you all right?" he asked, fighting back a grin.

She shook out her dress, then began dusting herself off. "Yes."

"I'm sorry. I never should have raised my voice." He slid his hands down her arms and took her hands, ceasing her movements. "But my frustration comes from having known you before."

Her embarrassment faded at his touch. His fingers were tender, yet strong, as they grasped hers. "I was a child," she whispered.

Slowly, he leaned into her. "That doesn't matter. I know you now, too. You said you never would have been at that brothel unless your life depended on it . . ." His gaze lowered, as did his voice. "I want to know why you were there. I want to know why you're so afraid of being hurt."

She swallowed, lifting her chin to meet his face. "When I come to help you with your father's files, I'll tell you every word. I promise."

When he leaned in closer, she realized he still had a hold on her. "How does a week from today sound? Say, around noon?"

Her eyes struggled not to close as he caressed her cheek with the back of his hand.

"It sounds . . . grand."

"Good. Now, may I ask you a question?" His delicious breath warmed her skin, like an exotic tea she just had to taste.

"Yes."

Her heart hammered against her ribs as he brought his face toward hers. Losing all resistance, she closed her eyes and parted her lips, tilting her head in anticipation. To her surprise, he bypassed her mouth and went straight for her left ear.

"When I kissed you weeks ago, did it really, truly mean nothing?" he asked softly, his lips brushing against her flesh.

Gooseflesh began peppering the back of her neck, spreading quickly throughout the rest of her body like wildfire. She let out a breath and searched for her voice with no success.

"Because if it did mean something—" He pressed his lips to the tender spot behind her earlobe. "I could always do it again."

His mouth felt like absolute *heaven* as he suckled and nibbled at her earlobe. When his tongue traced along the outer edge, then swirled fiercely around the center, a soft whimper escaped her lips.

"But *you* have to say it." His kisses moved down to her neck, where they grew harder and hungrier as he planted them on every inch of her tingling flesh.

She tried speaking again, yet the words wouldn't come, only her increasing breath as her body ached with desire. Her jaw line soon fell victim to his cruel, teasing kisses. His lips burned hot against her skin, each flick of his tongue sending waves of arousal crashing through her body.

"Say it," he murmured, his lips lingering on her chin.

It meant everything. Please kiss me. Oh, why couldn't she say the words aloud?

"Say it," he repeated, firmer this time.

Kiss me . . .

He planted featherlike kisses across her cheek and down to her lips, where he came to a halt. She shivered as his soft bottom lip brushed along hers.

"Say it, Ellie," he demanded against her mouth.

She'd never heard her name sound so beautiful as it poured like warm honey from his rich, sultry voice.

The sun's rays pricked her eyes when she opened them, bringing the reality of the situation crashing down on top of her. This beautiful man—now the most eligible bachelor in all of New England—stood before her with his lips inches from hers, and she couldn't bring herself to answer. It wasn't fair.

She looked into his eyes. He stared back in waiting silence. Despite how much her heart wanted to believe he'd never hurt her, her mind was an entirely different beast. *Papa betrayed Mama, what makes you think this man won't eventually do the same?* A deep pang spread beneath her ribs once she realized she wouldn't be able to say what he wanted to hear.

As if reading her thoughts, Gabriel released her and backed away. She cast her eyes toward the sand, shielding herself from the vast inches growing between them.

"I'm so sorry," she said, her voice dying off.

His face remained deceptively composed. He opened his mouth as if to say something, but snapped it shut without a word. Folding his arms across his chest, he faced the ocean. The blustering wind, the rolling waves, even the piercing sounds of the sea birds couldn't mask the agonizing silence.

She could no longer bear it.

Wringing her fingers, she took a small step toward him. "Please, say something. Tell me what you're thinking."

"I'm thinking several things," he said plainly. He pointed to a vessel so close to the horizon that it resembled a child's toy. "I'm wondering where that ship is headed, I'm thinking we should probably be turning back now, and—" He shot her a twisted smile. "I'm thinking about how incredibly stubborn you are."

"Stubborn!" She wished she were strong enough to send him straight into the water.

"Yes, stubborn. I don't know what's holding you back, but I'm willing to wait as long as it takes."

She swallowed hard, folding her arms around her midsection as if it would ease the sickness she felt. "You will find then . . . that it will be a waste of your time."

"It's my time to waste." He jerked his head to the left. "Now come on. It's getting late."

He didn't offer his arm. Instead, his hands remained at his sides as he strode several paces in front of her. Better for him not to see the frown she couldn't hide, nor her agitated nail biting, nor her fallen skirts snagging every piece of seaweed in her path. She didn't care anymore.

The only thing on her mind was Gabriel's perplexing persistence. What had he meant by saying he would wait? Would he wait for her to take him to bed, or could he have meant something more? Great God, perhaps their kiss *had* possessed deeper meaning for him. She'd been trying to hide from her own feelings of desire since the moment it happened.

Her heart began to race.

Suppose he truly did desire her? Her vow not to become involved would be shattered. Every glance, every touch and every word would make it all the more difficult to resist him.

Chapter Seventeen

Ellie focused on squaring her hips while urging Lincoln to a gallop. Crop in hand, flexing both ankles, she aligned her spine for balance. Three months might have been a long time to master the art of riding side-saddle, but it was an accomplishment nonetheless. Something had to make up for her spotty piano playing and amateur painting skills. The warm wind lashed her face, bringing with it a feeling of peace and triumph.

When she reached the top of the hill overlooking the estate, she peered back over her shoulder in search of Mr. Cain.

Nowhere in sight, thank God.

He'd surprised her with a visit following breakfast, intent on sharing a horseback ride on this glorious, sunny day. Except she hadn't done much sharing. Instead, she did the most unladylike thing she could think of: Challenge him to a race, then take off and leave him behind before he could answer. Not her finest moment, yet a necessity if she planned on escaping his pursuit.

She gave Lincoln's damp neck a pat, the sweet smell of solitude rushing her nostrils. What would Gabriel say if he saw the way she avoided her lawyer guest? Something wayward or humorous, most likely. She smiled to herself.

The way those lips had searched her neck and demanded a response that day at the beach hadn't left her for a moment. Every part of her had regretted resisting his kiss—that is, until she remembered how he'd called her stubborn.

She pulled her thoughts together, terrified of all she'd vowed to tell him come Sunday. Saying the words aloud meant admitting that Creekwood hadn't just been some nightmare. She'd have to release Jasper, Papa and all those other men from her vault, the one she'd buried deep beneath the sands of her mind, in hopes of losing the memory. Surely then Gabriel would understand the reason behind her assumed "stubbornness." He might take a step back and decide she wasn't worth pursuing—that she was beyond repair. He might stop looking at her the way that made her blood rush to the very places that had once been abused.

An unexpected pain squeezed her heart at the idea. The worry, turmoil and fear of the past had all but burned out her mind. She should stop associating physical intimacy with pain, to accept that Gabriel's touch held comfort and protection, where Jasper's held revulsion and evil.

She clicked her tongue three times, sending Lincoln down the other side of the hill toward the fishing pond, her designated finish line. When she rounded the hedges, she found Mr. Cain waiting beside the water.

Wonderful.

"Well, what a surprise," she said, pulling up on the reins. "Nicely done, sir."

"You gave me quite the run, Miss Baker." The man's grin gave him an unnatural appearance compared to his usual, bland expression. "Little did you know that I'm one of the most competitive people you'll ever come across. Mr. O'Hare was kind enough to provide me with a short cut or two."

She clenched her teeth. Tim would have to pay for this one, the traitor. "Two against one is never a fair race, you know."

He released a low, closed-mouthed chuckle. "Just this once, I shall call it a tie. Now that you've shown me that your riding skills are nearly superior to mine, would you do me the honor of accompanying me back up the hill?"

She glanced at the long stretch of green she'd just ridden. The distance had seemed so short at a gallop's pace, but walking it beside Mr. Cain would surely take an eternity.

"I'd love to, sir." She raked her fingers through Lincoln's coarse black mane. "But I can't guarantee my horse will feel the same way. He was bred for speed."

"I'm sure the animal won't mind." Mr. Cain led his tall gray mount over to her. With its regal stature, long face and dusty charcoal mane, the horse almost resembled him. "Shall we?"

Forcing a smile, she gave a tense nod of consent. She must be the worst at repelling men, for heaven's sake. There was nothing special about her, especially when prettier, better-bred girls could be found all over this town.

They started up the hill, creaking saddles and hoof beats muffling the vast silence between them. Hopefully the absence of conversation might last the entire way.

"Have my gifts been finding you well?" he asked after clearing his throat.

Darn.

"Yes. They're lovely, thank you. But you needn't trouble yourself, sir."

"Please, call me Magnus."

She found her hands squeezing the reins at the request. It would be so easy to send Lincoln flying . . . "If it's all right with you, I'd feel much more comfortable calling you Mr. Cain." Not wishing to completely insult him, she inclined her head and fluttered her lashes.

"As you wish, Miss Baker. Perhaps someday, you might feel otherwise."

The confidence in his voice tightened the knot in her stomach.

She stole a look at him out of the corner of her eye. He sat tall as a towering spruce, his thick dark hair flecked with gray and his skin pulled taught over the elegant ridge of his cheekbones. Even at his older age, Mr. Cain was too handsome a man to remain alone.

"May I ask you somewhat of a personal question?" she said.

"You may."

"Have you ever been married?"

He didn't answer right away. "You must think a man of forty eight years roaming the world alone is a bit odd."

"Not at all. I just assumed that a man of your caliber would have had several prospects at one time or another." Oh, dear. She was supposed to hinder the man, not flatter him.

"You are too kind, Miss Baker," he said with a grin. "It would be ungentlemanly of me to confirm your assumption, but I can tell you that I am indeed a widower. My late wife passed nearly twenty years ago."

She swallowed the sigh of relief threatening to exit her nose. So Mr. Cain *had* been married. Somehow, knowing that made him a little less unsettling.

She didn't ask any more questions, and after a brief discussion involving the weather, they reached the top of the hill. The Westgate mansion stood majestically before them, its four chimneys, multi-shaped roofs and stone balconies capturing her breath, no matter how many times she looked upon it.

"One of the loveliest views in the state, I'd imagine," Mr. Cain said plainly.

She nodded. "In the entire country."

The sun beamed off the glossy front doors as they opened.

Gabriel stormed outside, the tense outline of his shoulders straining against the fabric of his jacket. He mounted his horse, ran both hands through his hair and dropped his head. Ellie squeezed her riding crop. Everything inside her ached to ride down to him. He sat motionless for a moment, then spun his mount around and galloped across the drive, disappearing behind the trees.

Mr. Cain shook his head. "Poor Gabriel."

What did he just say? "Pardon?" Ellie stared at him, her mind whirling.

"That young man is Henry's nephew and my late client's son. Everyone in town had presumed him dead until he returned some months ago. He'd been gone for years." The sympathetic tone of Mr. Cain's voice only added to the pounding of her heart. "I could barely believe my eyes when I saw him again. I can only imagine Henry's reaction. Henry has never been the kind of man to adjust to change easily."

Ellie faltered, trying to comprehend what she was hearing. Her palms grew damp inside her gloves as her head swirled with confusion. The man pursuing her was the same man helping Gabriel? Dear God, no. Just thinking of it stirred blinding panic. If Gabriel ever found out—if he confronted Mr. Cain and severed their alliance—the chances of avenging his mother would prove impossible. After all he'd been through, she refused to stand in his way.

That's why she would put on a good face and remain silent, something she might be able to manage as long as Mr. Cain didn't take another step closer.

* * *

Gabriel reached into the washbasin and splashed cold water on his face. Clutching the dresser, he stared into the mirror, watching the beads of moisture drip down his neck and onto his bare chest. Slowly, he exhaled.

For the hundredth time, he glanced down at the opened note sitting beside the basin. When he'd written the headmaster at Harvard, requesting further details regarding the guest teaching position, he hadn't expected a timely response. Not only did the ink on the page drip with enthusiasm, but the offer appealed in every way. A handsome salary. A well-balanced curriculum. The career opportunity of a lifetime—were he to meet and impress the right people.

God, but the timing couldn't have been worse.

He reviewed the third line from the bottom again, willing the *six months* written there to magically change to two or three. Just when his patient numbers were increasing, he'd have to abandon them again. His family's case would grow cold, Jane would be eight months along by the time he returned, and Henry would become even more of a stranger. The weight of responsibility kept piling atop his shoulders like wet bricks. But thinking over it now had little point. The events of the past few days had left his brain drained, hollow and lifeless.

Pulling his shirt from the bedpost, he straightened to relieve the ache in his shoulders. Monday, Tuesday, Wednesday—they'd all consisted of routine doctoring and several house calls. He'd been glad to see so many new faces and familiar patients, their ailments all minor to moderate. But he hadn't been prepared for Thursday, when a visit to the Greene family had affected him in ways he'd long since forgotten.

David Greene, the owner of a gentlemen's hat shop in town, had been concerned when his youngest son Jacob had fallen ill. One glance at the six-year-old child and Gabriel knew that advanced scarlet fever had taken hold. There was no hope of recovery. Yet in the days that followed, he'd worked tirelessly to administer the best available treatments, trying to keep the boy as comfortable as possible as he clung desperately to life.

Gabriel closed his eyes, reliving the pain of that final scene this morning. It had been but five hours since he'd witnessed the child struggle for his last breath. Yet another life he'd failed to save.

"Dammit!" He pounded a fist against the bedpost and clutched his hair as if it would help him regain control. But the sense of grief was overwhelming.

He sank to the floor, allowing tears to drip from his tired eyes as he recalled the earth-shattering cries of Jacob's parents and five siblings. He'd tried to comfort them, but how could he, when every word fell so short?

Loss, illness, death. He'd forgotten how hard it all was.

Dragging a hand down his face, he peered at his father's old clock on the shelf. Nearly noon. Ellie would be arriving within minutes. If anything could lift his spirits, her jesting quips and radiant laughter could. But he wouldn't try kissing her today; he wouldn't do that for a while, after her resistance at the beach. He just wanted to spend time with her, to bask in the glow she exuded, while they sat in the privacy of his home.

Sporting a fresh necktie, waistcoat, and trousers, he reached the bottom of the staircase as the first of three knocks sounded from the door. His heart did an odd flop in his chest as he grasped the handle and pulled the door open.

Ellie's bright smile greeted him. His worries blew away like smoke as she held out her burgundy skirt and offered a comical curtsy. Could she possibly be more breathtaking than the last time he saw her?

He rewarded her with a larger smile of his own, then matched her with an exaggerated bow. "Did young Harry see to your horse, madam?"

"But of course, sir," she said. "The boy is impeccably attentive."

"And you managed to get away unnoticed?"

She wrinkled her freckled nose. "If you mean did I pay Jane an afternoon visit, then yes."

"Good." He stepped aside, extending an arm in a welcoming gesture.

She walked into the hall slowly, hips swaying, then turned to him once he'd shut the door. "Something's wrong. What happened?" she asked, a crease of concern on her brow.

He shook his head, baffled as to how she could have picked up on his mood so quickly. Unless he truly did look as plagued as he felt. "Nothing's wrong."

She removed her shawl, exposing the porcelain flesh of her neck. "I've known that expression for years . . . Ever since the day your old dog died." She moved closer to him. Heat spread up his arm when she reached out and touched it. "Besides, I can see it in your eyes. Please, tell me what's the matter."

He studied her face, feature by feature, wishing he could read her the same way. Despite his frustration, he appreciated her concern. "I lost a patient to scarlet fever this morning. He was a young boy . . . very young, and I've—" He felt his arm tense beneath her hand. "I've been having a difficult time accepting it."

"I'm so sorry, Gabriel," she whispered, her hand on her breast.

"His fever had become rheumatic. His heart was too weak to battle the infection. There was nothing I could do." His voice snagged on the last word and he cleared his throat. "God, I can't help but feel responsible. I always feel responsible for these things . . ."

To his astonishment, she wrapped her arms tightly around his torso and pressed her head to his chest. He shut his eyes, allowing her warmth to penetrate to his very center. As he slid his arms around her slender frame, he imagined that she was his, if only for a moment.

"You mustn't blame yourself," she said tenderly. "Some things are beyond our control, no matter how much we'd like to change them. I'm sure the boy's family was grateful for all you did."

Gabriel knew he couldn't control everything, yet he battled with that idea too often. "It's days like this when I fear the future most," he admitted, resisting the urge to stroke her back. "I fear what I'll see, what I might be challenged with, and whether I'll be strong enough to bear it."

"You are strong enough." She gripped him tighter. "You're passion for others is what gives you strength. You doctor because you care. I have such respect for what you do."

Bless this woman.

The floral aroma of her hair reminded him of his mother's rose garden—the way it would smell after a spring shower. It begged him to bury his face in it and inhale deeply. She was too close—too tempting. If he didn't let go of her now, he would surely lose all control. Reluctantly he released her, which allowed her to do the same.

A quick change of subject was in order.

"That means a great deal, thank you," he said, smoothing a hand across his brow. "Can I bring you anything before we get to work? The sooner we start, the better."

He forced himself to focus on the task at hand, not the subtle curves beneath her clothing. His father's documents wouldn't search themselves. Days ago, after pulling every box from the attic, he'd started digging through a few of them himself. The stocks, grants and labor reports had eventually blurred into one massive document. Even with Ellie's help, it would take a miracle to finish the job.

"No, thank you." She began removing her gloves, tugging up each fingertip, one-by-one. "I had a large lunch for the sole purpose of being entirely at your disposal." She stuffed the white gloves inside her reticule before tossing it onto a chair in the hall.

At his *disposal?* Christ, she had no idea how sensuous her voice sounded. He inwardly recited the names of all the states to keep the blood from swelling his cock.

She strolled into the study, gazing back over her shoulder with a smile so innocent that it made him ache all over. He flexed his jaw to keep from groaning. Damn if the woman's mixed signals didn't thwart him to no end, flirting one minute and pushing him away the next.

When he caught a glint of merriment behind those green eyes, he suddenly got the feeling she knew exactly what she was doing to him.

Chapter Eighteen

"I have some sort of contract here for the purchase of steel." Ellie held up the piece of paper she'd been struggling to interpret for far too long. "Where does this one go?"

"Put it in the construction pile over there," Gabriel said, gesturing to the tall stack three piles to her right. He pulled off his reading glasses and rubbed the space between his eyes. "How are you making out? Are you ready to jump off a cliff yet?"

She squeezed her eyelids shut, then opened them as far as they could stretch. Anything other than staring at ink on paper would be a welcomed relief. "Not at all, but I can't deny that my eyes might fall out of my head."

He held up his eyeglasses. "Maybe you should borrow these."

"Those would only make things worse," she said with a giggle.

"Suit yourself." He grinned and positioned them back onto his face. "No doubt I look much better in spectacles, anyway."

Sliding the frames halfway down his nose, he mimicked an old man's expression that should have made her laugh. Instead, she pressed her lips shut to prevent herself from drooling as she helplessly stared at him. When he dropped his head back down to immerse himself in the papers he held, a few brown locks fell across his forehead.

She studied his every feature as he scanned the ink lines and puckered his full lips in concentration. He was so very handsome. Only Gabriel could joke about wearing reading glasses without realizing how well they actually complimented him.

When his eyes caught hers, her heart stuttered. He dropped the remaining documents into the box beside him, pulled out his pocket watch and gave it a glance. "It's been nearly two hours. A break is well overdue."

"Agreed," she said quickly, setting her paper atop the construction pile.

She couldn't have brought herself to concentrate much longer anyway, not when she'd promised to tell him everything about the brothel. From the moment she'd stepped through his doorway, the urge to get the haunting story over with had pressed hard on her soul. But accepting what happened couldn't be much harder than hopeless denial, so she promised herself she wouldn't back down.

Gabriel rose to his feet, his gaze sweeping the cluttered library. "I never could have gotten through all this without you. You're a champion, Miss Baker." His hands moved to rub his firm, round bottom. "My posterior, however, is not."

A chuckle emerged from beneath her nerves as she joined him in standing. "Discomfort is but a small price to pay for good company. There's little else I'd rather be doing than spending time with you."

A bold choice of words, but Gabriel's nearness did kindle feelings of comfort and warmth, like a cheerful Christmas carol on a wintry night. When her eyes found his, she noticed a hint of pink had kissed the space atop his cheekbones. Did she actually make him blush? Her toes curled at the idea of affecting him in that way.

"Likewise," Gabriel said. The way he leaned on the desk's edge caused the fabric of his trousers to gather so tightly around his crotch that she had to tear her eyes away.

Admit it, Ellie. You're attracted to him.

"May we sit?" She gestured to the two armchairs beside the fireplace. "A week ago, I made you a promise, and I'd like to tell you everything now . . ." Her mouth went dry as she clasped her hands behind her back. "If you don't mind, that is."

"I don't mind at all." He stood up straight, relieving her of the distracting view. "Do you need anything before you—"

"No, thank you."

He nodded. A thousand butterflies batted against her ribcage as she rushed to the smaller chair and sank into the cushion. Without taking his eyes off her, Gabriel took the opposite seat and rested his back against the dark green upholstery. He placed his hands in his lap, fingers entwined, still as a statue.

"Now you're being too serious," she half-laughed, half-choked.

What's the matter with you? What's next, asking him to face the other way? Not to breathe? She offered him a look of apology.

Frustrated at her lack of words, she wished the ability to speak came as naturally as her ability to delay.

"It's only me, Ellie." His words were as cool and clear as ice water. "How's this? I'll tell you something that only I remember. Something that might ease your mind."

She sighed. Gripping the wooden arms of her chair, she inched her bottom toward the center of the cushion and allowed him to continue.

"It was early afternoon," he said, removing his glasses. "Your mother stood on our doorstep with a pie in her hands, chatting with my mother for what seemed like eons to a nine-year-old boy. I remember being crouched on the stairs, bored out of my mind, and bitter about our move across the states." He paused for a moment, then grinned. "Suddenly, a small girl emerges from behind your mother's skirt. When she spots me, she wastes no time or manners in strolling right into my house and up the staircase." His smile broadened. "She extends a tiny hand and says, 'Hello, boy. Come see my new ducklings!' How could I have said no? So I followed her down to the pond that day, and we watched the ducks play for hours." He gazed at her, his eyes soft with fondness. "That was the first day we met."

She couldn't believe it. He'd remembered everything.

Her heart swelled inside her chest, and she felt her smile grow so big it nearly reached her ears. No response on earth could properly show her appreciation for what he'd just shared with her. Perhaps he wasn't expecting one.

No, the best thing she could do for him was begin.

"Twelve years ago, my father died in a stampede. He'd barely opened the gate to the cattle pen when they all went wild." She breathed past the ache already settling beneath her ribs, but her throat constricted even tighter. "It was awful. Our animals had never done anything like that before. A part of me died that day. I was so angry at Papa for leaving me . . ."

She dropped her eyes before his steady gaze and shrugged. "Pretty soon, we could no longer afford to pay the ranch hands. A couple of them stayed out of kindness, God bless them. But no amount of work we did could put a dent in Papa's debts. The collectors came over the years, Mama got sick with cancer . . . and we watched the life we'd known disappear before our very eyes. When my mother died, I couldn't bear the memories surrounding me."

"You moved to Creekwood to get away," Gabriel said, his tone somber and concerned. "Your parents were both wonderful people. I'm so sorry you had to lose them."

She turned her attention toward the tree branches swaying outside the window. The vibrant green leaves fluttered happily in the summer wind, unaware that the encroaching fall would mean their demise. A shiver ran through her. She didn't want to be like those leaves—torn from her place of safety once everyone discovered her shameful secret.

She released a ragged breath. "Alone and penniless. The perfect combination that might lead someone to believe me desperate enough to become a whor—"

"Don't," he said. "Don't say it." He closed his eyes momentarily, displaying a mixture of frustration and sadness. "Just tell me what really happened to you."

"He threatened me," she blurted.

Gabriel shifted in his seat. "Who did?"

"Jasper." His name felt like poison on her tongue. "He approached me in town one day with a promising job offer. He said he'd known my father for years."

"Dear God." Gabriel's hands clamped onto his thighs, his eyes burning with outrage.

"He was a good actor. He'd seemed so . . . genuine," she admitted. "I knew I'd be hard-pressed to find work anywhere else. Besides, I was hungry and desperate." Folding her arms close to her body, she clutched her elbows. "Once I saw The Inn . . . Once I saw what it truly was, I rejected him and tried to leave. But Jasper didn't let me. He forced me into his office and told me exactly how he knew my father."

Gabriel stared at her, fists clenched, his chest barely moving with shallow breaths. He said nothing.

Avoiding his penetrating stare, she summoned the strength to continue. "Papa had visited Creekwood several years ago. He'd gone to The Inn and . . . *slept* with Jasper's sister. He enjoyed her so much that he returned several times, just to see her again. I can only imagine how long it continued before she became pregnant." An empty anger filled her, and she bit back the urge to scream. "Papa threatened to end his visits unless she aborted the child. She tried, but it ended up killing her."

"That can't be true," Gabriel said, his voice like cold steel. "I knew your father, Ellie. The man would have sooner died than sleep with some harlot. His family, his cattle and his ranch were his entire life."

"How can you be so sure?" She could feel her voice starting to shake. "He wooed my mother at a fair. A fair, for God's sake. She had a family, a life, and he pulled her away from it all just to chase some selfish dream!"

"You can't possibly know how your mother felt, Ellie."

"It doesn't matter how she felt because, either way, my father betrayed her. You weren't blind to what happened at that horrible place, where countless husbands and fathers pay right through the nose for a little piece of pussy."

Gabriel's eyes shot wide and his mouth fell open. Ellie didn't pretend to ignore what she'd just said. Never before had she used such vulgarity, but the tremors of emotion rocking her pulse kept her from caring. Every vivid recollection came back to her, as if she were reliving the terror all over again. But the urge to keep going burned like a hot coal inside her.

When she rose from her chair, he did the same. He drew in a breath to speak, but she stopped him with a raised hand. His mouth clamped shut and his jaw twitched.

Turning her back to him, she paced toward the bay window. "Jasper told me I owed a debt on my father's behalf. It wasn't money he wanted."

"No . . ." Gabriel growled.

She stared blankly through the glass. Her stomach tossed at the memory of Jasper's filthy, merciless thrusting—stripping her of her virginity, and her very life. Moisture filled her eyes, blurring everything she saw, like rain on fresh paint. This time, she couldn't stop it. She let the unshed tears spill in ribbons down her cheeks.

"I tried to fight him off, but I couldn't." She glanced back at Gabriel.

The man might as well have been witnessing a murder. The color had completely drained from his face, and he stood motionless in front of his chair like an expensive museum exhibit. "He held me down and . . ." Her voice closed off with an awkward squeak, and then she collapsed onto the window seat in a bundle of sobs.

Within seconds Gabriel had his arms wrapped around her like steel binding. She buried her face in his shoulder, allowing her sobs to continue in a much-needed release. Her secret was out, but among the guilt and shame she felt something much stronger— Freedom.

"You don't have to say any more," he said as he rocked her gently, like he'd comforted dozens of blubbering women in his lifetime. "The God damned son of a bitch. I should have killed him. I should have killed him when I had the chance."

She could feel the thrashing of his heart as he buried his fingers in her hair, sheltering her inside a cocoon of protection. His breaths were short, yet heavy. His body shook angrily against hers. Several minutes later, when her sobs finally faded into whimpers, she felt him relax a little.

Lifting her head, she looked down at the puddle she'd left on his shirt. "You might . . . need to wash this," she said, feeling a weak smile emerge beneath her tears.

"I could care less about a shirt." He clutched either side of her face, his eyes reaching deep into her soul. "What I care about is you. I haven't the words to tell you how sorry I am." Wiping the humiliating moisture beneath her nose with his thumb, he added, "I'll never forgive myself for assuming you'd chosen that life."

"That's foolish." She pulled his hands from her face and jerked to her feet so fast that her head spun. "Have you been so quick to forget that you're the reason I'm here? You fought to get me out of that place and into that coach. I owe you my life."

"You owe me nothing."

"You're the only person who knows this now." She brought the tip of her thumbnail to her front teeth. "The Westgates can never find out. Nobody can."

"They'd understand."

"No," she said. "They're the only family I have now. I won't take the risk in telling them something so shameful." She sank down onto the window seat cushion, her pulse finally slowing. "Jasper ruined every chance I had at a normal life. But he also opened my eyes to the betrayal I'd never known. I refuse to end up like my mother."

Gabriel pulled a handkerchief from his trouser pocket and smoothed it across her cheek. "And that is why you're set on not marrying?"

She nodded.

"Ellie—" He shook his head. "I know you've been hurt in ways I could never understand, but you have to know that not all men are unfaithful scoundrels."

"I don't know what I know anymore." She watched the sparrows hopping in the grass, trying to tame the bitter emptiness she felt.

"You don't know, because you've never experienced anything other than being ravaged and used." Tenderly, he brushed beneath each of her eyes with the kerchief. "What a shame it would be to live out your days alone, never knowing the true pleasure a good man could give you."

"There's no such thing as true pleasure," she said with a sigh. "Even if there were, I doubt I could feel it if I tried."

His gaze took an intimate turn. "Something tells me you've already felt it. You've just been too afraid to acknowledge it."

She tore her eyes from his. The harder she tried ignoring the truth, the harder it persisted. The night she'd succumbed to him in the cabin; the afternoon at the beach when he'd smothered her neck with demanding kisses—of course she'd felt something then. Her skin had tingled, her pulse had pounded and the most intimate place between her legs had awakened as if it had a mind of its own. Desire had filled her every bone. Those feelings must have been close to pleasure—perhaps the closest she'd ever get. But how could she know for sure?

She looked into Gabriel's azure eyes, then down to his stubble-coated jaw, then at his strong, masculine physique. Breathtaking. If she had any hope of experiencing so much as a hint of what Jane had carried on about, he'd be the perfect candidate to try with. Fatigued, liberated, exposed, Ellie had nothing left to lose. A lifetime of solitude didn't mean she couldn't enjoy one afternoon in the arms of a man she knew better than any other.

It would be like an experiment. A silly, educational experiment.

Drawing in a deep breath, she rose to her feet and backed slowly toward the center of the room. "All right, Gabriel. Show me what I don't know."

Chapter Nineteen

Her bluntness must have surprised him more than she'd thought, because he'd failed to stand when she did. He looked like she'd just struck him.

"I . . . beg your pardon?" he stammered.

"I want you to have me however you like." Ellie kept her voice steady, to show she wasn't fooling. "You seem so confident in proving to me that there's something I'm missing."

Surrendering herself to him should have made her feel insane. Yet as she took in Gabriel's bewildered expression, she tasted nothing but eagerness and excitement. This was something she wanted—something she *needed* to try for herself.

"You're being serious?" His tone remained cautious as he stared at her.

"Yes." She cast her arms out to the sides, opening herself up in every way. "Now, will you have me, or not?"

His gaze never left hers as he slowly, carefully rose to his feet. After two small steps he stopped, waiting for her reaction like a hesitant puppy.

She rolled her eyes. "I'm not going to change my mind."

"I was only making sure." He raised his palms in a gesture of surrender. One corner of his mouth curled into a crooked grin. "Otherwise, what kind of gentleman would I be?"

Tingles spread across her body as he approached, each step increasing her heart rate until she thought it would leap from her chest. He halted in front of her, just as he had at the beach. Only this time, she wouldn't resist him.

"Allow me to make one thing clear," he said, his gaze cascading down to her lips.

"And what is that?" She wondered if there would ever come a day when his close presence didn't make her heart pound and her breath catch.

Gabriel took hold of her shoulders, sliding his hands gently down her arms until he'd reached her fingertips. Clutching her hands, he lifted them to his mouth and pressed his lips onto each knuckle. She shuddered at the intimate contact, each kiss permanently branding her flesh like a hot iron.

"You said you wanted me to have you however I like . . ." He stared at her over the raised ridges of her knuckles, his magnificent eyes burning with passion. "Well, today isn't about what I like. It's about what *you* need, and you must understand that in order for me to continue."

Struggling for coherence, she couldn't bring herself to answer. She simply nodded, allowing her lips to part in anticipation of feeling his kiss pressed against her mouth again. He pulled her arms around his waist, and she instinctively clutched the thick fabric of his waistcoat.

Her eyes fluttered shut, and she leaned into his palm when he pressed a hand to her cheek. The moment his lips touched hers, she was swept away into another world. She returned the pressure of his kiss, moving her mouth in passionate rhythm as their lips embraced in a tender reunion. Those soft, caressing lips felt more exceptional than she remembered, and she savored every taste as she matched them, kiss-for-kiss. Each time she thought it couldn't get any better, he'd increase his pace, suckling and searching her mouth, while his delightful afternoon stubble chafed her skin.

Pulling away slowly, she allowed her breath to catch as the blood rushed to her tingling lips. The subtle scent of his musk roused her senses. He brushed his mouth against hers, wordlessly requesting permission to continue.

It was too much to handle.

Standing on her tiptoes, she reclaimed his mouth with reckless force. All at once the room started to spin, growing hotter by the second as their wet, starved lips combined in perfect unison. Gabriel moved his hands to her hair, sliding his fingers between her pinned curls as he slid his tongue inside her mouth. She parted her lips wider, coaxing him deeper, and she whimpered when he teased her tongue in a tender, yet dominating way. Her own tongue plunged and prodded back, lapping up every delectable flavor in his irresistible mouth.

Heavens, he was delicious, and the sound of his loud breathing against the silence of the room brought an unfamiliar wetness between her legs as she mindlessly melted into him. He pressed up against her, releasing a carnal moan from somewhere deep within his throat.

When she felt the hard evidence of his desire through her skirts, she held back the urge to rub up against it. She was no stranger to erections. In the past, she'd wanted nothing more than to run at the slightest chance of contact with one. But Gabriel didn't scare her like those men. For once, she found herself relishing every forbidden part of the male frame.

Clutching him tighter, she found herself longing to see his bare flesh—wanting to feel what she alone had done to his body, without the barrier of fabric in the way.

He tore his reddened lips from hers and searched her eyes. "How are you feeling?"

Breathless, she traced a finger along his coarse jaw in her best, flirtatious effort. "I'm not sure. I think you may need to try harder."

"Harder, huh?" His eyes sparked with wickedness. "That can be arranged, madam."

Within seconds, his powerful arms wrapped around her legs, just beneath her bottom. She laughed, holding onto his broad shoulders as he hoisted her straight up toward the ceiling. Drawing her arms around his neck, she kissed him, giving herself freely to passion as they stumbled carelessly about the room. Her body shivered and burned beneath her clothing at the hope of his caressing her naked skin in ways no man had before.

Gabriel lowered her onto a hard, familiar surface. Her eyes shot open.

"Wait," she gasped, tearing her lips from his.

He brushed the strands of hair from her face. "What is it? What's wrong?"

She lowered her hand to clutch the edge of the smooth mahogany beneath her, fingers trembling as she stroked the underside. Ellie had been roughly stripped of her virginity atop a similar desk, but now that seemed a lifetime ago, a hazy memory from a darker world.

Heart still pounding with desire, she gazed into the eyes of the passionate man standing before her. Sensual, beautiful and kind—three of the thousands of words she could use to describe him. The present moment couldn't be farther from the past. If anyone could doctor the infection Jasper had spread throughout her body, it was Gabriel.

Reaching up, she pushed the dark strands from his forehead, savoring the touch of his hair. So soft. She'd never felt it before. "Nothing's wrong. It's just that I'm . . . so hot."

He brushed his lips against her ear. "Allow me to help you with that."

She sighed as his mouth moved to the flesh of her neck, his masterful lips dancing around her beating pulse. She half-moaned, half-laughed at the contact, and her skin rose with plucked gooseflesh just as it had before.

Gabriel drew back and moved his fingers to the first button of her blouse. Thank God she'd chosen to wear simplistic clothing today. She unfastened her skirt as his hands worked swiftly and impressively down the front of the garment. He slid the open blouse down her shoulders, exposing her collarbone and bare arms.

She'd barely had time to suck in a sharp breath as he lowered his lips to the uncovered skin just above the laced line of her chemise.

He exhaled against her chest. "Better?"

"Not yet . . ." she whispered, finding the words came out with no effort at all.

He lifted his face and pressed a hard kiss to her lips.

"Bear with me on this part," he said with a low chuckle. The heat of his breath rippled across her mouth, causing every nerve to tingle with a need for more.

He toyed with the first busk of her corset, finagling the metal clasp every which way, until it finally popped open. The second busk opened faster, and the third even faster than that. Four, five, six. Each click sounded a desperate release.

He removed the whalebone encasing and tossed it to the floor. In the face of a newfound freedom, Ellie reminded herself to maintain slow, shallow breaths. The last thing she wanted to do now was faint, bringing an abrupt end to the only true intimacy she'd ever known.

Afraid that if he kissed her again she might lose consciousness, she turned her attention to him. "What about you?" She fingered the fabric between two of his waistcoat buttons. "You must be burning up."

The corners of his lips raised into a devastating smile. "Stifling."

He stood completely still, allowing her trembling fingers to unbutton his brown waistcoat, one button at a time. She parted the open seam to reveal the buttons of his shirt, hidden underneath. Then she lifted her eyes to his with a look of question, which he answered with a nod of his head.

This time her hands steadied with determination as she unbuttoned his tear-stained shirt, bottom to top. With one fair swoop, she pushed both waistcoat and shirt back over his broad shoulders, allowing him to shrug them off the rest of the way.

Leaning back, she gaped at his spectacular physical form.

Sure she'd seen his bare torso before, when the dim light cast by the fire had created playful shadows across his sound frame. Yet here he stood now, positioned before her in the light of day, leaving nothing to her imagination. She could barely breathe. Something— either his rough and tumble life in Colorado, or perhaps a daily routine of exercise—must have attributed to contouring his exquisite body.

Beautifully molded cords of muscle shaped his arms and chest, while his firm, chiseled abdomen appeared to have been carved from stone. A light dusting of coarse hair draped across his chest and formed a thin line just beneath his belly button, ending somewhere beyond the waistband of his trousers. Beside his left armpit, a uniquely shaped scar hugged the far side of his chest. She counted her blessings and gave silent thanks. Three inches to the right, and that shot would have taken his life.

Reaching for his torso, she ran her fingers along the ripples and crevices of hard muscle. His skin felt so warm that she wanted to press her face to it. "You must be the only man alive who looks like this."

He grinned. "Thank you for the compliment, but I can assure you I'm not."

"Well, you're the only one I care about."

"I won't argue with that," he murmured, lighting her skin on fire as he brushed his fingertips across her bare collarbone. "But I appear to have less clothing than you now. I wouldn't want to make you jealous."

She took his hand and guided it to the satin strap of her chemise. "Then you had best even the score."

His eyes smoldered. He slid both straps down her arms, causing the top of the garment to drop to her waist, revealing her bare breasts.

He settled his gaze on them, entranced. "Oh, Ellie. You're so beautiful."

She smiled, stunned that she hadn't tried to cover herself. For the first time in her adult life, she truly did feel like more than a piece of mere flesh. "Kiss me," she begged.

His mouth captured hers. She moaned against his lips as his rough hand covered one breast, bringing her nipples to harden beneath his stimulating touch. They fell back against the desk in tandem, sending books, papers and pens crashing to the ground.

Reaching down, she yanked up the hem of her chemise, all modesty vanishing. Her legs clamped around one of his thighs, and he groaned as she moved her hips against him in a most unladylike way.

"You have no idea what you're doing to me," he muttered.

He lowered his face to her breast and covered it with his hot, wet mouth. She arched her back and moaned, raking her fingers through his hair. The way he suckled and swirled his tongue around the sensitive peak of her nipple stirred a wild thrill inside her. It was as if every nerve in her body had suddenly awakened with the push of a button, starving her of both breath and thought.

"Oh . . . God," she whispered.

His lips moved to her second breast, while his hand toyed with the first. Ellie dug her fingers into his shoulders, abandoning herself to his every touch as he claimed her breasts simultaneously. Wrapping her legs tighter around his thigh, she pulled him even closer.

His hardness dug against her hip. She couldn't resist this time. Instinct drove her to grind up against him like a wild animal, her whole being flooded with desire.

Gabriel groaned and released her, causing an unwelcome surge of cold air to prick her skin. "Slow down, my dear," he rasped. "You might finish me off here and now if you keep doing that."

She gave an apologetic smile, yet a thrilling realization dawned on her. *I'm the one controlling him?* Every other man had controlled her, using their strength and sex as a means of power. But now the power rested in her hands—in her body. As much as she thrilled at the thought, she couldn't deny that Gabriel possessed something over her, too. A new, welcome sensation that sent her soaring to the stars at his every touch.

Slowly, sliding from the desk, he kissed a path down the center of her stomach before planting his lips right on her inner thigh. He gripped her hips, and in one swift motion, pulled her bottom to the edge of the desk. Ellie lifted her head as he parted her legs and cupped the space between her thighs with a warm hand. What could he be doing? Her nerves fluttered a little, but the confidence in his eyes told her to trust him.

"I'm going to show you what true pleasure is," he said, spreading her tender flesh apart with his fingers. He looked at her with a deep hunger that suggested he, too, was about to fully enjoy himself.

Lowering her head back down, she closed her eyes . . .

The warmth of his lips made contact. She held her breath, her mouth gaping wide with soundless cries. His tongue traced and lapped around her opening as if he were tasting her like candy, shattering the hard shell she'd built around herself so carefully.

"Breathe, sweetheart." His low purr vibrated against her flesh in a way that made her cry out.

She glanced up to find him staring at her. God, he was right. She hadn't been breathing. Her lungs pushed out a gust of air before sucking a new one into its place. He grinned with satisfaction, then lowered his head and reclaimed her flesh. This time, she made it a point not to withhold her whimpers and moans.

Squeezing her eyes shut, she reached out and clutched both sides of the desk as he suckled the most sensitive pearl of nerves beneath the folds of her flesh. She couldn't disguise her body's reaction. He'd found her very core. When he slid a finger deep inside her slick opening, she lost all control and cried out against the combined pressure of his hand and mouth.

The euphoric feeling was so powerful, so concentrated on that one part of her body, that it baffled her. Yet at the same time, it somehow managed to reach out and fill every other part of her as if she were under some kind of pleasure spell.

Finally she arched her body into him, allowing the ecstasy to consume her while she cried out over and over until the explosion gradually subsided.

Her head swam. She opened her eyes to find Gabriel staring at her.

"Incredible," he said.

Without another word, he rose to his feet, kicked off his shoes and began unfastening his trousers. Seconds later, they dropped to the floor.

She gazed upon his lower half, trying not to drool.

Between his strong, toned thighs and below his narrow hips sat the hard length of his sex, thrusting proudly in her direction. It was exquisite—and God, how she wished it had been the only one she'd ever laid eyes on.

Her body craved to have him inside her.

She reached out to him, spreading her legs eagerly as he climbed on top of her and covered her body with his. He pressed a kiss to her lips, the tip of his erection finding her wet, ready entrance.

"I promise I'll be gentle," he murmured.

"I trust you."

She sighed as he slowly eased himself into her body, filling her inch-by-inch with his thickness. The warmth of his flesh was intoxicating. He felt so big. For the first time, she could celebrate her absent virginity as he entered her entirely with one last thrust.

A perfect fit.

Face-to-face, man-to-woman, they were one.

He exhaled as his hips pressed a gentle, rhythmic motion into her, each thrust sending a greater ripple of pleasure throughout her than the last. She couldn't get enough of him. Digging her fingers into his lower back, she pushed her hips upward, sending him deeper into her body.

"Good Lord," he moaned. He shook his head, gazing at her in awe. "Whatever you're doing, don't stop."

Knowing how good she made him feel made her body respond in ways she never thought possible. The pressure of his pelvis—plunging and pulling in tandem—brought her right back to where she'd been before when his mouth and fingers had ravaged her. He lowered his lips to her face and they kissed, moving their mouths and bodies together in intimate, give-and-take waves against one another.

"Say my name," he panted against her lips.

"Gabriel." She loved the sound of it on her breathless tongue.

"Say it again . . ." he demanded, his thrusts growing harder and faster.

"Gabriel."

"Again."

"Gabriel . . . Oh, Gabriel!" she cried out to the heavens as she matched his pace and rode him hard.

The world spun and careened on its axis. Her wild shrieks of pleasure only caused him to move faster, and he panted and groaned against her lips as he devoured her mouth with passionate kisses. His tense, hard-working muscles glistened with perspiration, and when she reached a hand around to grasp his firm bottom . . .

His jaw clenched.

He pulled himself out of her, allowing her to watch as he spilled his seed onto his thigh.

Ellie lifted herself up on shaky arms, her mind numb with a deep feeling of inner peace. Part of her wished she could have experienced that last moment with him still inside her. But that wasn't an option. The blood flowing back into her head made her dizzy, and she watched Gabriel's chest rise and fall with heavy breaths while he shut his eyes for several seconds. He turned to face her with a soft smile that affected her down to her toes.

"Amazing," he said. He was still erect when he slid off the desk and got to his feet. "I have to clean up. I'll be right back."

Once he'd left the room, her gaze traveled from the doorway to the very window she'd wept beside several minutes ago. No more sadness filled her, no more pain, either. And mercy, had the afternoon sun been shining that bright before? Something new had awakened inside her—something moving, fulfilling and wonderful. She grinned and pressed a hand to her cheek, certain it was pure, satisfied elation.

Only what would happen now? What followed the act of making love? She knew how things had been done at the brothel, where the words *making love* had never existed. Her stomach sank at the thought of Gabriel sending her on her way. She'd been the one to throw herself at him with the ludicrous challenge. Whatever he did with her now was his choice, and she wouldn't blame him for it.

When she heard footsteps, she looked over her bare shoulder to see his naked form standing just inside the doorway. She clutched the fabric of her bunched-up chemise, her mind and heart racing. He cocked his head to one side as his gaze swept her exposed body.

"Come here," he said, holding out a hand.

She slid from the desk and went to him.

When her fingers slid inside his, he pulled her back into his protective embrace. Relief filled her. The heat radiating from his body thawed her skin as she wrapped her arms around his lower back and pulled him closer. Her breasts ached all over again as she rested her head against his bare chest. Thank the Lord he hadn't sent her away.

She lifted her head and kissed him. His soft, moist lips returned the gesture, while his gentle hands slid across her shoulders and down her back. She sighed into his mouth, astounded at her thirst for more after such a short time. With his hardening length pressed up against her abdomen, he must have wanted more, too.

"Come upstairs," he spoke against her lips.

Oh, God, how she wanted to. She wanted him to take her beneath his bed sheets so badly that her thighs clenched. Yet the grandfather clock in the corner served as a cruel reminder that she couldn't do so. Six o'clock. Mr. Westgate expected her back soon. The sneaking around and lies were exhausting, and the idea of no visible end made things all the more unsettling.

Ellie nuzzled her cheek against his, loving the scratch of his stubble. "If only I could. But it's late, and I must be getting back."

His palm flattened against the base of her skull, his fingers raking into her hair. "Lord. There isn't enough time in the day, is there?"

"Not nearly enough."

Gabriel unraveled his arms and stepped away, allowing that unpleasant surge of empty air to envelop her skin again. She bit the inside of her cheek and searched for her scattered clothing as he moved to snatch up his trousers. Her cotton skirt felt like a lead blanket around her waist, while each closing *click* of her corset busks deprived her of oxygen, binding her once-freed flesh.

"Ellie, I've—" Gabriel hesitated as he fastened the last button of his shirt. "I've been invited to guest teach at Harvard this year."

Just like that, reality returned.

She blinked. "Are you serious?"

"Quite serious, I'm afraid." His eyes darted with uncertainty. "And after reading their last letter . . . I'm seriously considering the offer."

Despite her wanting to jump for joy, the reluctance in his expression kept her from doing so. Still, she offered him a smile. "That's wonderful, isn't it? I think congratulations are in order."

"Thank you, but I assure you their reasons for summoning me can be traced back to my father. He donated a great deal of money to the medical program, both during and after my studies there."

"Still an honor, nonetheless." Her hands clenched at her sides, resisting the urge to touch him again.

"It's all political, Ellie," he said bluntly. He approached her discarded blouse, which artistically draped the inside of an empty bookshelf.

"Political, or perhaps—" It was high time to shake some sense into him. "Perhaps you are actually *good* at what you do." She slapped a hand to her cheek. "Well imagine that, Doctor."

His features relaxed measurably, and he held the blouse open for her arms to glide through. "How do you always do that to me?"

She went to him and turned around. "Do what?"

He slid the garment on, caressing the edge of her ear with his lips once the blouse fit her shoulders completely. "Ease my troubles with no effort at all."

The hair on the back of her neck rose as if he'd pulled some sort of trigger. Her head leaned into the space where his breath warmed her.

How do you always do that to ME, she wanted to reply. Every inch of her ached for him, and she wanted nothing more than to lift her arm and reach around the back of his neck.

"I suppose it's a gift," she whispered.

"A gift for you, or a gift for me?" His arms came around her, closing up each of her buttons in the slowest, cruelest way.

Damn him.

The last thing she wanted now was to have her clothes back on. She had to get a hold of herself, and quickly. "Are you going to take the opportunity, then?" she asked, nearly slurring. "After all you've endured, this could be the first step toward recognition. Just think of those you would educate, and the people you might impress."

She tensed when she felt him release her, something she never enjoyed. When she turned around she saw him standing beside the bookshelf, tapping his fingers along the cherry wood. It hadn't been her intention to cause him distress by asking a simple question. The man deserved happiness, and she couldn't fathom why someone in his position wouldn't be thrilled at such an opportunity.

"I've thought of that." He dragged a hand down his face. "I've thought of so many things that I can't think straight anymore."

"Then what may I ask is stopping you?"

"The timing," he said. "I would be gone six months."

So there it was.

It felt as if the very ground beneath her crumbled with one blow. *Six whole months?* He might as well have said forever. How could she exist without him that long? Her insides knotted horribly, making her nauseous.

"Oh. I see," she said quietly.

"If I go, it would place an enormous damper on the investigation, and I won't be here for Jane if she needs me." He shook his head, placing his gaze somewhere near her feet. "If something happened to her, I would never forgive my—"

"Gabriel."

His head snapped up. "Yes?"

"Jane will be fine. She has plenty of people to watch over her, myself included. And heaven knows you'll be home before the child is born."

He stared off blankly, as if her words were weapons for an ongoing inner battle. Not wanting him to go, yet convincing him to do so nonetheless, Ellie could feel her own inner battle beginning.

"As for the investigation—" She trembled at the thought of accidentally saying Mr. Cain's name aloud. "You said your father's lawyer is assisting you on the case. I'm sure he'll continue to do so in your absence."

"And you?" he asked.

"What about me?" Her attempt to remain unaffected must have looked pathetic.

All too suddenly his gaze bore into her eyes, with such intensity that it knocked her breath away. "If you tell me not to go, then I promise I'll stay."

She swallowed. The words she had to say might be the hardest to ever leave her mouth. Harder than pretending their shared kiss had meant nothing, and harder than denying it again on the beach. But she couldn't be selfish, and she couldn't keep him away from what he was destined to do.

"You must go," she said, trying hard not to frown. "I'll be right here when you return."

If she'd blinked, she'd have missed the disappointment that flickered across his face.

"Then it's settled. I leave Friday."

Ellie went to him and placed a palm to his jaw. She cared about his success as much as he did, maybe even more. "I won't keep you from this." She pressed a hard kiss to his lips, sadness filling her. "Thank you for today. A thousand times thank you."

Without turning back to look at him, she dashed into the hall, grabbed her reticule and ran out the door.

Chapter Twenty

A private meeting with Mr. Westgate always brought a certain level of intimidation. Ellie sat across from the man in his office, anticipating his reasons for summoning her with each tick of the German wall clock. With his statuesque posture and glass of sherry in hand, he captured the very essence of authority, while gazing at her across his antique desk.

Ellie wondered why Mr. Westgate asked to speak with her. Certainly Hanlon had not been forthcoming when she was called.

"I was highly impressed by your playing this afternoon" — pride layered Mr. Westgate's voice— "as were our lunch guests. Your piano skills have become something of which you should be quite proud, my dear."

She rejoiced at his paternal praise. Despite her qualms about his intractable nature, she could tell the man had grown increasingly fond of her, and she returned the admiration equally. Bull-headed or not, he was the closest thing she had to a father.

"Thank you, sir. I've been practicing every day."

"Your efforts have paid off." He sipped his drink, swallowing audibly, as if savoring every taste. "The radiance you exuded while playing and throughout the luncheon were quite different than I've seen before. You were a true social delight."

He must have been referring to the insuppressible giddiness that hadn't left her since the moment she'd made love. "I enjoy spending time in the Maxwell's company, and seeing Jane and Matthew always puts me in good spirits."

Mr. Westgate straightened against his tall-backed chair and raised his chin. Suggestion ruled his expression. "And there is no other reason for the additional air in your step?"

Oh, there is. She glanced at the desk in front of her, her face heating at the memory of crying out Gabriel's name to the heavens as he claimed her in fiery passion three days ago. What that man had done to her in his library, how alive he'd made her feel—consumed her body and mind. She shuddered at her underestimated feelings. Her heart was stronger than she'd thought, because when she had told Gabriel that she trusted him, she'd meant it.

Now, she'd have to endure six months without his incomparable presence. She twiddled her fingers, already mourning the loss. Despite Gabriel's modesty regarding his teaching opportunity, his brilliance had attracted the attention of Harvard Medical School. The hope for his success stirred a thrill inside her.

If only she knew whether to laugh or cry at the fact that she'd given part of herself to the one man who'd secured her heart. Nothing could have prepared her for the overwhelming urge to share even more with him.

"No reason, sir," she fibbed, resolving to act aloof.

"Very well," Mr. Westgate raised an eyebrow. "How have you been enjoying your time with my good friend?"

Unconsciously she moved back a little. "Your friend, sir?"

"Magnus Cain, of course."

The dreadful sound of the man's name—and the look on Mr. Westgate's face as he mentioned it—made her stomach drop. "He's been very gracious and kind ... yet I would still consider him little more than a stranger."

He wagged his finger at her blithely. "Your humility is endearing, my girl. I may not possess the perceptive skills of the fairer sex, but I can still confirm when one is indeed taken."

"Oh . . ." An awkward chuckle flew from her throat as she squirmed in her seat. "I assure you I'm not being humble when I say that my heart has not been given away just yet."

"Perhaps not, yet common interest grows into respect, and then I assure you the heart soon follows," he stated plainly. "That is the way of an arranged marriage."

"I—"

"Ellie, dear. I summoned you here because Mr. Cain has grown very fond of you. This morning, he told me that he's interested in your hand."

Was she too young to have a heart attack? A sudden, burning sensation radiated from the base of her throat down to the pit of her stomach, and she swore she could die. "I'm . . . very flattered, sir," —she wouldn't lose control— "But, wouldn't a younger man be more suitable?"

"My girl, I'm afraid that at nearly twenty-four-years-old, the odds of marrying a man less than forty are not in your favor." Mr. Westgate reached up and twisted one end of his mustache, looking on her with empathy. "Even if you were to formally make your debut in society, the competition of young women who have recently come of age would present an enormous challenge."

"I enjoy a good challenge," she said, her tone higher than usual. She held her breath, praying for him to show the slightest hint of mercy.

But he shook his head. "You've suffered with debts and poverty in the past, but now that you've returned to your roots, life is going to be much different. I want to see you well taken care of. Magnus might be older than thirty, but he will provide you with a lifetime of security and protection. Age is but a number these days."

Ellie clutched the dark blue satin of her skirts, her crossed ankles digging into one another beneath her chair. The urge to refuse—to cry out—pressed hard on her tongue, yet she struggled to remain silent.

"Unless of course," he tilted his head, "There's another prospect you had in mind."

The situation felt like a deep puncture in her side. Panic settled in, and her mind somehow fabricated the image of Gabriel standing behind his uncle, wearing the very smile that made her melt as he gestured to himself.

Yes, I could marry you, her heart answered just before he vanished. *I could have always married you.*

Her face tingled as warmth enveloped her body. God, she really was stubborn and blind. It seemed as though every awakening emotion had been put into a pot and poured all over her. When she was with him, she could feel again. Committing to anyone but Gabriel Peterson would undoubtedly impair her very soul.

But what could she say? Mr. Westgate wasn't speaking to him. If she rejected Mr. Cain and exposed her history with Gabriel, then the family she'd grown to love would crumble for good. She'd butcher Mr. Westgate's trust, annihilate any chance of a reunion and find herself tortured over an impossible choice: Losing one, or the other.

"No, sir," she replied. "But Mr. Cain's visits are so scarce and abrupt that I haven't had a moment to consider his intentions. I would need to get to know him better if I'm to make such a decision."

"Perhaps spending a little more time together will help." Mr. Westgate encouraged. "All I ask is that you give the man a chance. I'd like to rest easy knowing you'll be provided for, and given time, you'll be happy, as well."

Happy?

Despite his good intentions, she could never be happy. An unbearable mass of bitter frustration settled in Ellie's throat as she looked at him. This man had done so much for her. She should be thankful that he had her best interests in mind.

She dipped her head in respect, urging her forming tears to hold their place just a little while longer. "Yes, perhaps you're right, sir."

He took another sip of sherry. "Wonderful. Now that that's settled, you're excused to dress for dinner. I'll see you in the dining room shortly."

He rose from his chair when Ellie stood, but she feared taking a single step might send her to the floor. She pushed her weakened joints to work as she made her way to the door and slipped into the hall, unable to look back at the man who had unknowingly plunged a dagger into her heart.

Once the door had shut, she pressed her back to the wall and clutched her sickened, tossing stomach. The mahogany chair rail bruised her spine as she slid to the floor, unable to hold the tears any longer. Her ribcage beat against her corset as she wept, the thought of Magnus Cain's condemning expression on their wedding night tormenting her mind.

Shutting her eyes, she brushed shaky fingertips along the bare space atop her high neckline, summoning calmness by imagining Gabriel's touch there. What started off as an absurd quest for pleasure had immersed her in feelings so deep that friendship could never be considered again. The only arms she wanted were his, even if it meant risking betrayal. Gabriel could be right—all men couldn't be bad. But a lifetime without him meant nothing but darkness.

She wiped her wet cheeks and buried the crushing news deep inside her. Gabriel could never know about her arrangement—not right before he left for the best career opportunity of his life. He wouldn't go otherwise, and she refused to hold him back.

In the meantime, she could darn well try her hardest to delay the dreaded nuptials until Mr. Cain grew tired, or better yet, Mr. Westgate's veil of resentment toward his nephew finally lifted. No way on God's earth would she surrender without a fight.

* * *

Buckling the straps of his old suitcase, Gabriel could practically hear his mother scolding him for the aimless way he'd thrown everything inside. He'd never claimed to enjoy packing, hence his habit of waiting until the last moment. He wrenched the heavy luggage from atop his bed and glanced at the time. Seven o'clock in the evening; twelve more hours until he'd board the train to Massachusetts.

A strange feeling overcame him as he surveyed his bedroom. The last time he'd taken a trip, he hadn't returned for four years. This embarkment would be different. Breathing deeply, he imagined a secure future, one that would undoubtedly rebuild his life were he to play his cards right. Stability sat just beyond his reach.

He ran a hand across his jaw and glanced in the mirror, and decided not to shave until after he'd traveled. His reflection stared back at him, a different man. Gone were the privileged aristocrat, the lost, belligerent fool and the man struggling to reclaim his place in society. The past would always be part of him, yet he'd be damned if he let it define him.

A magnificent friend reminded him of that. She'd believed in him when he doubted, and after all the heartbreak she'd endured, her strength inspired him to better himself. He would prove to her that he believed in himself again.

Determination filled his blood. He raced down the stairs to his examination room, where his medical bag sat open, atop a wooden stool. Bottles and instruments clanked as he yanked open cabinets and pulled out drawers, while thoughts of Ellie's refreshing encouragement spurred on his packing. Few people, including his own family, had embraced his career choice once they'd learned he'd no intention of adopting his father's profession. Railroad expansion just never appealed to him the way medicine did. With Ellie, no judgments or qualms existed—he'd half a mind to think she'd support him if he were a cobbler.

He recalled her astounding behavior this morning, during his farewell breakfast with his cousins. The gold flecks in her eyes had glimmered with unspoken passion, and she'd smiled at him as if he were the only man in the world. And in Jane's parlor, when she'd hugged him goodbye, the affectionate words she'd bestowed in his ear had undoubtedly weakened even his most masculine parts. His willpower to leave had diminished significantly.

Pride swelled inside him at the idea of his lovemaking affecting her mood like that. He still couldn't pull the sensation of every touch from his own imagination. If he'd made her feel but a fraction of what she'd made him feel . . . then he must have done something right. No woman had fit so perfectly beneath his body.

Of course he'd had affections for her before, but once her tears had stained his shirt, once she'd trusted him in her most vulnerable state, he ached to conquer that heart of hers once and for all. She didn't have to deem herself unworthy of a husband, and she sure as hell didn't have to pretend to be guarded anymore. He would show her that he'd always be there, and he'd become the best damn doctor in the Northeast if it mean giving her what she deserved. Somehow, he'd prove himself to her. He'd prove himself to his uncle. He'd prove his worth to everyone . . . including himself.

Clutching his stethoscope, the last instrument to be packed away, he vowed to teach everything he knew, and to continue his own studies until he'd branded a lasting impression into Harvard's walls. He'd be back well before Jane gave birth, and Ellie would be waiting just as she'd promised. Christ, was he actually feeling optimistic? A grin crawled up his face as he shut the black leather bag.

He'd barely reached the library to retrieve his medical journals when the front door rattled with a series of urgent knocks. He tensed, concern claiming the forefront of his mind. A patient wouldn't call at this hour unless it was an emergency.

"Who is it?" he asked, marching toward the door.

"It's Magnus, Gabriel," Cain's grim voice announced from the other side. "I apologize for the undisclosed visit, but it's—"

Gabriel grabbed the door and swung it inward, bringing himself face-to-face with Cain's urgent expression.

The man lifted his satchel and gestured to it. "It's of great importance."

Chapter Twenty-One

"What do you think of these for the nursery?" Jane asked, setting three different strips of fabric on the empty seat beside her.

Ellie dipped a spoonful of golden honey into her tea. "I like them." She wished she could pay attention to the conversation, yet Gabriel occupied every corner of her thoughts.

Saying goodbye to him this morning had challenged her composure, especially when circumstances forbade them from spending a moment alone together. If only she could have felt his arms close around her one more time. She would have nestled her head in the crook of his neck, where the scent of his musk could bathe her in comfort. She wanted to tell him how happy he made her, to thank him for mending her cantankerous, inflexible heart. Perhaps she could put her emotions in writing and mail them to him.

"I liked this one for the baby's cradle." Jane held up a swatch of mint green fabric. Next, she held up a strip of white with yellow floral design. "And I was thinking of having curtains made from this one."

"And a blanket from the other?" Ellie pointed to the remaining piece of cream lace. She'd promised to help Jane decorate, so she willed herself to return her fleeting attention.

"Yes! What do you think?"

"I think they're all lovely choices."

"I don't think the baby will care if the room is painted black," John said as he appeared in the doorway. "All they want to do is eat, sleep and soil their diapers."

Ellie twisted sideways to glare at him. "Must you always be so ornery?"

"Only when the occasion calls for it." He smiled wide. "Besides, if I don't say these things, who will?"

"Why aren't you in the library with Father and Matthew?" Jane asked, putting the fabric back in her reticule.

"They're discussing business and politics, which bores me to tears." He sauntered into the parlor and tossed himself into a Louis XVI wing chair. "And the smoke from their cigars smells something awful."

Ellie flinched when he nearly knocked over the porcelain figurine on the table beside him. Still, the boy's meddling presence was a nice distraction from the woes associated with Mr. Cain. "I'm afraid you'll be just as bored with us in here."

"Not if I begin a new subject of conversation," he said, plopping his legs onto the colorfully embroidered foot rest.

She raised an eyebrow. "Such as?"

"Oh, I don't know . . ." He gripped the chair's arms and leaned forward, his cheeky grin turning into an accusatory stare. "Such as Father telling Matthew that Mr. Cain wants to marry you. He said you've known about it since yesterday."

Jane gasped. "Mr. Cain? Oh no, Ellie. No, no, no." Tears of emotion—an effect of pregnancy no doubt—wet her hazel eyes.

"Oh, John, now see what you've done." Ellie rushed from her seat and squeezed in next to Jane. "There, there, Jane. Everything will be all right."

"How can it" —Jane sniveled— "when Father is so foolishly pressuring you into marrying someone twice your age? Honestly, he should be giving you at least a year to be social. Surely you're going to refuse . . ."

"I'm sure Father's intentions are for the best," John muttered. When his sister turned to gawk at him, he recoiled and added, "However ridiculous and far-fetched they may be."

Ellie had to be tough. The last thing she wanted was uncertainty and despair—Colorado had given her more than a lifetime of that. She handed Jane a handkerchief, patted her shoulder and said, "Your father has done more for me than you'll ever know. I'd feel like an ingrate if I refused his proposition immediately. But you're right . . . I can't marry Mr. Cain. I won't marry him. As far as I'm concerned, this is the farthest this silly idea will go."

John hauled his feet back to the floor with a thump. "You're going to sabotage the proposal?"

"I'll make him see that I'm wrong for him. He'll be so through with me by the time I'm done that he'll never propose. And if that doesn't work, I'll avoid him for the next six months."

"Why six months?"

Jane pulled the handkerchief from her face. Her flushed cheeks raised above a wide, glowing smile. "Because that's when Gabriel returns . . . and she loves him." She clutched Ellie's wrists and did a little bounce. "I was right all along, wasn't I? You do love him, don't you?"

Warmth coated Ellie's bones and an ache spread throughout her chest. Her heart fluttered madly. Could this indescribable feeling be attributed to love? She wasn't sure yet.

But she'd never felt so strong, so in control of her life, as she did now. And that life was nothing without Gabriel Peterson. Fourteen years of separation hadn't pulled him from her thoughts, because deep in her heart, she had always been his. A tangible, unspoken bond would always exist between them, one that would never need justification. As long as Gabriel was around, her trust in humanity stood a fighting chance. There was still a way for her to grow whole again.

She summoned a deep breath, urging the drumming of her heart to dissipate. Hopefully, her confession wouldn't be too embarrassing. "You were right, Jane. I have to be with him."

Jane pulled her into an affectionate embrace. "Oh, thank God."

"I knew it all along," John said. He leaned back, seemingly pleased with the situation. "Miss Tuttle's tittering and nonsense would have put Gabe in an early grave—or any man for that matter. At least one of you has finally admitted your feelings."

The words spelled relief in a number of ways. How refreshing that John and Jane saw right through her with frightful clarity. Ellie shouldn't have underestimated their support. For the first time in months, she'd set something free. She must have looked a fool, because she couldn't stop smiling.

"Gabriel and your father have gotten nowhere by doing things their way. The time has come to take matters into my own hands," Ellie said. "Somehow, I have to bring them together, just as I have to fend off Mr. Cain." She sat tall and shuffled her gaze between her companions. "Now I ask you, will you help me into battle?"

The eager boy sprung to his feet and saluted her. "At your service, m'lady. My loyalty lies beneath the family tree, so I'll do whatever it takes to ward off suitors."

She rushed to him, planting a kiss atop the scar on his forehead. "You're an exemplary young man, do you know that?"

"Before he left, Gabe told me to take care of you and Jane. That's precisely what I'm going to do."

Jane rose to her feet. "I promise to help, too. To the gutter with confinement . . . let it try and stop me. I won't see your glorious destiny ruined by a pointless feud."

"Hear, hear," John declared.

Ellie reached for John's hand and extended her other to Jane. She grasped her cousins' hands, squeezing tightly. The parlor glowed in warm gaslight. A sense of family connection, determination and unwavering courage filled the air.

"Together, we can accomplish anything," Ellie said.

The ache in her heart was replaced by beats of valor as she began conjuring a plan.

* * *

Gabriel stared at the last note atop the vexing pile of letters in his hands, willing the most disheartening words he'd ever read to dissolve right off the page.

"There must be some mistake . . ." His eyes snapped up to Cain, who sat across from him. "Where did you find these?"

Cain buckled the last strap of his satchel and placed it on the floor against his chair. "Patrick appointed me to hold onto his most private documents . . . were any of his misdeeds to come back to haunt him years later." He frowned, letting out a deep sigh. "I never would have shown them to you unless I'd felt it completely necessary."

Even while sitting, Gabriel needed to steady himself, as his mind floundered at the insufferable truths revealed by his father's pen.

"No, I—I'm glad you did," he stammered through the cannon ball-sized blow to his chest. He gripped the chair's arm, feeling his dinner fight its way up his esophagus as he took in the agonizing papers on his lap. "So, my father slept with all these women . . . then paid them for their silence?"

"I'm afraid so."

"And this one," Gabriel snatched the most gut-wrenching paper from the pile—the one he'd been staring at the longest—and held it up. "Fourteen years ago, he went under the assumed name of his neighbor, Samuel Baker, to bed a prostitute who later died aborting his child? Is this true?"

Cain extended a hand toward the crackling fire. "Your father is probably pitching in his grave, knowing what I've shown you."

"Is this true?" Gabriel repeated firmly.

"Yes." The man nodded gravely. "He knew the brothel owner was an impetuous man, and with you and your mother living close by, he didn't want to risk your safety."

"So instead, he risked the safety of another man and his innocent family!" Gabriel crushed the letter inside his fist. "Samuel Baker died a few years later, and chances are it wasn't a goddamned accident."

Rage twisted inside his gut as he squeezed the paper even harder. Christ, that was the reason his family had left Black Hawk so abruptly. His father had declared that his business was finished out west, and as a fourteen-year-old boy with little knowledge of the man's occupation, Gabriel hadn't questioned him.

He didn't know what made him more furious—his father's unforgivable, gut-wrenching offenses, or how he'd tell this bitter truth to the woman who'd stolen his heart. He wanted to erupt . . . to hurl his chair across the room, pummeling everything in its path.

Tearing his reading glasses from his face he glared up at Cain, battling to keep from demanding that he be left alone. He'd nothing more to say, and he didn't care that any one of the corrupted letters could bring him closer to answering his questions.

The way Ellie had looked, so shattered, while sharing her darkest secret, harassed his memory. The tragedy that befell her—and her poor father—his own flesh and blood was responsible for that suffering. He couldn't have been angrier on the day of her confession, but what he felt at the present moment deserved a classification of its own.

"If you're determined to solve this crime, no stone can be left unturned . . . even if it means discovering truths you didn't know were there," Mr. Cain said. "Your father was only human, Gabriel, and he still cared for you and your mother very—"

"You don't have to speak on his behalf," Gabriel snapped, awash with a combination of anger and betrayal. "At twenty-eight-years-old, I'm far from a boy in need of consoling."

The man stiffened. "Of course you aren't. Forgive me . . . at times I still forget."

Gabriel exhaled and shut his eyes, feeling as though his mind were floating ten feet above his body. Surely one hell of a headache was on its way. His father's position of power, combined with the travel demands of an industrial profession, created the perfect recipe for an unfaithful marriage. Part of him had always known. Yet it had been far easier avoiding thoughts of his mother having a disloyal husband.

"Well, I could certainly use a drink," Mr. Cain said. "I'm sure you could use one, too."

"I've regrettably quit," Gabriel muttered, disgraced at his yearning for a bottle more than ever. Hell, he remembered why turning to the drink involved little effort.

"Quit? How admirable."

"Not admirable. Necessary."

"I understand." The lawyer scratched his jaw and peered at his pocket watch. "It's later than I thought. I should leave you to rest for tomorrow."

Rest. That's rich, Gabriel thought, as Cain rose and gathered his satchel.

Gabriel followed him to the door, wanting nothing more than to heave the letters into the hearth instead of dropping them onto his desk. God only knew how many of Patrick Peterson's illegitimate children roamed the country. As for the haunting note concerning Ellie's father—Gabriel shoved the miserable piece of paper into his waistcoat pocket, sickened by the idea of Jasper Cogs having anything to do with the man's death.

"Thank you for bringing this to my attention," Gabriel said, while retrieving Cain's hat off the rack beside the door. "I'll study the letters on the train and stay in correspondence while I'm away."

"Anything I can do to help, dear boy." Mr. Cain took his hat from Gabriel's hand. "Yet I'm curious as to how you heard of Samuel Baker's death. I certainly didn't know, and I doubt your father did."

"I've . . . remained in contact with his daughter—" Gabriel squeezed his eyes shut and pinched the space between them "—who I'm certain you've learned is my uncle's ward."

Cain grew silent for a moment. Then, tilting his head he said, "Strange, Miss Baker never mentioned you. Why, just last week we spotted you on our ride around the estate, and she seemed ignorant when I spoke of you."

Gabriel's stomach clenched. "You've spent time with her, then?"

When Cain nodded, he held his breath.

"I've called upon her a time or two, but I've been sending her gifts often." The man displayed a lewd smirk that made Gabriel want to lunge for his throat. "I've always been somewhat adept at the art of wooing. A striking, audacious little creature, is she not?"

Gabriel lurched the door open, feeling as if a hand were wrapped around his heart, digging its fingers into the beating tissue. A fire ravaged the space beneath his ribs, and it was all he could do to not grip his chest.

"Not that your Miss Tuttle isn't a rose among weeds," Cain added. "Your arrangement still continues, I'm sure . . ."

"I'm afraid not."

"I'm sorry to hear that. Well, all the more reason to enjoy your time away from the burdens of courtship."

Gabriel strained to fake a smile. "Men like us are the envy of those poor, love-struck fools."

"Don't speak too quickly. I dare say you're looking at one of those poor fools now." With a smug look, Cain placed his top hat on his head and stepped outside.

"You can't!"

Cain spun around, his perturbed expression demanding an explanation. Gabriel held firmly onto the knob, praying this were some sort of hellish nightmare, as he stared back at his collaborator-turned-rival.

"What I mean to say is—" Gabriel cleared his throat. "You can't hurry these things. Women are complex, intelligent creatures who require extensive patience."

"I don't doubt it for a young man such as you, but at my age, experience takes precedent over time." Cain backed away with a tight-lipped, almost mocking smile. "However, the wedding can most certainly wait until you return. Good evening, Gabriel, and safe travels to Cambridge."

"Good evening." Gabriel waited for the man's carriage to roll off. He hurled the door shut and pounded a fist to the oak. "And God, help me."

Chapter Twenty-Two

Turning back into the hall, Gabriel paced six heavy steps and stopped. He whirled back toward the door, his hands digging ruthlessly into his scalp. Six more urgent paces—then five, then three—until he finally let himself collapse into the nearest chair. He leaned forward, elbows on his knees, and dropped his forehead into his hands.

"Get a hold of yourself," he said aloud, something he hadn't needed to do in a long time.

Cain wanted to marry Ellie—his Ellie. God, how could this be?

He thought back to his own parents. His father had been fifteen years older than his mother, and just like the other women of her class, she hadn't seemed to care. Cain's age barely mattered when he had good looks and wealth to recommend him. The years had been kind to his refined features. But if he so much as lay a finger on Ellie . . .

"No," Gabriel growled against the silence. No, it would never happen.

The idea was so disturbing that it was nearly hilarious. So much, in fact, that Gabriel let out an unnatural chuckle. He urged his lungs to continue functioning as he strove to convince himself that she'd never surrender to such an offer. Yet his convictions brought little comfort.

Gabriel cared for Ellie deeply, that much he knew. Now, as his fractured heart thudded mercilessly against the walls of his chest, and the thought of losing her hit beneath his ribs, he realized how much.

His childhood friend had blossomed into pure beauty, but her kind heart and playful nature remained the same. It wouldn't make a difference if she truly were a prostitute. She had pulled him from his dark despair, accepted him for who he was, and made him quake with pleasure every time she touched him. Ellie Baker was far more than someone familiar, for whom he wanted to care for. She was his heart, his soul, his happiness . . .

God, he loved her.

The unexpected realization sent him straight from his chair. He paced the hall again, his strained breathing almost like accompaniment to his frantic steps. Good Lord, his once-numbed heart truly could feel love. How could it not for the woman with whom he'd spent his best childhood years, the only woman who'd stand by his side through darkness and light? He yearned to wake to her large emerald eyes gazing back at him each morning, to see her bear and raise his children, to spend every waking hour in the glory of her presence. Yes, he loved her—with every part of his substance, he loved her.

But the grave reality of the situation restrained his heart from lovesick pitching. Why hadn't she told him about Cain's interest? She didn't have to tell him—not if she didn't love him. The time he'd spend in Massachusetts only made things worse. He was still at odds with his uncle. He wanted the one woman in Henry's protective care. Oh yes, and she kept her heart sealed, for reasons caused by his own father. Christ, he was in over his head.

A long-forgotten sense of wretchedness fermented deep within him. He could no longer think. Just this once, he needed to escape—to drink until silence claimed his mind. It was too easy, too tempting. He faced the door, balling his fists and waiting for the voice of reason to stop him.

Nothing.

The promising taste of liquor ruled his desires, and he imagined the alcohol saturating every crevice of his mouth like sweet, forbidden nectar. Loathing himself for his sudden lack of control, he snatched his high hat off the rack.

"You're worthless," he mumbled to himself as he reached for the handle and yanked the door open.

Later, as he trudged through the dim confines of the alehouse, he avoided eye contact as he brushed past patrons and claimed the nearest cast iron stool. He tugged the brim of his hat down over his forehead and folded his arms atop the counter, reluctant to be recognized by anyone he knew.

"Evening," the bartender said as he approached. "Can I get you a lager?"

Gabriel shook his head. "Whiskey."

The bartender plunked an empty glass in front of him. "You look like you could use a double. No extra charge."

"Much obliged."

When the man began pouring the amber liquid, Gabriel's stomach churned oddly. He wrapped his fingers around the glass and lifted it to his nose, nearly recoiling as the familiar aroma numbed his nostrils. He'd never hesitated to drink before, yet now the alcohol itself appeared to stare him down—reminding him of the dark places it had taken him.

He glanced up to find the bartender studying him while polishing a beer glass.

"I've never seen a man look so guilty for having a drink in his hand," he said.

Gabriel groaned. "I don't know what I'm doing anymore."

"Rough day?"

"Unimaginable."

"In that case, I can only assume it involved a woman."

"Involved, that's the simplest way of putting it." Gabriel placed the untouched glass back down in front of him. "Tell me, what would you do if you discovered that the woman you loved was arranged to another man?"

"Simple." The bartender shrugged. "Marry her first."

"Right." Gabriel let out a tense chuckle and slapped a few coins onto the counter. "Yet suppose you were leaving the state tomorrow morning, and would be gone for several months."

The bartender grimaced. "Then I would drink up, just as you're about to, and hope for the best. There are plenty fish in the sea, my friend." He slid the money into his hand, tapped the counter twice and made his way back down the line of patrons.

Gabriel cursed beneath his breath, snatching up the foul glass. Yet the closer he brought the whiskey to his mouth, the more his head refused to tilt backward; his lips would not part. Dammit all!

No matter how long he sat there, he knew he couldn't bring himself to take a single sip. He just . . . couldn't do it. Hell, he didn't even want to. In an instant, the common sense he'd been searching for rattled him. An old adapted response to stress had tricked his brain into thinking he needed alcohol as a release. But he could never allow the habit to ruin him as it had before.

"Here, take this." He slid the glass to the man sitting beside him. "It's already been paid for."

After staring for several seconds, the puzzled patron bestowed an appreciative grin. "Er ... thank you, sir."

Gabriel slid to his feet and gave the man's shoulder a friendly pat before leaving the building. Fresh evening air replaced the smoke in his lungs. He untied Roger from the tethering post while unease ate away at him.

He'd been satisfied with Ellie's tender goodbye several hours ago, but now, after hearing the confident way Magnus Cain had announced his intentions, Gabriel needed to speak with her alone. Why hadn't she mentioned Cain's visits? Why hadn't she mentioned Cain at all?

He climbed into the driver's seat of the buggy, deciding that sleep was something best saved for tomorrow's train ride. Attempting to lay his head down tonight would prove useless anyway. Lovesick jealously devoured him. He guided Roger toward the main street, the unfathomable urge to sneak into Ellie's room outweighing the risks.

If he left without hearing her reason for keeping such a secret—without knowing her true feelings for him—he would all but lose his mind.

* * *

Ellie knew she was dreaming. The white, two-story ranch house stood out like a beacon in the middle of an open field, with no mountains, fences, nor barn surrounding it. Every visual lacked in detail and appeared as gray as a photograph.

She ran toward the house, her feet bounding at an unnaturally slow pace through the knee-high grass. When she reached the front door, she stopped. The knob wouldn't turn. She twisted over and over, yet even her mind couldn't will the dream door to open. Suddenly, a child's laughter drifted from behind the house.

The muted sky turned even bleaker as she hurried in the direction of the sound, and when she rounded the corner, she saw her. A little girl, her black hair in two braids tied off with ribbon, laughing merrily on a tree swing. Papa smiled as he pushed her five-year-old self from behind.

He'd just built her the swing that morning. Ellie remembered everything about this day. She folded her arms, the sounds of their happiness filling her heart with bittersweet pain.

"Higher, Papa!" the little girl cried.

He laughed. "Ellie Bear, if you swing any higher, you'll reach the clouds."

"Could I really reach them?"

"Maybe." He sprinted around the tree and stopped in front of her. "You'll never know unless you try. On the count of ten, leap as high as you can and I'll catch you."

Ellie jumped as the window beside her slid open with a squeak. Mama poked her head out, completely unaware of her presence. Invisible. This must have been how Ebenezer Scrooge felt with the Ghost of Christmas Past.

"Samuel!" Mama pointed her wooden spoon at Papa. "If she breaks a single bone, so help me."

"I'll let you break the same bone of mine, dear." His voice held an infinitely compassionate tone.

"I'm going to reach the clouds, Mama!" the girl squealed.

"Well, once you've reached them—" Mama's mouth twitched with humor. "—bring your papa inside for a fresh slice of pie."

She retreated back into the house, and Papa held out his arms and took a step backward. "Are you ready, my child?"

The girl gripped the ropes tightly. "Yes!"

"One . . . two . . . three . . ."

As Papa counted, Ellie forced herself to move closer to the action. She'd just reached the halfway point when a boy's voice echoed eerily through the fields. "Ellie Bear! Ellie!" it called out several times. But Ellie's eyes remained on Papa and the little girl.

"Ten!" Papa said.

The child leapt from the swing, soaring high into the air with infectious laughter. Papa caught her in his arms and fell backward, holding her to his chest as they tumbled against the ground together.

"Did you touch one?" he asked, chuckling and hugging her close.

"I was so close! Let's try again, Papa!"

Every bark of their laughter twisted Ellie's heart a little tighter. Slowly she continued approaching the happy pair until she hovered just above them. Sprawled out on the grass, Papa looked so young, alive and happy. The child grabbed his face between her small hands, smashing his cheeks playfully. She had loved him more than anything.

"If only you'd known what you'd do to me." She knelt down beside them, searching his kind, loving eyes. "You were a good father."

The little girl's head shot up and she stared right through Ellie. "Look, Gabriel's here!" she exclaimed, springing up from Papa's chest.

Ellie turned to see young Gabriel no more than ten feet behind her, waving a scrawny little arm. His dirt-stained knee socks and blue satin knickerbockers invited warm memories of how they'd always manage to ruin their clothes. It was his voice that had been calling out her name. Papa grinned and propped himself onto his elbows, a tender expression on his handsome face. He watched the girl skip to Gabriel.

"I swear that boy will take my place someday," he said with a contented sigh.

"Oh, God," Ellie whispered, pain swelling inside her. She reached out to touch his shoulder. "Papa . . ."

Tap, tap, tap!

Her hand retracted at the sudden, obnoxious sound.

"Gabriel," Papa said, getting to his feet and brushing himself off. "Come on inside with us. Mrs. Baker has just baked a delicious blueberry pie."

Tap, tap, tap!

Gabriel smiled. "Blueberry's my favorite. Thank you, sir!"

"Mine, too!" the girl exclaimed, grabbing the boy's hand.

Tap, tap, tap!

Ellie's eyes shot open. The grooved ceiling of her dark bedroom stared back at her. She pulled the jostled covers over her body, her half-conscious brain struggling to adjust to the present.

Tap, tap, tap, tap, tap!

Dear Lord, the sound had been real! She froze when she realized it had come from the far bedroom window. If only a tree with outstretched branches sat close enough to serve as a logical explanation. But nothing more than a garden view was on other side.

She got out of bed and crept cautiously toward the drawn curtains, afraid that lighting a lamp would give away her position. Crouching against the wall beside the window, she slid a finger beneath the drapes and inched the fabric away, trying to make out a form in the darkness. But it was too small a space, and the angle wouldn't allow her to see more than a fraction.

Just open it. It's most likely nothing.

She shook her arms for the jolt of courage she needed. Then, stepping in front of the window, she took a deep breath, grabbed hold of the curtain and threw it aside.

Chapter Twenty-Three

Gabriel's startled face stared at her through the glass, and she leapt back with a gasp, as he lost his balance and fell out of sight.

"Oh! Oh, no!" she whispered, lunging forward and unlatching the lock.

She yanked the window doors open to find him dangling nearly twenty feet above ground, gripping the sill like a clumsy tomcat. Clutching one of his arms, she pulled with all her might, enabling him to use the momentum to hoist himself inside. One final tug and he hit the floor with a thunk. She prayed the sound wasn't loud enough to wake the house.

"Why, in God's name," he groaned as he rose to his feet, "would you ever open a curtain like that?"

"I hope you're joking." She combed her fingers through her embarrassing, bed-wrangled knots. "You terrify me in the middle of the night by rapping on my window, and then expect me to casually draw the curtain with a smile on my face?"

"You looked like you had the devil in you," he said, shrugging off his coat and tossing it onto a nearby chair.

She was beyond thrilled to see him again. When midnight rolled around, she began losing hope that he might see her one last time. She fought a smirk as she lit the nearest lamp. "Well, I do apologize for nearly killing you."

"Serves me right for acting like a burglar." When he smiled back at her, his mouth took the same shape as the nine-year-old boy in her dream. "Now, if you'll please come here."

He needn't ask twice. Ellie rushed to his open arms, succumbing to the bliss of his embrace. Sturdy and warm, he felt like home. Gripping his waistcoat, she buried her nose in the smells of sandalwood, thyme and even tobacco smoke.

If only there were a way to meld closer to him. "I'm so glad you're here."

"I couldn't very well leave without saying a proper goodbye, could I?" he said, brushing his fingertips along her arms.

Her skin tingled through the soft silk of her gown. "Or perhaps you just missed the sight of me in my nightgown. I believe this is the exact one I wore when I ran after you, screaming."

"I thought it looked familiar." He moved back, took her chin and guided it upward until their eyes locked. "You don't know how badly I wanted to kiss you that night, you insane little woman. But I'm afraid that if I kiss you now, I won't want to leave tomorrow."

This man couldn't be real. Queen Victoria herself might be inclined to snatch him up if she had the chance. The more his stunning blue gaze bore through her, the more her stomach sank. Six months was such a long time. But she would not beg him to stay. Instead, she distracted herself by counting the stray hairs of his eyebrows.

"You have to go," she said, shutting her eyes as he slid his hands up her neck and held her face. "Doctoring and caring for others . . . It's in your blood. It's part of you. You deserve to be successful at the things that make you happy."

"You make me happy." He brushed his thumb across her lips, coaxing her to part them eagerly. "Everything about you inspires me to better myself."

"It does?"

"Yes. It's been that way since the day you approached me in that miserable, hellish saloon." His chest vibrated against her as he laughed softly. "How you recognized me behind that shaggy hair and grizzly beard, I'll never know."

It was those eyes, vibrant and deep, the same as she'd remembered. She looked up at him, memorizing the man he'd become. The tired creases below his eyes, the smooth curve of his chin, the bow in his upper lip. "I'd thought I didn't matter to anyone anymore," she said. "It was a dark, empty feeling . . . a loneliness I wouldn't wish upon a single soul. But then I saw you."

"And I saw you." He planted a soft kiss to her forehead, grazing her skin with his stubble.

"Not only saw—" She sighed and rested her head against his lips. "But rescued. You rescued me in so many ways."

He stepped back, a gleam of curiosity in his eyes.

"Of course, there were the times you literally saved me," she said. "From The Inn, from my fear of dancing, from the thunderstorm—" She rolled her eyes. "Though I hadn't wanted to admit it at the time."

He shook his head with a quiet, low chuckle.

Heavens, she could barely focus on anything when he aimed that devastating smile in her direction. "But most importantly, you saved me from fear. When I learned about my father . . . when Jasper hurt me without a thought or care, I swore I'd never trust another man for as long as I lived. How could I, when the most important man in my life proved nothing than a grueling disappointment."

She closed the window, shut the latch and turned around. Her gaze never left his as she reached out and clutched his hand. Pressing his palm to her chest, she covered that hand with both of hers, allowing his heat to penetrate her gown. "But a wise man once told me that 'a life alone is no life at all.' You've helped me see that there are good men in this world, and I shouldn't deny myself happiness just because of a few corrupt scoundrels. So for that . . . for all of that, I say thank you."

Gabriel stared at her for a solid five seconds. "My, but you certainly know how to humble a man."

He blew out a breath, and she moved her gaze from his eyes to his lips. Oh, how she longed to kiss them. The prolonged anticipation was almost unbearable. "There's . . . just one more thing I must say."

He tossed his head back and slapped his free hand to his chest. "My dear, you're going to cause my heart to explode."

"I promise it's short.."

"All right." He grinned. "Go on."

Standing on her toes, she wrapped her arms around his neck and pressed a hard kiss to his lips. "I only want to say that, ever since I was five-years-old, my heart has belonged to you. And it will remain that way long after eternity."

* * *

As Gabriel gazed back into the pair of eyes that rendered him speechless, he could only question whether he'd heard correctly. The events of the past couple hours must have really warped his mind.

"Would you care to repeat that?" he asked.

Her smile deepened into laughter. She took his face into her hands and gazed at him with intent. "Gabriel, my heart is forever yours."

So he *hadn't* imagined it. His own heart grew so warm that it nearly ached. "Dear God, you might have done it." He pressed four fingers to the pulse on his neck. "Yes. Yes, I'm officially dead."

"Well then," she wrapped her slender arms around his waist. "You're the happiest dead man I've ever seen."

At this moment, happiness was all he craved. Well, happiness and Ellie. He didn't want to question her loving words, but the longer she kept Magnus Cain a secret, the more he wouldn't be able to help it. But he was keeping something from her, too, wasn't he? He'd have to tell her about his father eventually. About the numerous ways the man had destroyed her . . .

But not now. Not this moment.

"More than that," he said. Holding her close, he savored the delicate curve of her back. "I just might be the happiest man in the world."

"And what does the happiest man in the world wish to do now?" Her playful eyes searched his face, and she pressed against him in a way that made him ache.

A sensuous light passed between them. His pulse quickened.

Christ, how he wanted to reach forward, grasp the fabric at her neck and tear that gown in two. "What will you have me do?"

Releasing him, she took a single step back. Then she clutched her nightgown, pulled it up over her head and tossed it to the floor. His jaw might as well have hit the ground beside it. Perhaps she'd read his mind. Ivory skin, perfect breasts and beautiful curves stared back at him, ready and eager to be taken. Her eyes glowed with a savage inner fire, and he swore he'd never seen a more beautiful woman in all his life.

"Make love to me," she whispered, dragging her fingers down the forbidden valley between her breasts.

He clenched his fists at his sides. He would not lose control and carry her straight to bed.

Tonight, he would take his time.

"Is that a request?" he asked.

She tilted her head and peered up at him longingly. "Yes."

"Only a request?" He narrowed his eyes, challenging her. "Are you sure?"

Something flickered inside her gaze, and she drew closer until they nearly touched. "A demand."

"That's more like it," he voiced in a low reply, snatching her by the arms and pulling her into him.

He brought his mouth down on top of hers, relishing her soft, succulent lips, and her bare skin beneath his hands. His hunger for her was bone-deep. She felt so incredibly good. Before he could deepen the kiss, her lips parted further and her tongue found the inside of his mouth. Softly, she whimpered.

He savored the sensation of her in his arms, the notion of her wanting him—and just knowing the risk they took seemed to increase his arousal ten-fold. Quiet, secret, dangerous.

His hand slid down to her small round bottom and gave it a squeeze. She gasped in delight, tugging on the lapels of his waistcoat. "You do things to me," she purred. "To my body. Things that I can't explain."

He took her hand and pressed it to the hard bulge beneath his trousers. "One might say the feeling is mutual."

To his surprise, her grip tightened. He groaned instantly. He spun her around and guided her backward toward the wall, where he braced his hands on either side of her head. "That's mighty dangerous territory."

"I'm brave enough. Besides, tonight is supposed to be about you."

"Oh, is it?" he asked, just before pressing a wet kiss to the side of her neck. When she sucked in a breath of pleasure he added, "Well then, forgive my poor manners."

He dropped his arms and pulled away, allowing her to fiddle with the buttons of his waistcoat without his interference. They came undone at an impressive rate, and he relished the sensual look on her face as she slid her fingers beneath the wool and pushed it back over his shoulders. When it fell to the floor, and she began untying his necktie, the battle to keep his hands off her became impossible.

He reached out and stroked the soft skin along her side, making her recoil with laughter as she pulled the black tie from around his neck.

"You're a cad," she whispered, slinging it around her own neck.

"And you're beautiful."

There was a depth to her smile that had been missing for too long. Lord, he'd compliment her every minute of every day if it meant he got to see that expression over and over again.

She tugged hard on his suspenders, causing him to stumble forward. Releasing all thoughts he kissed her again, pressing her up against the wall and bringing her to squirm as she tore at the buttons of his shirt. He snuck a hand between their bodies, traveling downward until he slipped two fingers between her thighs.

A soft cry of pleasure came from her lips, one that shot an arrow of arousal straight to his aching, confined cock. Shutting his eyes, he drove his fingers upward until he could feel her slick inner walls spasm against him. So warm. So wet.

She moaned as he massaged his palm against her, the movement of his fingers working with every sway of her hips.

Parting the fabric to expose his bare chest, she planted a hot, wet kiss to his collarbone, breaking his concentration. When her lips searched along the muscles of his chest, he thrilled at the idea of her fighting for control.

"You really are—" he clenched his jaw and sucked in a breath as she swirled the tip of her tongue around one of his nipples, "—determined, aren't you?"

"Very," she murmured, torturing him with her close breath against his roused skin.

He thrust his finger deeper inside her, making her gasp. "Tell me why."

Her red, swollen lips parted as she looked at him in earnest. "Because I have never, and will never, want to please any man but you."

I love you, Ellie Baker. Pride filled him as he repeated the words in his head. Slowly, he removed his hand from the warm haven between Ellie's thighs. "Then for God's sake, woman, have me."

"Finally." She offered him a smile, then covered his nipple with her hot mouth, brushing her fingers across his tense abdomen.

Every suckle, every permeating lick on his flesh made him throb harder inside his trousers, and he prayed for the strength to resist. He'd let her have her fun before he took over, even if the feel of her wet tongue tasting him made resistance damn near impossible.

He met her lips, entranced by the sweet flavors of her mouth, the passion and energy of her kiss—that is, until he felt the tug of her hands on his waistband. He really should stop her. Yet as he lifted a hand to fondle one of her round, supple breasts, he somehow couldn't bring himself to do so. So he cupped her flesh and teased her pebble-hard nipple instead, delighting in her moans and how perfectly she filled his hand.

Somehow, the little minx still managed to unfasten his trousers.

He tore his mouth from hers. She slid his suspenders down his arms, her eyes sparkling as though she were playing her favorite game. He tensed when she reached around and untied the back of his drawers. No, she couldn't be doing what he thought she was doing . . .

Oh, yes, she was. Her right hand dove beneath the loosened garment, and his breath hitched when he felt her digits wrap around the hard length of his shaft. He squeezed his eyes shut and shuddered as she stroked down over him—one, two, three times.

"Lord. You're about to bring me to my knees, woman," he said through clenched teeth.

"Not if I get there first," she purred, just before suckling a tender spot beneath his jaw.

As she trailed her lips along his neck, across his chest, and down to the bottom of his stomach, Gabriel almost forgot all the trying news he'd received earlier that night. Ellie's touch was the only thing that mattered now. She was his endless escape.

He opened his eyes, watching in awe as she dropped to her knees and tugged all clothing covering his bottom half down his thighs, springing him free in one swift motion. Slowly, she lifted a hand to grip the base of his erection and peered up at him with a small, shy smile.

"I've only done this once before," she said.

"Ellie, you don't have to do any—"

Before he could finish, she wrapped her lips around the length of his cock and took him in her mouth.

"Oh . . . my God," he moaned, slapping a hand to the wall for support as a blinding wave of pleasure rocked him.

He bit back a cry as the warm, wet cavern of her mouth slid further down, taking even more of him inside. The blood draining from his head made him stagger as she pulled back up the length of his shaft, swirling her tongue around the sensitive tip, while her hand simultaneously stroked him.

The moisture pooling round her mouth and down her fingers felt so good that he might easily come if he wasn't careful. Over and over she plunged his shaft deeper into her mouth and pulled back again. He could feel his seed beginning to stir as his body tensed with surge after surge of concentrated, mounting satisfaction.

Good God, she was incredible. It was as if she'd always known exactly how and where to satiate him, but he knew he couldn't last much longer. As much as he craved immediate release, he craved the feel of her pulse beating against him even more. Tonight he belonged buried within her, to feel her tight, warm sheath envelop him once more before he left her for the demanding world of lectures and medicine.

He took a step back, and she gazed up at him with a small frown.

"Did I do it wrong?" she asked, rising slowly.

"No, my darling." He lifted her chin to meet his face and kissed her. "Quite the opposite. Unimaginably perfect."

She blushed. "Truly?"

"God, yes." He pulled his trousers back up over his erection. "But you've had your fun with me, and it's my turn now."

He wrapped an arm around her waist and reached beneath her knees, bringing her up into a cradling hold. She clung to his neck as he brought her to the bed and lowered her onto the rumpled bedcovers. Her trusting, desirous eyes greeted him as he turned back around, and he trembled at the thought of how much she moved him. No woman had come close to doing that before.

He tore off his clothes and climbed on top of her naked body, stopping himself from entering her just yet. As her legs spread further apart, he leaned into her and brushed his lips against her flushed cheek.

"Lord, I'm going to miss this. I'm going to miss you."

"Lord," she breathed, imitating his tone. "You can't imagine, my darling."

He couldn't bear the torture of being outside her any longer. She sucked in a gasp and arched against him as he slid forward and entered her wet, eager body in one steady thrust. Once he'd filled every inch of her, he reminded himself to maintain control as her legs closed in around him. Tonight he wanted to cherish every look, every move, and every touch that he'd be without for the next six months.

Entwining his fingers with hers, he pinned her hands over her head. Her hips rocked upward to match his thrusts. He could feel her sheath tighten and pulse around him as her tension grew, her breasts rising and falling with every pleasure-filled breath.

She squeezed his hands and orgasmed, biting down on her lip to stifle her cries while her hips slammed against his. It was too much to handle. Releasing his grip, he braced his hands on either side of her and increased his thrusts, harder, faster, allowing his own pleasure to completely consume him.

"W-wait Gabriel, not yet," she panted.

"Why on earth not?" he rasped, curling his toes to keep from bursting right then and there.

"Put me on top of you."

He jerked his head back and stared at her. There might never be a time when the woman wouldn't completely catch him off-guard.

Without a word, he took her by the shoulders and flipped their bodies so that she straddled his hips. Waves of ecstasy throbbed through him. She immediately began grinding down against him, plunging him deep into the heat of her receptive body. Her slick inner walls clenched, and her breasts bounced heavily as he pounded up into her with hard, possessive strokes.

Her hands latched onto his arms as she climaxed a second time. She leapt off him and took him in her mouth, and he groaned deep within his chest before erupting into a warm, wet cavern. If he hadn't been so consumed, his jaw might have dropped when he saw her swallow.

She collapsed on top of him. He wrapped his arms around her, their racing heartbeats pounding against one another as she nuzzled her face into the side of his neck. They rested in blissful silence, neither of them uttering a word until their heavy breathing returned to normal.

"Never in my life . . . would I have ever imagined feeling this way," she whispered.

He stared up at the ceiling in contentment, trailing his fingers along the ivory skin of her back, comforted by the heat of her body. "You deserve to feel it every day."

She sighed, then reached up and raked a trembling hand through his ruffled hair. "I only wish you didn't have to pull away." Her breasts pressed against him as she chuckled softly. "I suppose I'm far too taken with bliss to consider the consequences."

"Yes, well—" He gave a small chuckle himself, wrapping his arms tighter around her. "After the way I drank over the past four years, I can only question the potency of my seed."

A hard smack branded his chest, followed by her head snapping up to scowl at him. "Don't you ever say that. Heaven forbid, Gabriel."

"Such worry." He smiled at her. "If I didn't know any better, I would think you wanted to have my child, Miss Baker."

A pinkish hue swept over her cheeks. "No, I—I only meant it for your own behalf."

He pressed a kiss to her mouth. "Liar."

"Well, I can't very well have your child now for heaven's sake," she murmured, brushing her velvet lips over his. "Forgive me if the idea of becoming pregnant, shamed and cast from the house while you're away doesn't have me beside myself with joy."

"And forgive me, but the only words I seemed to understand just then were 'I can't have your child now.'"

She smirked and kissed him. "Such utter arrogance."

"Naturally, my dear."

Removing himself from the sanctuary beneath her body. Gabriel gently shifted their bodies so they rested on their sides, facing each other. Her creamy skin, the lamp light reflecting her eyes, that disheveled mane of ebony hair—he intended to keep this perfect image with him forever.

"You must write to me often," he said, tracing a finger along her arm. "And Ellie, if anything dire happens while I'm gone . . .

anything at all—" Involving Mr. Cain. He hesitated, a jealous sickness washing over him. "Promise you'll tell me immediately."

"I promise," she replied, her eyes darting for a millisecond—just long enough to unnerve him.

He tensed, every part of him burning to question her about the lawyer's visits, why she hadn't mentioned them, and more importantly, whether she knew about Cain's intentions. Silent second after second passed. Ellie caressed his chest, the strokes of her fingertips somehow driving him deeper into trepidation. He could no longer stand it. He was going to ask her.

"Gabriel," she said lightly, before he could open his mouth. "Is blueberry pie still your favorite?"

He relaxed a little. "What on earth led you to ask that?"

"A dream I had tonight—a dream and a memory. You were a boy, and you said that blueberry pie was your favorite."

"And it was, up until I discovered pumpkin."

They shared a smile, and he felt his heavily flogged mind and recently satiated body succumb to exhaustion. He'd ask her at dawn.

As he rolled onto his back, she drew in close, placing a tender hand on his chest and whispering soft endearments into his ear. Despite the battle to keep his eyes open, the soothing, melodic lullaby of her voice relaxed him, and he was quickly seduced into slumber.

It seemed he had barely shut his eyes when the sounds of shuffling—loud enough to wake him—pervaded throughout the room. His eyes fluttered open to find that the morning sun had not yet breached the horizon. When he discovered no warm body beside him, his groggy gaze shifted to the far corner of the bed where Ellie stood, hastily slipping her arms back through the sleeves of her nightgown.

"What time is it?" he asked with a yawn.

When she whirled around, he saw the terrible flames in her eyes.

"How convenient you should ask." Her accusing tone immediately jolted him upright. "I was wondering the same thing when I woke, so I decided to search your waistcoat for a pocket watch."

"Shit," he muttered, his throat going dry.

"Instead—" Her hand flew in the air, clutching his father's letter. "I found this."

Chapter Twenty-Four

Gabriel scrambled from the bed and grabbed his trousers, staring at her like a worm on a hook as he pulled them on hastily. "Ellie, I can explain."

"Explain?" she choked through the rising lump in her throat. "Everything is spelled out right here."

This must be some kind of terrible joke. She stared at the toxic words on the page, yet she could barely read them. *I've regrettably taken the name of my neighbor, Samuel Baker, in order to engage in less than honorable activity. Now, I fear that I may have gotten him into trouble . . . Charlotte Cogs. Dead. Re-locating. Regards, Patrick Peterson.* The rest of the black lines blurred into something resembling an archaic language. How, in the span of a blink, could her world have shaken with such blinding force?

He approached slowly. "Christ, I know, and I didn't intend for you to find out this way."

"I doubt you intended for me to find out at all," she said, hearing the chill in her own voice.

"I was going to tell you, Ellie."

"How long have you known?"

"Only since tonight, I promise."

He reached for her, but she retracted. Gabriel had a history of lying in order to protect himself—so did his father, apparently. How could she believe him when he'd kept something so personal—so crucial—from her? The strange sense of betrayal brought her to shiver. She bit back the urge to cry. Tears would only make things worse.

"So all this time, it was your father . . . behind everything." She clutched her stomach, barely able to breathe at the cold realization of the truth. Her papa—the man she'd bitterly blamed for ruining her, the man who tortured her memories—was innocent. Oh, God, he was innocent. She sickened with regret. "I know our fathers weren't friends, but what did my family ever do to deserve something so horrible?"

"Nothing," Gabriel growled. "My father was a selfish, entitled, power-hungry son of a bitch. I couldn't be sorrier for what he did."

She scoffed at his answer, but he reached out and caught her by the arm before she could walk away. "Don't think for a moment that this wasn't devastating for me. Not only did my father stray from the marital bed at least two dozen times, but he completely ruined your life, as well. How in God's name was I supposed to waltz right in and tell you that?"

She yanked her arm free. "I don't know, but it clearly wasn't the first thing on your mind when you so eagerly took me to bed. How very typical."

"You seduced me." His nostrils flared.

Why, when he was clearly in the wrong, did he look so angry?

"You could have refused."

"Forgive me for not thinking clearly with your breasts in my face."

"Well, I'm glad my breasts provided you an escape from all your—"

"Enough," he barked in a tone that made her flinch. He washed his hands over his face, anguish darkening every feature. "Do you want to know where I was before I came here?"

She said nothing, her stomach knotting under his withering glare.

"I went to the alehouse. I felt the world crashing down on me, so I reacted the only way I knew how."

Gabriel, no. For the first time since reading the letter, she truly looked into his eyes. They were dim and bleak with sorrow. She'd been selfish to ignore his feelings, because if the tables were turned, she'd have crumbled. She drew in a breath to speak, but he held up a hand.

"I know what you're going to ask, and the answer is 'no,' I didn't. I couldn't bring myself to take a single sip."

Relief washed over her, despite the hurt she felt.

He took a bold step toward her, paralyzing her with his presence. "That's when I knew I'd damn well changed. I sat there with a drink in my hand, repulsed by my weakness. I hated myself more than I hated my father. The choices I made before destroyed me, and I wasn't about to fall back into something that would strip from me all the good I have left in my life." She made no move to stop him as he snatched the paper from her hand and hurled it away. "The most important thing being *you*."

His breath was shallow, and he kept his arms pinned to his sides as he searched her face. She could barely look at him. With every glance, the pain in her heart became a sick and fiery gnawing. Somehow, she almost found herself wishing she'd never discovered the truth.

"Tell me how I can trust you . . ." She dashed a stray tear from her cheek. "How, when I know that your past is linked to lies? And now, your blood is linked to betrayal."

He reached out and seized her face between powerful hands. "I am not my past, Ellie, just as I am not my father."

She could feel her lip beginning to tremble. She wouldn't allow herself to trust the wrong person again. In a last grab for strength, she stepped back, removing herself from him like pulling tar from a shoe. A cold, painful separation. "My heart wants to believe you, but I . . . I'm going to need some time."

"Then it seems this worked out perfectly, because time is something you're about to have plenty of."

The words were playful, but their meaning was not. Gabriel picked his shirt up off the ground, slicing the air with his footsteps as he gathered the remainder of his clothing. A painful, agonizing silence lingered between them. It grew worse by the second, yet Ellie feared that uttering a single word might cause an eruption of tears. She sank deep into her chair, praying for temporary blindness so she wouldn't have to see him leave.

He finished dressing as the warm beginnings of light started filtering the dark morning sky. Averting her eyes, she heard the click of the window latch. Her gaze settled on the abandoned letter crumpled near her feet.

"Wait." She snatched it up and handed it to him. "This is yours."

He took the battered paper. "Oh yes, I almost forgot." He hesitated, cold dignity creating a stony mask of his face. "No matter. I'm sure that if I'd left it, you would have found a way to get it back to Mr. Cain somehow."

Ellie flinched. The icy emphasis behind his voice contained no sympathy, and not a soul could have doubted that he questioned her fidelity. As he continued to stare at her, he'd never felt more distant.

"Excuse me?" she answered him thickly.

"And yet you regard me as untrustworthy. Well done, Miss Baker. I must say this deception is very unbecoming of you."

She held her breath, unable to blink as he pulled the window open and slipped outside. This couldn't be happening. Say something, you nitwit!

"I was—I was afraid to tell you . . ." But her voice broke miserably. How ironic.

"Take care of yourself," he advised, sounding nothing more than professional.

He grabbed hold of the cast iron downpipe and disappeared, leaving her to the silent confines of her lonely room. She didn't attempt to follow. She rushed to her bed and buried her face in the pillow that still carried his scent, surrendering herself to pain. The tears she'd fought so hard to repress started spilling in torrents. She didn't care.

Her heart was breaking, and she couldn't have felt more alone.

"Dreary day, isn't it?" Mr. Cain remarked.

Ellie looked up at the cloudy October sky where a gaggle of geese migrated in perfect V formation. "I prefer the gloom," she said.

A slight exaggeration, but of all the seasons, she did enjoy autumn most. Today seemed especially dark and chilly. It was certainly a terrible afternoon for a stroll through the estate's orchards, yet she'd recommended it nonetheless.

"And why is that?" he asked.

"Because it gives one incentive to reflect on the more forlorn parts of life."

She tugged at the sleeve of her frock coat and glanced up at him, hoping to see some degree of a frown. Instead, the man chuckled slightly. "Ah, but we're so alike, Miss Baker. Though I can't say I encourage your troubling yourself with desolate thoughts. It's highly unhealthy for a woman your age."

She forced a soft smile, masking her boredom by plucking an apple from the nearest tree.

Four months had passed since Gabriel left, but it felt more like ten. When she wasn't out riding, visiting with John, or calling on new friends, she distracted herself in Jane and Matthew's company. Solitude allowed time to think, and when there was time to think, Gabriel dominated her mind. Jane knew little about the situation, and thankfully, preparing the baby's nursery took precedent over her prying questions.

Jane had come to wear the signs of impending motherhood beautifully, a blessing bestowed on very few women. Little else had grown round other than her middle. As for Matthew, he'd outperformed the role of expectant father long ago, when he'd ventured out in an evening rainstorm to fetch his wife an assortment of butterscotch, licorice and taffy.

Mr. Cain cleared his throat. "I hope I'm not being too forward, but I have detected a trace of melancholy in you since our last encounter. Did something happen while I was away?"

His three-month trip to France to care for his newly widowed sister hadn't been planned. Before that, he hadn't come to call. She'd seen him in town the week after Gabriel left, but thankfully, too many people milled about for privacy.

But God, even this stone-faced lawyer noticed her heartache? She mustn't be holding herself together as well as she thought. "I suppose this weather reminds me of Colorado. I find myself missing my parents quite often during this time of year." It wasn't a lie. She especially thought of Papa—the wonderful way she used to remember him.

"The forlorn parts of life . . . I now understand what you mean. Grief is an ongoing struggle, Miss Baker. Time certainly heals, yet there is no single moment in our lives where we truly recover."

"The scars on our hearts remain with us for eternity."

"Until we all meet again."

Breathing in the sweet scent of ripe apples, she watched the fallen leaves brush against the hem of her skirt. Reds, yellows and oranges, a vibrant palette of autumn hues crunching beneath their feet. Perhaps it was the weather, or maybe loneliness, but somehow, she enjoyed spending time with Mr. Cain today. He was always so matter-of-fact. Who needed playful jokes and passionate conversation anyway?

She squeezed the McIntosh in her hand, the image of Gabriel's grim face haunting her for the hundredth time that afternoon. Whether awake or in dreams, the memory of their last few moments together still clung to her.

She'd written him last month. She asked about Harvard, apologized for keeping Mr. Cain a secret, then explained that she had absolutely no intention of marrying him. Papa was innocent, but even if he weren't, Ellie would sooner die than hurt Gabriel. So why couldn't Gabriel be faithful and true? She'd been wrong to assume the worst. She didn't deserve a response from him, but every day without a letter made her ache like an old wound on a rainy afternoon.

"Miss Baker," Mr. Cain said.

"Sir?"

"I pride myself on facts and logic. I've never been the most romantic type of man . . . but I must say that your beauty is unmatched. Helen of Troy herself would be jealous."

A bit much, Mr. Cain. "Thank you."

Truthfully, the man probably saw little else in her. She wasn't exactly the friendliest around him. A man of his position wanted a delicate prize to parade around on his arm, one who would bear him attractive children to carry on his legacy and inherit his wealth. It wasn't his fault; it was the way he'd been raised.

She increased the pace of her steps, but his large hand wrapped gently around the crook of her arm to stop her. His dark gray eyes glimmered with romantic intent.

"If the sun is out tomorrow, I'd like to call on you, if I may. There's something important I've been meaning to speak to you about." The deep tone of his voice rattled her bones.

"Oh?" Her mouth felt like old paper, dry and dusty.

"Unless you'd like me to speak about it now—"

Thwak! A stray apple careened into the back of his head.

"What the—!" He released his grip and spun around, clutching the spot of impact as he stared off into the vacant rows of trees.

Don't laugh. Don't laugh. "Are you all right?" she asked.

The air remained crisp and still, the silent marksman nowhere in sight.

Mr. Cain turned back with a scowl. "Who the devil threw that?"

She shrugged. "I barely knew you'd been hit."

"Mark my words, whoever you are," he roared out to the space around them. "I'll get to the bottom of this and make you pay!" He peered over her shoulder, his gaze latching onto something.

She turned to see Tim sprinting toward them.

"Miss Baker!" the boy hollered through laden breaths. He slid to a halt once he reached them. "I was sent to find you. You're needed at the house right away." Turning to Mr. Cain, he dipped his head. "I'm sorry, sir, but it's urgent."

"Well, what are you waiting for?" Mr. Cain conceded with a flick of his hand. "By all means, go on. I'll stay behind you young bloods and find you shortly."

As she glanced from Mr. Cain to Tim, she could tell this wasn't a trick. Orange brows level with his green eyes, Tim looked genuinely concerned. "Thank you," she said to the older man while gathering up her skirts.

Tim bolted and she followed, dodging fallen apples and barreling through rows of trees as fast as she could manage with a bustle and corset.

Slowing his strides to match her pace, Tim snickered. "That was a direct hit, wasn't it?"

Ellie's mouth fell open and she laughed, despite her struggling breath. "So it was you who threw the apple! How did you manage to appear behind me?"

"You're quick to forget who you're speaking to."

She laughed again. "You're right, and I adore you. Now, what's the matter at home?" "See there." Tim pointed toward the house's entrance, where a handful of servants worked to unload suitcases from Jane and Matthew's parked carriage.

Chapter Twenty-Five

Ignoring the burn in her legs, Ellie raced faster until she reached the portico. She clutched one of the pillars near the doors, heaving to catch her breath. Tim assisted a servant who was carrying a large antique chest. Matthew strode out the front door with Henry Westgate on his heels. Both men looked on with tired, burdened faces.

"Is that the last of it?" Mr. Westgate asked.

"Yes, sir," Hanlon replied, helping the two young men maneuver the chest up the steps.

"Thank you for your help, gentlemen." Mr. Westgate watched them enter the house. Then his weary gaze latched onto Ellie. "Ellie? I thought you were out. Where is Magnus?"

Clutching her bodice, she straightened. "He allowed me to go ahead when Mr. O'Hare told me it was urgent." She looked at the empty carriage, then to Matthew. "What's wrong? What happened?"

"Jane hasn't been feeling well of late," Matthew said in a dull, troubled voice. "As a precaution, we'll be staying here until the child arrives. We'll be closer to the doctor by twenty minutes, and Jane insisted on being with the entire family."

"I told him they're welcome as long as they like," Mr. Westgate added, his eyes bleak and unguarded as he looked at his son-in-law.

He trudged to the top step and sat on the cold marble, gazing blankly out at the estate grounds. That alone sent alarm bells ringing. A gentleman of his age and station didn't simply sit on steps like that. How strange to find him so . . . vulnerable. It chilled her seeing him this way.

As steadily as she could manage, she turned to Matthew and asked, "Where's Jane?"

"Upstairs, with the doctor." He gave a weak smile. "I know she'll be happy to see you."

"I'll go to her at once."

She rushed inside, bounding up the grand staircase and slipping past busy servants. Reaching Jane's old bedroom, she knocked. No response. She spun back into the hall as the door nearest the staircase opened. A bald-headed doctor made his exit, and she waited for him to descend the stairs before she darted to the door.

Pressing her ear to the wood, she tapped three soft knocks. "Jane? It's Ellie. May I come in?"

"Please do," Jane's sweet voice answered from inside.

Ellie opened the door, her heart contracting. Pale and situated in the middle of an enormous bed, Jane looked so delicate. Although she smiled, she seemed frail.

"Oh, dear girl—" Ellie crawled onto the bed and wrapped her arms around her. "Are you all right? Tell me what happened."

Jane leaned her head against Ellie's shoulder. "I'm fine, darling, really. I just had a bit of a fainting spell last night."

"What?" Ellie nearly shrieked.

"I don't know what came over me. One moment I was standing in the drawing room, and the next, I was on the ground with several people hovering over me."

"And the baby?" She pulled away, thinking of Mama, of little Walter and Martha . . .

"The baby is fine," Jane said with a smile. "In fact—" she took up Ellie's hand and held it to her perfectly round belly, "Can you feel all that kicking? It hasn't ceased since you came in."

"Oh, yes." Ellie shut her eyes, melting with relief as she felt the tiny foot push against her palm. A beautiful, wondrous experience. She could only imagine what it felt like to Jane. Despite her worries and reservations, she'd come to love this child like a niece or nephew.

"Doctor Davis insisted I spend the remainder of my confinement in bed. So, by telling Matthew that I'd much rather do so in the company of family, I came up with the perfect way to keep you far too occupied for . . . other things."

Ellie tucked a few strawberry tendrils behind Jane's ear. "Are you really that selfless?"

"Or selfish."

"Oh, Jane, I promise to spend every minute of every day with you."

"I'd like that very much." Jane's eyes twinkled and she squeezed Ellie's hand. "I only hope you aren't angry with me for spoiling everything."

"Can't you tell how furious I am? You dreadful girl . . . I'll never forgive you for this." A laugh—no . . . a snort shot from her nose.

Jane stared at her, and then burst out laughing. Ellie covered her face, erupting with laughter herself. Joyful warmth flowed through her. It was just like old times, when she and Jane would sit in bed and giggle about the stupidest things until their sides ached. She hadn't felt this free in a while.

"It's so nice to see you laughing again," Jane said, once their chuckles had subsided. She leaned her head against the pillows and sighed, her smile fading a little. "Now, since I've done you this favor, it's only fair that you owe me one."

Ellie inwardly cringed. She knew what Jane wanted to ask. "Please, any favor but that one."

"Honestly, can you blame me for wondering why you never want to talk about him? I know something unpleasant happened, you've told me that much. But I wish you wouldn't hide the reason from me."

Ellie folded her arms—as if that would keep her from falling apart. The sadness slipped back in, the hurt as fresh as the day he left. "The reason involves the past. I've always been afraid to tell you about it, and now, in your condition . . . it's out of the question."

Jane sat up and leaned forward. "I promise I can endure it."

"You don't understand." Ellie moved to open a window in the stuffy room. "It's far worse than anything you've known. You may never want to speak to me again after you hear it. Besides, I can't bear the thought of causing you so much distress that something goes terribly wrong with the baby."

Jane's light, feather-like brows creased with disappointment. "Fine. You will tell me eventually, though. And when you do, I promise I'll still speak to you afterward."

Ellie gritted her teeth and slid the window halfway open. Fresh air flowed in and across her bare hands, chilling her skin as if it were ten times colder. "Gabriel found out about Mr. Cain," she rested her forehead against the glass, "and now . . . I'm afraid I've ruined everything."

"But surely you told him why you kept Mr. Cain a secret. You didn't know the man would set his sights on marrying you, nor that Father would actually encourage the idea. What's so wrong with trying to avoid trouble?"

"Mr. Cain was the only person who could help Gabriel with what he wanted to do. He's had enough trouble in his life." She turned around. "I didn't want to ruin his chance at peace and rebuilding the future he deserves. I wrote a letter telling him all of that."

"Well, that's good then, isn't it?" Jane asked.

"It's been several weeks, and I've yet to receive a response."

Pursing her lips, Jane pointed to the colorful duffel amidst a pile of luggage near the fireplace. "Bring me that carpet bag, will you?"

An odd request, but perhaps pregnancy made a woman scatterbrained. Thankfully, the bag was light despite its large size.

Ellie carried it to Jane and reclaimed the spot beside her. Jane rummaged through the bag, pushing aside fabrics, ribbons and papers until she found a sealed envelope.

"This came to me last week," she said. "It appears he's written to you."

Ellie stiffened, staring at the envelope. "But he's . . . he's only written you all this time."

Jane pointed to the scribble on the front of the post. "Not anymore, see? It's specifically addressed to you."

Swallowing, Ellie finally reached for the letter. She ran her thumb across the terrible handwriting, her heart pounding at the sight of her name written by him for the first time. This letter was for her. He had replied.

"Well, what are you waiting for?" Jane gave her a playful shove. "Go read it."

"Right . . . I suppose I should."

Ellie's skin felt numb. Jane grinned like a child hearing the end of an enchanted fairy tale, but no happily ever after existed in a world of secrets and family rivalries. Not wishing to worry Jane, Ellie thanked her, kissed her forehead and walked calmly out of the room.

Once she'd shut the door to her own bedroom, she dropped like an anvil to the upholstered bench at the foot of her bed. She stared at the letter in her hands. The paper almost felt warm—a connection—as if part of him were touching her. Never before had she so wanted to read, yet *not* read something, at the same time. She could only imagine what he might have to say after their last encounter.

Biting her lip, she tore the envelope open and unfolded the letter.

Dear Ellie,

I apologize for not writing you sooner. Out of respect, I decided to give you the time you requested until you were ready to correspond. It was anything but easy—I've had many sleepless nights to prove it. But I was very happy to receive your letter.

Regarding the unforgivable things my father has done, there are no clean words to express my feelings on the subject. Yes, his blood runs through my veins, but his mind and his heart DO NOT. You have more reason to fear an attack from an African lion than betrayal from me. I could never blame you for your reservations, given the countless stories I made up to preserve society's idea of me. Being a Peterson was all I'd ever known. I was blind to change until you reminded me how liberating it felt to be myself. When your letter came to me, I had never felt a greater relief.

Furthermore, I understand your actions with regard to Mr. Cain, but I still wish you hadn't kept it from me. I would have much rather heard it from your lips instead of his. The way he spoke of you made me go mad with senseless suspicion and jealousy. Yet the childish way I brought up the subject was uncalled for, and for that, I am truly sorry. Please, my dear, promise to tell me everything from now on, just as I promise to do the same.

The weeks here are long, yet fulfilling, and so much has changed since the days of my own education. I've seen substantial growth in my students with their intensive laboratory work. I enjoy teaching those classes far more than I enjoy lectures, as they allow my pupils to not only engage in hands-on learning, but also facilitating the discovery of knowledge through their research. Pardon the dull medical blather.

Now that you've written me once, I expect it to continue, madam, as I am missing you terribly. December can't come soon enough.

Yours,
Gabriel.

She hadn't lost him.

A rogue tear splashed onto the page, blurring the "G" of his name. She wiped her cheeks clean, sinking forward with relief. She read the letter a second time, then a third, allowing every word to embrace her in place of his arms. If he were with her now, she would tell him how terrified she'd been when he left, how unbearable it felt to be apart, and most importantly, how much she loved him.

There was no more denying it. She'd probably loved him since the day they first met, when watching the ducks swim had been the most important thing in the world. It didn't matter that Patrick Peterson was his father, just as it didn't matter what he did during those years in Creekwood, or whether he was a wealthy heir, or a middle-class doctor. He had always been hers, and she loved him.

But how to resolve this hopeless mess? She slumped back against the footboard. If marrying Gabriel only affected her, she would do so in a second. But she had to think of Gabriel, and of Mr. Westgate, Jane and John. She wouldn't involve the Westgates in scandal, abandon the man who'd taken her in, and sever all ties with the family she loved so dearly—and neither would Gabriel.

No, he would wait as long as it took to make things right. Kind, patient and understanding, the man wasn't his father—not even close. She'd seen enough bad men to last a lifetime, and several memories would likely stay with her forever. That she had come to terms with. But a door in the darkest part of her heart had opened, allowing for a wide shaft of light to spill into every corner.

She hurried through the room on jittery legs and pounced onto her desk chair. Words, words, words, so many words she ached to write! Scrambling for paper, she swore she wouldn't stop until her hand fell off.

"Ellie?" Mary tapped on the door. "I was asked to tell you that Mr. Cain has left for the day. He spoke to Mr. Westgate, and he insists that your time with Jane should take precedent over him. I don't doubt you'll be seeing much less of him for a while."

Bless the man.

Chapter Twenty-Six

Ellie stared out her bedroom window, watching sheets of snow pummel every which way in heaps. According to Gabriel's last letter, he was scheduled to arrive home sometime yesterday. But the early December blizzard had barely let up at all during the past forty hours. How was she supposed to know if he made it back safely? Her mind churned with anticipation and worry. She'd seen her share of lengthy winter storms in Colorado, and Mr. Westgate said it was common for New England to experience a terrible one every couple years or so.

She yawned, her breath fogging the frosted glass. It was late, and she should be asleep instead of willing the weather to stop. She doused the lamp and slipped beneath the bedcovers, pulling them up to her chin for warmth as the fire dwindled in the hearth. Shutting her eyes, she counted sheep until she got frustrated, then pondered the events of the day instead. Embroidery, warm potato soup, a game of checkers with John, followed by several rounds of cards with Jane.

Sweet Jane, always smiling, even now when she'd grown large and uncomfortable. In the morning, Ellie had received a letter from Mr. Cain full of concern for Jane's well being. He'd been kind enough to keep away for the most part. Her thoughts blurred into silence, and she finally succumbed to sleep. She dreamt of her parents in bright, vivid colors. Hand-in-hand, Mama and Papa strolled through a flowery park, happy, youthful and romantic. They'd given up so much for love, but Ellie knew it couldn't have compared to giving up each other. They looked so peaceful, so perfect. Oh, how she loved them . . .

"Ellie!"

She shot up with a gasp. Pulse pounding, she struggled to adjust her eyes to the dark as John's silhouette barreled towards her. "John? What is it? What are you—"

"You have to come, quickly." He threw the covers off and grabbed her by the wrist.

"Why?"

"It's Jane. The baby's coming."

He tugged on her arm, but she couldn't move. It felt as if time had frozen around her. The baby couldn't be coming now. Shutting her eyes, she listened to the howling wind outside. Not tonight. No, not tonight!

She gripped his shoulders. "What are you talking about? The baby isn't due for another month."

"I know!" he yelped in a shrill voice. "Please, you have to come, now!"

She struggled out of bed, but her legs felt like pudding. Somehow she couldn't run, she couldn't hear and she certainly couldn't think. Sheer black fright swept through her.

She followed John through the hall; each step seemed to drag as though she trudged through thick molasses. When they rounded the corner leading to Jane's room, Mr. Westgate and Matthew greeted them with pale faces.

"Is it true?" she asked, wedging herself between them.

"Yes . . . yes, it's time." Matthew dragged a hand through his hair.

Fatigue had settled in the pockets under his eyes. His blond locks looked a mess; he wore nothing more than trousers and an untucked shirt. She'd never seen the man so disheveled. Though fully clothed, Mr. Westgate appeared even worse off than his son-in-law. Stark and vivid fear glittered in his dark eyes.

"I've sent two men out into the storm," he said. "The doctor lives on the other side of town. The ground is covered in several feet of snow, and the blinding conditions are near impossible to maneuver through. Of all nights . . . of all the blasted nights, it had to be this one."

Turning sharply, he began pacing like a frantic madman. Silence seeped into the hall like a heavy mist. She could only imagine how things were on the night that Mrs. Westgate . . .

Stop it! She whirled back to Matthew before images of what-could-be flashed through her mind. "What can I do? Tell me what to do."

Matthew sighed. "See to Jane. Make sure she's comfortable."

She reached out and clutched his arm. "I won't leave her side."

Slowly, she inched the door open and slipped into the room. A lively fire crackled inside the hearth, bathing the space in a warm glow. Mary rushed to her, holding a stack of clean towels to her chest.

"Thank goodness," she whispered, a crease of worry on her brow. "Any word on the doctor?"

"Not yet," Ellie answered softly.

She peered over Mary's shoulder to look at Jane. Her eyes were closed and she sat completely still, clutching the hand of her maid, Libby. Ellie clenched her fists until her nails dug into her palms. The child was coming, and there was nothing she could do to stop it.

"How long since this began?" she asked, her gaze still attached to the distressing scene.

"An hour or so. But her pains are growing closer—"

"Ellie," Jane called out, relaxing back into the pillows. "I'm so relieved to see you."

When Libby moved away, Ellie rushed to take her place beside the bed. "Of course I'm here, darling. What can I do for you?"

Jane looked her dead in the eyes, desperate and terrified. "Please, tell me everything will be all right. I'm so . . . afraid."

The plea was like a stab to the heart. Swallowing her fear, Ellie smiled softly. "Do you think you're the first woman to give birth in a silly storm? You're going to be fine, Jane, I promise. I won't let anything happen to you."

Jane leaned into her, and they pressed their foreheads against one another.

"Thank you," Jane whispered.

Ellie slid her hand beneath Jane's. This wasn't fair. Why was this happening to someone so gentle and kind? She choked back the urge to cry out and scream a slew of curses. Several seconds of silence followed, neither of them moving until Ellie felt Jane's grip tighten.

Ellie drew back as Jane shut her eyes, lurched forward and moaned. Stroking her arm, Ellie spoke soft, comforting words until it was over. She felt so helpless. She didn't know what else to do.

"Oh, Ellie," Jane released a breath and relaxed her grip, "the pain seems to be getting worse every time."

"If I could do anything to take it away, I would. But you must remember that you're not alone. Every mother goes through the same pain, fear and uncertainty. I do hope you realize how much stronger than men we are."

Jane smiled for a moment—then began to cry. "My mother wasn't strong enough. What if I'm not, either? I don't want to die the way she did. Oh, God, I don't want to die."

Her sobs grew louder. She was unraveling.

Ellie's heart pounded up into her throat. She locked eyes with the two maids, both appearing as fearful as she. Suppose Dr. Davis didn't make it in time? The truth about Helen Westgate's death froze in her mind, cold as winter ice. She couldn't just sit around and wait for help that might never arrive. Jane was panicked and frail, and the baby was coming no matter what. Something had to be done.

She had to see if Gabriel was back.

Her heart ached for his comforting presence, his soothing voice and calm demeanor. He needed to be here. He'd know exactly what to do.

But Matthew and Mr. Westgate would sooner trust her to deliver the baby than Gabriel. Matthew had told Jane on numerous occasions that he didn't trust the man's sanity, nor did he feel comfortable keeping secrets from his father-in-law. And Mr. Westgate might very well erupt if she mentioned Gabriel's name tonight. She wouldn't risk asking them.

So who could she send out into the storm? Tim, perhaps. Yes, hardy and strong, the young man could easily—Oh, God, but he didn't know where Gabriel lived. Suppose he got lost? Suppose he found the house but ran into an obstacle, or he didn't try knocking on the door hard enough?

Icy fear twisted round her heart. The only way she could be sure nothing went wrong was to go herself. This was insane . . . this was irrational. But she'd made up her mind.

"Jane, listen to me." She took the girl's face into her hands. "You're not going to die, do you understand me? You're not going to die."

Jane nodded through her sobs.

"I'm going out to find help. You must promise me that you'll save your strength for when you need it. Stay calm, and all will be well."

The words must have been enough to pull Jane out of it, because her watery eyes stared on in disbelief. "Ellie, no. It's too d-dangerous."

"I'll be fine. I'll take Mr. O'Hare with me." Ellie turned to the maids. "Watch over her. Make sure she rests whenever she can, and has everything she needs."

"Yes, miss. Please, be careful," Libby said.

Jane stirred restlessly. "You can't go out there, Ellie. If something happens to you, I'll—" She gripped the bedpost with one hand, a pillow with the other, and cried out. Ellie's stomach clenched. Dear God, the pain looked unbearable.

Sickened with guilt, she dashed out the door. Yet guilt wouldn't stop Jane's agony. She rushed past the men in the hall, explaining how she had to fetch Jane's favorite book from the library. They'd panic when they found her gone, but she couldn't worry about that now. Her strides echoed throughout the cold, dark corridors, and when she reached the servant's quarters, the entire staff stood to greet her.

"Please, Tim—" she located the boy among the anxious group, "—I need you to dress as warmly as you can and fetch two horses. And no side saddle for heaven's sake."

"Yes, ma'am," he said, wasting no time in bounding right over the wooden table and disappearing into the hall.

Hanlon frowned. "Surely you're not thinking of going out there, Miss Baker."

"I have to find Dr. Peterson," she declared.

The wrinkles around his eyes stretched wide. "Does Mr. Westgate know about this?"

"I know it's ludicrous, but Hanlon, you've serviced this house for fifteen years. You were there the night Mr. Westgate lost his wife, and you and I both know that Dr. Peterson lives several miles closer than Dr. Davis. Jane needs help, now. Wouldn't you rather have her safe, than worry about your employer's reaction upon seeing his nephew?"

He averted his gaze, then nodded.

A young cook stepped forward. "You'll be needing warm clothes, too, won't you, miss?"

Ellie looked down at her robe. Drat, she couldn't go back upstairs now. "Yes, I will. I'd be forever grateful if I could borrow some."

"No problem at all," the girl said.

Seven minutes later, Ellie left the cook's room in a simple frock with thick wool stockings, boots, a bonnet and a heavy brown coat. She couldn't remember the last time she'd dressed in under ten minutes—or without a maid's assistance.

When she yanked the kitchen door open, it flew back to reveal a winter nightmare. The freezing wind howled and the ice pelted her face, yet steadfast, she trudged through the thick snow to where Tim approached with the horses.

"Where are we going?" he called out, before handing her a glowing lantern and helping her into the saddle.

"Jane needs help, and soon," she replied. "I'm afraid the others won't return in time, so we're going to find another doctor."

Her numb hand cracked the reins, and she gripped the saddle with her thighs while coaxing a snow-covered Lincoln to canter. Standing in the storm had been bad enough, but speeding through it only reminded her of what a dangerous idea this was. The blizzard raged on angrily, the biting cold attacking and stinging her exposed flesh like a swarm of wasps.

She couldn't see more than three feet in front of her. Flurries of snow darted every which way in the lantern's light, and her lungs burned from the icy air, while her irritated eyes watered. The dense trees provided a moment of shelter, allowing just enough time to make sure Tim's light still glowed somewhere behind her. But all too soon they reached the clearing, and the blizzard pounded back against their frozen bodies with merciless force. They were so close, and Ellie pushed herself to press on.

When she reached the iron gate leading to Gabriel's house, she dismounted so quickly that she fell deep into the thick snow. Pulling herself up, she reached out with frozen hands, ignoring the sting of the metal as she gave it a hard shove.

The stupid thing barely budged.

"I'm not strong enough to open it!" she called out, as Tim rode up behind her.

He leapt from his horse. "Let me try." His red fingers curled around the bars, and he pushed as hard as he could, creating a space barely large enough for a person to squeeze through. "The snow's too thick. It won't move any more."

"I think I can fit. You wait here with the horses and I'll go get help."

Thankfully, Tim didn't protest. She slipped an arm, then her shoulder, then the rest of herself through the small opening. She stomped through the bulky snow as fast as she could, each heavy step more difficult than the last. Her toes stung by the time she made it to the icy doorstep.

Please, Gabriel. Please be home.

She lurched for the door and pounded her fist against it. Only now did she realize she was trembling.

Chapter Twenty-Seven

"Gabriel! Gabriel, are you in there? Wake up! Gabriel!" Ellie slammed both hands on the wood and hollered like a banshee. "Please, open the door! Open the door, Gabriel—"

The latch clicked from inside, and the door whipped open as if it were on a spring. Lamp in hand, Gabriel stood in the dark frame, shirtless. His face dropped.

"Great God."

"It's J-Jane," she half-chattered. "The baby. You m-must come quickly. She n-needs you."

He stared out at the violent storm, then pulled her inside and shut the door. "Christ, are you insane? What were you thinking going out in this weather? I have half a mind to shake you, Ellie!"

"I know it was crazy, but Dr. Davis might not make it to Jane in time. You have to help her."

"Jane's having the baby?" His eyes widened with alarm, as if he just now understood the situation. "Christ. Wait here. I'll be two minutes."

She nodded, rubbing her frozen hands together as he sprinted up the staircase. Heavy footsteps beat the floor above her head, and several seconds later, he thundered down the stairs fully dressed.

"Put these on, for God's sake." He tossed her a scarf and large pair of gloves while rushing to the examination room.

She slid her stiff fingers into the leather gauntlets, appreciating the warmth.

"The stable boy came here with me. He's waiting outside with the horses," she called out, coiling the scarf around her neck until it covered her chin.

"Does he have gloves?" Gabriel's voice hollered back.

"No."

"The blind leading the blind! Check the table by the door. There should be an extra pair inside the drawer."

Wonderful. He must think them both idiots. She found the gloves just where he'd said. When she turned back around, Gabriel had returned with his doctor's bag. He threw on his winter things and she followed him outside. His arm clung firmly to her waist as he guided her toward the gate. She handed Tim the gloves, and all three of them tugged on the metal bars until it opened wide enough for Gabriel to fit through.

He hoisted her into the saddle, climbed up behind her, and grabbed the reins. Nestled in the protective cradle of his body, the ride home seemed almost tolerable. When they finally reached the service entrance, she'd no clue how much time had passed since she'd left. Hopefully not more than an hour.

"Go on inside," Tim said as they dismounted. "I'll get someone else to help me with the horses."

"Thank you, Tim!" She would find a way to repay him handsomely.

Her mind swirled with mixed emotions as she bolted inside with Gabriel. She dreaded Mr. Westgate's reaction to all this, but more importantly, she prayed nothing had gone wrong with Jane. If

Mr. Westgate decided to tar and brand her, she'd take full responsibility for her actions.

They raced up the curving staircase, and she stopped abruptly at his heels the moment her gaze locked with Mr. Westgate's. Eyes red, expression broken, he sat slumped in a chair like a worn-out rag doll. Her stomach lurched when he didn't stand.

"Uncle." Gabriel knelt down beside him.

Jane's screams rattled the door, and Mr. Westgate shut his eyes in agony. "In all these years . . . I've never felt so helpless since the night your aunt—"

"That's not going to happen again."

"John couldn't bear hearing her like this, so Matthew had to take him away and calm him. As for me, well, I haven't been able to leave this spot. I had to stay here with my daughter. My Jane. My little girl . . ." Tears spilled from his eyes as he clasped Gabriel's hand. "Please, you have to help her. I'm begging you."

Gabriel covered Mr. Westgate's hand with his own. A moment of peace followed—uncle and nephew united at last. Rising to his feet, he looked at Ellie. "When we go inside, your job is to see to Jane. Do what I say, and don't leave her side."

"Yes," she whispered, her pulse pounding.

He reached for the handle, and she silently followed him into the room.

Jane gasped as Mary dabbed a wet cloth along her forehead. "Gabriel! Oh, God. Oh, thank God!"

Dropping his bag, he ran to her and kissed her damp, flushed cheek. "Hello, my Jane. Doesn't this child know that it's bad form to debut in the middle of a snowstorm?" he said with a warm smile. "I'm here now. It's all right. Everything's going to be all right." Libby handed him a glass of ice water, and he held it to Jane's lips. He turned to the maid. "Have you been timing her contractions?"

"Yes, sir," she answered. "They're coming every minute or so now."

"And I can't bear them anymore," Jane cried. "Please, give me chloroform!"

Gabriel shook his head. "I'm so sorry, Jane, but I need you conscious. I don't want to use forceps unless absolutely necessary." He held her limp hand and looked at Mary this time. "Have her waters broken?"

Mary nodded.

"There are two bowls of hot water and clean towels on the dresser," Libby said.

"Thank you both. You've done a marvelous job." Gabriel kissed Jane's cheek again before moving across the room to shed his coat and jacket. "Now, go take a well-deserved break for the rest of the evening. I'll call you when you're needed."

"You'll tell us when the baby's born?" Libby asked.

He shoved his sleeves up past his elbows. "Absolutely."

Once the maids left, Ellie clutched Jane's hand as another horrible pain struck. She watched Gabriel's shoulders tense and his jaw flex as he vigorously scrubbed his hands in the basin. Clearly, he hated seeing Jane in this condition.

Jane squeezed Ellie hard, her groans escalating into awful shrieks as her suffering intensified. Ellie could barely breathe watching her squirm and thrash about the bed. It wouldn't be long now. When the unbearable pain finally ended, Ellie took the wet cloth beside the bed and wiped perspiration from Jane's reddened face.

"Jane, I'm going to examine you now," Gabriel said, approaching the foot of the bed.

Jane made no sound, only nodded weakly as Ellie stroked her damp hair.

He slid his arms beneath the bed sheets, keeping his eyes focused elsewhere and working by touch alone. "It appears we made it just in time. You're ready to begin pushing."

"No," Jane whimpered, her eyes ridden with terror.

Ellie's hands trembled. She couldn't imagine having to go through this without Gabriel. Mama had been midwife to a friend once, and she'd always said that assisting a birth wasn't for the faint of heart. Only now did Ellie understand what she meant. Leaning into Jane, she whispered, "You can do this, my darling. It will all be over soon."

"Please, don't leave me," Jane begged, clutching her wrist.

"I'll never leave you."

"Now listen to me carefully," Gabriel said in a calm, soothing tone. "When the next pain comes, I want you to draw your legs up, take a deep breath, and bear down as hard as you can. Can you do that for me?"

Jane nodded. She sucked in a gasp, and Ellie helped hold her into position as she pushed down with all her might. Gabriel counted to ten. He instructed Jane to release her breath, draw in another one and start the entire process over again.

Half an hour later, the strain had taken a toll on Jane. She seemed to grow more exhausted by the minute. After yet another feeble push, she collapsed onto the pillows, her body shivering and her chest heaving in surrender.

Gabriel moved his hands between her legs, but Ellie couldn't see what he was doing. He looked so calm and professional. After a moment of silence, he expelled a small breath of relief. "The head is out, Jane. I know you're tired, but just a few more pushes and you'll—"

"I can't! I've no strength left . . ."

"Yes, you can. You've come too far to give up now."

Ellie squeezed her trembling hand. "Just think of the baby."

"No. I can't do it," Jane cried, hysterical.

"Jane, look at me," he demanded. "Look at me!"

The tears died down, and Jane's eyes snapped open to stare, while her teeth chattered in distress.

"You can do this," he said. "I damn well know you can, because you've always been the strongest one in this family. I saw the way you cared for John after Aunt Helen died. I read the encouraging poems you wrote to my mother when my father took ill. You accepted me when I deserved the cold shoulder. I've seen the courage in you since the day you were born. Don't let that change. Don't let me down."

His expression brimmed with love and authority. A spark of determination settled beneath Jane's gaze, and she nodded her head. When the time came for her to push again, she worked hard without stopping.

"That's it, keep going," he coaxed. "Almost there. Almost . . ." His shoulders lowered. He broke into a wide, open smile as the gurgling cries of an infant rang throughout the room. "It's a girl! And she's—oh, she's beautiful, Jane."

Ellie burst forth in tearful laughter as Jane collapsed against the pillows. Joy, pure and tender, bubbled through her. As she met eyes with the doctor across the bed, she'd never felt a deeper love.

"Come here," he said, his grin as intimate as a kiss.

She rushed to him, her breath catching when she saw the precious pink newborn in his arms. The child was so beautiful, so innocent and new. A mother's work was truly the most rewarding. Ellie loved her so much already. She couldn't wait to play with her and watch her grow. Someday, when no one was watching, she might even teach her to ride like a western.

Handing her a pair of medical scissors, he instructed her to cut just above the spot where he'd tied off the cord. Ellie did so carefully, and she gently washed the baby clean before wrapping her in a blanket, then giving the infant to her mother.

"She's perfect, isn't she?" Jane whispered, her eyes heavy with fatigue as she stroked the infant's tiny cheek. "How can something so precious cause so much discomfort? I can't tell you how grateful I am for both of you."

"We're grateful for you, Jane. You should be so proud of yourself," Gabriel said, still grinning from ear-to-ear.

Once he'd finished tending to Jane's medical needs, Ellie gingerly washed the new mother and covered her with fresh blankets. Then she settled down on the bed, watching the new baby in pure wonder. "She looks just like you. Do you know what you're going to call her?"

"Well—" Jane smiled. "Since Matthew's mother and I share the same name, we thought it would be silly having a third Jane in the family. I'd like her middle name to be Helen, in honor of Mother. But as for her first name . . . I was thinking of calling her Victoria."

Gabriel stopped scrubbing his hands in the basin and peered over his shoulder. "You were?"

"Only if you don't mind."

"No, I—" His blue eyes glistened as if some raw emotion had touched him. "I don't mind at all. That means the world to me. Thank you, Jane."

Ellie wished the tender moment could last an eternity, but three very worried men waited patiently outside. Matthew especially deserved admittance. With Gabriel nearly finished packing his bag, she kissed Jane and the baby and slipped into the hall.

Matthew and Mr. Westgate sprung to attention like a couple of well-trained terriers.

"It's all over," she announced. "Matthew, you have a beautiful daughter. Jane is doing just fine, too."

Matthew slapped a hand to his chest and collapsed against the wall. "Praise the Lord!"

Mr. Westgate covered his eyes and turned away. Part of her longed to embrace him, despite the man's obvious need for a personal moment. She couldn't imagine the overwhelming relief he must feel.

"May I?" Matthew asked, gesturing to the door.

She nodded with a smile, and he reached for the knob just as Gabriel stepped out into the hall. The two men stared at one another. Slowly, Matthew extended a hand. Gabriel shook it.

"I don't know how to thank you for what you've done," Matthew said, his voice strewn with shame. "I only hope you can forgive me someday for my cold behavior."

Narrowing his eyes, the corner of Gabriel's mouth twitched. "I'll consider it, Mr. Tiller. But for now, don't waste another second away from your wife and child."

Matthew cleared his throat anxiously, then slipped into the bedroom and closed the door behind him.

"I suppose I should be furious with you."

She turned to find Mr. Westgate standing behind her.

"I'm sorry, sir," she said. "I promise I can explain everything."

"I'm sure you can, and you certainly will. Only, not tonight." He reached out and held a hand to her cheek. "Tonight, my dear, is a celebration. I thank you from the bottom of my heart."

He kissed her forehead, and she shut her eyes as warmth embraced her heart. If this were how Mr. Westgate behaved at his happiest, she could certainly become used to it. Taking a step back, he glanced at his nephew, then to her.

"John is still hiding away in that spare bedroom," he said, pointing to the door at the end of the hall. "Would you mind telling him he's an uncle, and keeping him company while I speak with Gabriel for a moment?"

In all these months, she'd only heard him speak Gabriel's name once—the night she and Jane had listened to them shouting outside. A nervous flutter battered her stomach. Please, let this be the day. No more hiding, no more pain, bitterness and anger. Only forgiveness. She prayed for forgiveness.

"Of course." she said, her eyes meeting Gabriel's for a short second. They exchanged a subtle look of passion, one that weakened her knees even after he'd returned his attention to his uncle.

Every part of her quaked with anticipation as she walked the ten long paces to the door and went inside.

* * *

Gabriel set his bag down and dropped his coat on top of it. He should be more serious, but his heart still swelled with optimism. In the course of three hours, he'd seen Ellie again, delivered a beautiful baby girl—a girl named after his mother—and cleared his tension with Tiller.

Holding the infant in his arms, he couldn't help but wonder what it would feel like to cradle his own child. He'd always assumed he'd become a father someday, yet that's all it was—an assumption. Marrying within his rank and producing an heir was part of a privileged man's duty. But producing a family shouldn't only be about duty—it should be about love. He loved Ellie unconditionally. The enchanting way she smiled at that baby made his loins ache to create new life with her. No more assumptions. He wanted to become a father.

"I've become so accustomed to our arguments, that I now find myself at a loss for words." Henry's voice halted his thoughts.

Only now did Gabriel notice how gray his uncle's sideburns and mustache had gotten over the years. The lines on his forehead and around his eyes had deepened, yet his stare seemed much less harsh than in times past. Something told him the man wasn't about to kick him out this time. Every grueling encounter, every disgraceful shouting match and insulting word had led up to this very moment. He couldn't deny that he'd given up hope long ago. Who knew the recipe for civilized conversation included a blizzard, the birth of a child and one very foolish—yet incredible—woman?

He sighed. "Would you care for me to start?"

"No, no." Henry held up a hand. "I can manage. I've wanted to mend things for quite some time, yet I've been too cowardly and stubborn to do so. But first and foremost, I must thank you for helping Jane when I failed to do so. I called you uncaring before . . . but tonight, I saw how much you still love her." He hesitated, his eyes darting to a pair of framed silhouettes on the wall. "I know I wasn't the most supportive of your choice of profession, but may God strike me down if I ever think ill of it now."

Gabriel released a quiet chuckle. "I've waited years to hear those words."

A shadow of guilt crossed his uncle's face. "I know I've never been the best at conveying my emotions. Tonight, I'll admit that I was truly afraid. I feared that yet another person I loved would be taken away from me, and that this time, I might not be able to endure it."

"I'd be lying if I said I wasn't afraid myself."

"It's astounding, really." Henry folded his arms and rocked back on his heels. "We assume we have control over our lives, yet all it takes is one frightening situation to make us realize how truly powerless we are."

"But we can control how we react to those situations. I, for one, acted incredibly poorly by abandoning my family . . ." The bitter taste of regret filled Gabriel's mouth. Though he looked toward the future now, it would still take a long time to forget. He could accept that.

"We learn from our mistakes, Gabriel. We all make mistakes." Slowly, as if walking on egg shells, Henry stepped toward him. "I made the mistake of shutting you out when I should have cherished the chance to have you back. I made the mistake of convincing my sister to travel with you to Chicago, because I didn't trust you to handle everything on your own. I was the one who told her to go. The guilt I had to live with after losing both of you was . . . unimaginable."

Gabriel stiffened. All this time, he had no idea what lingered beneath his uncle's anger. Four years ago, he might have been furious. Now, watching the great Henry Westgate shrink before his very eyes, Gabriel only wanted to reach out to him.

"When your property went to auction, I bought your house and everything in it," Henry continued in a slightly shaken voice. "I'm not sure why I did it. I must have thought that by some miracle, I might knock on the door and find you there again. The passing months eventually quenched my hope, yet it still killed me to accept your death. So, I did my best to shut you out of my memory. I hid every photo of you, I told the children never to speak of you . . ." He shook his head and stared off somewhere. "If you never existed, then I'd never have to mourn you."

Gabriel understood. He could never blame Henry, because he knew exactly what hiding from grief felt like. Something was always missing. Part of him was always cold.

"When I saw you again, it was like the strangest of dreams. Suppose I let myself love you again, only to lose you to something unforeseen? I'd never recover. In my confusion, anger and fear, it seemed less painful to remove the burden of Victoria's death from my shoulders and place the blame with you."

"I felt blame enough," Gabriel said. Shutting his eyes, he let Henry's painful words sink in. The confession was a jagged sort of comfort, but at least he knew the truth. In some strange way, it helped him understand.

"It was wrong of me to do that to you," said Henry. "I wasted so much time in anger, instead of embracing that, regardless how long it took, you had chosen to return. I'm just as guilty of running as you."

"If I could change the past, I wouldn't hesitate," Gabriel said. "But the truth is I can't, and neither can you, Uncle. Not everyone gets second chances. What good are they if we don't take them?"

"Useless, I gather."

"Then . . . does this mean I'm forgiven?" Gabriel asked.

Henry gazed at him, his eyes shining with unshed tears. "Nephew, it is I who should ask you that question."

Gabriel blinked. There was no need to consider. Tonight, he'd finally get his "real" father back. He closed off the space between them and gripped his uncle hard. Henry hesitated a second before slapping his arms around Gabriel's back and clutching him. The air around them cleared, months of pent-up tension and grief floating away. Gabriel bit back a groan of emotion. For the first time since his return, his family felt complete. Or, almost . . .

"Uncle." He released Henry, his heart aching with a different kind of love. "I need to speak to you about Ellie."

Henry's eyebrows shot up. "Ellie?"

"I mean, Miss Baker. You see . . . there are a few things you should—"

The door opened and Matthew popped his head in, wearing the proud smile of a new father. His contentment was contagious enough to melt Jack Frost and end the snowstorm. Little Victoria certainly created a glow bright enough to warm the whole house.

"Come see the child," he said. "Bring John. Bring the staff. Bring everyone, for all I care!"

Gabriel patted Henry's arm. "Go on, Uncle. I'll get the boy."

When Henry grinned, he looked ten years younger. "Right. We'll continue this conversation tomorrow, after you've had a good night's sleep in one of the guest rooms. You deserve proper rest after all you've done."

"Thank you, sir, I look forward to it," Gabriel said, grateful for the hospitality—grateful for everything good in his life.

He turned for the hall, his heart thumping madly, his legs unable to walk fast enough. There were so many things he wanted to tell Ellie. The past six months felt like the longest of his life. How did he endure those fourteen years without her? He didn't know, but God, how blessed he'd been to find her again. So very blessed.

Now, as he reached for the doorknob, he swore he'd never lose her again.

Chapter Twenty-Eight

John pounced on Gabriel the moment he entered the room.

"Gabriel! It's so good to have you back, old chap. Is Jane alright? Can I see the baby yet?"

Gabriel laughed. Damn if the boy hadn't grown taller already. "It's good to see you, too, Uncle John. And yes, your new niece is waiting to meet you."

"Bully!" Tugging the tie of his robe, John bounded full-steam out the door.

Ellie rose from the chair beside the window, her dark hair draped softly around her pale shoulders. She gave him a smile that sent his pulses racing. He swore she became more beautiful every time he saw her. It was time for a proper reunion.

Without a word, he marched to her, lifted her off the ground and covered her mouth with his. He remembered those lips as if he'd just kissed them yesterday. Warm. Full. Familiar. Lord, how he'd missed them. And that subtle floral smell—heavenly.

She wrapped her arms around his neck, and he twirled her once before setting her back down. Pulling away, he opened his eyes to find a pair of sparkling emeralds gazing at him. "You don't know how long I've been waiting to do that," he confessed, grinning like a buffoon.

Tilting her head to one side, she said, "Actually, I think I might have an idea."

He'd never grow tired of seeing her blush. He knew she'd missed him—her letters had told him that much—but to truly see the longing in her face, the passion and glow in her eyes as she held him, made him bubble over with joy.

"When I saw you on my doorstep tonight . . . I literally thought you'd gone insane. You're going to give me gray hair, you know." He pulled her close, cherishing every touch. "You brave, beautiful woman."

"I'm sorry. I know it was dangerous, but Jane was the only thing on my mind, and—"

He silenced her with a kiss. "No need to explain. You saved the day, Ellie Bear."

"No, you did," she said, pressing a warm hand to his cheek. "You handled everything with such confidence, as if you weren't afraid at all. How many times had you done that?"

"Only once, back when I was an apprentice."

"You're a brilliant doctor, Gabriel. I've witnessed plenty of calves and foals being born, but watching you deliver that baby was the most incredible thing I've ever seen."

He covered her hand with his. "We work well together, don't we?"

"Yes." The howling wind rattled the window, and she winced. "Only, what happens now? Tell me your uncle isn't sending you back out there. Tell me you've spoken to him."

"He opened up to me about everything, and I now understand the reasons behind his distance. It turns out he and I are not that different. We both had fears and terrible regret to sort through. I'm thrilled to say that all has been forgiven."

Joyful relief shone in her face. "Oh, Gabriel."

Slowly, he took up her hand. Her eyes, bordered with tears, glistened with happiness and affection. It was time to tell her how much she meant to him. "First thing tomorrow, I'm speaking to Henry." He pressed his lips to the underside of her wrist. "I'm going to make sure he calls things off with Mr. Cain."

"You are?"

"Yes, and I'm going to tell him about our childhood years together, when we splashed in mud puddles and played hide-and-seek in the barn. I'll tell him how you found me a lost, drunken wretch several years later—" he kissed her cheek, trailing several more down her elegant jaw line, "—that you alone inspired me to return to the things I ran from, and how you helped shape me into the man I am today."

When his lips reached her mouth, he stopped. His heart drummed wildly. "And, after all that is said and done, I'll tell him how much I love you. Because I do love you, Ellie Baker. I've loved you since the night I taught you how to waltz at that ridiculous party. You could have trampled my feet a hundred times for all I cared. To me, your imperfections are perfect."

* * *

He loved her!

Never had she heard more beautiful words spoken. And God, she loved him, too, so much that she couldn't even remember how long ago it had started. Most likely her entire life.

A year ago, the world was a cruel, unforgiving place. She hadn't felt worthy of things like love, and romantic confessions meant nothing more than false promises and lies. How drastically things had changed since then.

She ached to do something she never would have dreamed possible—to completely and irrevocably open her heart.

"Say something, sweetheart," he said with a nervous chuckle. "I get the impression you're trying to murder me with your silence."

She laughed, squeezing his hands. "It's your own fault for making me speechless. Yet, if you would care to repeat what you just said, I'd be happy to respond this time."

"Gladly . . ."

His sharp exhale should have served as a warning. He swept her up off the ground again, and her head spun as he kissed her hard. She felt his pronounced smile beneath her lips, lasting all the way up to the moment he placed her on the bed.

"Now, listen carefully this time," he said, narrowing his eyes and bringing his face inches from hers. "I love you. I will love you forever, and long after that."

She reached for his hands, lacing his fingers with her own. "I love you, too, Gabriel. With all my heart, no matter what the future may bring."

His eyes lit, and that charmingly crooked smile stretched the farthest she'd seen. Brushing his lips against her ear, he asked, "Well then, love of my life, will you stay with me tonight?"

She gripped his waistcoat, pulled him forward and kissed him deeply. Releasing all the love she felt for him, all the emotion she'd been afraid of, she never wanted to let go.

* * *

The following afternoon, she waited outside Mr. Westgate's office, her stomach twisting into knots. The house felt quiet today. Everyone had gone to bed so late that even the servants were allotted an extra hour of sleep. Mr. Westgate must have been at his utmost leisure last night. Hopefully, his merriment would carry on for a very long time.

Folding her arms across her chest, she tiptoed into the adjacent library, peering at the grandfather clock for the third time in ten minutes. It had been more than an hour since Gabriel left to speak with his uncle. No doubt they had plenty to discuss, and catch up on. They deserved all the privacy they wanted, yet every minute the door remained closed felt a little like torture.

What were they talking about at this very moment? How much had Gabriel revealed, and how had Mr. Westgate reacted upon hearing it? Suppose she had to answer questions she wasn't prepared for? Nonsense. Gabriel would never mention the brothel, nor the time they'd spent alone together . . .

The door swung inward and she jumped. Gabriel stepped out, his expression calm, yet unreadable. He looked so handsome in his wool frock coat. Seeing him fully dressed made her cheeks burn, because mere hours ago, not a scrap of clothing had stood between them. They'd made love three times last night; she'd fallen asleep in the safety of his arms.

She rushed to him. "How was it? How did it go?"

He leaned in, planted a kiss on her cheek, and whispered, "So many questions. You'll find out soon enough."

The answer didn't help, but at least he'd kissed her. That had to be a good sign.

He backed down the hall, and she blew him another kiss, which he caught before disappearing round the corner.

"Beautiful day, isn't it? The storm ended this morning. The sun is finally out again. I'm half-inclined to go make snow angels."

She spun around to find Mr. Westgate standing in the doorway.

Despite the dark circles beneath his eyes, he grinned. "We might benefit from a little fresh air after being indoors so long. Why don't you bundle up, and we'll rendezvous out back?"

"Yes, sir. That sounds lovely," she said. Somehow, the thought of conversing in open air as opposed to the dark confines of an office helped quell her nerves.

She ran upstairs and put on her winter coat, not only remembering to wear gloves this time, but a nice warm muff, as well.

When she stepped outside, Mr. Westgate was waiting, and she took his arm as they walked down the shoveled steps and into a field of white. Their shoes crunched the glistening snow. Fresh powder rested on fences, and ice-encased tree branches looked like glistening glass. A pleasing stillness filled the air.

"Doctor Davis arrived an hour too late," Mr. Westgate said, his voice light. "You should have seen the look on the man's face when I told him everything had turned out all right. I hope you realize it was all thanks to you."

"I felt so horrible keeping it from you."

"Yet you were right to do so. To think that I might have refused Gabriel's help. Had you not gone to find him, I can't imagine what might have happened." His breath fogged the air as he stared off. "Jane is my only daughter. One meaningless grudge might have cost me so much."

Yes, it could have, but he understood that now. She reached over and patted his arm with her free hand. He led them into a cast iron gazebo, where the elevated view made the trimmed hedges look like snaking white mounds.

"It warms my heart to see you happy, sir. I don't think I've seen you this content since the day I arrived."

He studied her in a fatherly fashion. "That was the most outspoken thing I've heard you say. Helen was quite outspoken at your age. Never afraid to share how she felt when others would only pretend. It was one of the traits I admired most about her."

"I wish I could have met her."

"Me, too."

They glanced at each other and grinned.

"Now, my dear," he said with a significant lifting of his brows. "As you well know, Gabriel and I had a lot to talk about this morning. Truths, grievances, confessions, and simple topics I feared I'd never share with him again. Then, after all was said and done, there were a few more" —he tilted his head— "surprises."

Dear Lord. She went blank, mind and body benumbed. Preparing her answers had seemed much easier in the absence of his presence.

"Would you care to confirm of which I speak, Ellie?"

She latched her hands together inside her muff, scrambling for coherent thoughts. Just start at the beginning. Yes, the beginning might be a good idea.

"I met Gabriel when I was four-years-old. We were neighbors during the five years his father worked in Colorado." She was already doing a terrible job. "He was my best friend, and I thought we'd be playmates forever until his family—"

Mr. Westgate held up a hand. "Yes. I heard every detail pertaining to a most fascinating past between the two of you, and if you'd like, we can discuss more of it later. Perhaps I didn't make my question clear enough." He folded his arms and peered at her. "Are you in love with my nephew?"

Oh . . . so that was what he meant. How blunt of him to seek a simple answer—one she would gladly give over and over again.

"Yes. With all my heart."

He didn't answer. He only eyed her with a stoic, calculating expression. Her chest tightened and she held her breath. What was he thinking? When she thought she might pass out, his face softened, and a slow grin raised the corners of his thick mustache.

"How sentimental."

The dry, unmistakable voice came from behind her.

A chill struck her spine. She froze. Her nerves must have caused her to hear things. Her heart began pounding, and she turned around slowly.

Jasper stepped out from behind one of the gazebo posts, wearing a deadly smile.

CHAPTER TWENTY-NINE

"Who the devil are you?" demanded Mr. Westgate.

"An old friend." Jasper's cold, dark eyes took Ellie in. "Isn't that right?"

She couldn't speak. Icy fear seeped into her bones at the sight of him standing in the snow like a poisonous black stain. He moved toward the steps with a slight limp, surveying her clothing from head-to-toe.

"I must say you've done well for yourself. No wonder you left me for dear old H. Westgate here."

"Leave him out of this," she rasped, finally finding her voice.

Oh, God, this couldn't be happening.

Mr. Westgate must have seen the terror in her eyes because he took her arm with gentle protection. "Ellie, how do you know this man?"

Jasper regarded her with amusement. "Yes, Ellie. I think an introduction is necessary after all we've been through."

A shiver shot down to her toes, numbing them. She couldn't say what she wanted to. She couldn't scream and shout that Jasper had raped her. Somewhere beneath his long black coat, a loaded gun waited. Jasper always carried one. Mr. Westgate would become enraged, and he had no idea what Jasper was capable of. She did.

Reluctantly, she said, "His name is Jasper Cogs. I worked for him in Creekwood."

"Yes, and what a marvelous member of my staff she was, too. I missed her so much that I thought I'd pay her a visit while I was in town. I'd love a moment to catch up with her if you don't mind."

Mr. Westgate's stare drilled into him. "As a matter of fact, I do mind, because she doesn't look at all thrilled to see you."

A shadow of irritation crossed Jasper's face. His patience was wearing thin.

"Actually, sir, I would like to speak with him." She pulled her arm free. "If you'd be so kind as to give me a minute with Mr. Cogs, I would greatly appreciate it."

Mr. Westgate stood his ground. Bless him for trying to protect her when Jasper could kill him in the blink of an eye.

"Stubborn old man, isn't he?" Jasper shot him a cautionary smile. "You'd be wise to do as she says, friend, since I can speak to her with or without your permission."

"How dare you threaten me on my own property!"

Mr. Westgate stepped forward, and she saw something in Jasper snap. His hand slid beneath his coat, and her panic yielded to terror. Mr. Westgate's life was in danger—right now.

"I was a harlot!" she cried out, desperate to save him.

It worked.

Jasper removed his hand, and Mr. Westgate spun around to stare at her. The shock and confusion on his face killed her, but she reminded herself of what was at stake. She had to get him out of harm's way, even if it meant hurting him.

"I worked for Jasper at a brothel. I've slept with dozens of men, including him." She pointed to Japer, trying not to vomit at every putrid word spewing from her mouth. "I'm so sorry I didn't tell you. Please, allow me to spare you the humiliation by leaving and never coming back."

She felt the pain everywhere. She couldn't bear seeing the look on Mr. Westgate's face, so she dropped her eyes and pushed past him. Heaven help her, this was for his own good. Biting her lips to keep from sobbing, she glared at Jasper and hurled her muff to the ground.

"I'll go with you, alright? I know that's what you want. Just leave him alone."

Jasper chuckled, seemingly pleased with her decision.

His bony fingers wrapped around her elbow, and her heart pounded so hard that it made her light-headed. As they moved through the snow, the sinking feeling of anguish caused her to stumble. Somehow, some way, she'd get out of this.

"Send for the police, and she dies," Jasper called out over his shoulder. Yanking her close, he leaned into her ear. "Such bravery. My, my, little dove, how you've changed."

"Where are we going?" she asked.

"Back where you belong," he said, his grip tightening on her arm. "Did you really think you could stab me in the ass and live happily ever after? I told you that you couldn't run from me. I told you I'd always find you. You made it so easy too, leaving that letter behind and all."

He ushered her into a cluster of trees, where their every movement caused heaps of snow to smack her face and saturate her clothing.

"Aren't you going to ask me how my leg is?" he spat bitterly.

She wanted to tell him she was sorry he hadn't gotten an infection, that she wished he was dead and rotting in a shallow grave. But there was no telling what awful things Jasper would do once he had her alone. The further they moved from the house—and from Gabriel—the more her heart hurt. *Just know how much I love you.*

"You seem to be walking just fine," she said, with as much disdain as possible.

Jasper barked a short, sarcastic laugh.

Then he stopped walking and jerked her to a halt. His eyes narrowed suspiciously, as if her answer had disturbed him in some way. After recoiling at his every move a year ago, had she fooled him into believing she wasn't afraid?

"Did that big fancy house and expensive clothing make you feel good, Ellie? Did it make you forget everything I've done to you, and how little you'd be worth once your rich little friends learn the truth? They don't care about you like I do. They don't see your potential."

His lips twisted into a cynical smile, but she wouldn't allow his mind games to work. Not this time.

"You're wrong. They do care about me," she threw the words at him like stones. "Even if I never see those people again, they'll have meant more to me than you could in a hundred lifetimes. You can't force me to fear you by pointing a gun in my face. And no man respects you out of choice, either. You're the one who's worthless, Jasper."

He slapped her.

"It's been a while since someone's shown you your place. You seem to forget who you're dealing with, missy."

"I know exactly who I'm dealing with—" her cheek was on fire, but she lifted her chin to meet his icy gaze head on, "—that's why I'd like to ask you something important."

"What?"

"Did you murder my father?"

Reaching out, he gripped her face like a small child's. "Why would you want to know a thing like that? Don't you fear me enough? Aren't you already tortured inside by the thought of what your punishment will be?"

She didn't flinch. "Tell me."

He tilted his head, his mouth spreading into a mocking smile. "His animals killed him. Whether or not I happened to spook them into a frenzy as he opened the gate is something entirely different."

Devil!

Fury choked her as she tore away from him. "And when did you realize my father wasn't the man you were looking for? When you saw his lifeless face?"

Jasper's expression darkened. "What the hell are you talking about?"

"You know exactly what I'm talking about. My father had nothing to do with your sister. You killed an innocent man and lied to me about everything . . . just so you could own me!"

The long, deep look they exchanged made her sick.

"Clever, clever girl," he said, reaching for her again. When she jerked away he retracted. "Oh, now don't act that way. It's not my fault your father got himself impersonated. I only knew I wanted to kill Samuel Baker. All men look the same in hats. It took me years to find the real son of a bitch responsible for Charlotte, and when I did, he was nearly dead from pneumonia." Seizing her arm, he continued to pull her through the trees. "Since I couldn't kill the old bastard myself, I did the next best thing."

Gabriel. She pressed a hand to her mouth and squeezed her eyes shut.

"He was rich as hell, leaving behind a spoiled widow and privileged son. So I hired someone to track them down, kill them and destroy the family's inheritance. No one double crosses me and gets away with it."

He went on and on. She did all she could to keep her legs from giving out as she listened to him confess everything.

" . . . So I burned the will, and let the fine state of New Hampshire distribute the assets however they saw fit."

"And you're proud of yourself."

He smiled in a satisfied way.

They reached a clearing. His horse-drawn cart waited in isolation. This was really happening. Her tiny amount of courage withered. She dragged her footsteps, wishing she could scream.

"You're trying my patience," he growled, nearly yanking her arm from its socket. "Walk faster."

"Or what? I don't care what you do to me anymore."

Her body hit the snow before she realized he'd thrown her. Seizing her throat with his big claw, he closed in. "Don't be so quick to assume," he warned, tilting her head back. "You act so tough, but I can feel your heart pounding like a frightened little fawn. As useless as you are to me dead, don't think you can't push me too far."

Click.

The sound of a gun cocking pierced the atmosphere. Jasper released her as Gabriel pushed through the trees with a revolver in his hand.

"Who the hell are you?"

Gabriel's eyes burned like hot coals. "You tell me, Cogs."

Jasper stared at him, confused.

"I suppose I can't blame you for not recognizing me." Gabriel took a step forward. "You hired an assassin to kill me and my mother, didn't you? And you certainly couldn't have known that drunk who beat you to hell in your own brothel was the same man. Lucky me, I guess."

"No . . ." Jasper went pale and stumbled backward. For the first time, dread looked out of his eyes. "All those years. You were supposed to be dead . . . but you—you were right in front of my face the entire time."

"Feel stupid, don't you?"

"Shit," Jasper hissed. "I should have killed you when I had the chance!" As he reached into his coat to draw his weapon, Gabriel's gun roared. Jasper screamed, and he dropped in the snow, holding his crotch. "You son of a bitch!"

Gabriel stormed over and grabbed him by the collar. "That's for all the women you've put through hell during your lifetime."

He threw Jasper down, pulled back the hammer of his revolver and took aim. There was an insatiable hunger for vengeance in his eyes. Jasper groaned like an angry bear, and the blood on his trousers began staining the snow a bright red. Blood. So much blood.

Ellie averted her eyes, but it was too late. The nausea and sweating started. She struggled to control her reaction, but she must have failed, because she barely noticed Gabriel fire one last shot. He rushed over and scooped her up, his arms trembling noticeably.

"It's all over," he said. "Let's get you inside."

She held onto his neck and buried her face in his shoulder, shutting herself away. The dizziness subsided quickly, so did the nausea. He smelled so wonderful. If Jasper had kept her from smelling Gabriel ever again, she would have died.

Something—a feeling of dread—told her to look up. She lifted her head and saw Jasper pulling his gun. She screamed as he struggled to aim. "No!"

Gabriel dropped her, and she hit the freezing ground moments before she heard the shot. A long, eerie silence followed. She started to cry. The snow stung her face, yet she was too paralyzed to move. Please, God, please let Gabriel be alive!

She felt a hand on her shoulder. "Ellie."

Lifting her head, she opened her eyes to see Gabriel kneeling close. He smiled, brushing the flakes of snow from her cheeks. No blood stained his clothing. She searched his chest for marks, watched his breathing and took in the color of his face. He was all right. Relief washed over her, so powerfully that she sprung up and wrapped her arms around his neck, tackling him to the ground.

"I thought I'd lost you," she choked through tears.

The snow might as well have melted around them, because all she felt was warmth as he held her close. She never, ever wanted to be that afraid again, just as she never wanted to be without him. He wasn't just her love, he was her heart, her soul.

He lifted their bodies up into a sitting position. "I'm not going anywhere, thanks to my lookout. You saved my life, sweetheart." He pressed a hand to her cheek, and she leaned into his cold, damp palm.

Branches rustled. Matthew and Mr. Westgate burst through the trees with pistols. They stared at Jasper's body and froze, their eyes wide with shock.

"Good God, are you two hurt?" Mr. Westgate asked.

She tried looking at Jasper, but Gabriel took her chin and turned her away. "You don't need to see that, not unless you really want to."

Perhaps it was best if she didn't. All that mattered now was that Jasper couldn't hurt her, nor anyone else, anymore. She thought of the girls at The Inn—Rebecca, Lydia and Mattie. What would they do now? They didn't have someone like Mr. Westgate to take them in, or a man like Gabriel to love them. She could only hope their lives might improve.

"We're all right," Gabriel said, helping her up.

"Thank God," Matthew said as he moved to where Jasper lay. "What a mess."

Mr. Westgate scowled. "I never would have let him get away with it."

The words surprised her. She folded her arms, recalling the terrible things she'd confessed earlier. "Mr. Westgate, about what I said before—"

"My dear, I may not have known you for twenty three years, but I'm not stupid. I saw the way you looked at that disgraceful man. When I went inside, Gabriel explained everything to me. I gave him my good revolver and let him go ahead while I found and loaded the other guns."

Gabriel shoved his gun into his pocket. "I've never spoken so fast in my life."

"Thank God you knew what you were doing, my boy." Mr. Westgate gathered Ellie into his arms and hugged her. "As for you, my dear, your strength astounds me. I hope you're proud of yourself, because you deserve to be. I only wish I could change the past."

"We never look back, sir," she said as he released her.

She locked eyes with Gabriel, and a shiver ran through her. When that gun had fired, she'd never felt so terrified, so broken. Knowing how close she'd come to losing him made her want to drop to her knees and cry out thanks. She loved him so much.

"I'll call the authorities. The man had two guns and a knife on him," Matthew announced as he trudged back to the group.

Gabriel reached for her hand and wove her fingers through his. "Let's get you cleaned up before you're questioned."

"Questioned?"

"You won't have to say much," Mr. Westgate assured her. "Cogs violently assaulted and attempted to kidnap you on my property. That's all anyone needs to know."

Gabriel's eyes darkened. "Uncle, there are a few other crimes Cogs is responsible for …"

"We'll discuss it later." Mr. Westgate shot him a commanding look. "For now, take her inside. Matthew and I can handle matters from here."

Gabriel nodded. He placed a hand on her back and escorted her to the house.

"Will you meet me in the parlor when you're finished cleaning up?" he asked when they stepped into the foyer.

"Give me ten minutes," she said.

Once in her bedroom, she threw off her winter things, washed her face and began fixing her hair. As she tucked and pinned the wet tangles atop her head, her mind felt like porridge. Jasper Cogs had actually found her. And the strangest part of it all? She barely cared about what he'd done to her in the past. The love and acceptance from Gabriel and the Westgates had helped her find the strength she needed to face his abuse. But when she'd learned about Papa and Gabriel's mother, she'd never known such evil.

She buttoned up a dry pair of boots, then rushed downstairs.

In the parlor, newly decorated ready for Christmas, Gabriel stood facing the window. He didn't seem aware of her presence, so she knocked twice on the doorframe.

He turned around, his mouth curving with tenderness. "Do come in, madam."

She didn't care about the tree or the holly; her eyes never left his as she crossed the room to his side. Taking her hand, he guided her to a green chaise lounge and sat beside her.

He frowned, studying her cheek. "Did he hit you?"

She shrugged. "Just a slap. I'm all right."

"And you'll be all right from now on," he said, his eyes dark and serious. "I don't know what I would have done if something happened to you."

"I feel the same way about you—" she squeezed his hand "—which is why you must promise me that the next time you kill someone, you'll first take his weapons away."

"I haven't had much practice with shooting people."

"Promise me."

"I promise, my love." He grinned for a moment, then turned his profile to her. "That day in my library, when you told me how your father died . . . I knew Cogs was responsible. But I couldn't prove it. Worse than that, I could do nothing about it."

She lowered her gaze. Despite the ache she felt at the truth about Papa's death, she appreciated Gabriel's sympathy. Papa had loved her and Mama with all his heart, and there was comfort to be had in that. He also approved of Gabriel long before he had hair on his chest. Although Papa was gone, she still felt him with her. She would always feel him with her.

"It's funny," Gabriel continued. "I barely thought of Jasper when I found out about my father. Attaching him to the assault in Chicago seemed so far-fetched. I didn't think he had it in him to pull off something like that. I couldn't have underestimated him more."

"You heard Jasper confess?" she asked.

He nodded.

Her heart broke for him as she gazed into those soft blue eyes.

"Avenging my mother's death . . . your father's death . . . your rape . . . That was all I gave a damn about," he said. "I never cared about my fortune, not really. Had I returned home with her body like I should have, the state would have issued me the inheritance. But what would I have done then? I would have kept my wealthy status, married for appearances and lived a fake, miserable life." Shaking his head, he lifted a hand to caress her slapped cheek. "I never would have known what it felt like to truly share my heart with someone."

She closed her eyes and sighed. She couldn't imagine what her life would be like finding Gabriel married to someone else, of never sharing a single intimate touch. Material possessions didn't matter to her, either. She didn't need a mansion, handfuls of servants and fancy carriages to keep her happy. The only thing she needed was him.

"Ellie," he whispered, taking her chin as she opened her eyes. "The past is the past, and we cannot change that. But I swear I'd live those four miserable years all over again if that were the only way I could be with you."

Emotion dripped from every word, and as she looked into his eyes, she let him see into her soul. He still hadn't told her whether Mr. Westgate approved. If he didn't, she'd surely fall to pieces. "And can you be with me? Truly?"

Gabriel lifted her hand to his mouth with an easy smile. She didn't try to calm her beating heart when he pressed a tender kiss to the inside of her wrist. "Truly, the decision is yours. Will it be the doctor or the lawyer, Miss Baker?"

Her heart soared. She threw her arms around his neck and kissed him.

He chuckled against her lips. "I assume you're choosing the doctor, then?"

Instead of words, she answered him by claiming his mouth again. He cradled the back of her head as she clung to him, releasing all the emotion, all the love they had for each other.

He pulled away, narrowing his eyes. "I should warn you that my uncle has insisted that I court you properly. That means no more sneaking around, and no more doing other things for a while." He pressed his soft, warm lips to hers and lingered there. "No matter how much we want to . . ."

"Don't worry," she murmured, "You're well worth the wait."

Epilogue

Christmas Day

John pulled a glass of mulled wine from a passing tray and held it up. "To special occasions. Merry Christmas, Ellie."

Ellie laughed, recalling the way his face had lit during that very first dinner—the night Mr. Westgate had allowed him a drink due to a special occasion. She clinked her champagne glass to his. "Merry Christmas, John, and thank you again for the mirror and hair barrettes. I truly love them."

"I'm so glad. Jane might have helped me a little with your present."

"Really? I never would have guessed." She squeezed his arm. "Speaking of Jane, where is she?"

"In the drawing room, but good luck getting to her. She and Victoria are surrounded." He grimaced playfully, and then bounded off to join the handful of people singing carols with the orchestra.

John was probably right. The house had come alive with an endless sea of party guests, all of them set on meeting the new baby. Mr. Westgate had spared no expense celebrating Victoria's public debut. Embellished wreaths and holly draped the walls. A string orchestra played holiday favorites in the hollow between the grand staircases. Chandeliers burned brightly, and a towering tree, laden with candles, treats, ornaments and tinsel, overwhelmed the center of the foyer.

Standing near the tree . . . was Mr. Cain. He mingled with an older couple, who appeared to be introducing him to their attractive daughter. When he glanced at her, her breath hitched. He bowed his head with a polite smile. She did the same, relieved to know that even if he despised her, he'd never show it. Still, something told her he wouldn't despise her for long.

She finished the last of her champagne and passed her glass to a servant. When she looked up, she saw Gabriel. He stood at the parlor's entrance, laughing heartily with Mr. Westgate and the elder Mr. Tiller. She'd seen him dressed up twice before, but it never ceased to amaze her how marvelous he looked in that black evening coat.

His eyes found hers and he smiled. Mr. Westgate took Mr. Tiller's arm, muttered something into his ear, and pulled him away. Gabriel didn't seem to mind the strange departure at all. In fact, he looked quite content as she approached.

"Dare I ask what that was about?" she asked, clasping her hands behind her back.

"Of course not." He sipped his drink, and she squinted at him. "It's plain cider, my dear. You can taste it if you'd like."

He knew full well that her look wasn't meant for the cider. Something felt suspicious. "I've been looking for you since dinner."

His deep chuckle warmed her. "Well you must not have looked over here, because I've been standing in this very spot for quite a while." He pointed above their heads to where a bushel of mistletoe hung from the doorframe. "There's only one berry left. I had to be sure to guard it with my life."

"That must mean you're waiting for someone to kiss you."

"Why yes, I am." He plucked the bright red berry and brought his face down to her level. "As a matter of fact, the woman I've been waiting for has finally arrived. Will you do me the honor?"

She shut her eyes and kissed him, grinning all the while. Everyone knew Gabriel was courting her now—society never slacked when it came to fresh gossip—but this was the first kiss they'd shared in public.

"That was lovely, thank you," he whispered. He drew in a long breath and exhaled. "Now, would you mind coming with me for a moment?"

She nodded, taking his arm. He led her down the hall to the empty library and closed the doors. When he turned to face her, he looked almost nervous.

"Have I mentioned how exceptionally beautiful you look this evening?"

She traced a finger along his smooth jaw. "I could say the same thing about you, sir."

"Beautiful, really?" he asked, raising an eyebrow. "Not dashingly handsome or majestically noble?"

She laughed. "All three of those descriptions suit you just fine."

Pulling her close, he leaned down and kissed her gently. "I have something to tell you. The president of Harvard wrote to me. It appears their eldest funder was born and raised in this town. He was so impressed by my work, that his foundation is issuing me a grant to build and operate this town's first modern hospital. Construction begins in the spring."

Her mouth dropped open. "Oh, Gabriel, that's wonderful!" she cried, wrapping her arms around his neck.

He lifted her off the ground and held her against him for several seconds. "I needed some time to sort things out in my life before making any major decisions," he said as he lowered her back down. He ran a hand through his hair and cleared his throat. "Now that all is said and done, I can finally give you your real Christmas present. I've wanted to give you this one for a very long time."

Their eyes met, and she felt a shock run through her. She didn't move when he took her left arm and gently pulled off her glove. Then, dropping to one knee, he reached into his coat pocket and pulled out the most perfect ring.

Her heart fluttered. As his smile faded, hers grew.

"Ellie, so much has changed from the days we played together. I have no doubt that things will continue to change in the years to come." He reached out and held her hand. "But there's no one else in the world I'd rather take that journey with. My love for you is unconditional. It would be the greatest honor of my life if you would be my wife."

His mouth twitched and he blushed. "Lord, I just said a rhyme, didn't I?"

"I wouldn't care if you sang the words." She laughed, cupping his cheek with her free hand. "My answer is yes, a thousand times yes."

He chuckled as he slid the ring on her finger. He rose to his feet, brought his arms around her, and she surrendered to his kiss.

"Merry Christmas, my love," he whispered.

As she looked into his passionate blue eyes, she tried to imagine what a lifetime of loving Gabriel Peterson would be like. But she couldn't, which made it all the more wonderful. Whatever came their way, whatever victories and obstacles they might face, they would face them together. The future felt as bright as it was exciting.

"Merry Christmas," she replied, and then her lips met his again.

Made in the USA
Lexington, KY
17 November 2014